W9-BOM-171

"Take off your glasses," she murmured. "They make you look too scary."

She leaned toward him. He made an inarticulate sound as he slid his arms around her. His lips were warm and firm, taking possession of hers with an appealingly shy reticence that frightened her far more than the hard muscled embrace. She heard the low growl in his throat and experienced a rush of emotion so overpowering her knees actually buckled.

Her knotted muscles relaxed one by one. The fingers that had been clenched against the heavy twill of his shirt eased their frantic grip. His big hands were under her jacket now, stroking her back, his palms skimming the bumps of her spine. Exerting only the barest fraction of his strength, he urged her upward with those big, brutal hands until she was molded to him. . . .

TAMING THE NIGHT

Paula Detmer Riggs

FAWCETT GOLD MEDAL • NEW YORK

A Fawcett Gold Medal Book
Published by The Ballantine Publishing Group
Copyright © 1999 by Paula Detmer Riggs

www.randomhouse.com/BB/

Library of Congress Catalog Card Number: 98-93426

ISBN 0-449-15019-4

Manufactured in the United States of America

First Edition: January 1999

10   9   8   7   6   5   4   3   2

For Tricia Adams and Diane Dunaway,
who taught me the craft of storytelling
and the glory of precision in language
and who, along the way, enhanced my life.

For Catherine Anderson,
the sister of my heart, patient friend, and wonderful writer,
who never stopped believing.

For Nancy Yost, the calm in the midst of my storm.

For Elisa Wares and Carolyn Nichols, who took a chance.

And always, for Carl, my rock.

Thank you all.

PROLOGUE

Oh God, it's too early. Please don't let me have my baby here.
Summer Laurence curled forward over her swollen belly, awkwardly cradling the baby with her shackled hands. Gradually the sharp pain eased, and she let out a shaky breath. It didn't feel like a labor pain, not like the ones described in the book she'd been reading the morning of her arrest, anyway.

Closing her eyes she rocked gently, trying to soothe the little love who'd been restless since morning, when they'd taken Summer from her airless, sour-smelling cell in the Metropolitan Jail for the trip downtown to the courthouse. She'd had the first cramp in the van and begged the marshal to take her to the ER, but the hulking cop had only laughed. She was a frigging prisoner, he'd said through the wire grid. They'd take the kid the minute it was born, so what the hell? Why sweat it?

"I'll never give you up, my sweet baby," she crooned, careful to keep her voice low so that it wouldn't carry to the marshal who sat nearby, reading the morning paper. "But guess what, sweetie. Today—this very morning, in fact—Daddy's coming to get us."

Kyle would make the nightmare go away. *Trust me on this, babe. Just keep your chin up and your mouth shut until I work things out.*

"Your daddy is a wonderful man," she whispered, rubbing the spot where a tiny fist had pummeled. According to the ultrasound

1

technician at the free clinic, the baby was a little girl, sucking her thumb in the Polaroid picture Summer kept propped next to the studio couch in her one-room apartment.

Across the anteroom, the grossly overweight man with the acne-scarred face looked up from the sports page and snorted. According to her cell mates, Corporal J. T. Jessop was every female prisoner's nightmare. The worst of the worst. Summer had cringed when she'd seen his name tag.

"Way I hear it, ain't no way of knowing who 'Daddy' is," he said, deliberately staring at her breasts until her skin crawled.

"I know and so does h-her father."

"Don't jerk your chin at me, bitch." Jessop's voice was as painful as the slap she'd gotten last week from the matron in charge of her cell block.

"I'm . . . sorry," she managed to get out. Whatever you do, don't piss off the guards, her cell mate Rosalie had warned that first awful morning when they'd locked her up with three other women. *We be workin' girls, too, honey,* Rosalie had said with that world-weary laugh. *Though from the looks of that big belly, it 'pears like you ain't quite got the hang of it, yet.*

Everyone thought she was a hooker. Only Kyle knew the truth. Feeling the panic rising again, she twisted around to look at the clock. In ten minutes she was to go in front of the judge.

"Getting anxious, babycakes?" The guard scraped back his chair and lumbered to his feet. Summer shrank back as he loomed over her. Chuckling, he reached out a hand to grab her chin, and she felt the sweat on his palm. The terror she'd been fighting since dawn surged to her throat, constricting her windpipe until she felt light-headed.

"Be nice to me, little girl, and I'll see you get all the shit you want." Jessop's voice was greasy, like the stuff plastering his thin hair to his scalp. "Crack, speed, you name it, sweetcakes. Only cost you what you been givin' out to them suckers on the beach. Me and you, alone in a nice private van on the way back to the lockup."

Summer fought down a rush of nausea. At the jail he'd taken

his time shackling her. While the matron pretended not to notice, he'd groped Summer's swollen breast, pinching her hard when she'd flinched away. When he'd bent to fasten on the leg irons, he'd slid one beefy hand up to stroke her thigh. During the short drive across town he'd described in graphic detail exactly what he'd like to do to her.

"Please let me go," she whispered, squeezing her eyes tight. "The baby . . ."

"What are you, sixteen?"

"S-seventeen," Summer admitted, feeling fully twice that and more.

"Seventeen and already knocked up." His oily grin revealed teeth so stained they appeared rotten. "Always did have me a taste for the young stuff. Break 'em in right." He snarled a laugh. " 'Course that ain't possible with you, is it, sweetcakes? Seeings how you was already well broken in afore you turned sixteen." His thumb rubbed her throat, making her skin crawl. "Give me some sugar, green eyes, and I'll see you get to have your brat in the infirmary 'stead of on the floor of your cell like the last bitch who refused me. She was real upset when the kid strangled to death afore the matron got around to calling in the doc."

Summer felt faint with horror. Surely he was lying. He had to be lying. Such things didn't really happen. Or did they? *Oh dear God, please give me courage to get through this before Kyle comes for me. Please, please help me.*

The guard leaned forward, bathing her face with his foul-smelling breath. "How 'bout a little somethin' on account?" He reached out to fondle her breast with his fat fingers.

Somehow Summer kept from gagging. "Please don't," she begged, squeezing her eyes closed. "I'll be sick—"

The door leading to the courtroom opened, causing the guard to straighten quickly. The man in the doorway was tall and well built and blond. For an instant her heart all but stopped, and her spirits soared. *Kyle!* Except that it wasn't, she realized with crushing disappointment.

" 'Morning, J.T.," the officer drawled, his expression mocking.

"Sorry to disturb you, but we got us an arraignment coming up in about six minutes. Old Judge Ramirez don't take kindly to cooling his heels while one of his marshals grabs a quickie in the anteroom."

Jessop's fingers tightened until Summer felt as though her skin would split before he released her. "You heard the man, Ms. Laurence. On your feet."

Summer obeyed, but her movements were slow and ponderous. The bulge of her seven-month pregnancy made her feel unbalanced, which she might have found comical if she hadn't been so scared. The agile athlete who could hang ten over the edge of a surfboard and waltz with the waves suddenly found it tricky to keep her footing on level ground.

The courtroom was icy. Most of the seats were empty. Heart thudding hard above the now quiet baby, she searched the huge room, desperate for the sight of the man she loved. Instead, she saw a few lone spectators in the rear, reading the morning paper or chatting while waiting for the show to start. Desperately, she shifted her gaze to the front where the blond cop was chatting with a plump, gray-haired lady in a blue suit. The court reporter, Summer registered absently. Like in old "Perry Mason" reruns she used to watch in the middle of the night when the craving to use again got so bad she couldn't sleep.

Today was simply a formality, she told herself as she cast an uneasy glance at the twelve vacant seats in the jury box. Seats that would remain empty unless the judge ruled there was enough evidence against her for a trial. But that wouldn't happen, she reminded herself. Kyle would make everything right again. But where was Kyle? Surely he knew what time she was to appear.

Please don't let me faint, she prayed silently as she gripped her manacled hands tightly together in front of her and waited for the marshal to remove the handcuffs. The chains around her ankles would remain. To keep her from hauling ass, Rosalie had explained.

"Put that sweet young butt in the chair and behave yourself,"

Jessop said in a low voice only she could hear. "When this is over, we'll have us a party. Just you and me, little girl."

He clamped a hand over her shoulder and led her to one of the tables in front of the low railing. Resisting the urge to rub away his clammy touch, she slowly settled her pregnant body into the seat next to her court-appointed attorney.

Tall, skeletally thin, and already balding in his mid-twenties, Leon Finkle was considered one of the best public defenders in the city by her streetwise cell mates. She was lucky, they'd assured her. Lucky? When her father could afford a team of the best defense attorneys in the state? In the country, for that matter? Yet refused to give her even one penny for bail or her defense.

The news of her arrest had sent ripples through the entire upper crust of upscale Point Loma. Montgomery and Doris Laurence were decent people, generous with their time and their money to several local charities. Monty was on the board of directors of the West Bay Yacht Club. Doris headed the Junior League. Everyone agreed that Summer had been pampered and spoiled, but to become a common drug addict? And a pusher? Someone who'd sold drugs to her friends? And now, about to bear an illegitimate child? It was an abomination, that's what it was.

Those same neighborhood friends who'd smoked pot with her and shared bottles of cheap wine around beach bonfires now no longer knew her. When she'd finally gotten through to her big brother, Phillip, at the La Jolla brokerage firm where he worked, he'd called her a slut and a disgrace and warned her never to call him at the office again. No doubt he was afraid he'd lose clients if his name was linked with hers.

Every time she thought about her family she bled a little more inside. Over and over she'd begged them to forgive her. If she had to, she'd crawl on her knees from here to Point Loma to show how sorry she was. She'd begged her father to forgive her. For the sake of their first grandchild, if not for her own. But the father who used to call her his little princess and give her sips of his martini just to make her giggle hadn't let her get out more than a few words before slicing her hopes to bloody ribbons.

"Are you okay?" Leon whispered, his sparse eyebrows pulling together beneath the wire rims of his glasses.

"I couldn't sleep," she admitted, pressing her hand against her belly. The pain had subsided, thank God. "I was sick most of the night."

"Why didn't you ask the matron for some Kaopectate or something?"

"I did. She . . . she told me to shove my pillow in my mouth and shut up." The woman had said other things, too. Obscene, filthy things that had made Summer feel even sicker.

Leon hesitated, then pressed his hand over hers where it rested on the table and squeezed gently. "Summer, if you'd just agree to plea-bargain—"

"No," she whispered fiercely around the sick fear in her throat. "I can't—I won't—admit to being guilty when I didn't do anything wrong."

Leon's sigh was weighted with disbelief. "Summer, you were expelled from Point Loma High School for bringing marijuana onto the campus. Your parents kicked you out when you stole your mom's credit card and maxed it out to buy dope. Norvell knows all that and more."

According to Leon, Assistant District Attorney Cleve Norvell held the record for the most convictions in San Diego County. Around courthouse circles he was known as a man who hated drug dealers with a crusading passion.

"But I've been clean for over a year! I have a job, I pay my bills."

"With drug money, Norvell will claim."

"I'm a waitress, Leon. I live on minimum wage and tips. My apartment's smaller than . . . than that room where I was waiting just now. The only new clothes I've bought in a year were for the baby. And I swear to you, I've never, ever sold so much as a joint, not even to my friends. Ask anyone who knows me, and they'll tell you the same thing."

"Now, that would be a wise move wouldn't it?" he said in an impatient whisper. "Calling a bunch of whacked-out dopers as character witnesses?"

Summer stared at him, her heart thudding hard. "If that's what you think, why did you take the case?"

He shrugged one shoulder. "Someone had to. It was my turn in the barrel."

"You . . . you mean you think I did all those horrible things?"

His pale-blue eyes narrowed, but his expression was pitying. "You told me yourself you'd lure a likely mark to the rocks at the end of Sunset Cliffs and get him to take off his pants, then throw his clothes in the surf and steal his wallet."

She felt the heat rising from between her breasts to stain her throat and then her face. "Yes, and I'm not proud of it. But I never slept with those men, and I never sold drugs. I swear it on my baby's life."

Finkle snorted. "Get real, Summer. They caught you holding the goods in your hand. Remember the L.L. Bean satchel full of rock cocaine in neat little baggies you had clutched to your chest when the cops showed up? Estimated street value in excess of two mil."

"I've already explained that, Leon," she rushed to remind him. "Someone else gave it to me. To hold for him."

"Oh yeah, right. This mystery guy you keep telling me is going to make this all go away. This knight in shining armor whose name you can't tell me because you don't want to 'blow his cover.' " His mouth twisted as he glanced toward the next table where the burly prosecutor had just taken his seat. "You'd better produce him in the next three minutes, or your ass is grass."

"I'm sure he'll be here any minute." Fighting the panic clawing at her, she turned toward the double doors in the rear. *Please, please,* she prayed, her heart thudding in rhythm to the passing seconds. After what seemed like hours, the door opened and Kyle walked in, looking impressively solemn in a dark-gray suit and a tie the color of a morning surf. His thick golden hair had been recently styled to the contours of his head, and the scruffy beard he'd worn as part of his cover was gone, revealing a deep cleft in his chin.

His gaze met hers, his brown eyes hooded beneath tawny brows. Though she waited for that special smile he reserved just for her, his face remained impassive as he turned to close the door behind him. Her heart skipped a beat as a wave of love rolled over her, and tears welled in her eyes as she clutched Finkle's thin forearm. "See, I told you he'd come," she whispered, relief making her a little giddy. "I knew he wouldn't abandon me."

Finkle turned to follow her gaze. "Is this a joke?" he demanded in a strident undertone. "Because if it is, I'm definitely not laughing."

"What . . . what are you talking about?"

"Detective Bogan, that's what I'm talking about. The star witness for the prosecution."

"But that's . . . there must be some mistake. Kyle is here to help me, not them."

Summer twisted around, waiting for Kyle to come to her side. Instead, he slipped quickly into a seat directly behind the prosecution table. She waited for him to look at her again, but he stared straight ahead, his jaw locked, his expression grim.

"Leon, quick, go tell him to come over here and sit with us." When Finkle didn't move, she gave his arm a frantic shake. "Hurry up. I need to talk to him before the judge comes in."

"Summer, listen to me. You are in deep trouble, and Bogan is part of it." Leon's voice was lashed with urgency.

"Of course he is, but not in the way you think. Like I keep telling you, if you'd just listen for once, instead of telling me to hurry up because you have another appointment."

Something like guilt glinted behind his glasses before he nodded. "Okay, I'm listening, but make it fast."

Summer took a quick breath. "Me being on the beach that morning with that satchel, it was all part of Kyle's plan." She leaned closer and lowered her voice. "I couldn't say anything before, on account of his plan, but he was going to arrest this pusher he'd been watching for months. A real sleazeball named Enrique, from Baja, who was selling to the junior-high crowd. I was to pretend to be his accomplice. That's why I had the rock cocaine."

Finkle looked almost kindly as he drew a deep breath. "The word I got is that he's going to say you were the pusher he was after."

For an instant Summer was shocked speechless before she rushed to correct him. "No, he wouldn't do that to me. We're going to be married. I'm carrying his child. We . . . we're going to name her Kyla Marie."

"According to what our esteemed assistant DA told me outside just a few minutes ago, your fiancé has just gotten engaged to the daughter of the deputy commissioner. He's also received a promotion and a plum assignment to a new anticrime unit downtown. Do you understand what I'm saying, Summer? Bogan is on the fast track. A real comer. The last thing he needs is a pregnant, teenaged bride with a murky past."

Summer felt dizzy. She had trouble drawing in air past the sick constriction in her throat. "No." She drew more breath. "I don't believe you."

"There's more."

"No," she pleaded, twisting around to look at the man she loved. As though sensing her gaze, he turned his head and regarded her impassively. Deliberately she smoothed her hands over her distended belly, reminding him of the precious baby they'd made together in her tiny room. A smile trembled on her lips as she put all of her love and hope into her expression. Instead of the answering smile she so desperately sought, his face twisted into a grimace of distaste before he returned his gaze to the front of the courtroom, rejecting her and their child. Summer felt the blood drain from her face. Her skin grew clammy and cold, as though drenched in ice water.

Leon continued, his voice relentless and harsh. "He said

you've slept with so many 'johns' before relieving them of their wallets he doubts even you know the father's identity."

"I . . . see." Very slowly, she turned her head and stared directly ahead. The court reporter was readying her equipment while the bailiff chatted with the guard and another man in uniform. There was a buzzing in her ears, and her throat felt raw. But her eyes were dry. As dry as her dreams.

"Think of your baby, Summer," Finkle said, as though from a great distance. "Do you want to have your baby in prison?"

Be nice to me and I'll see you get to have your brat in the infirmary 'stead of on the floor of your cell. Terror raced through her, causing her to shiver. She wanted her mother. Or her father. Somebody who cared about her. But there was no one. Only a jaded public defender who wanted to cut a deal and be rid of her. She'd never been more scared in her life. Or more alone.

"I swore . . . when I found out I was pregnant . . . that I was going to make myself into a person my child wouldn't be ashamed to know," she said, her voice jerky and nearly soundless as she forced herself to look at her attorney. "If I admitted to doing what . . . what they claim, I'd be branded as a drug pusher for the rest of my life. I can't do that to my angel baby, no matter what her father does."

Finkle regarded her closely, something very like respect glimmering in his eyes for a moment before he sighed. "Then you'd better brace yourself," he said softly, "because your baby's so-called father over there is about to nail you to the wall."

CHAPTER 1

The big old house itself was fantastic. A shining masterpiece under the layers of grime and weather stress. Well, okay, maybe the facade was a little seedy, and maybe the roof could use patching, but the place had presence—and thick redwood siding that would make a southern California contractor's mouth water.

"Yes, yes, *yes*!"

Spreading her arms wide, Summer took a deep breath of the crisp air and held it, loving the oxygen high. Slowly, reluctantly, she exhaled, feeling almost giddy. Grinning like a besotted idiot, she turned a slow circle in the yard and listened to the birds happily warbling their little feathered hearts out in the surrounding trees. Lush trees that made the straggly, smog-strangled eucalyptus outside her bedroom window in San Diego look positively anorexic. During the summer, the foliage of these babies would provide havens of shade on the rolling acreage.

This was where Phoenix House would rise from the metaphorical ashes. Right here in this beautiful spot nestled under the protective slopes of the Cascade peaks. She allowed herself a moment of pure bliss before she hauled herself up short. Nothing was settled. Nothing was certain. A lot of obstacles had to be overcome before she could have her miracle.

They'd met six months ago at a women's retreat at Big Sur. Three days of meditation, soul-searching, and fasting—all served

11

within the context of a basic New Age mysticism. Summer had been a guest speaker, her topic the scourge of teenaged drug addition. Dottie Hollister had been one of the facilitators, an imperious, albeit tiny, female Napoleon with a surprisingly lush figure, a big heart, and a bawdy sense of humor that belied her sixty-one years.

Summer wasn't much for trusting anyone on first meeting. In fact, the ability to trust in anything but herself was dead last on her list of personal character traits. Perhaps it had been the subtle aura of loneliness that surrounded the woman that had gotten through Summer's defenses, or the faint echo of sadness in Dottie's ready laughter that had touched a similar chord. Either way, Summer had cautiously allowed herself to consider the older woman a friend.

Over foul-tasting tea and some kind of mushy grain dish on the last night of their stay, Summer had told Dottie about her arrest and conviction—and about the promise she'd made herself in prison. Somehow, she would devote her life to helping other teenaged addicts turn their lives around. If she saved only one person from the same hell she'd experienced, it would be worth it. When she'd made that promise to herself, she hadn't known where or when or even how she would make that dream come true. She only knew that she would.

Over the years the "how" had formed into a plan for an inpatient drug rehabilitation center geared especially for adolescents. A different kind of facility that would combine the best bits and pieces of others she'd studied. She intended to call it Phoenix House.

The "when" had first depended on her acquiring the necessary training and experience, and then, later, on money. For the past five years, since she'd earned her doctorate in adolescent psychology and substance abuse and gone to work at the Mc-Donald Center in San Diego, she'd been putting aside every spare cent in a trust account. At the same time, she'd begged for donations everywhere—from service groups, corporations, private citizens. By her reckoning she now had enough for a bare-bones start.

The "where" had been a sticking point, however. Even renting a place in southern California was beyond her paper-thin budget. And then she'd met Dottie, who'd mentioned the property she owned over the mountain from the Seattle sprawl. Thirty-five acres of ranch land near the mountain community of twenty thousand listed in the AAA book as "a quaint and charming Alpine village in a picturesque setting on the dry side of the magnificent Cascade Range." The land and the ranch house were Summer's for as long as she wanted it, and at a phenomenally low rent.

By the time her face was tingling from the wind and her usually tidy French twist was a mess of trailing tendrils fluttering around her neck, Summer had made two circuits of the main house and was completing a third. Writing as fast as she could, she'd filled four notebook pages and was all but jumping up and down.

The house had gingerbread on the back porch, for heaven's sake, and twenty-seven double-hung, oversized windows, most of which offered a view of the valley beyond. She'd also uncovered a profusion of wild roses growing on the split-rail fence that separated the yard from the barn lot. There was a whole mess of plants she thought might be daffodils poking through the dirt near the equipment shed. Several stalks had fat buds on the ends, ready to pop open any minute, hopefully before she had to catch the return flight to San Diego nine days hence.

Impatience ran through her like a fever, and she gnawed at the left corner of her mouth. Most of the items on her list of things to check required more than cursory attention—like a thorough, detailed search of the county records pertaining to zoning laws and land-use ordinances and an in-depth evaluation of nearby medical facilities. And, of course, she would need at least five bids for the work that was required before she could move in.

Move in? The thought brought her up short. All during the long flight from San Diego to Seattle, she'd been congratulating herself for being so mature about this. After all, she'd been practical enough to schedule her trip to coincide with her speaking engagement, even though the eager little kid inside her had wanted to hop on the same plane that had taken Dottie home from the retreat.

Between then and now, she'd read all she could find on the Pacific Northwest, particularly about the Wenatchee Valley where Osuma was located. She knew all about the pretty little town and its struggle to survive after the timber bust that had started in the seventies. With painstaking determination, the citizenry had laboriously changed their logging community into a replica of a Bavarian village, complete with oompah music, German cooking, and the most elaborate Oktoberfest outside of the Tyrol. From boomtown to bust and back again to prosperity. She loved the very idea of it. The majesty and resilience of the human spirit. The sheer rightness of it all.

A glance at her watch told her that it was nearly four, well past the time Dottie had set for them to meet. Impatient to see the wonders she was sure she'd find inside as well, she decided to fetch her camera from her bag and take some exterior shots while she waited. Halfway to the front again, she paused to survey the property's layout. It had a rough sort of symmetry, with the house, equipment shed, and a large sturdy-looking barn arranged in a lopsided triangle. Dottie lived close by, on another section of the property that would remain separate from their agreement. "We'll be neighbors," Dottie had written. In fact they would share the same driveway.

She was nearly at the front again when she heard a car pull up and stop. Quickening her pace, she hurried around the side of the building, a greeting already forming on her lips. She saw the mud-spattered white Blazer with the pine-tree-and-mountain logo of the Osuma Police Department emblazoned on the side first, then the giant of a man standing with feet spread and body braced next to the left front fender.

Beneath her jacket's hand-stitched lapels her heart thudded, and bile rose in her throat. For an instant she was seventeen again and terrified. Her frantic gaze took in the shiny gold badge pinned to a worn leather bomber jacket, the lethal blue-steel pistol riding one lean hip, the heavy black boots polished to a mirror finish. Though the wide brim of a brown Stetson shaded much of his face and his eyes were hidden behind the dark lenses of gold-framed aviator sunglasses, she felt the sharp scrutiny of suspicious eyes. Black, sharklike eyes, she had no doubt. Mean and hard and unforgiving.

She narrowed her own gaze, even as she forced steel into her backbone. She was thirty-three now, a respected psychotherapist with three degrees and a slew of honors. A woman determined never to be a victim again.

"May I help you, ma'am?" His voice was scratchy and coolly polite, with just enough of a down-home twang to grate on her already jangling nerves.

"No thank you, Officer. I'm waiting for a friend."

He came closer, and she wished he hadn't. She hadn't felt so defenseless in years. Of course, she understood the dynamics of intimidation full well. At five feet two inches and one hundred six pounds soaking wet, she was no match for a man with the chest and arms of a logger.

She hated feeling dwarfed by a man's towering body, which was probably the reason she'd always featured leaner, more compact heroes in her private fantasies. Fair and even-tempered instead of dark and angry. Sun-bronzed, whipcord-thin surfers instead of brawny mountain men. This particular specimen had to be well over six feet, with monstrous shoulders that blocked out the sun, and thickly muscled thighs and calves stretching the seams of his cowboy jeans.

Another emotion snuck under her guard, more complex than an instinctive fear. She recognized the first tentative tendrils of a purely involuntary sexual attraction. But the man was a cop. The worst of the worst. A bully with a badge. Like Kyle. And therefore not to be trusted.

"May I see some identification, please?"

She blinked, then frowned as she reached into her shoulder

bag for her wallet. There was something odd about the way he strung his words together, she realized as she drew out her driver's license from its compartment and extended it toward him. As though he were hesitating over each syllable.

After taking her ID, he drew a small spiral notebook from his back pocket and flipped to a clean page, then retrieved a pen from his shirt pocket. As he transferred information, she couldn't help noticing his hands. Large, callused, brutal hands. Wide and square, with close-clipped blunt nails and prominent blue veins riding atop sinewy muscle. Beneath the crisp cuffs of his khaki shirt were thick, powerful wrists. A working man's hands, she thought, watching his gaze flick for an instant from the picture on the license to her face. Hands that were no stranger to violence, she suspected. And utterly incapable of gentleness. Too many times she'd seen the results of hands like those, on the kids she fought to protect—ugly, swollen bruises on tender skin. And even uglier bruises on already wounded souls.

"California," he said with something that sounded like disgust sneaking into that calm voice. "Figures."

"I beg your pardon?"

"We get a lot of you people up here," he said as he handed her back her ID. "Mostly tourists looking for local color."

"Then they're bound to be disappointed, aren't they?" she muttered, slipping her license back into her wallet.

One black eyebrow traced an arrogant arch above the dark lenses. "Ma'am?"

"In the local color."

He returned the notebook to his pocket, his gaze still on her face. "Is that a fact?"

She nodded. "Your local color is almost all green, with a few black gashes here and there. Every shade of green in the spectrum, and maybe a few that aren't. It's rather startling at first glance."

He cast a look around, as though trying to see the valley through her eyes. His profile seemed hewn from the rocks he studied, hardened features on a hardened man. It was an angular, roughly put-together face with an aggressive bone structure, an autocratic nose, and high-riding cheekbones. His jaw was stubborn, his mouth a bit too wide, with controlled corners, and seemed fashioned for angry words and biting commands—even if the blatantly sensual lower lip suggested otherwise.

His hair, curling against the jacket's worn collar, was the color of jet. Shadowed by the brim of his hat, his brows seemed to slash across his forehead without a hint of curve to soften them. Even at first glance, he had the look of a man who would always stand slightly apart, even in a crowd, like the lone majestic pine silhouetted against a barren slope. Or a street-tough taking on all comers with only his fists and grit as weapons.

"Guess it's green at that," he conceded after a moment's study. "Most likely because of the trees. We got a lot of those."

"I've noticed."

He glanced toward the road, then returned his gaze to her face. She sensed a shift in him. A sudden edge, a hint of danger. "About this friend you're meeting. Would you mind telling me his name?"

"Ms. Dottie Hollister. I expect you know her?"

Instead of answering he stood silent and still, one hip cocked and his big boots firmly planted. A classic stance of a man used to the privilege of command. A consummate power play. He who speaks first, loses. He was good at it, she acknowledged with reluctant admiration. Better than most, in fact.

Schooling her features, she debated the wisdom of stonewalling. This time the law, such as it was, was on her side. On the other hand, a cop with an attitude made a powerful enemy. If she should in fact settle here, the last thing she needed was trouble with the authorities.

"Ms. Hollister owns this property. Sixtyish, about my size, with reddish hair? She usually wears a lot of big, clunky jewelry and has the most wonderful laugh." She waited for a response, and when one didn't come, she added a bit impatiently, "She's the head librarian in Osuma. You know, the town you work for?"

"Oh, that Miss Hollister." Though his mouth remained firmly

compressed, she had the distinct impression he was laughing at her.

To her utter chagrin, she felt her temper start to sizzle. Worse, she wasn't sure why. Stress, she decided. Too many hours buttonholing judges during the two and a half days of the conference, trying to win them to her philosophy of treatment, not punishment. Nothing she couldn't handle, of course. She knew any number of stress reduction techniques—and had practiced them all at one time or another. Remaining centered and firmly in the moment was her favorite. Still, it took her a few seconds to achieve the necessary equilibrium, no doubt because she was tired from the long drive.

"I'm waiting for Miss Hollister to arrive," she amplified with only the tiniest edge to her voice. Just enough to let the big man with an attitude know she didn't intend to be pushed around.

"She's expecting you, then?"

"Yes, of course. Didn't I just say so?"

"No ma'am," he said gravely. In contrast to her own firm tone, his seemed disarmingly gentle, quiet, a mellow rumble that seemed to originate well within that huge chest. Summer had to salute his skill. Trust me, he seemed to say. I'm really on your side here. She knew better. "You said you were waiting for her to arrive. You could be planning to surprise her."

"I assure you she knows I'm coming, because I called her at the library right before I left the Bellevue Hilton. She told me how to find this place and said that she'd be here by three-thirty. She's late."

He nodded but said nothing.

"Phone her yourself if you don't believe me," she suggested. "I have both her work and home numbers in my planner."

"Now, that just might be tough to do," he said in that odd way he had. "Calling Ms. Hollister, I mean."

"Why is it tough? I assume you have a radio in that macho machine—along with your shotgun and truncheon."

He smiled slightly, a crease appearing in one hard cheek. It humanized him just enough to give her defenses a nasty little shake. "Oh, yes ma'am, I have a fine radio, with lots of buttons and lights. Gives me something to play with while I'm cruising for innocent citizens to beat up."

More truth than fiction, in spite of the sarcasm, she thought sourly. "Well, then, this is easily cleared up, isn't it?" she managed to toss back calmly. "Just use your radio to call your dispatcher and ask him or her to put a call through."

"According to you, she's on her way here. And sixtyish ladies generally don't carry cell phones."

Summer had forgotten about that. Somehow this man had a way of disorienting her. "Well, yes, I feel certain she is." She frowned. "On her way."

"To show you the house?"

"Well, yes. And because I'm to be her guest for the next week." She paused, then corrected herself. "Well, nine days, actually."

Oddly, he looked as though that annoyed him. "You being a friend of Miss Dottie and all, I guess you know she has a tendency toward impulsive generosity?"

"Meaning what, exactly?"

"Meaning she just might have forgotten about that 'invitation.'"

"I doubt—"

The sound of a blaring horn startled them both into turning toward the road. At the same time, his hand had gone to his holster. "Hell," Summer heard him mutter as a vintage convertible the size of an ocean liner and the color of pea soup careened up the graveled driveway. She gasped aloud as the big car stopped only inches behind her rented Neon, sending stones and mud spurting from beneath the tires. The door flew open and Dottie Hollister emerged in a burst of energy and color, a gauzy skirt in shades of Day-Glo pink and purple swirling around surprisingly sexy ankles.

The hair that had been an auburn bob the last time Summer had seen her friend was now as black as the cop's and coiled in a chignon at the nape of Dottie's slender neck. Her ears sported silver hoops the size of silver dollars and a bright silk scarf was looped around her neck, vivid greens and yellows and fuchsia which would have clashed on a less confident woman.

"Dear heart, you made it," Dottie trilled, her toothy Pepsodent grin spreading ear to ear. "You're actually here!"

Summer braced herself for one of Dottie's patented bear hugs and found herself impaled by the cop's gaze as she returned the embrace. Something about the annoyed way he was looking at her through those dark lenses had her face warming. It wasn't sexual. She wouldn't let it be.

"Dottie, I'm so glad to see you," she murmured when her friend drew back, leaving Summer enveloped in a cloud of Obsession. One of her signature scents, Dottie had told her. For days when she was feeling particularly buoyant. "And you look absolutely marvelous."

"You don't think the image is too youthful?"

"Not at all," Summer assured the older woman. "It suits you."

Dottie pirouetted on tiny, sequined sneakers, her skirts flaring and her earrings swinging, then patted her bangs into place again. "See, I told you she was an absolute darling," she cooed, gazing up into the officer's dour face.

"Was that before or after you 'forgot' to tell me 'the absolute darling' was coming for a visit?"

"Now Brody, don't fuss."

"I don't fuss."

Summer blinked. The man she'd considered human granite sounded utterly offended.

"Sure you do, dear, but I realize you can't help yourself, so I forgive you," Dottie chided, patting that rock-hewn jaw.

Summer saw the color wash up from the strong column of his neck and realized she was gaping. "I take it you two are acquainted?"

Dottie laughed. "Yes, indeed. Brody's my nephew."

Summer felt a thud in the vicinity of the third button on her jacket. The nephew who had built Dottie the house just down the road? The widower nephew who lived in that same house with his teenaged daughter? The same house where Summer was to be a guest?

"I didn't realize." She directed a pointed gaze at the left side of his chest. "You're not wearing a name tag."

His big hand flipped open the jacket to reveal the silver bar imprinted with his last name pinned over his shirt pocket. She caught a whiff of leather, the barest whisper of musky aftershave before he let the jacket fall closed.

"Oh, dear, you mean he didn't introduce himself when he stopped by to welcome you?" Looking anything but annoyed, Dottie beamed as she glanced from one to the other. "Shame on you, Brody. It seems your manners could use a little brushing up."

"Don't push it, Auntie."

The cop's scowl turned lethal. Summer couldn't resist flashing him a gay smile. "Actually, your nephew seemed to be under the distinct impression I was some kind of second-story person, come to rip you off."

As Dottie swung her gaze his way again, her features sharpened. "Brody, you didn't!"

The color in his lean cheeks deepened, and Summer could have sworn she glimpsed a sheepish look settling over his hard-bitten features. It came and went so quickly, however, that she decided she must have imagined it.

"What did you expect me to do when I saw a strange car parked in the drive? Invite the driver home to some of that god-awful tea you set such store by?"

"Well, of course you had to investigate. It's part of that job of yours, but that's no excuse for insulting one of my dearest friends."

"I didn't insult her." He sounded little-boy sullen, and Summer fought an urge to grin and stick out her tongue.

"I'm sure you did, dear. You go into Papa Bear mode. It's one of the things that I find most endearing about you, as well as the most exasperating."

Bracelets jangling, Dottie reached up to adjust his collar,

oblivious to the fact that he was a monster of a man with a surly attitude—and the most impressive set of pectoral muscles Summer had ever seen.

"You'll have to forgive him, dear," Dottie said, turning her way. "Just last Christmas—or was it the Christmas before?—well, it doesn't matter when exactly. The point is, he surprised a transient trying to sneak in through that boarded-up window next to the chimney—only, of course, it wasn't boarded up then—and Brody nearly got himself killed when the nasty man pulled out a shotgun. Blew a limb off of Mama's apple tree." Twisting around, she pointed toward the bay window Summer had admired earlier.

"I understand," Summer hedged, glancing his way. Perhaps the man was only doing his job. And as much as she wanted to dislike him for his choice of professions, she found his protectiveness toward his fey aunt endearing. "I apologize if I was rude, Officer Hollister."

"It's Chief Hollister, dear," Dottie corrected gently. "Not that Brody stands on ceremony. Like he always says, 'Osuma's too small for crap like that.' "

"Damn it, Auntie, watch your language," he grumbled.

Dottie blinked. "I will if you will."

Touché, Summer thought, smiling a little. The cowboy cop shifted on those long legs, then glanced at the sky as though calling down divine assistance. Summer suspected he'd lost more than his share of skirmishes in what appeared to be an ongoing battle.

"Care to tell me why you arranged to meet your visitor here instead of at the library?"

"Pay attention, dear. I've already explained everything."

"No, ma'am, you did not," he drawled, moving slightly to put his wide chest between the chill wind and the two women.

"Silly of me. How could I possibly forget something like that?"

"Quit stalling, Auntie. What's going on here?"

"Nothing you need to worry about, Brody, I assure you."

Summer could almost hear his patience thinning. "Try me."

"It's just business, Brody. Nothing to concern you. Summer is looking for a place to relocate her practice—she's a psychotherapist, you see, and a very good one, I might add." She beamed a fond smile Summer's way. "You should have heard her talk at the Ashram. She had us all spellbound." She blinked. "Where was I?"

The cop shifted his gaze to Summer's face. "Relocating her practice," he prodded with surprising gentleness.

"Oh yes, of course. I suggested she might like Osuma."

"Dumb question, but indulge me, okay? How come you didn't arrange to meet her in town?"

"Because I've told her all about Grandpa's house and she asked if she could see it."

"Why?"

"I just told you. She's looking for a place to rent, and this house is perfect."

"Waste of time."

"Brody!" Dottie chided. "You'll make Summer think there's something wrong with the house."

He shot a disgusted look at the sagging porch. "It's a damn good thing she didn't break her leg on those steps."

"They're more solid than they look," Summer said.

"Maybe for your weight," he said, his gaze sliding over her like the slow brush of his callused hand. Summer felt a pulling sensation in her belly and told herself it was simply hunger because she'd skipped lunch.

"Summer's right," Dottie chimed in, her earrings bouncing. "The house just needs a few licks with a hammer here and there and it'll be as good as new. Better."

He shook his head. "I've told you before, Auntie. The place is a fire trap. Best thing for it is dynamite."

"Don't be ridiculous. Your grandfather built that house for his bride, and your father and I were born here. Right upstairs there in the east bedroom. And you grew up here." She glanced toward a shuttered dormer window, her face softening. "You used to climb down that oak at night and sneak over to the creek to catch frogs."

Something very like bitterness crossed his face. "You're not going to budge on this, are you?" His gaze shifted from one woman to the other. "Either of you?"

"No." The word came out in chorus and Summer laughed. The cop didn't.

Using two stiff fingers, he nudged the brim of his hat higher and offered his aunt a glimpse of that half smile Summer had seen earlier. A hard man with a shy grin was a powerful combination, she thought.

"In that case, I'll leave you two ladies to your grand tour."

"You're welcome to join us," Summer offered, feeling more than a little guilty that she'd painted him with another man's sins.

"No thanks, ma'am. I'm not much for hanging out with bats."

"Bats?" she repeated in a thin voice.

"Don't worry. They're not plentiful. Not more than a dozen or so, last time I checked."

Oh God. Rats were bad enough, but at least you knew where to look. Bats could come at you from anywhere. "You're . . . that's a joke, right?"

He studied her for a beat, bringing heat to her cheeks, and a nervous feeling in her stomach. His grin was more than a little unsettling. "If you have a hat, you'd best wear it. Wouldn't want to get that big city hairdo any more mussed than it already is."

Summer drew a swift breath, but before she could find her voice, he turned on his heel, climbed into the Blazer, and fired it to life. While the two of them watched, he backed around the huge Olds, then took off in a spray of gravel and exhaust.

"I do apologize, dear," Dottie murmured, her voice flavored with what sounded suspiciously like laughter. "Brody has a good heart, but he's been a policeman for more than half his life. His mood isn't always the sweetest, especially when he's taken by surprise." Dottie shook her head, then brightened. "Well, about that tour, I'm game if you are. Or would you like to freshen up?"

Summer realized she'd been staring at the Blazer tearing

along the twisting road and jerked her gaze back to the big old
house. "Definitely the tour," she said, straightening her shoulders. "If the inside is as great as the outside, I have a feeling I'm
about to fall in love."

CHAPTER 2

Brody Hollister headed back to town at his usual ten miles over the limit. It was close to five o'clock, and he was dog tired. The temperature was unseasonably warm for early spring, with just enough bite in the air to add color to winter-pale cheeks and stir the blood. Consequently, Osuma was filled with tourists from the Seattle side—"coasters" out for a day in unpolluted air.

A cautious man who'd learned to expect the worst from both society at large and people in particular, Brody had six officers working instead of the usual four per shift. Even so, they'd had trouble keeping up. Since he'd gone on duty at six-thirty, he'd handled everything from the disappearance of a garden gnome from the sidewalk outside Lucy's Alpine Garden to a brawl at Sarge's Place, a seedy watering hole near the old abandoned mill on the wrong side of the river.

When the dust settled. Brody had hauled two of the three drunken bikers to the county lockup and charged them with assault. The third, fingered by the others as the instigator, had been a minor, not yet eighteen, but with a mouth on him that would put a seasoned bullwhacker to shame. That one was now in juvenile detention in Wenatchee, and Brody was more than happy to let the juvie cops deal with the wiseass remarks.

Maybe a night in detention would take some of the sour piss out of him, though Brody doubted it. Yet there'd been an instant when Brody had seen something besides venom in the kid's eyes, something painfully familiar. For want of a better word, he'd labeled it desperation. The kind that soaks into the bone after too many years of fighting back against rotten odds. Whatever it had been, it had kept Brody from booking the kid as an adult, though the courts had recently granted him that right. He doubted the ungrateful punk even knew he'd been cut a break. Brody was too cynical to think he'd ever hear from the boy again. But sometimes, in his lonelier moments, he wished that just once he might be part of someone's happy ending.

Spying the sign for the rest stop overlooking the Wenatchee River at milepost 14, he decided to pull over and do his end-of-watch paperwork where he had something to look at beside the stacks of performance reviews and reports on his desk. The parking lot was deserted as he pulled into his favorite spot near a stand of spruce and killed the engine. After tossing his hat onto the passenger's seat he shifted his gaze to the river a hundred yards below. The water was up from last week and tinged with a deep iridescent green, the first tentative sign of a high-mountain thaw. In the sunlight the surface showed only gentle ripples, but beneath, the current had a wild core, tinged with winter's lethal chill. Like Dr. Summer Laurence's eyes.

An interesting woman, Dottie's friend. A . . . what was the word? Enigma? Yeah, that's what she was. A classy enigma.

A cop on assignment might look at the lady and see a tough career woman who gave as good as she got, and yet there'd been something intensely vulnerable about the thrust of her chin and the set of her slender shoulders. A man who lived his life on the lonely side just might notice hints of a buried sadness in that not quite perfect face. If he were really looking, he might even have seen a moment of purely feminine interest, which was probably the deluded imaginings of a horny widower, he thought as he sat up and reached for his logbook.

Setting his jaw, he ran his pencil down the neat entries designed to account for every minute of every shift. By his calculations he'd spent thirty-five minutes at the ranch. Long enough to realize he hadn't quite turned to stone.

Any lawman who'd been on the job a decent number of years

had pretty much seen everything by the time he'd earned his first five-year stripe. But the lady's reaction when she'd come around the house had surprised him. The quick flinch, the look of revulsion—both could have been nothing more than surprise. Or something else entirely. A guilty conscience maybe?

He'd decided to lean on her a little harder, just to see how she reacted. Damn if she hadn't leaned back. He wasn't much for aggressive females, but this one was different somehow. Maybe because she had the nicest legs he'd seen in recent memory. A little on the short side for some, but long enough for his taste, with an interesting flare to her hips and perfect ankles. His mouth had watered at the thought of seeing those sleek legs bared to the sun. He pictured her stretched out on a sunny patio wearing perfume that cost more per ounce than he made in a day—and nothing else. When he added himself to the image, he nearly groaned aloud.

He signed the log and toyed with the idea of strangling his softhearted, unpredictable aunt. She knew better than anyone why he hated to open his house—and his life—to strangers. Nine days, the lady had said. Which meant eight nights, sleeping in the guest room, which was directly across the hall from his. Eight nights of slipping between the sheets half-naked after one of those endless showers women seemed addicted to, her skin still pink and soft from the torrents of warm water.

Shit, he thought as he stowed the clipboard and fired the engine. What had he done recently to deserve such punishment?

Hell, he went to church most Sundays, showered every day, and watched his language when ladies were present. He'd even changed old man Felderson's tire in the pouring rain just last week, while the miser-mean bastard had gleefully recounted every damned thing wrong that had happened in Osuma in the nine years since Brody had become chief.

He backed around, then let the Blazer idle while he checked out the '88 white Civic four-door pulling in. Washington tags, current sticker. A young couple in the front, a baby in a carrier in the back. All were safely belted in.

Catching sight of him watching, the woman looked startled, then raised a hand in a tentative wave. He returned her wave with what he hoped was a decent enough smile and pulled away, his gut twisting.

His Meggie had been dead for eleven years. He'd grieved hard and he'd grieved long, but he'd finally accepted the empty place in his life. So why did it still hurt so damn bad to watch others enjoying what he'd lost?

The road was clear ahead and behind as he pulled out, and he punched it. The souped up V-8 responded instantly and the Chevy surged forward, a greedy momentum shoving him back against the seat. The speedometer needle shot to the right and was climbing fast when the radio crackled to life.

"Son of a bitch," he muttered, braking hard at the sight of a widened place on the shoulder. Five-thirty on a sunny Sunday in April was a rotten time to have a two-car pileup on the busiest road in the city limits.

Traffic on Highway 2 westbound was a tangled nightmare. Even with lights and sirens, it had taken Brody twenty minutes to reach the accident scene. On the way he'd heard rookie patrolman Rich Keegan call for more units and then a heartbeat later, an ambulance.

The site itself was controlled chaos, radios crackling out noise at sporadic intervals and powerful strobe lights assaulting the eye with white and blue pulses of light. Three OPD vehicles were lined up in a ragged row on the west berm just shy of the sign marking the city limits. Fire and rescue trucks were parked a few yards farther west, their lights adding glaring red slashes to the confusion.

The sun had already dipped behind the peaks as Brody pulled up behind Sergeant Slate Hingle's dusty white Taurus and killed the engine. He saw Hingle first, a dark-skinned, steady-eyed giant in an immaculate uniform, standing on the white line bisecting the two lanes, directing traffic westbound. Farther west,

Keegan's partner and training officer, Corporal Paul Sawyer, was handling the eastbound flow, which was much sparser.

From what he could see, there'd been only two vehicles involved. The maroon Jaguar XJ 12 traveling in the westbound lane had apparently left the road at a sharp angle and smashed into a huge white-bark pine standing approximately ten yards from the shoulder. The other vehicle, a '99 Toyota pickup, its shiny paint as red as blood, had plowed through a fence on the opposite side of the highway, coming to rest about twenty feet away in a thick stand of brambles. The twin sets of skid marks on the pavement, both starting in the right lane, indicated that the driver of the Jag had swerved to avoid the truck and hit the tree instead.

On the way to the scene, he'd heard Keegan run the plates and drivers' licenses. The Jag was registered to a Martin Oates at an address in Kent. A routine check of the owner had come back clean. The Toyota was listed in the name of Dr. Anson Finley of Bellevue, also clean. The name on the Washington driver's license had been one Joseph Anson Finley, seventeen, same address, no outstanding warrants.

Tall, bony, and red-haired, with the bulging Adam's apple and awkward grace of a modern-day Ichabod Crane and a Howdy Doody face, Keegan stood next to the open door on the driver's side of the truck. Next to him stood a young man—Finley, Brody figured—who was dressed in a sloppy sweatshirt and baggy shorts. The young man was visibly nervous and kept running his hand through the lank hair hanging in his face. At the same time, his gaze kept darting to the truck's interior. Looking for what? An open container? A loose joint? The hard stuff?

Brody knew the signs. The same signs he'd first seen on the streets of L.A. when he'd been working drug intervention. The bastard was a doper. A goddamned junkie!

Jesus, he hated scum like that. Right down to the bone despised them with every ounce of emotion left to him. There'd been a time when he wouldn't have trusted himself in the same room with scum like that.

After keying dispatch to announce his arrival on the scene, he opened the door and got out. A familiar odor of tar and burned rubber kicked up from the graveled shoulder to hit him full in the face. Hingle spied him first, and lifted a hand in acknowledgment. The sergeant's expression was grim. Brody braced himself for the worst.

A blue pall of exhaust fumes from the slow-moving vehicles hung over the scene and filled his nostrils as he headed toward the back of the red-and-white ambulance up ahead. While two firemen in full turnout gear stood close by to render assistance, three blue-clad paramedics, two men and a woman, worked feverishly over someone lying on a gurney. A female Caucasian, smaller than most by the size of the blue deck shoes peeking out from blood-soaked khaki slacks.

Brody felt a moment of sick rage before he clamped a lid on it. He waited until one of the medics, the oldest of the three, had time to spare him a look, then asked brusquely, "Is she going to make it?"

"Yeah, maybe. Her baby didn't," one of the other EMTs answered without looking up.

Brody clenched his jaw and looked down at the victim lying so still and white on the gurney. She looked surprisingly serene, as though sunning herself in her own backyard. Above the trach tube in her throat, her freckled face was untouched save for one small cut on her temple.

He saw the rounded tummy beneath the blood-soaked shirt and felt a slam of pain that took his breath. Megan had worn that same angelic expression, even as her blood was congealing on the new living room carpet she'd wrangled out of him for their fifth wedding anniversary. A familiar mix of emotions expanded inside him, threatening to blow a hole right through twenty-five years of professional discipline. Cops didn't cry on duty—at least not this cop.

"The driver?" he managed to jerk past the knot in his throat.

"Never had a chance." The medic nodded his head toward the open doors of the van where another gurney containing an adult-sized body covered by a sheet had already been loaded. Brody wanted to plead with them to save the young mother, but they were already doing the best they could. Later, he would deal with the images filling his head—and the anguish they invariably evoked.

"Jag's got a child's seat in the back," he prodded, glancing back at the wreckage.

The female EMT glanced up from the syringe she was preparing, her face pinched with strain. "Boy about four survived with just a few scratches from flying glass. Nothing serious."

"Where is he now?"

"In the back of Keegan's vehicle. This one's triage priority. As soon as we're done here, we'll check him out."

Brody glanced behind him at the souped-up Taurus, but the child was nowhere in sight. "Does he know—did you tell him about his folks?"

The medic shrugged before plunging the needle into the woman's limp arm. "Far as I know, no one's said the words."

"You get his name?"

"No time." Brody couldn't fault her for that. He thought about radioing for someone from Children's Services to take over. They were trained for stuff like this. But with traffic snarled and it being Sunday, it might take hours to get someone out here. What the hell did he do with the boy in the meantime? Let him sit in the back of a smelly patrol car while the ambulance drove off with his family inside? Take him into town and plunk him down in an office somewhere where every face he saw was a stranger's and every voice alien? Handle it himself? He panicked at the thought.

"I'll take care of it," he said quietly before heading back toward Keegan's car. He was reaching for the door handle when he heard an angry shout. Spinning toward the sound, he caught a flash of movement near the Toyota as Keegan slammed its driver against the front fender.

Brody shouted a warning, but too late. The driver had already exploded into action. In one furious motion, he plowed a fist into Keegan's gut, then kneed the officer in the groin. Keegan sank to the ground, his body bent double. At the same time, Finley spun around and hauled ass toward the plunging slope of a ravine twenty yards to the north.

Brody was already running when he saw Hingle take off in the same direction. Finley was fast, but hampered by the panicked looks he kept darting behind him. Brody had the advantage of a longer stride and gained steadily. Close enough now to hear the rasp of the young man's tortured breathing, Brody dug for one desperate burst of speed, gauged the distance, and launched himself at the suspect's knees. Though it was far short of a textbook tackle, his weight and momentum sent the fleeing man forward onto his belly into a patch of weeds and mud. Mostly mud, Brody realized, spitting out dirt.

Beneath him, pinned by Brody's two hundred forty-five pounds, the junkie lay momentarily motionless, gasping for air. From the corner of his eye Brody saw Hingle approaching. At the same time, the man under him exploded into action—arms and legs flailing wildly as he struggled to escape. Things were hairy for several seconds before Brody managed to plant his knee in the suspect's back, pinning him against the dirt.

"Don't move, asshole," he grated close to the suspect's ear. "Don't even twitch."

"Hell of a tackle, Chief," Sawyer exclaimed as he joined them, his round cheeks fiery red.

"Yeah, great show for the civilians," Hingle chimed in, jerking a pugnacious chin at the traffic, which Brody saw was now being handled by the firemen. "Gives 'em something to talk about besides how bad our crime scene is messing up their day."

Brody moved back, ready to slam Finley to the ground if he moved again, but all the fight seemed to have gone out of the bastard. "Too bad the media didn't get it on tape."

"Oh yeah, I can see it now—a prime example of police brutality in Osuma-fucking-Washington," Hingle replied with a sneer. "Don't shoot the bastard. Huh uh. No way. Sit down and have a quiet dialogue instead and see if the hyped-up fucker will consent to being arrested."

"Consent or not, this fucker isn't going anywhere but jail," Brody declared as he snapped his own cuffs on Finley's wrist and jerked them tight.

"Hey, that hurts, man!" The suspect's cry was muffled by a mouthful of weeds. Brody hoped he choked on them.

"Be gentle when you pat him down," Brody jeered as he got to his feet.

Hingle did as requested, then none too gently jerked Finley to his feet. "Bastard's lit up like a Christmas Eve." His expression was bleak. "Probably doesn't even know he wiped out most of a nice family."

But he *would* know, Brody vowed. And he *would* pay. If there was any fairness at all left in the justice system.

"It's your collar, Chief. You want me to book him for you?"

Brody nodded. "But give the collar to Keegan, only don't let him know about it right away."

Hingle's ebony countenance creased into a sudden grin, transforming his mean-looking face. "Let him sweat, huh?"

"Do him good." Brody moved his jaw, testing for damage where the heel of Finley's sneaker had clipped him when they'd fallen. "Miranda him and get the blood and urine levels as soon as you get there, then call the deputy DA and give him a rundown. Tell him I'll call him when I get back to the office. Soon as *Daddy* gets the word, this place will be crawling with Dream Team types."

"Will do."

"My father's gonna have your badge, butt hole," Finley muttered as Hingle pushed him toward the Taurus. Sweat was dripping from his chin, and his eyes were sunken and bloodshot, the pupils so dilated they all but obliterated the lighter irises.

"Save your breath, Mr. Finley," Sawyer ordered, his disgust obvious as he glanced Finley's way, " 'cause there ain't nobody here who cares."

"By the time he and his lawyers are finished with you pigs you'll be lucky to find a job as a crossing guard."

Walking on Finley's other side with Sawyer, Brody caught

his sergeant's eye and shook his head. "Sounds pretty good about now, doesn't it, Sergeant?"

"Yes sir, it surely does at that."

Red-faced, halfway recovered, Keegan met them at Hingle's car. "Found this in plain sight on the floor," he said, holding up an evidence bag that contained a handmade crack pipe and a small packet of a crystalline rocklike substance. "Soon as he realized I'd seen it, he went crazy."

"You log it?"

"Yes sir." He cleared his throat. "Guess I blew it, huh?" he muttered, watching glumly as the sergeant shoved the prisoner into the back.

Brody withstood the urge to lecture the rookie about proper procedure. That would come later, after Keegan calmed down enough to really hear him out. "Mistakes happen, Keegan. You got lucky this time."

"Yes sir."

"After you finish your paperwork, I want you to write an essay for me. About what you should have done that you didn't do."

"Yes sir."

"You get a next of kin on the victims yet?"

"A Mrs. Blanche Oates, address in Kirkland. Listed as the driver's mother. Dispatch is trying to contact her."

This was Keegan's first fatality, and from the pallor on the young man's face, Brody figured the kid was fighting a perfectly natural need to puke his guts outs.

"Let the guys from fire handle traffic. You help Sawyer secure the crime scene." Even as he issued the order, Brody knew it was a losing battle. Trying to preserve evidence for the coroner and the investigators in the midst of chaos was damn near impossible. But he ordered it done anyway.

The rookie's relief was more than evident. "Yes sir."

Brody watched Hingle maneuver into the space Keegan cleared then walked along the berm to the remaining Taurus. He caught sight of the pale little face looking at him through the tinted window of the backseat.

The youngster was a redhead like his mama, with saucer eyes that were more gold than brown and a spray of Dennis the Menace freckles on his cheeks. He was sitting near the door, sucking his thumb. A small yellow-and-white quilt with ragged edges and chocolate stains lay next to him on the seat. The youngster's security blanket.

Brody's gut twisted as he reached inside the driver's open window to release the back door lock. He heard the routine radio chatter at the same time and shut off the set, furious that Keegan hadn't thought of it. The last thing the child needed was to hear the desperate messages darting back and forth to the hospital about his own mother.

"Hi," Brody said when he'd opened the door and squatted to the boy's eye level. He remembered the dark glasses and removed them so the boy could see his eyes. Experience with Kelly when she'd been a little girl had taught him he wasn't so scary that way. Gentling his voice after years of deliberately honing it to a protective edge was difficult, but he gave it a shot. "I'm Brody. What's your name?"

The child pulled his thumb from his mouth and blinked. He was dressed in jeans and a T-shirt under a miniature Seahawks windbreaker. He'd lost one of his high-top sneakers, and he had a hole in his sock. Brody caught a whiff of little-boy sweat and felt a tug in the vicinity of his heart.

"I'm not a-spos'd to talk to strangers," the little one said in a small, scared voice.

"Did your daddy tell you that?" Moving slow and easy, Brody placed the glasses on the floor.

"Uh huh. And my mommy, too."

Good people and loving parents, he was sure of it. The kind that invariably paid the price instead of worthless scum like Finley. "Your mommy and daddy are right about that." He paused to clear his throat, but the tight thickness was still there. "See this badge on my jacket?"

"Uh huh." The boy stuck his thumb back in his mouth.

"That means I'm a policeman. Did your mommy or your daddy ever say it was okay to talk to a policeman?"

The youngster considered that solemnly for a while, then nodded.

"Do you think you could tell me your name, then?"

After another long considering moment, the thumb popped free. "Trent Adam Oates," he singsonged.

"Okay if I call you Trent and you call me Brody?"

The boy's head bobbed.

"How old are you, Trent?"

"Four and a half. I'm a big boy."

"I'll bet you're strong, too, right?"

"Uh huh. I help Daddy carry in logs for the fire 'cause I'm so strong. And he's proud of me, 'cause I'm such a good helper."

Brody swallowed hard. He was doing this all wrong and didn't have a clue how to do it right. Give him a bad guy to chase or a crime to solve and he handled it. But words were a struggle for him. Sometimes they came out wrong. Usually, when it mattered most, they didn't come out at all.

"Uh, I'll bet he is proud," he blurted when he realized the boy was looking at him expectantly. "Real proud."

Through the window's tinted glass, Brody saw that the ambulance was still there, parked just beyond the fire truck, which obscured his view—and the boy's. He decided to take the youngster into town with him while he waited for dispatch to reach the grandmother.

Maybe Trent didn't understand what was happening now, but someday he'd know. And he'd remember the last glimpse he'd had of his family. Sorrow tore through him as the memory of another ambulance in another place crowded hard into his mind.

"Uh, are you hungry?" he asked casually, keeping his voice low and nonthreatening. "I am. I missed lunch, you know, and uh, maybe . . . how about we drive into town and get some ice cream? You like ice cream?"

Brody knew he'd made a mistake the instant the boy darted a frantic gaze toward the opposite door. His parents must have told him not to accept candy—or ice cream—from strangers. Even cops.

"It's okay, Trent—"

"Where's my mommy? The other policeman said I was a-spos'd to wait for my mommy here."

Brody felt something cold grinding in the center of his chest. "Uh, how about we go find your grandma instead?"

"No! I want to go see my mommy! The p'liceman said she was gonna be right back." The small chin with the promise of strength jutted forward.

Brody closed his eyes and wished desperately that for this one moment, his throat wouldn't close up on him. Please God, not now, when he needed words to comfort the boy. But the jagged constriction he never stopped dreading was already starting. Desperate, he took a breath and tried to push out the words. The effort only locked them tighter inside his throat.

"I want my mommy!"

The boy scrambled across the seat to the opposite door and grabbed for the handle. Brody leaped forward and hooked one arm around his skinny waist. Still screaming for his mommy, Trent struggled wildly, smashing an elbow into Brody's nose. All arms and legs now, he tried to escape. Gently, so as not to crush small bones or bruise tender flesh, Brody turned him around and onto his lap. Folding himself around the small body, he hugged him tight, even as the panicked child dug small frantic fingers into the back of his neck. At the same time, he rubbed the boy's bony back in slow, measured circles.

The boy hiccuped, then snuggled his cheek against Brody's wet shirt. He was calmer now, exhausted from the crying. "I want to go home," he mumbled against Brody's neck. "I want to see my mommy and my daddy."

I know, baby, Brody wanted to tell him. But he couldn't. Not without stuttering like a jackass, which would only frighten the boy more.

Trent tried to lift his head, but Brody pressed a gentle hand against his bright curls to keep him from seeing the activity beyond the tinted windows. The firefighters were buttoning up the truck, preparing to leave. Ahead, the ambulance with lights flashing was just nosing out of its spot. As the ambulance passed, he caught sight of the weariness in the female EMT's face and had a hunch she wouldn't get much sleep tonight. He doubted any of them would.

A moment later, he saw Sawyer approaching the car. The corporal hesitated, then crouched down to say softly through the open window, "Dispatch called. They've been trying to reach you." He glanced at the silent radio, comprehension dawning in his eyes. "The grandmother is on her way to the station. ETA, three hours."

Brody nodded. Sawyer hesitated, then asked, "Accident investigation just arrived. You want to talk to them?"

Brody shook his head. Instead of taking the hint, Sawyer stayed put, waiting for orders. With a grim resignation, Brody unlocked his jaw and reminded himself of the hours of speech therapy he'd put in so he wouldn't spend the rest of his life as a silent, miserable outcast. Sometimes, though, the tricks he'd learned through painstaking practice failed, especially when he was emotionally drained.

Seeing Sawyer's expression turn uneasy, he took a breath and let it out slowly, speaking with the flow of air the way he'd been taught. "You . . . handle it," he managed to get out, his voice jerky as hell. Until he got himself under control again, however, anything more was beyond him. He nearly sagged with relief when Sawyer nodded and got to his feet.

Brody felt Trent's small body relaxing against his and glanced down. The boy was curled into a fetal position against his chest. Trent's eyes were closed, and his cheeks were wet. Once again, his thumb was tucked securely in his mouth.

Brody let out a stream of air, then slowly pulled the quilt from beneath his thigh. As gently as he could, he wiped the tears from the boy's pale cheeks. And then, far less gently, from his own.

CHAPTER 3

The sun had slipped behind the mountains while Summer and Dottie had been inside the old house, and though the sky was still light, the trees blocked all but occasional glimpses from sight. It had grown colder, too, an odd sort of cold that seemed far more penetrating than the occasional chilly day in San Diego.

Driving at a snail's pace behind Dottie's huge land boat, Summer cast an anxious glance through the open sunroof and made herself take a slow, deep breath. It didn't help. The towering pine trees on both sides of the graveled access road formed a black, impenetrable canopy overhead, one that made her feel smothered. She'd driven through tunnels before—lighted, concrete structures that made her shiver inside. But this tunnel seemed endless—and frightening.

To distract herself, she thought about the house she'd just left. The high ceilings and spacious rooms that would be filled with light once the plywood had been removed from the windows. The huge kitchen with the wonderful bay window looking out over what must once have been a garden. The dated cabinets and faded wallpaper would have to be changed, of course, and two more bathrooms added. Just as she was mulling over their exact placement, Dottie put on her brakes, then swung the Olds into a sharp turn to the left. Summer followed, and seconds later emerged from the murky darkness into a clearing that, in comparison, seemed flooded with light.

40

Following Dottie's lead, she parked under a huge oak tree, bare now of leaves, that was twice as big as anything she'd seen in the city.

After killing the engine Summer exhaled a noisy sigh of relief, then found herself gaping at the scene in front of her. Smack dab in the center of parklike grounds sat the kind of house she'd always coveted when watching those old black-and-white movies on the classics channel. As neat and tidy as a doll's house, it was two stories high, with sparkling white shingles and a terrific wraparound porch. It even had a swing.

"It's perfect," she murmured, charmed by the snowy lace curtains that adorned every window, reminding her of delicate bridal veils. There would be roses in summer, too, neatly trimmed bushes lining the stepping-stone walkway, their bare canes already putting out the crimson shoots of spring.

To the right was a double garage, both doors open. Inside was a midnight blue pickup truck and a huge motorcycle, the kind of muscle machine ridden by the Hell's Angels. A perfectly maintained, vintage hog. Hollister's, of course—although some imp inside her was already busy imagining Dottie perched on the wide seat, her small hands twisting the throttle to a full roar. Next to the garage was a fenced area with a swing set and jungle gym that looked a little rusty, but serviceable. Tucked into one corner was a miniature version of the house itself, complete with the same intricate trim along the eaves. It seemed an idyllic life in an idyllic setting. But it wasn't a life for someone who had debts to pay, she reminded herself as she stepped from the car.

"Your house suits you, Dottie," she exclaimed as she walked around the Neon to open the trunk. "Especially the annex."

Dottie looked puzzled, then grinned when she saw that Summer was referring to the playhouse. "Brody built that for Kelly before we moved in. She'd just turned four and was still missing her mama. She still hides out there when she wants to be alone."

"I used to have a place at the beach like that. It was in the rocks below Sunset Cliffs. This is much more private." Summer tried to remember if Dottie had told her what happened to the child's mother. An accident? An illness? Something sad, at any rate. Dottie sometimes muddled her stories, breaking off one in mid-tale to begin another. It was part of her charm.

"I keep hoping there'll be more children playing there, but Brody seems determined to remain a bachelor. Over the years I've introduced him to a number of lovely young women, but . . ." She sighed as she grabbed the small carry-on case containing Summer's laptop. In spite of the resignation in Dottie's expression, Summer felt a whisper of suspicion.

"Dottie, I sincerely hope you don't have any ideas about fixing me up with your nephew, because—"

"Oh, no dear! That never crossed my mind, I assure you. No, I remember distinctly your telling me that you're far too busy to marry."

Summer studied the guileless eyes fixed steadily on hers, looking for the telltale signs of deception, but Dottie gave every appearance of telling the truth. "Well, good. Fine," she told her friend before retrieving her tote and closing the trunk. Side by side they ambled up the flagstone walk toward the wide steps. The pine-scented breeze tugged at her hair and rustled through the needles overhead. It smelled like Christmas morning.

"By the way, did I apologize for being late?" Dottie asked as they climbed the wide front-porch steps. "I was researching Renaissance sexual mores for an author in Dryden and lost track of the time." She glanced around, then lowered her voice. "Did you know that a dapper gentleman of the fourteenth century expressed his individuality by the kind of codpiece he wore?"

Summer blinked. "No, actually I didn't."

Dottie's blue eyes sparkled with mischief. "I found the most wonderful book full of illustrations. Knights even wore them under their armor. Some even had an entire wardrobe of codpieces. They even had little faces drawn on them. With different expressions." Dottie's own expression turned quizzical. "For different occasions, do you suppose? Like weddings or beheadings or whatever?"

Summer choked out a laugh. "The mind boggles, doesn't it?"

Dottie actually giggled. "I imagine women of those days could judge a man's personality by his codpiece. Rather like a man's tie today." Dottie bobbed her head, reminding Summer of a tropical bird. "Brody hates ties, you know. Refuses to wear them unless he absolutely has to. Do you suppose that means he would have been naked under his armor most of the time?"

"I really have no idea." Summer had always been a visual person. Before she could stop herself, her mind had formed a graphically detailed image of long, sinewy thighs and heavily muscled calves clothed only in chain mail, tight hose, and boots. Exerting every ounce of mental discipline she possessed, she managed to stop herself before the rest of the picture took shape.

"I'm so pleased you're finally here," Dottie exclaimed as she opened the heavy front door.

"So am I," Summer told her, even as she silently wished that her friend's beloved nephew lived someplace else. Like Alaska, perhaps—with the other timber wolves.

"I'm still fine-tuning the interior," Dottie said, ushering her inside. "Every time I move a stick of furniture, it drives Brody crazy. But you know how men can be. They hate change."

"It looks tuned just fine to me." Summer looked around her. "Perfect, in fact."

"Oh, please, don't say that," Dottie said as she closed the door. "Perfection is so dreary."

"Not to mention impossible."

Dottie laughed. "There is that, though one does try."

And inevitably fails, Summer thought with a touch of leftover sadness for a shallow, thoughtless girl who'd sought solace from her parents' indifference in the perfect wave, the perfect high.

The entry was spacious, the walls a lovely ivory trimmed in misty green. The thick rug on the wide-planked floor was a darker shade of the same green tone, bordered with heavy fringe. Ahead was a sturdy oak stairway, its wide handrail just begging to be ridden.

"That's Brody's office," Dottie said, indicating a closed door on the left of the entry. "He claims he goes there to catch up on the paperwork he brings home from the office, but Kelly is always teasing him about hiding out there because he feels outnumbered, especially when the house is filled with teenaged girls."

Summer nodded politely. What the man did behind that closed door was his business, not hers. "Your niece is what now? Fourteen?"

"Yes, at the end of March. I'm sure I must have written you about the fun we had in Seattle shopping for her present. Brody swears the two of us all but melted the numbers off the credit card before we were finished."

The end of March. Summer fought off a searing jolt of pain. She'd gone into labor on a March day. . . . She drew a breath and fought to ground her thoughts in the here and now. "Dottie, would you mind if I changed into something more comfy before we continue the tour?"

"Of course, dear. Here I am chattering away like a silly old lady while you must be desperate to put your feet up and relax. It's just that I've so looked forward to your visit and I've got hours of conversation stored up." Her laugh was self-conscious. "Not that I don't love Brody and Kelly dearly, you understand, but they have their own lives. You're such good company. Such a sympathetic listener, but then that is your job, isn't it?"

"With you it's simply a pleasure."

"You are a sweet child," Dottie murmured, looking a bit embarrassed. "It's going to be such fun introducing you to the Fearsome Foursome."

Summer blinked. "Pardon me?"

"The Fearsome Foursome is Brody's name for myself and three of my closest friends. We've been together since grade school, you see. On occasion we've been known to cause a little harmless mischief. Like the time we filched Deirdre Fleener's padded bra from her gym locker while she was taking a shower and strung it up on the flagpole."

Summer choked a laugh. "I take it Deirdre was not a close friend?"

"Oh no, dear, just the opposite. You see, she was the most terrible gossip, and she'd started this rumor that wasn't true about this sweet Negro girl who had just moved to town." Anger shimmered for an instant in Dottie's eyes. "Deirdre was so mortified she transferred to Wenatchee and had to drive forty miles back and forth. Ruined her father's Plymouth."

Still talking, Dottie led the way up the stairs. The landing was larger than Summer expected, with a wide hall, both walls of which were covered with framed photographs, some obviously dated and others of more recent vintage. A quick glance at the nearest photo had her gaze clashing with the smiling eyes of a much younger Brody Hollister standing straight and tall in sailor's whites. For a few seconds she stood frozen, her heart thudding loudly in her stunned body. The man with the lumberjack's body and the unyielding jaw of a medieval warrior had the eyes of a poet. Gentle, compassionate eyes the color of amethysts in the sunlight. Eyes that seemed to see unerringly into her soul.

"Impossible."

Only when Dottie turned her head to look at her did she realize the word had slipped from her lips. "What's impossible, dear?"

"I . . . your nephew's eyes." She drew a breath to steady her still-racing pulse, then tried a small laugh. "Are they really violet? I couldn't tell behind the sunglasses."

"Only in certain lights. In others they look almost purple. And I have to warn you he's extremely sensitive about them. Women tend to gush, you know, especially over his eyelashes."

Summer could see why. His ebony lashes were so thick they seemed to tangle at the corners. A dramatic frame for those disturbing eyes.

"It's the curse of the Hollister men, those eyelashes." Dottie let out a long-suffering sigh. "Mine, as you can see, are puny and thin, as were my aunt Naomi's. Even Kelly wasn't blessed. But my father and my brother, they had lashes like Brody's. It's enough to make one quite peevish."

Summer smiled. "How long was he in the navy?"

"Six years. He was sixteen when he enlisted, had to lie about his age, which is the only lie I've ever known him to tell. Not that I blame him, you understand. His life was pretty miserable here. His father, my brother, Ray, was not a kind man." A shadow crossed her face, and for a moment, she looked every day of her sixty-one years. "Brody was a good sailor, even though he got violently seasick every time he went on cruise. Even so, he made first-class petty officer before he got out. His specialty, I guess you could call it, was the shore patrol. He was hired by the LAPD the day after his discharge came through."

Beneath the stiff white hat, his black hair was much shorter and his smile cocky, revealing the beguiling crease in one hard cheek. Though he was clearly standing still, he seemed to swagger somehow. Like the biggest, toughest dockhand on the meanest wharf. Only belatedly did Summer notice the woman standing next to him. No bigger than a minute, she had curly red hair, a pearly complexion, and laughing eyes the color of a clear Celtic lake.

"That's Brody and his wife, Megan, on the day they became engaged," Dottie said softly, watching her. "She was a nurse at a hospital in Long Beach. They met when she helped the ER doctor sew up a knife wound in his thigh."

"She's very pretty." Adorable really, with a Madonna's un-lined face and a shyly innocent smile. "She must have been very young when she died," she added softly. And deeply in love.

Dottie drew a slow breath, and all vestiges of a smile left her face. "She was twenty-nine. Kelly had just turned three a few weeks earlier. She doesn't remember her mother at all."

"Did you tell me she was ill?"

Dottie shook her head. "She was killed by a man who broke into their house one night when she was alone."

Shock jolted through Summer's tired body. The empathy that made her a good therapist also made her far too susceptible to the suffering of others. "I'm so sorry," she murmured, her gaze fixed on the young mother's laughing eyes. "That must have been horrible for B . . . for all of you."

"It was. Brody blames himself. I don't think he's ever really gotten over it."

"No, I can imagine." Summer didn't want to feel Brody Hollister's agony. But she did. "Is that why he left L.A.? To get away from the memories?"

"That was part of it, I think. A larger part than he cares to admit. His primary reason was to give Kelly a stable upbringing, something that he felt would be impossible for a single father in the city."

"In other words, he brought his daughter home to you."

Dottie smiled, and her blue eyes were soft with affection. "I like to think that was part of it, yes."

Summer touched her friend's arm. "It's a lovely tribute, Dottie. I suspect your nephew doesn't bestow his trust easily."

"No, Brody has learned the hard way to guard his heart well," she said before turning away. After one last look at the young lovers, Summer followed, cursing herself for arousing sad memories in her friend.

"There are four bedrooms," Dottie said briskly, pointing as she strode toward the room at the end of the hall. "Only one bathroom on this floor, I'm afraid, though there's another three-quarter bath downstairs."

The door was ajar, and Dottie nudged it open. The bathroom was larger than most and smelled like soap. The same clean scent she'd sniffed when Brody Hollister had crowded into her personal space.

The tile was white, the fixtures chrome. A window at one end admitted the soft glow of the setting sun, splashing light over the octagonal floor tile. An enormous claw-foot bathtub was tucked into its own alcove, like an artifact in a museum. A good six feet long, it was deep enough to swallow her whole without leaving a ripple.

"The ivory towels are yours," Dottie said while denuding a

hanging fern of one brown frond. "They're all natural fiber, of course."

Summer followed the direction of her friend's glance and saw two thick ecru bath sheets edged with eyelet lace, hanging on a brass rod next to a standard shower stall. With one exception, the other towels were a pretty yellow tone, but without the lace. The exception was large, dark chocolate in color, and neatly hung over the shower door to dry.

Suddenly she had a vivid fantasy of a virile male body stepping wet and slick from a steaming shower, water beading on those massive shoulders and running over that wide chest. She felt an unwelcome pull of pure lust, and scowled.

Her need for a man's touch, a man's kiss, was so deeply buried, so heavily layered over with guilt and pain and shame, she'd thought it gone forever. But within the space of a few seconds in the presence of a man she had every intention of avoiding, those long-buried needs had surfaced with a vengeance. Later, when she had the time and the privacy, she would explore possible reasons. Emotion examined was emotion understood—and therefore capable of being controlled.

"This was one of the first porcelain bathtubs in Osuma County," Dottie confided proudly, running caressing fingertips over the tub's rolled lip. "I found it in the basement of Ma Nightingale's bawdy house a few months before Brody started building this place. Of course, the poor thing had been horribly neglected."

"Ma Nightingale?"

Dottie laughed. "The tub." She frowned down at the antique as though seeing it as it had been. "Covered with layers of dirt it was, and one foot had come loose. I scoured it with Comet and pumice, then had it reporcelained."

Summer struggled to catch up. "Ma Nightingale ran a bordello?"

"The best in the county, I'm told. Percy Gilbride used to be her doorman. He swore that Ma hired only the prettiest girls and treated them like her daughters. Unfortunately, she had to close down in the early twenties when a Methodist became mayor."

"What happened to Ma?"

Dottie grinned. "She retired to Arizona and married a rancher. Legend says she started the first home for unwed mothers in the state."

"Good for her," Summer commented as she followed Dottie from the bath and into the next room on the right. Like the rest of the house, the room was spacious and airy, with high ceilings and a bleached pine floor.

"Good heavens, don't tell me that came from Ma's, too," Summer exclaimed, her gaze on the huge bed with four posters, situated between two dormer windows. She'd never seen a bed with roses and cherubs carved into the headboard. And entwined initials. A *G* and a *D*, she thought, though the calligraphy was inordinately flowery.

"No, it's eighteenth-century French. It belonged to a courtesan in the court of Louis something-or-other. I forget which one. I bought it ages ago when I had thoughts of marrying." A look resembling pain crossed Dottie's face. A lost love? Summer wondered. And yet, Dottie was a contented old maid—or so she herself had proclaimed on more than one occasion.

"Kelly's room is next door to this one, and mine is the first one on the left," Dottie went on quickly, flicking a small wrinkle from the bed's embroidered counterpane. Which meant that the nephew's room was opposite hers, Summer thought, hiding her dismay behind an appreciative smile.

Dottie opened the drop-front desk and set the laptop case on the gleaming surface before bustling past Summer to open the closet door. "I've cleared out this half for your things, but if you need more space—"

"No, that's fine. I didn't bring much that needs hanging." Summer deposited her tote on the floor in front of the closet.

"There are extra blankets on the shelf in case you get cold."

"I'm sure I'll be fine." Summer was beginning to feel acutely uncomfortable. She was usually the one obsessing over details.

"I put an extra lightbulb in the drawer of the nightstand. There's nothing worse than settling in with a good book and having the light go out."

"Dottie, I'm fine. Really."

Dottie nodded, then cleared her throat, her expression more serious than Summer had ever seen it. "Summer, there's something I probably should have mentioned before. About Brody and this plan of yours."

Summer felt her shoulders tense. "You think he would object to your renting me the property for a treatment center?"

Dottie nodded. "He has a reason. A good reason."

"Everyone always does."

Dottie nodded, then cleared her throat. "Calvin Williams, the so-called man who killed Megan, had just been released from a drug rehab facility similar to yours," she said quietly. "Apparently the therapists there knew he was dangerous, but his Medi-Cal had run out, and they couldn't keep him."

Summer stared down at the vivid mix of color and texture swirling over the big bed. The stitches were neat and even, a pattern within the pattern. "Was it a robbery?" she asked when she trusted herself to speak calmly.

"No. Revenge. Brody had arrested Williams for selling drugs to minors. Because Williams was only nineteen and had managed to keep from getting into trouble previously, his attorney plea-bargained it down to possession. Ironically, that slimy weasel was one of those people who really did belong in prison instead of rehab. But he was smart enough to play the system."

Crossing her arms over her chest to ward off a sudden chill, Summer walked to the window and stared out at the snow-covered peaks. The puffy clouds that had seemed so benign earlier were now tarnished and sharp with menace. Beyond the trees, the mountains loomed like great hulking beasts ready to prey on the innocent.

"Brody wasn't home that Friday night because he'd gone to a retirement party for his sergeant. Kelly was at Meggie's parents' house for the weekend, because Meggie was suffering from morning sickness."

Summer stiffened and fought down the acid rising in her

throat. But the face she turned Dottie's way was composed, her eyes steady. A therapist's mask. "She was pregnant?"

"Six months along. She was still alive when Brody got home, but she died in his arms—along with their unborn son."

Summer realized her lungs were burning and she slowly released the air trapped in her chest. "Oh God, Dottie," she murmured, pressing her hand against the sudden knot in her womb. "Why didn't you tell me all this earlier?"

"Because I knew you'd have those second thoughts I already see forming in your eyes."

"Second thoughts that are justified, as you know perfectly well," she said quietly as she returned to the bed and perched on the edge.

"Forgive me, dear." Guilt glimmered in Dottie's eyes for a split second before, surprisingly, they took on a definite twinkle. "One of the advantages of being over sixty and a recognized eccentric is the right to be downright pushy when I think the situation warrants it."

"I'm sorry about Megan. Deeply sorry."

"I know you are, dear." The amusement in Dottie's eyes faded, to be replaced by an abiding sadness. "And I know you can understand why Brody hates anything to do with illegal drug use. One of his first acts as chief was to go after the meth labs in the hills. He nearly got himself shot more than once before he managed to close them down and keep them closed. His men have orders to come down hard on anyone suspected of selling drugs. No mercy for dopers is the rule of the day here."

Summer traced a curving crimson thread with her fingernail. "Dottie, I love you dearly, but you must have known you would be putting me in a terribly awkward position by offering to rent me your property."

"I disagree." Her friend's smile was edged with steel. "We'll never know for certain, of course, but suppose Calvin Williams had been sent to Phoenix House instead of that other place? Megan would still be alive, wouldn't she? And how many other families will be saved the agony we suffered?"

Even though she was sitting down, Summer suddenly felt as though she'd been neatly backed against a very solid wall. "There's no right answer to that, and you know it."

"I know I believe in you, Summer."

"I appreciate that more than I can say, but I also don't want to do anything that would hurt you." She raised her head. "I mean that, Dottie."

"I know you do. Just as I mean it when I say I didn't offer you my family's homestead on a whim. If you want it, it's yours. I do, however, have some advice for you—if you want that, as well."

"I always listen to advice from my friends," Summer said with a smile that felt disturbingly shaky.

"For the time being let Brody think you simply want the house for an office. Don't say anything about a treatment center."

"You mean lie to him?"

"I was thinking more in terms of a judicious evasion. After all, you're only investigating possibilities at the moment. And I do so want us to have a nice visit while you're here, which would be impossible if Brody got his back up."

"I can handle him." A feeling far too much like doubt ran through her before she shoved it away. "But what about the resentment toward you he's almost certainly going to feel if we go forward with this?"

"I'll do what I always do when he gets prickly about something—let him fuss and growl and lecture, then ignore him."

Summer decided that Dottie was far braver than she looked. "Think a minute, Dottie. Idealism can sometimes hurt—and hurt badly. If your nephew considers your actions a betrayal, he could strike back. Maybe do something rash or even ugly."

"No dear. He can be obstinate and opinionated and sometimes downright infuriating, but he hasn't a mean bone in his body."

Summer wanted to argue further, but knew all too well how love could block out reason. "What about my prison record? How's he going to react to that?"

Dottie gazed into the mirror over the dresser and took her time adjusting the folds of her scarf before turning to look Summer squarely in the eyes. "Why even mention it? After all, it's past history."

"It might not be to your nephew. He is a cop, remember? And cops always expect the worst."

Dottie's smile was gently chiding. "Not all of them, dear."

"Not all of them have reason to hate drug pushers. And according to my record, that's what I am. Or was."

"But you weren't."

"You have only my word on that, Dottie."

"I've never doubted it for a moment."

Summer released her stomach muscles from the hard, urgent knot and thanked whichever angel looked after friendships for sending her Dottie. "I'm not proud of the person I was then, but I can't change the past."

"That's what's so interesting about life, though, isn't it? The way human beings patch themselves together."

Summer smiled. "A lot of my patches are fairly ugly."

"So you made some bad choices." Dottie shrugged. "You accepted the consequences and moved on. It's where you moved on to that counts."

How many times had she herself said those very words to a sullen patient? Dozens? Hundreds? Summer got up and began to pace. The room that had seemed so spacious earlier was suddenly confining and airless. Too much like the cell that had been her home for more days and nights than she wanted to remember.

"I never thought I'd hear myself saying this, but Chief Hollister has good reason to feel the way he does," she said softly, stopping at the desk to grip the carved back of the chair.

"He's also wrong. He's spent the last eleven years hating people he doesn't even know. It's twisted all the gentleness out of him and kept him from getting on with his life." Her bracelets jangled as she made a sweeping gesture. "You, of all people, should understand the crippling effects of hatred."

"Yes, I understand." Summer let out a sigh. She was suddenly exhausted—as emotionally wrung out as if she'd been through a grueling therapy session. "If he asks me a direct question, I won't lie," she said, turning to face her friend.

"Nor should you. But a little artful shading of the absolute truth couldn't hurt, with others as well as Brody, I might add. There are a lot of people in this area who agree with Brody. A lot of others who resist change of any kind. It would be better to ease them into it rather than ramming it down their throats."

Summer sighed. She'd gone into this expecting opposition. No one wanted a drug treatment center in their backyard. Or a prison. Or an AIDS hospice. "All right. After all, nothing is really settled, is it?"

"No dear, not yet. But I have high hopes." Dottie grinned. "Take your time settling in, dear, and in the meantime I'll go down and make us a nice pot of tea." With a flurry of skirts and the violent swaying of the silver hoops in her tiny ears, Dottie was gone.

CHAPTER 4

Twenty minutes later, her hair freed from the formal French twist she preferred when working and her thighs grateful for the release from panty-hose hell, Summer was on her way downstairs when a photo on the wall caught her eye. Curious, she paused to take a closer look. A head-and-shoulders shot done in black and white, it was of a lady with aristocratic cheekbones, a true heart-shaped face, and, she realized with a moment's whimsy, the proverbial swanlike neck.

Opulent ostrich plumes waved from the glossy ebony of her thick, curly hair, and the bodice of the shimmering light-colored dress was low cut and beaded. Stardust glittered in her eyes, signaling to even the casual observer that she was an innocent girl deeply in love. And yet, it was a woman's eyes that smiled into hers, and the full lips were curved into a smile worthy of Eve herself. Summer drew a breath and felt a bittersweet tug of abandoned dreams.

"That's a picture of my aunt Dottie." At the sound of the young female voice, Summer turned around to see a petite teenager in baggy jeans and the pink-and-white striped smock of a hospital volunteer standing in the doorway of the room next to hers.

"I thought it was," Summer said, returning the girl's endearingly shy smile. An inch or two taller than Summer, she was as cute as a storybook pixie, with masses of black hair piled haphazardly on top of her head and a heart-shaped, adorably freckled face that gave promise of a mature beauty. With the exception of the deep-blue eyes, which seemed oddly shadowed, she might have been a very young Natalie Wood.

"Hi, I'm Summer Laurence," she added as the girl came to stand next to her. The scent that clung to the flawless skin was light, with just a hint of sass. Hidden currents, Summer thought. A girl who kept much of her personality beyond public scrutiny, as though to guard herself from hurt.

"I'm Kelly Hollister," she said, openly assessing Summer from head to toe as only the young can do. "Aunt Dottie said you were coming to visit. You're a shrink, right?"

"Yes, a psychotherapist actually. I work with teenagers mostly."

Kelly dropped her gaze to her sneakers. "Dad went to a shrink once, after my mom died. They made him, Aunt Dottie said."

" 'They' who?"

"His bosses at the LAPD. He kept losing his temper and all. Busting up things."

Summer was surprised. Hollister didn't seem like a man who would allow himself to lose control. "I can see why they were concerned."

Kelly lifted her head and grinned. "Have you met him yet? My dad?"

"Yes, while I was waiting for your aunt at the house next door. He thought I was a prowler. For a minute there I thought he was going to frisk me for assault weapons."

Kelly giggled. "Really?"

"Well, not quite. But I think it was a near thing."

"Dad has that effect on people. It's 'cause he's so big, Auntie says. That and the fact that he tends to scowl a lot. That's 'cause he's shy around strangers, especially women."

Summer had her doubts about that. Most cops she'd met, including Kyle, had been anything but shy. A few had been about as crude as a man could be. The stories she'd heard from her patients paralleled her own.

"That's my dad when he was in high school." Kelly moved a

few steps to her right and pointed to one of the other photos. "Tiff—that's my best friend—thinks he was a real hunk before he got old and all."

It was a candid shot of a much younger Brody Hollister dressed in an old-fashioned white undershirt, much like the muscle shirts today, and jeans tight enough to be illegal, both tattered and spattered with grime. Shoulders and arms bulging with strength, his burnished skin gleaming with what appeared to be sweat, he held an axe in one huge hand and stood with a sturdy work boot planted on the incredibly wide stump of a tree that he'd apparently felled. Shaggy dark hair trailed over his brow, and he was scowling ominously at the camera as though furious at the interruption.

"Aunt Dottie took the picture," Kelly rattled on. "She says it's her favorite of him, next to the one of him and me when I was a baby. See?"

This was the handsome young husband with the spectacular eyes, now so full of love it hurt Summer to look into them. A man clearly smitten with the rosy-cheeked cherub tenderly cradled in arms so brawny they stretched the ribbed sleeves of his red knit shirt. Something about the set of that hard jaw and the slight curve to his mouth suggested a man still dazzled by his good fortune. For all his faults—and she had no doubt he had some fairly nasty ones—Brody Hollister clearly adored his child.

Knowing she shouldn't, Summer let her gaze linger on the angelic face of the laughing infant. She'd never seen her own child smile. She never would.

"My mom was really pretty, wasn't she?"

The longing in the girl's voice pushed a lot of buttons Summer had never quite managed to disconnect. She knew all about the need to feel a mother's arms around her when life pushed in hard. "Stunning," she said with a warm smile. "You look like her."

Kelly's pleasure in the compliment was obvious. "She was a nurse, you know, and I'm going to be one, too, so I can work with babies like she did."

"Good neonatal nurses are worth their weight in gold."

"Yeah, that's what Grandma Mary says." Kelly's gaze drifted again to the photo of her parents. "Grandma and Dad don't get along."

"I'm sorry to hear that," Summer said carefully, studying the girl without seeming to. The impression of sadness she'd caught at first glance seemed to have deepened. Yes, something was bothering Dottie's niece. Something that had dimmed what Summer suspected was a natural vibrancy.

"Sometimes mothers of daughters have trouble letting go," she suggested gently.

Kelly pulled her dark brows together in a thoughtful frown before she shook her head. "She thinks my mom died 'cause of him."

Summer went still inside. Was that it? The reason for the haunted look? A deeply buried conflict between her love for her father and suspicion planted by her grandmother? She ... Whoa, Laurence, she reminded herself firmly. She'd been invited into this family's world as a guest and not a professional.

She was about to change the subject by asking about another photo of Dottie and a rough-looking man who looked a lot like an older, angrier Brody Hollister, when somewhere below she heard a door slam and the rumble of a man's deep voice.

"Kelly?"

"Up here, Dad," Kelly shot over her shoulder. "I'm just showing Summer our picture gallery."

Summer sensed movement a moment before Hollister himself reached the top of the stairs. He was bareheaded, his glossy black hair windblown and curling over his forehead. Along with the Stetson, he'd shucked the bomber jacket—and the badge. His uniform shirt had lost most of its starched crispness, and the cuffs had been rolled back nearly to his elbows. She noticed a fresh bruise on his jaw and muddy stains on his jeans. There was a long rip in the denim over the knee and darker stains that looked like blood. His gun belt was slung over one shoulder, giving him the look of a war-weary mercenary trudging home after a rough battle.

A scuffle with a prisoner? she wondered. Or a barroom brawl after hours? She could easily visualize both. Without question, there was a potential for violence in this man, though she sensed a rigid control keeping it in check. He could—and would—kill. Exactly the kind of man she abhorred. And yet . . . She found herself glancing again at the young father cradling his baby. Which was the real Brody Hollister? she wondered, returning her attention to the man himself.

"What happened to you?" Kelly asked, eyeing the dark smudge on his jaw.

"A difference of opinion with one of the bad guys."

"Gnarly." Kelly grinned, looking for a brief time like a mischievous six-year-old. "Did you shoot him?"

He scowled. "No. I sweet-talked him into giving up the way all good cops are trained to do."

Kelly giggled. Summer frowned. Sweet talk? Him? When pigs fly, she decided.

"Settled in, Dr. Laurence?" he inquired, his tone more weary than rude.

"Almost, Chief Hollister. Your aunt is an excellent hostess."

He nodded, then shifted his attention back to his daughter. When he spoke again, his tone was softer and the lines bracketing his mouth less severe. "I was supposed to pick you up at the hospital, young lady."

Kelly shoved her hands into the pockets of her smock and shrugged. "When you had someone call to say you'd be late, I got a ride."

"Twenty minutes late, max, and Mrs. Wyles said you'd already been gone for ten. In a red sports car."

"Dad, it's no big deal, okay?" she said, her voice turning sullen. "A friend happened to come by, and I hitched a ride."

"Which friend is that?"

The girl's hesitation was slight, the flicker of her lashes

subtle. Summer suspected Hollister had caught both. "Mark Krebs."

"The kid you met at Christmas? Doc Krebs's grandson?"

"Yes, and he's not a kid."

"If he's old enough to drive, he's too old for you."

Summer heard the exasperation in Hollister's voice and felt a reluctant sympathy. Being a single parent could be excruciatingly difficult during the teenage years, when hormonal surges and a child's natural need to detach joined forces.

"Dad, chill, okay? It was just a ride. No big deal."

In the fourteen years and one month since Kelly had been in his care, Brody had never lost his temper with her, just as he'd never lost his temper with Meggie. But unlike her sweet-tempered mom, Kelly had a way of pushing him right to the edge. Before he could figure out where to go from here, he was interrupted by Dr. Laurence's quiet voice. "If you two will excuse me, I was just on my way downstairs. Dottie's promised me tea."

"It was nice meeting you," Kelly said, brightening. "Maybe we could talk more later? About California and stuff?"

"I'll look forward to it," Dr. Laurence said with a smile that tugged at things inside him better left buried. Without looking at him again, she headed for the stairs, her cute little bottom swaying just enough to have a man swallow his tongue.

"Dad, I'm sorry about not waiting," Kelly said stiffly when their guest had disappeared down the stairs.

"Apology accepted." He rubbed a hand over the hard stubble on his cheek, searching for words to make her understand, to maybe cut him some slack in the dad department. But those that came to mind painted ugly pictures of sweet, innocent girls laid out on slabs, their once-pretty smiles battered into silent horror. Or, God help him, of Kelly's own mom desperately clutching his hand, begging him to look after their little girl. He managed a breath and tried for a smile instead. "I'm going to let you off the hook, but there'd better not be a next time or you'll spend your free time in your room or doing chores for your aunt."

Kelly gave him a frown that was her mother's, right down to the twin lines between her eyebrows. "Dad, it's cool, honest. Mark's a really nice guy. Only his father killed himself last Easter, and Mark's still, like, all torn up and stuff. He needs a friend, and you always said being there for your friends was sacred."

Brody felt his neck getting hot. Sure, he was sorry for the boy. And he understood grief maybe better than most. But Kelly was just a little girl, not a therapist like Dottie's friend. And like all little girls, Kelly trusted too easily. Maybe she thought Doc's grandson was harmless. But he didn't. A sixteen-year-old male was a walking hard-on. The thought of some sweaty adolescent relieving himself in his precious little girl filled him with panic.

"Kel, we've been all through this. No dating until you're sixteen."

"Dad, I'm almost fifteen! Tiffany's been dating for two years."

"You're barely fourteen, and Tiffany is not my daughter."

"What can happen on a ride home from school?"

"More than you can imagine. Kel, I want your word you'll obey me on this."

At the word *obey*, Kelly stuck out her chin and gave him one of those disgusted-to-the-depths-of-her-soul looks that he hated. "Do I have a choice?" she muttered.

"No."

"Whatever," she spat out before clamping her jaw shut.

Brody caught her arm just as she was turning away from him. "Baby, I—I'm just trying to keep you s-safe."

"I'm not a child anymore, Dad. I can keep myself safe."

"Kel, things happen. Accidents—"

"I have homework to do before dinner." She jerked her arm, trying to free herself. Brody let her go, the hand that had held her fisting at his side as she flounced into her room and slammed the door. Slowly, he turned, his gaze finding his wife's face. He was trying, he wanted to tell her. As hard as he knew how.

Through the years he'd done all he could to crowd Kelly's life with so much love she wouldn't miss having a mom in her life. Dottie had helped. But there were times when Kelly needed a mother's gentle smile. A mother's wisdom. He'd die for his daughter. But a mother's love was the one thing he couldn't give her.

An old ache settled in his chest, and he lifted a hand to rub at the spot before he realized what he was doing and dropped it to his side again. Damn, but he felt lonely sometimes.

Dottie loved the cozy window seat with its cushy chintz pillows and lacy curtains where she curled up at night to read—or sometimes just to dream impossible dreams.

It was past ten and the house had the hushed solid feeling of an impenetrable bulwark standing between her and the terrors of her own black regrets. At Summer's quiet, but decidedly firm insistence, Dottie had taken her shower first, then made her usual rounds to wish her family good night.

Brody had been closeted in his lair, muttering over paperwork, his always unruly hair even more disheveled by impatient fingers and his mood a little dangerous. A few minutes ago she'd heard him leave the house and roar off on his beloved 1969 Harley. Trying to outrace the demons that drove him so mercilessly, she suspected.

With a sigh, Dottie brought her knees to her chest and linked her arms around them. It was all those potent little chemicals rocketing around the dining room earlier that had her feeling melancholy, she decided, her gaze tracing the familiar outline of the Big Dipper, star by star. Definitely a pheromone moment. A first for this house.

Poor Brody, surrounded by women chattering away about hairstyles and makeup and teenaged heartthrobs. It had almost been comical, the way he and Summer had avoided looking at each other during dinner, but Dottie had seen that stiff, I'm-not-a-bit-interested look around Summer's mouth. Just as she'd seen the way Brody had attacked his pot roast as though it had somehow threatened his masculinity.

Enjoying the image, Dottie laughed softly, deep affection for her bull-headed, battle-scarred nephew bubbling inside her. It was both touching and amazing that he was still shy around women he found attractive. And he *did* find Summer attractive. Dottie would bet her Olds on it, with her entire collection of Navajo jewelry thrown in.

Leaning back, she rubbed her shoulder blades against the window frame and listened to the sound of the guest room door opening and closing. Summer had been in the bathroom when Dottie had come back upstairs, the bathtub taps running and wisps of steam escaping through the crack at the bottom of the door.

The sweet soul had looked worn-out by the time they'd finished stacking the dishwasher and wiping down the counters. Dottie had done everything but tie the woman to the dining room chair in an effort to keep her from helping on her first night as their guest, but Summer was as tenacious as she was smart—and as breathtakingly lovely as Dottie's prized hybrid tea rose.

Perhaps most important, though, was her kindness. It had been the first thing Dottie had noticed about her. Closing her eyes, she thought about the flicker of surprise in Summer's eyes when they'd met, followed by a flood of genuine delight and curiosity. Dottie knew all too well that more often than not she was viewed as an oddball. An eccentric spinster who still dressed in bright colors and hippie jewelry more suited to a woman half her age. Whose hair was never the same color from year to year, sometimes month to month. Who was essentially harmless—and slightly pathetic.

But Summer, bless her heart, had seen through the defiant facade to the lonely woman beneath who'd longed for a happy marriage and a houseful of children. Just as Dottie had seen the sadness that Summer cloaked in professional courtesy and brilliance. In some inexplicable, wonderful way, the two of them had formed a bond. It wasn't something they'd ever discussed, but it was there nonetheless, a feeling of kinship, of sisterhood in spite of the difference in their ages.

It was sometime late in the evening on the last night of the retreat that Summer had told her about her life's goal. Her dream, really, of healing the bodies, minds, and hearts of the lost souls she'd come to know so well. Kids who'd filled their bodies with vicious poison.

As Summer had talked, her words carefully chosen and her face somber, Dottie had sensed a deeply buried pain beneath the determination. She suspected that there was more to her story. A chapter that was perhaps too personal, too painful to share, even with her friends.

Dottie felt tears prickle her lids and drew a long breath. Another thing they had in common, she thought.

Summer had never been in a room that just reached out and took her in, like a smiling, full-breasted mama opening welcoming arms to a wayward child. It was the lush colors of plum and pink violets on the wallpaper and the lavender scent on the sheets, she decided, smoothing her palm over the pillowcase on the right side of the bed. It was real linen, the color of aged ivory with a wide edge of hand-tatted lace. One shade darker, the lace had been carefully mended, as though it had gone through some hard times.

Now *that* would be a hoot, she realized. A thirty-two-year-old semi-virgin snuggled down between sheets that looked as though they'd started life on a courtesan's bed. If only those pillow slips could talk, she thought as she drew back the plum-and-ivory quilt. Had the woman who'd first slept between these sheets welcomed her lover with an open heart and a willing body? Had her dreams been in her eyes, or had she lain rigid with humiliation, sick with shame after the man using her had gone?

Summer let her face relax into a self-deprecating smile. Even in the depths of her addiction she'd managed to keep from selling her body. There had been a time or two, however, when she'd come very close. Expelling a sigh, she nudged her shoulders back from the disgusting slump that had more to do with past sins than exhaustion. How many times had she lectured a patient about letting go of the past? Hundreds, at least. Only sometimes, like tonight, it wasn't so easy.

A teenager's sad eyes. That's all it had taken to bring it all back. The reason she worked twelve hours a day every day. The reason she lived like a nun, denying herself a normal life. The comfort of a man's touch in the dark. Children of her own. Love.

Sometimes she felt so tired of it all. The long hours, the loneliness. The struggle to beg, cajole, or charm start-up funds. The snatches of time devoted to researching treatment methods. The nights spent refining her mission statement. But if she saved one child—just one—from the hell she'd endured, it would be worth it.

The quiet rap on the door roused her. "Summer, it's Dottie. May I come in?"

"Of course." She was already moving when Dottie rattled the doorknob and found it locked. In her haste, it took Summer a moment to twist the little button.

"Sorry about that," Summer said when she'd finally gotten the door to open. "A function of living in the city."

"Don't apologize, dear," Dottie said as she breezed in on a wave of Obsession and the lingering aroma of the Wild Turkey bourbon she'd sipped while fixing dinner. Over a plain cotton nightgown, she was wearing a hot-pink peignoir decorated with purple ostrich feathers that fluttered when she walked. Summer had to work hard to keep from gaping.

"Brody is always lecturing me about forgetting to lock the front door when I leave. I suspect that's one of the reasons why he always makes it a point to come by the house at least once a day when he's on duty."

"He's right, you should."

Dottie shrugged, setting the feathers forming the gown's lapels to shivering. "I've lived here my entire life—well, with the exception of eighteen months in Las Vegas."

Summer blinked. "Las Vegas?"

"Hmm. My rebellious period. I had dreams of becoming a showgirl. This robe is a keepsake of those years." Her eyes sparkled with mischief. "I keep losing feathers every time I wear it, though, which is why I only bring it out on special occasions."

She lifted both arms, and as though on cue, three wispy feathers floated free to drift slowly to the floor at her feet. "See what I mean?"

Summer took one look at the mournful expression on her friend's face and burst out laughing. "Why don't you just glue them back on?"

"I've tried. The darn things just come loose again." She emitted a long-suffering sigh before bending to pick up the tiny purple wisps. "I just came in to wish you a good night."

Summer ran her hand over the coverlet, enjoying the soft brush of the fabric. "Dottie, I've been thinking it might be better if I moved to a motel."

Alarm ran over Dottie's countenance. "Is something wrong? Is it the room? I'd be happy to change—"

"The room's great. In fact, I think this is just about the nicest room I've ever been in."

"The bed? I know the mattress is softer than normal."

"It's fine, honestly. It's just that I feel as though I'm intruding."

"Of course you're not."

"Please don't take this wrong, Dottie, but tonight at dinner it was pretty obvious your nephew doesn't want me here. Not that I'm hurt by that, you understand. I've been through too much to be offended if someone takes an instant dislike to me. But it's silly for you and Kelly to be stressed out when it would be just as easy for me to stay someplace else."

Another feather floated free, and Dottie reached out to capture it on her palm before adding it to the collection in her pocket. "I admit he's uncomfortable with people he doesn't know very well, but that's got nothing to do with you personally. He's very sensitive about his stuttering."

Summer's jaw fell open. "Your nephew's a stutterer?"

Dottie nodded. "Since he was a little boy. My brother made his life a living hell because of it. Brody eventually learned to identify the sounds that gave him the most trouble, and he's good at working around them." Dottie hesitated, then sat down at the foot of the bed and folded her feathers around her, like a small bright bird. "It wasn't really a problem when he was little. He was always a curious child, always interested in something new. He was also clumsy, like a St. Bernard puppy that hadn't grown into its big feet, and he stuttered badly when his mind got ahead of his tongue. Nobody thought anything of it until he went to school and the kids started teasing him. One day he came home with a bloody lip, crying for his mother." She paused.

"Kids have a way of zeroing in on even the most hidden vulnerability," Summer offered with perfect truth.

Dottie nodded. "Ray happened to be home from work with an injury, and he made Brody go back and fight the boys who'd taunted him, even though they were older and bigger. Gunnar Stenner was the biggest of the bunch, and Brody took him on first." She grimaced. "Gunnar owns a bar down by the old mill. Sarge's Place. Gunnar was in the Marines, you see. Brody's men are always breaking up brawls there. Gunnar's still a bully." A smile flitted over her mouth, then faded. "Brody never had the knack of making things easy on himself, and he lost that fight. Ended up with a split lip and two black eyes. Ray was humiliated. He took it out on the only target who couldn't fight back. His five-year-old son. Called him terrible names and then whipped him so hard he couldn't walk for two days."

Bastard, Summer thought. It was a story she'd heard in a dozen variations over the years. She'd gotten used to it, but she'd never stopped feeling a hot rage at the damage done to tender souls. "Which only made the stuttering worse," she guessed.

"Exactly. In fact, there were times when Brody couldn't speak at all, no matter how hard he tried. It was as though his throat had just closed up tight." She drew in a long breath. "It was so agonizing to watch him struggling. I . . . well, I tried, but . . ." She shook her head.

Summer felt a kind of sickness settle into her own stomach. "When I was in graduate school, I did a rotation at Children's Hospital. One of my first patients was a stutterer. Jason. He was fifteen and the sweetest boy. By the time his parents brought him

to me, they were frantic. He'd been through three speech patholo-
gists without improvement."

She still remembered his terrible frustration when he'd tried
to force out even the simplest of words—and the rage that tore at
him when he failed. Desperate to give him relief, she'd tried
every technique she'd learned. Role playing, hypnosis, even
massage therapy for his throat.

"Did you help him?" Dottie asked quietly.

Summer shook her head. "He drank a bottle of drain cleaner
on his sixteenth birthday. A classic example of symbolism."
She took a ragged breath, fighting back the pain. "It's one of my
deepest regrets that I wasn't skilled enough to help him."

"You mustn't blame yourself, Summer," Dottie said firmly,
sounding exactly like the nurturing parent she might have been.
"You did all you could."

Had she? It was a question that had tormented her for years.
She still didn't have an answer, but she'd learned to detach from
the worst of the pain. It was either that or end up in the same ward
with other severely traumatized patients.

"Obviously Brody had better luck," she said briskly, shoving
aside the memory. "Or a better therapist."

"What he had was guts," Dottie said, her voice reflecting a
mixture of pride and anger. "I begged Ray to get him some help,
but he refused. He thought the stuttering was a flaw, a weakness,
and he made Brody believe that, too."

"What about your parents? Didn't they see what was
happening?"

"My mother was dead by then, and my father had the men-
tality of most of the older generation in these parts. Ray was the
head of his family and Dad wouldn't interfere. So I borrowed
money from . . . a friend and paid for his therapy myself."

"Good for you!"

"It was an awful struggle at first, but finally Brody learned to
control the worst of his problem by regulating his breathing. I'm
not sure of the mechanics, just that it works. Most of the time,
anyway. He still has trouble when he's tired or upset, so that's

when he comes off a little prickly. I don't know why it's easier for him to talk when he's growling like an old bear, but it is." She studied Summer with quiet eyes that missed little. "Maybe he doesn't show it—Brody doesn't show much—but he's a very lonely man. When Megan died, he simply shut down inside. He works, he sleeps, but he rarely laughs and I can't remember the last time he really relaxed."

Summer stared at her friend. She didn't want to imagine the suffering Brody had gone through. "How can he do his job?"

"I don't know. I just know he does. And well. Even Fat Phil Potter who edits the local newspaper and who's never forgiven Brody for replacing his brother as chief admits that the crime statistics in this town have gone down every year since he took over."

Summer didn't want to be impressed, but she was. "I can see why he'd be uncomfortable with someone he didn't know living in his house."

"You'll be good for us, Summer. Very good for us. At dinner Kelly seemed happier than I've seen her in years, and I feel wonderfully alive, just thinking about helping you to make your dream come true."

Summer glanced around, drawing in the room's warmth. "It's almost too nice here. I'm so used to fighting."

Dottie reached out to smooth back a stray lock of Summer's hair. "Let me help with that fight, Summer. The way I helped Brody with his."

Summer understood the need to feel useful. "You are helping. Inviting me here, offering me your property. Being my friend." She allowed herself the luxury of a grin. "I hated to give up this bed anyway."

Dottie's smile was radiant. "I can tell you're tired, dear, so I'll trundle off—after you promise me you'll treat this house as your own. *Mi casa,* uh, something something."

Summer grinned. "I promise, *mi amiga.*"

Looking delighted, Dottie enveloped her in a smothering

bear hug that had feathers flying. Somehow one ended up in Summer's mouth.

"I'd definitely try staples," she suggested as she handed it back.

"I think I will at that." With a fluttery wave, Dottie padded to the door and closed it behind her.

The sickle moon was almost overhead, and the wind from the north had an angry bite. Bathed in the glow from the propane lantern nearby, Brody sat on an upturned log in front of the woodshed at the old house, his forearms braced on his knees while he flexed and unflexed his stinging fingers to restore the circulation. In spite of the thick calluses he'd layered on over the years, he'd managed to add a few blisters during the last three hours.

Damn, but he was out of practice, he thought, glaring at the axe stuck into one of the logs yet to be split. There'd been a time when he'd felled trees all day and still had juice left. He must be getting old. Sure as shit he'd be stiff and sore by morning. Still, he'd chopped enough wood tonight to keep them in roaring fires half the winter. His body was about as tired as it could be, yet his mind wouldn't give him peace. He kept thinking about Trent Oates, wondering how the little cuss was doing.

By the time the boy had cried himself out, Brody had gotten a handle on his emotions and figured out a decent enough plan. He'd take Trent into the office and wait with him there until the grandmother arrived. Except that Trent had started crying whenever Brody had tried to ease him off of his lap. It ended up with Keegan driving back to the department with Brody and Trent still in the back. One of the parking control people about to go off duty had gone back out to Nugget Creek to pick up the Blazer.

The grandmother, Mrs. Oates, seemed like a nice lady. Sensible, his aunt would call her with one of those quick decisive nods Dottie gave when she was sure her instincts were on track. A woman of breeding and, well, grace, he figured was the right word, Mrs. Oates had been accompanied by her priest, who'd had calm, intelligent eyes and a strong handshake.

Brody had talked to them privately first, using one of the interrogation rooms since Trent had been sacked out on the couch in his office. Because he hadn't wanted Trent to wake up and find himself alone, he'd asked Max to stay past her usual quitting time to watch over him.

Brody had been prepared for the questions and tears. As much as a man could be. It had been awkward at first but he'd gotten through it without making a total ass of himself. Though clearly distraught, Mrs. Oates had held it together fairly well, only breaking down once, when she'd asked him about the baby her daughter-in-law had been carrying. He'd had a few rough moments then himself.

The priest had helped, holding her hand, speaking words about God's will and the hereafter that Brody sensed the man truly believed. Anyway, Mrs. Oates had seemed to find comfort in them.

There'd been paperwork enough to give him a whopping headache, so Max had walked the woman through the maze with a compassion Brody respected. Release forms for Osuma PD and the state. Notification forms for Children's Protective Services. All very impersonal and tidy. Not even a hint of the months of grieving ahead. Or the hollow emptiness of a house still filled with baby furniture and toys and maybe the lingering aroma of a pan of fudge brownies set to cool on a kitchen counter.

Brody cast a tired look at the shadowed spot where the glow from the lantern faded into the darkness and told himself the little guy was tucked up in a soft bed in his grandma's house, sound asleep and safe from the pain for a few hours. No doubt sucking hard on his poor thumb, with that tattered scrap of quilt someplace close. Brody had nearly lost it when Trent had pulled his thumb from his mouth to give him a hug good-bye.

Poor kid didn't have a clue what it was going to be like when he was too old to suck his thumb. If he was lucky, he might find a generous and loving woman to cuddle up to in the middle of the night when he was feeling scared or lonely or burdened with too many lousy memories. If he were really lucky, he'd never find himself standing at the edge of a grave with his baby daughter sobbing in his arms while the best part of his heart was being lowered into the ground forever.

Brody braced his shoulders and slowly climbed to his feet. Turning his head, he gazed over the chunk of real estate that had been in his family for close to a hundred years. His great-grandfather had logged the slopes. His grandfather had directed his timber crews from here, in a big corner room in the house he'd built to house a dozen kids. A family dynasty of Hollister men that stopped with Brody.

Big Malcolm had been a tough bastard. Hard as hickory. Brody had admired his grit. His grandfather hadn't been as physically or emotionally brutal as his son, but Brody still woke up in a cold sweat sometimes, tortured even in his sleep by the disgust in his grandfather's eyes when he looked at his only grandson.

Damn it, boy, stop stammering like some kind of pussy retard and spit it out. I got more important things to do than wait all blasted day for you to get out one half-assed sentence that don't make sense nohow.

His granddad's words had hurt worse than his old man's curses. So much, he hadn't been able to hold back the hot tears the way he'd learned to do when Ray'd taken after him. Blubbering like a baby, he'd stood mute while Big Malcolm damn near shredded him to hamburger.

He'd been all but seven or maybe eight when he'd started sneaking out to do his crying down by the creek where no one could hear. The first time he'd climbed out onto the roof and swung onto the rough branch of the oak had nearly been his last. The damned clumsiness that still sometimes caught him unawares had caused him to tumble a good eight feet to the ground. He'd hit hard and sprained the hell out of his wrist. It hurt almost more than he could stand, but he'd known better than to go running to his mother. Even when his wrist had swollen to twice its normal size, he'd managed to hide the pain. For two days no one noticed—until his aunt had come home from college on spring break. She'd been the one to take him to the doctor. Bless her, she'd always been the one to see to his hurts. Until he'd met Megan.

His stomach clenched as he fought free of the bad memories. He was years past those days—with a lot of battles fought and won behind him. His men respected him, and on a good day, he even respected himself. Maybe he wasn't the best-liked chief in the ninety-six-year history of the OPD, but he was the best for the job at this particular moment. He had the lowest crime stats in the state. Maybe in the entire Northwest.

It hadn't been easy winning the trust of people who'd known him all of his life. Hardnosed, hardworking, fiercely independent folks who'd witnessed the nightmare that had been his childhood. People like Sarge Stenner who'd taunted him as a child and gotten away with it.

Nobody called him names now. Not to his face anyway. And he no longer cared what they called him in private. He knew who he was—and who he wasn't. But sometimes, when he met someone new, someone special like Summer Laurence, he was tempted to forget.

Why the hell did she have to be a Ph.D.? he thought, as he jerked the axe free of the wood. One of those scary ladies with brains who'd always made him worry about his grammar, even when he had no damned intention of uttering a single word. Worse, she'd made him wish he was twenty-five again, with a body that didn't creak when the barometer fell and a tongue that didn't get tied in knots. Not that she'd be interested in the likes of him, he reminded himself with the ruthless honesty his kind of disability had forced on him a long time ago.

As days went, this one had worked out damned lousy. He'd smacked up against the obscenity of two deaths that shouldn't have happened and met a little boy who'd chipped off another piece of his heart. His daughter, his little girl whom he loved most in the world, wasn't speaking to him. And to cap it off, his damn house was being invaded by a woman he didn't know, who had his head all tangled up with things better left alone.

Yeah, his aunt had mentioned Summer Laurence, all right. Talked a lot about how bright she was and how generous she'd been to a lonely old woman. What she hadn't told him was how his body would react when he saw the woman. Or that he would take one look and ache all the way to his soul.

CHAPTER 5

Alone in the kitchen, Brody leaned against the counter and sipped his second cup of high test while watching the early morning sun edge across his aunt's spotlessly clean floor tiles. When he'd come down twenty minutes earlier, Kelly had still been asleep and his aunt had been listening to the news on her clock radio. Dr. Laurence was taking a shower.

It had been a hell of a start to his day, walking out of a steamy bathroom just as their guest was leaving her room looking like innocent sex bundled in a fluffy yellow robe big enough to hold two. Something about the regal way she'd held her head made him want to muss her up just a little. Maybe wind a hank of that butterscotch hair around his fingers and kiss the frown from that tart mouth.

"Scowling already, dear heart?" Dottie chided as she swept into the room on a cloud of perfume. She was wearing a one-piece coverall thing with red and white stripes that made her look like a walking, talking barber pole. Red, white, and blue beads hung like Christmas ornaments from her ears, tinkling like wind chimes with each step.

"Just thinking about the damn budget projections," he hedged, feeling far too much like a kid hiding evidence of a wet dream. "Max threatened to chain me to my chair if I didn't get them done today." Needing to move, he opened the fridge and took out a carton of eggs, butter, and a package of bacon.

Dottie filled her mug. "I have a meeting with the library trustees that will take up most of the day so I was wondering, if

75

you're not too terribly busy, if you'd show dear Summer the right places to go for information on zoning and land-use regulations. You know, dreary stuff like that."

He thought about spending the day in "dear Summer's" company, breathing in the scent of her, watching the sun in her hair. No way did he need that kind of aggravation. Not even for his aunt.

"With Maifest coming up fast, I don't have a lot of discretionary time, Auntie." He found a bowl and started cracking eggs into it. "Besides, I imagine Dr. Laurence is perfectly capable of handling things on her own."

"Of course she is." The voice belonged to the lady herself and held a subtle edge of warning. He suspected the good doctor didn't much care to have her life arranged for her. Since his well-intentioned aunt couldn't resist taking care of people she cared for, whether they liked it or not, he figured they were in for a rocky eight days.

"Good morning, dear heart," Dottie trilled, her voice warm and her expression welcoming. "I hope you slept well."

Summer's stomach rumbled at the enticing smell of strong coffee. "Very well, thanks." In fact, she'd slept like a baby with her tummy full of pot roast and lemon meringue pie—until the sound of Hollister's Harley had jerked her awake in the wee hours. After that she'd had trouble drifting off again. Instead, she kept seeing a sad, bewildered little boy rendered mute by the prejudice and stupidity of the very people who were supposed to protect him.

"I was just about to make tea, dear. It won't take a minute."

At that, Hollister glanced over his shoulder. He caught Summer sneaking a desperate look at the coffeepot. "Help yourself, but be warned: I was taught to make coffee by a navy chief from the hills of Kentucky. Claimed coffee wasn't really strong unless the spoon stood by itself in the cup."

"I'll risk it," she murmured before she caught herself. "Not that I don't like your tea," she told Dottie quickly.

"I understand, dear. Brody's a bear in the morning without his coffee."

An apt description, Summer thought as the man snorted. He did look grumpy and rumpled, with his uniform shirt hanging open over an olive-drab undershirt and yet another pair of faded jeans. His jaw was shiny from a recent shave, emphasizing the obstinate jaw. His glossy hair had been combed into a rough order, with a natural part falling about an inch right of center, and shaggy ends curling against his neck at the nape. There were a few strands of gray mixed with the black, shining silver in the bright light of morning. In the intimacy of the homey kitchen he seemed even larger and more intimidating, his strength and sensuality disturbingly blatant. She felt a sizzle of sexual interest in her chest, and a warming in her fingertips. She felt a distinctly annoying need to rub against him like a lovesick cat.

More distressed than she cared to admit, she shifted her attention to her hostess, who was adjusting one of her earrings. "Dottie, I wondered if you might have a list of contractors I could contact this morning."

"Of course, dear. I'll—" The phone rang before Dottie could finish, drawing Summer's gaze to the two wall phones—one white, one black—hanging next to a door opening into what Summer took to be the utility room.

"Mine, I think," Dottie said, catching up the white one. Summer took the opportunity to head for the coffee.

"Oops, wrong one," Dottie said, hanging up. "Want me to answer it, Brody dear?" she asked when the black phone continued to shrill.

"I'll get it," Hollister said, turning abruptly. Summer jumped back, but not fast enough to avoid a collision with his hard chest. The coffee she'd been pouring splashed over her fingers, and she yelped as pain seared her skin. Glaring at her as though it were her fault, Hollister plucked the pot from her with one hand while reaching for the hand towel with the other.

"It's fine, really," she protested as he gently wiped her fingers. "It's nothing."

"Quit wiggling!"

"I'm not wiggling." She glared at him, then winced. "Ouch, that hurts."

"Thought you were fine."

"I was until you started scrubbing off my skin with that darn towel." She tried pulling her hand free. His strong fingers held her fast.

"I'll get some ice," Dottie interrupted, her tone definitely more amused than concerned.

"Answer the phone first," Hollister ordered before manacling Summer's wrist with hard fingers so that he could drag her to the sink.

"Hey!" she protested, but she might as well have been shouting into a roaring surf for all the good it did her. With one twist of his powerful wrist, the tap spilled cold water over her fingers, easing the stinging pain. Behind her she heard Dottie informing the caller that the chief was involved in a family emergency and would call back in a few minutes.

"Really, that's not necessary—"

"Jesus, Laurence, you're as antsy as a two-year-old." He spared her a glance that showed equal parts impatience and disdain. She stiffened, and tried to pull free. His jaw hardened as he warned her with a look designed to send strong men to their knees. She refused to be cowed. Just in case, however, she locked her own knees.

"You're the one who smacked into me, *Hollister*!"

He drew his black brows together. "If you didn't go around sneaking up on a man, I would have known you were there."

"I was simply making myself at home," she maintained stiffly.

"Who was it?" he asked, glancing toward his aunt.

"Max. She said to tell you the mayor has called an emergency meeting of the Maifest committee for this evening at seven and commands your presence."

He snorted his thanks as he turned Summer's hand to direct the spray onto the red blotches. The contrast between his big hand and her much smaller one was oddly beguiling. Hers was tanned to a nice golden brown, but his was burned the color of fine leather. Scars crisscrossed his knuckles. No doubt from slugging helpless prisoners, she thought sourly. But even as she tried to fuel her anger, she knew she was fighting against herself instead of Hollister. The man tempted her in ways no one else ever had. Not even Kyle.

As part of her training, she'd studied the underlying mechanisms of involuntary sexual response in all of its various components. She knew, for instance, that her senses had responded to Brody Hollister within four seconds of their first meeting, specifically to the pheromones excreted through the pores of that huge body.

"Please don't let me detain you," she said in a taut voice. "I'm perfectly capable of taking care of myself."

"Book says five minutes under running water, five minutes is what you're getting, so give us both a break and behave."

She blew out a long breath, ruffling the bangs that usually fell in a smooth wave over one eyebrow. She was close enough to see the strain around his eyes. It disturbed her to think she might be the cause, which disturbed her even more. Nothing on this trip was turning out the way she'd planned. "Nobody asked you to play paramedic, you know," she said with great dignity.

"I'm a first responder. I didn't have a choice."

"But my hand's getting numb!"

"That's the idea." She stared at his mouth. Unbidden, her tongue made a quick swipe over her own lower lip. "It'll help your anxiety level if you relax," he said.

"My anxiety level is fine, thank you very much," she informed him a little more tartly than she'd planned.

"Guess it's just my good-old-boy charm that's got your heart beating like crazy." He rubbed his callused thumb over the pulse point in her wrist. She inhaled swiftly and caught a whiff of soap and squeaky-clean man. Nice, sturdy, practical scents. Nothing to jolt her system into overload. Yet she found herself wanting to nuzzle her face into the hollow of his neck and let those brawny arms close around her.

"*Charm* isn't exactly the word I would use," she muttered, angry at herself.

"Enlighten me, then." He grinned—a wicked flash of imperfectly aligned white teeth and deep male dimples—and her heart stopped. My God, she thought, stunned to her toes. He was gorgeous. "I'm waiting."

"Stop that," she ordered, glaring at him. He let the grin fade, and she felt . . . bereft.

"Ma'am?"

"Stop flirting with me," she said slowly and distinctly. "I don't appreciate it."

He shook his head. "Damn, that's what all the p-pretty ones say."

A choked sound came from behind her and Summer jerked her head around to find Dottie laughing. As soon as their gazes met, Dottie's mouth sobered, but her eyes continued to gleam.

"Here's the ice," Dottie murmured. "There's some antiseptic ointment and gauze in the first-aid kit upstairs. I'll just run up and get it."

"Make sure Kelly hasn't slept through her alarm again while you're up there."

Summer stiffened at the arrogant command. Dottie, however, seemed unruffled. "Yes, dear," she said with a tranquil smile.

Summer waited until Dottie was gone, then turned on him. "It's truly inexplicable to me why a woman like your aunt puts up with a tyrant like you."

A muscle twitched in his jaw. "She thinks I need her."

"Do you?"

"No, but don't tell her that." He smiled a little—just a comma at the corner of his mouth, as if he were mocking himself. Suddenly she was ashamed. Brody Hollister hadn't done a thing to hurt her—other than make that crack about the bats yesterday afternoon. Moreover, he was clearly concerned about his aunt's well-being, just as he'd been concerned about his daughter's safety. Not that she owed him a real apology—exactly. More like an olive branch. She had to clear her throat a couple of times, however.

"Chief Hollister, I realize we got off on the wrong foot," she ventured in a cool voice, only to stiffen when he snorted.

"If that's an apology, it needs work, Doc."

"An apology for what? You were the one who treated me like a criminal yesterday. And now you're acting like . . . like a bully!" The words were out before she remembered her intention to be pleasant.

His rough-textured fingers shifted against the delicate skin of her wrist, distracting her for a split second before he spoke. "At least I'm not a snob."

"Are you suggesting that I am?"

"Not suggesting, Doc. Flat out saying it."

"Don't be ridiculous. I'm anything but."

He gave her a disgusted look that had her forgetting all about her resolve to be civil. "You want a list, we'll start at the top."

"Please do." The chill outside couldn't hold a candle to the ice she put into her tone. It didn't appear to faze him.

"How about yesterday, at the homestead, walking around with that freckled little nose wrinkling like you just ran across a load of manure?"

"I most certainly did nothing of the kind!"

He snorted again. "I might not be as educated as you ivory-tower types, but I can recognize snobbery when I see it."

"Aha," she crowed, pouncing gleefully. "Now I get it. You resent me because I have a Ph.D."

His thick black-as-sin lashes flickered only slightly. She admired his control. "Bullshit."

Bull's-*eye*, she corrected. "I've met men like you before, Chief Hollister. You carry a big gun and think your badge gives you the right to push your weight around, but the fact that I have those three little letters behind my name automatically makes me the enemy, doesn't it?"

"Not yet, but keep talking and you'll get there."

"Look, I didn't mean to imply that I'm special just because I managed to make it through grad school."

"Didn't you?"

She felt the barb hit home, and realized he'd seen through her false modesty as though it were as clear as the mountain air.

"Look, I admit I'm proud of my degrees," she backtracked, "but I worked hard for my education. My career means a lot to me, yes, but it doesn't make me better than someone who . . ." She stopped abruptly when she realized she had no idea of his own academic history.

"Who didn't even make it through high school?" he suggested blandly.

She blinked, then drew a breath as the truth dawned. Feeling ashamed to the soles of her Top-Siders, she tugged her hand free. "I take it you're referring to yourself," she said, deliberately adopting the objective tone of doctor to patient.

He gave her a mocking look before turning off the water. "Quit halfway through the tenth grade."

She began to suspect a trick. "I saw the pictures in the hall. You were in the navy. Dottie said you lied to get in."

"Half the deck crew on my first ship had shit for brains. Made me feel right at home."

Before she could respond, he was walking away from her, his long strides impatient as they ate the distance. It was then that she saw Dottie standing in the doorway, holding a white metal box the size of a small suitcase.

"Is something wrong?" Dottie asked.

"Don't wait dinner," he grated impatiently. "I'll be late."

"But I'd planned to take Summer to The Black Forest tonight."

"No reason not to. I'll snag something to eat in town." His brutally large hands were gentle as he set her aside. His boots tapped angrily on the hall runner, and the sun that had shone through earlier beat a hasty retreat behind a cloud.

"That boy." Dottie clicked her tongue as she handed Summer

the first-aid kit. "During the busy season I swear he never sits down to a regular meal."

After placing the heavy box on the counter, Summer opened the lid and surveyed the contents. The only thing lacking seemed to be a nurse to assist. After a moment's rummaging she found antiseptic suitable for burns.

"I don't want to offend you, Dottie, but your nephew is . . . is . . ." She stopped, unable to come up with a word that wouldn't hurt her friend.

"Difficult?"

"That's one way of putting it, yes."

Dottie gave a delighted laugh before retrieving her mug. After taking an eager sip, she said, "You find him interesting, don't you? I can see it in your eyes whenever you look at him."

Summer didn't quite snort. "I find grizzly bears interesting, too, but I wouldn't want to spend much time with one."

"What a perfect analogy! That's exactly what Brody has reminded me of since you arrived, a grizzly with a thorn in his paw. In this case, a thorn in the guise of a pretty little crusader who thinks she has no time for love."

This time Summer did let out a snort. "Are you sure that was sugar you spooned into your coffee?"

"I know what I saw. Sparks and flames hot enough to singe the walls." She lowered her cup and stared at the contents. "I'm not so old that I don't remember what it's like. Or how rare that kind of attraction really is."

Summer heard the wistful note in the other woman's usually vibrant voice and felt an instant empathy. She also felt the pull of curiosity. "Whatever you saw or thought you saw hardly matters. I don't have time for personal relationships."

Careful not to rub too hard, she applied ointment to the scalded places on her hand and fingers. In spite of the cold water and ice, a blister the size of a teardrop had formed on the back of her index finger. She hesitated, then carefully sorted through the neatly organized box for a Band-Aid. "I thought I'd take measurements of the rooms this morning, if that's all right with you, and then walk the grounds before I check on the zoning laws."

"Of course, dear. Remind me to give you the key before I leave." Dottie paused to refill both their cups. Summer capped the antiseptic ointment and returned it to the box before taking a long, greedy sip.

"I'll need to take pictures of both the exterior and interior, too, as well as the barn and that funny little shed with the missing door. To show to my principal backers."

"Parents of some of your former patients, I believe you said?" Radiating energy and bright-eyed interest, Dottie put down her cup and picked up the fork Brody had discarded earlier.

"Primarily, although I've written several grant proposals to interested foundations. So far I've received two positive replies. The next step is to submit a detailed start-up plan and a five-year projection of operating costs."

Dottie finished layering the bacon in the skillet and set it to frying. "I had no idea it was so complicated to help people who need it."

"By law, adolescents are still considered children in nearly every state, which makes licensing requirements even more stringent." Summer retrieved butter from the fridge, then sorted through a selection of homemade jams and jellies on the door. Her throat watered at the sight of raspberry preserves in an old-fashioned mason jar. "Though God knows most of my patients left childhood behind years ago."

She put the jam next to the butter and started setting the table. The place mats Dottie had jammed into the drawer the night before were now sadly wrinkled. Summer did her best to smooth them flat. "Paper napkins?" she asked, rooting through the drawer that contained only a jumble of mismatched mats.

"In the pie safe."

Summer found them behind the bottle of Wild Turkey Dottie had dented during last night's dinner.

"Sad, isn't it?" Dottie mused before retrieving her cup for another sip. "All those kids just wasting something as precious as youth and . . . innocence." Still holding the cup, she looked at Summer thoughtfully. "I admit to being a bit of a rebel when I was a teenager. But even so, the most daring thing my friends and I did was smoke my father's cigarettes and sneak sips from his hip flask."

Summer bit her lip, then blew out air. "Dottie, I've been thinking about your advice not to tell your nephew the whole truth about my plans and I'm very uncomfortable with the idea of keeping secrets. My instincts tell me we're both asking for trouble here."

Dottie's smile was a bit absentminded. "Snip some chives into those eggs, will you dear? The scissors are in the crock by the flour canister."

Summer bit off a sigh as she snagged the scissors and reached across the sink to shear off an inch of lush growth from the pot of chives on the windowsill. "You aren't listening to me," she said as she snipped the strands into bits over the bowl.

"Remind me to give you a copy of the preliminary research I've done on the place."

"What preliminary research?"

"Zoning laws, well and septic capacities. All within acceptable parameters. And of course, the water rights allowing access to the river for irrigation go back nearly to the beginning. In a dry year that's pure gold."

Summer blinked. "You have been busy."

"Not really. I had Hank O'Dell down at the planning commission run the numbers." She offered Summer a sly look. "Somehow Hank got the idea I was thinking of renting my place to a group from the coast looking to start a church camp."

"Somehow?"

"There'd been some interest. Two years ago, about this time of year, come to think of it, a prissy little man in a dowdy suit waltzed me around for a couple of weeks, quoting scripture and rhapsodizing about strengthening little bodies as well as souls. Even waved an option check in my face."

"A big one?"

"Low six figures."

"Really? I had no idea hills and rocks were worth that much." She saw Dottie's gaze flicker and apologized profusely. "That came out wrong. It's just that it's so hard for a Californian to judge . . . uh, mountain real estate."

Dottie's smile forgave her. "Actually that's well below market value. What with growth and all, there aren't many parcels as big as mine left so close to town."

Summer winced. All that and Dottie was willing to lease it to her for a thousand dollars a month. "I was worried that I might be taking unfair advantage of you if I accepted your offer. Now I realize I was right."

"Now, you put that right out of your mind this instant. I know very well what I'm doing. Besides, some things are more important than money."

Dottie turned off the burner and wiped her hands. "Dear little Mr. Trusdale apologized for the low offer, of course. But explained that the church was depending on donations in order to raise even that much."

"I can relate to that," Summer muttered.

"Naturally I was considering his proposal. I even went so far as to have Hank change the zoning. So many little ones growing up in the city have no idea how beautiful this country is or how wonderful it feels to run through a field of wildflowers or jump into huge piles of autumn leaves and feel those prickly little bits trickling down your neck." She grinned. "I was already figuring out how many saddle horses I should donate."

"What happened?"

"Brody saw the Rolex."

"What Rolex?"

"The one on Mr. Trusdale's wrist." Dottie clucked her tongue. "His act was almost perfect, but he'd forgotten about his watch. Brody ran a check and found out that he was really a real estate broker representing a consortium of Japanese businessmen who wanted to use my property and my irrigation rights for a golf resort."

She laughed softly. "You should have seen it, Summer. Brody grabbed the man by the back of his coat and the seat of his pants and actually stuffed him into his little Japanese car like he was a sack of grain. All the time, Trusdale was sputtering about police brutality and legal action. I imagine he was still sputtering as Brody escorted him to the county line."

Summer choked back a laugh. "Did Trusdale sue?"

"Of course not. No one in his right mind would take on Brody when he's in protective mode."

Somehow Summer didn't find that a bit consoling.

It was nearly noon when Dottie glanced through the open door of her office to see Brody approaching from the west end of the main reading room with long, impatient strides. Though her glasses were perched atop her head, she could see well enough to know his strong features would be tensed into a frown, and his jaw would be taut. She was also pretty sure he was glaring at her through those dark lenses he thought hid his soft heart from a world he'd never really learned to trust. He was annoyed. Very annoyed, in fact.

"A good sign," she murmured into the telephone receiver she'd forgotten for a moment she was holding.

"Dry rot is a good sign?" Summer's voice carried a hint of surprise to her through the wire.

"No, no," Dottie hastened to reassure her as Brody walked in. "Someone just came into my office with a problem."

"Then I won't keep you. We can talk more over lunch. As soon as I finish inputting my notes, I'll head into town. How's twelve-thirty for you?"

Dottie glanced at her watch. Forty minutes. "Sounds good," she said before giving directions to the restaurant across from the library while Brody leaned against the doorjamb and crossed his arms over his chest. She smiled and wagged her eyebrows. His scowl deepened. Another good sign. He'd shown more emotion in the last two days than he'd shown in all the years since his return. She knew why, of course. Summer Laurence had come to town.

"Well, this is a lovely surprise," she all but chirped as she hung up. "Have you come to take your favorite aunt to lunch?"

"No, I've come to take my favorite aunt to task," he said, his voice under the tight control that warned of a steely anger riding just below the surface.

"Now, Brody—"

"Don't waste your breath, Auntie. We both know you're busted." He straightened and walked to the desk. "I want your word you'll end this game now."

"What game is that, dear?"

"Pretending to be busy so that I would have to baby-sit your guest."

"I *am* busy."

"You're matchmaking again."

She really must learn to be more subtle, she thought as she got to her feet. "Wanting to see you happy isn't a game, dear heart."

"I *am* happy. No doubt Dr. Laurence is happy. We're both *happy* going our separate ways. Got that?"

"Of course, dear. If you say so." She plastered on a placating smile and patted his arm. A hickory trunk had more give.

"Auntie—"

"Although I'm quite sure dear Summer is far from happy." She allowed the smallest of sighs to escape. "Something—or someone—has hurt her very deeply in the past. So deeply I think she's still bleeding a little inside. Like you, dear."

At his quick frown, she hastened to lift a hand. "Before you start growling again, I want you to know I did not invite Summer here as a possible romantic interest." She angled her head and sighed. "Although I was hoping . . ."

The muttered obscenity was distinctly annoying, but she forgave him. Brody didn't have a cruel bone in his big body. He just needed idiots like Sarge Stenner to think he did. Sometimes she thought he even tried to make *her* think his growls were real. But then, he'd spent the first third of his life protecting himself from the kind of emotional battering no one should ever have to endure.

"Now you listen to me," she declared, drawing herself up to her full sixty inches. "Summer is *my* guest, not yours. She's worked hard for her degrees and now that she's finished her internship and several years working for others in San Diego, she's interested in starting her own practice."

"In Osuma? C'mon, Auntie. Give me a break."

"And what's wrong with Osuma?"

"It's about a million light years from upscale, for one thing."

He swept off his hat and plowed impatient fingers through the inky thickness of his hair before dropping the hat atop a printout of new releases. Though the day was still young, he looked rumpled and tired and just a little sad. The lingering effects of yesterday's double fatalities, she suspected, the story on the radio news still fresh in her mind.

"Are you suggesting that Summer is a snob?" she asked, her voice tempered by empathy.

"No, I'm trying to keep you from being too disappointed when she hands you a polite 'Thanks, but no thanks' and heads back to the fast lane."

"Aren't you being just a bit prejudiced here?"

"I'm being realistic, something you find all but impossible when you're on a mission."

Dottie sighed. "If Summer decides that Osuma is not to her taste, I'll be disappointed, but I won't be crushed. Does that make you feel better?"

He eyed her critically for a long moment, then nodded. "And no more m-matchmaking."

"If that's what you want, dear."

"That's what I want."

Dottie allowed herself to look disappointed. Brody was not an easy man to fool. "Now that that's settled, how about lunch?"

The wariness that had faded from his eyes returned. "Sounds to me like you already have a lunch date."

She leaned forward to power down her terminal before retrieving her purse from the bottom drawer of her desk. "Summer's joining me for a quick bite," she said as she rose, "but since we've already established your total lack of interest in her as a lover, that shouldn't present a problem now, should it?"

Brody stiffened. "Jesus, Auntie," he muttered, his face turning the color of a painful scalding.

Dottie arched her eyebrows. "You're a man in your prime, Brody. You need sex. Even my father, God rest him, needed a woman after Mama died." She smiled a little as she remembered her father's unpredictable moods when the need was on him. "Wearing yourself out chopping more firewood than we can possibly use is no substitute for a willing woman."

His glare could have stripped paint. Dottie managed to stifle the grin that wanted to burst free.

"Just remember what I told you." He jammed his hat on his head before spinning around and stalking out.

"Whatever you say, dear," she called over the thud of his boot heels. Aphrodite was in her heaven and all was right with the world.

Weekends were the only time Brody worked a regular patrol schedule. The rest of the time was spent on the administrative duties he hated. By the time the three-to-eleven shift was getting under way he was in a foul mood and didn't much care at the moment who knew it. Spending eight solid hours with his ass stuck to his chair would put a saint on edge. It didn't help that the officers just emerging from the briefing room were having themselves a jolly old time.

"You want to hold it down out there," he shouted at no one in particular, then scowled when his officers exchanged long-suffering looks. Telling himself they could all go to hell, Brody scribbled his name at the bottom of his quarterly report to the city council and slapped it on top of the stack already awaiting Max's attention. He'd lost count of the number of things he'd signed, initialed, or dictated since he'd unlocked his office door at seven that morning. Damned papers were probably breeding at night, he thought as he jerked open his top drawer in search of the bottle of extra-strength aspirin he kept there.

"Uh oh, looks to me like the man needs him a triple whiskey." Slate Hingle grinned as he came forward to plop his linebacker's body into the visitor's chair. Monday was the sergeant's day off and he was dressed in civies. Brody wondered what he was doing in the office, then remembered it was payday. No doubt Slate had come in for his check and stopped by to harass the poor, overworked chief.

"You try running a twenty-five-man unit on a budget for twenty, and see how you like it," he told the sarge with a scowl.

"Guess they'll be pushing you to cut back on personnel again."

"I'd put money on it."

Hingle slid down in his chair and stretched out long, massive legs kept powerful with daily workouts at Osuma's only gym. "Gonna do it?"

"What do you think?"

Brody marked the slight easing in the tension ringing Hingle's mouth and figured the sergeant had gotten what he'd come for. "I think the rookies don't know how lucky they are."

"Tell that to Keegan."

Hingle grinned. "I heard you're making him write a report on proper arrest procedures."

Brody flexed his shoulders. "The way he handled that arrest yesterday the damn kid could have ended up in a box instead of nursing sore balls."

Hingle's chest rose and fell in a heavy sigh. "Yesterday was a rough one for all of us."

Brody didn't try to deny it. "One way or another, fatals are always rough."

"Max said you spoke to Mrs. Oates's doctor this morning?"

Brody nodded. "She's still in critical condition, but it looks good. Barring complications she should make it."

"Does she know about her husband?"

"Not yet. They have her sedated. One problem at a time, the doc said."

"Ain't that the truth?" Hingle unfolded his body slowly from the chair, stretching to his full height. "Guess I'd best let you get back to your paperwork."

"Don't do me any favors, Hingle."

The sergeant laughed. It was a rich sound that started deep in his flat belly and rolled all the way up his chest. It never failed to make Brody grin whenever he heard it.

"One more thing," the sergeant said, sobering a little too quickly for Brody's peace of mind. "It's probably nothing, but coming into town I passed a red ninety-eight Miata driving a good ten miles over the limit on that narrow stretch of Orchard Road between mileposts six and nine. The driver looked to be high-school age, or maybe a little older. I didn't stop him because I was in civies, but I thought you ought to know."

Brody felt his gut tighten. "Any particular reason?"

Hingle hesitated, then added in a gentler tone, "The top was down. Kelly was in the car."

"When?"

"About twenty minutes ago."

Brody was out of his seat and reaching for his jacket before a rank obscenity exploded past the constriction in his throat.

CHAPTER 6

Patience was part of a therapist's persona. Ask anyone at the McDonald Center and they would say that Summer had more than most. Dealing with contractors, however, was rapidly taking its toll. Contractors, it seemed, were never in their offices. They also took their time returning phone calls, which meant she'd spent most of the afternoon sitting at the kitchen table, waiting for the phone to ring.

While she waited, she worked on the brochure for Phoenix House, which she intended to send off to every adolescent therapist on the West Coast as soon as her plans were finalized. By four o'clock only two of the four men and one woman she'd contacted had returned her call. While she waited out the other three, she decided to reward herself for her diligence and discipline with a cup of Austrian dark roast she'd found in a specialty shop next to the restaurant where she and Dottie had had lunch.

She was standing at the sink measuring coffee into a fresh filter when she heard a car drive up. Looking out the window, she saw Brody's Blazer pull up next to the gate in the fenced-in backyard. Almost before the vehicle came to a complete stop, the passenger's door flew open and Kelly leaped out. Without a backward glance, she jerked open the gate and raced up the walk, her hair flying. Summer had time for a glimpse of Brody's angry expression before Kelly came charging through the door, her face a becoming pink and her eyes blazing.

"I hate him!" she said when she caught sight of Summer. "I wish he wasn't my father." She threw her purse and her books onto the table and stalked to the fridge. One of the books toppled over onto the floor with a thud. "He's mean and insensitive and . . . and I'll never, ever forgive him," she cried as she all but jerked the door off the hinges.

Somehow managing to keep a poker face, Summer glanced back at the window in time to see Brody gun the Blazer into a tight U-turn before taking off with a gravel-spraying fury. It seemed that neither father nor daughter was having a great day.

"Care to talk about it?" she said, picking up the book on her way to the table.

"Why? Nobody ever listens anyway!"

"I do," Summer said as she watched Kelly slop milk into a glass.

"Yeah, well, that's your job."

Summer heard the hurt mingling with the anger and backed off. "I bought cookies while I was in town having lunch with Dottie," she said, stacking the books in a neat pile on the table. "They're in the pie safe with your aunt's Twinkies."

Kelly glared at her as though she'd suggested a root canal. "Cookies are full of fat."

"These aren't. A very nice lady at the bakery assured me they were made with applesauce instead of butter."

"I hate cookies," Kelly muttered, returning the milk carton to the refrigerator. "But since you bought them, I might as well have one."

"I'll have one, too, please," Summer told her as she retrieved a mug from the cupboard. Too impatient to wait until the coffee finished dripping, she snatched the pot from the hot plate and poured.

"So, what did your father do to tick you off?" she asked.

"Nothing much," Kelly jeered as she plunked the bakery sack onto the table while at the same time planting her fanny in a chair. "He only, like, totally humiliated me in front of the entire school."

Summer winced. "That sounds heavy."

Kelly tore into the bag and pulled out a cookie. Eyes narrowed, she studied it very much the way Summer imagined an exterminator studied gnawed wood. "Are you sure this isn't filled with fat calories?"

"Absolutely. In fact, I think the woman at the bakery mentioned something about taking them to the Sunday school class she teaches, so I feel sure we can take her word."

Kelly made a throaty noise that approximated her father's more intimidating growl, before taking a small bite. "Yuck, you're right. It tastes like nonfat."

Summer carried her cup to the table and sat down. "There're always Twinkies. They're loaded with fat as well as preservatives."

Kelly gave her a disgruntled look. Some of the angry color had faded, and much of the temper in her eyes had backed off. "Life sucks," she muttered before taking another bite.

"In general or specifically?"

"Both. He's totally ruined my life."

"Your father?"

Kelly devoured the cookie, her hand already digging into the bag. "I'm not going back to that stupid school no matter what he says. I'll run away first." She glared at Summer with stormy eyes, daring her to object.

"Perhaps I could be more helpful if I knew more details," Summer suggested.

"You'll just take his side! I know you will."

"Not necessarily."

"You will so. Everyone's afraid of him when he gets that look on his face. Even Aunt Dottie sometimes, and she's not afraid of anything."

In times of heightened stress or emotional volatility Summer had always found a slow, thoughtful nod to be a wonderful tool in a therapist's bag of tricks. Now was one of those times, she decided, and used it. "What look is that?"

"That . . . that 'You'll do what I say or spend the rest of your life spitting out teeth' look."

Summer had just taken a sip of coffee and had to use a great deal of control to keep from spraying it all over the cookies.

"Kelly, you know your father would never hurt you," she protested when she'd swallowed.

"No, but he wanted to. I could see it in his eyes. So could Mark."

Aha, Summer thought. The plot thickens. "Mark, the young man who drove you home from the hospital yesterday?"

Kelly nodded, her expression turning more morose with every second that passed. "I wouldn't blame Mark if he, like, never spoke to me again, you know?" she mumbled into her milk. "Dad totally humiliated him."

Summer leaned back and cradled her mug against her chest. Teenagers tended to clam up when asked a direct question. Fortunately, Kelly began speaking again.

"It wasn't like Mark was speeding or anything," Kelly muttered, directing her glare at the bakery bag as though one of the cookies had just called her a dirty name.

"I thought you said your dad humiliated you at school."

"No, on Orchard Road. He pulled Mark over, right in front of Tiffany's house."

"Ah."

"The bus was just dropping Tiff off. It was awful. Everyone was watching." Her face flamed. "Dad, he just stalks up to the car and opens the door." Her nostrils flared as she drew in an agitated breath. "Then he yelled at me like I'm some kind of . . . of criminal."

"I hear what you're saying." Summer sympathized. She, too, had had an up close and personal view of Brody Hollister at his most intimidating.

The teenager huffed. "It's like, Mark had just put the top down and everyone could see."

Summer nodded—and did some more waiting.

"Mark was real polite, telling Dad how it was his fault I missed the bus, and how he felt responsible and all."

"And was it his fault?" Summer inquired before bringing the mug to her lips.

Kelly's gaze slid away from hers, and Summer had her answer. "It's not fair," she cried. "All the other girls get to date and ride home with guys. I'm a . . . a freak!"

"Kelly, you listen to me! You are no such thing. You're a lovely, sweet girl whose father loves her very much."

"Right in front of Mark he told me to . . . to get my butt in the Blazer before he paddled it a good one."

So Papa Grizzly had been driven to discipline the little she-cub, she thought, hiding a smile. "I can see why you'd be upset."

The self-righteous triumph in Kelly's eyes had yet to flame its brightest before Summer added, "But I can also see why your father was angry."

"I knew you'd take his side," Kelly mumbled sullenly.

"Perhaps I misunderstood what he told you yesterday about not accepting rides with anyone without his permission."

Kelly's lower lip edged out and for an instant Summer was afraid she was going to bolt. "It's a dumb rule."

"But one he has a right to make."

"Mark's a careful driver."

Summer drew a breath. The clock in the other room chimed the half hour. Dottie would be home soon. And perhaps Brody. She felt an odd little flurry beneath her breastbone at the thought. "Kel, did it ever occur to you that your dad has seen a lot of things on his job that most of us never have to face? Things that make him worry about the people he loves."

Kelly stared at the stack of textbooks for a long time before she shifted her gaze to Summer's. "It's not . . . it's just that . . . oh, forget it."

"If you're not comfortable talking about your feelings with me, I understand. But I'm willing to listen if it would help sort things through for you."

"You mean, like shrink listening?"

Summer laughed and leaned back. "No, like friend listening."

A look Summer couldn't decipher ran over Kelly's face. Guilt was the closest she could come, which made her wonder. "You'd probably think I'm awful."

"Not even if you did an awful thing. There's a difference, you know, between who we really are inside, and the things we do. Sometimes good people do bad things. Or at least things that make them feel pretty awful inside."

Kelly traced a meandering film of milk residue in the empty glass with her index finger. "He was yelling at me, and all of a sudden he started stuttering real bad. You know, like he does sometimes when he's really, really upset."

"I see."

"It used to scare me," Kelly said, staring at the glass. "It's like his face gets all red, and the veins stand out on his neck. Like he's going to explode. I used to hide behind the couch so I wouldn't have to watch."

"I imagine that was difficult for you both," Summer said carefully.

Kelly dropped her gaze. "He caught me hiding one time, like with my hands over my ears. He looked so hurt."

"I'm sure he didn't blame you."

"Summer?"

"What, sweetie?"

"Mark asked me to meet him in town Friday night. I told him I would."

Summer looked down into the inch of now tepid coffee remaining in her cup. How would a mother handle this? she wondered. "Have you asked your dad's permission?"

Kelly shook her head. "I'm grounded for the next month. I can go to school and church and the library. No place else unless he or Auntie's with me. He'd bust a gut if I even mentioned going out with Mark."

"It sounds to me as though you have yourself a problem. Any idea how you're going to solve it?"

Instead of answering, Kelly got up to put her glass in the dishwasher. "I heard Aunt Dottie tell her friend Lucy on the phone last night that she was taking you out to dinner in town Friday night, and I was thinking, maybe I could tell Dad I was with you guys."

"No, Kelly. I sympathize with your dilemma, but no. I won't

be a party to deceiving your father, and I very much doubt if your aunt would be either." Summer left her seat and went to stand next to the now silent teenager. "Kelly, look at me, please," she said when Kelly continued to stare through the window.

It seemed to take forever, but finally Kelly complied. "I lied to my father once, and he never forgave me. In fact, he . . . he told me he never wanted to hear from me or see me again. I'm not saying that would happen with your dad. In fact, I doubt it very much, but the point is, it could." She took a breath and went on. "Trust is such a precious thing, especially between a child and a parent. I'd do almost anything for you, sweetie, but I won't help you destroy something so special."

Kelly dropped her gaze, her teeth worrying her lower lip. "I don't know what to do."

"Want some advice?"

Kelly nodded without looking up.

"Call Mark and cancel the date."

Rebellion ran over her features. "He'll think I'm a dweeb," she said sullenly. "He probably won't ever talk to me again."

"Maybe not, but if he doesn't, he's not the boy for you."

Kelly was silent, her expression troubled. Finally she heaved a sigh and lifted her gaze to Summer's. "I'd never get away with it anyway," she muttered. "Sooner or later Dad would find out, and he'd ground me for the rest of my life."

"It's hell making grown-up decisions, isn't it?"

"I hate it."

Summer smiled. "I'm proud of you, Kel. You're a great kid."

Kelly flushed with pleasure, but muttered, "I'm not a kid." She looked a little brighter when she collected her books and went upstairs to study.

Seconds later, the sound of screaming guitars filled the house and rattled the windows. Was this what it was like living with a normal teenager? Summer thought as she got up to refill her cup. Noise and drama and tears? Typical problems of adolescence? A sad smile curved her lips as she realized she would have loved it.

* * *

"Ah shit. Three men on base and Griffey strikes out."

Slumped on the leather sofa in his grandfather's pine-and-glass family room, Mark Krebs muted the sound of the between-innings commercials and wondered why he even bothered to watch the frigging Mariners in the first place. Everyone knew the American League sucked sewer water and always had, which was why he'd always rooted for the Cubs instead of the wimpy, candy-assed White Sox.

"One of the docs on staff has season tickets," his granddad said from the bar built into an antique armoire. "I can probably talk him into selling me a couple if you'd like to take in a Sunday game."

"Yeah?" Mark wanted to be pleased. Instead, he found himself wondering what kind of number the cagey old guy was running on him. Dr. Greydon Krebs—Doc to his patients and Grey to his fellow physicians and friends—was a tall, rangy sort with a rumpled thatch of iron-colored hair and calm nut-brown eyes one shade darker than Mark's own.

His sixty-fourth birthday had been only a few weeks after Mark had come to live with him, but to his fitness-conscious grandson, he seemed much younger, more like a tough, well-seasoned outdoors man in his early fifties. Though he would rather choke on his own tongue than admit it, Mark was a little afraid of him. Consequently, he kept his voice respectful as he added, "I thought you hated baseball."

"We haven't had much time together, son," his granddad said over the sound of glass clinking on glass. "I'd like to change that."

"It's okay. I know you've been busy. Mira said you had a lot of responsibilities."

His grandfather looked pained at Mark's use of his mother's Christian name, but instead of handing him a load of shit about it the way Grandfather Conneaught always did, the old guy let it pass. "Trust me, Mark. I'd rather spend time with you than listen to a bunch of accountants and auditors explain why a hospital that serves most of the south county can't possibly afford a new MRI."

"Sounds like being the top guy sucks."

"It does indeed." His grandfather's grin was lopsided and easy, showing even, white teeth and a shallow dimple in one tanned cheek that Mira had called "delicious" one Christmas when she'd had too much mulled wine. It made Mark sick to see the way she all but drooled over her own father-in-law. Not that Granddad let on, though Mark figured the old guy was too savvy not to notice. Unlike Mark's dad, his grandfather was a real straight-arrow. No late nights out and about, except at the hospital. No parties. As far as Mark had been able to figure out, the man lived a damned dull life.

Take booze, for instance. In the four months since Mark had come to live in the big yellow house on River Road, he'd never seen the doc take more than two fingers of Chivas Regal, neat, before dinner, or a small snifter of B & B before bed.

Conscious of his image, Mark's dad had preferred the same brands, but hellfire would have been buried in icebergs before his old man stopped at one. Everyone always said that good old G. Markham Krebs knew how to hold his liquor. It was a sign of a real man, he'd told his only son more than once, usually when he was about to pour himself another belt. Always claimed the Krebs men had too much class to become sloppy drunk. *Class and brass balls, kid. It's in the genes.*

Mark figured his old man had been right about the class part, anyway. "Good old G. Markham" had used a priceless nineteenth-century dueling pistol to spatter his brains all over the French-walnut paneling in his own den.

It had made all the papers, and even the Sunday evening news on WGN—right after the highlights of the Bears-Detroit game. The first reports had been sympathetic, claiming that prominent stockbroker G. M. Krebs, Jr., son-in-law of Alderman Truman Conneaught, had been depressed over a recent illness—and then the truth had started trickling in. Rich, well-respected, "classy" Markham Krebs had been on the brink of a double indictment for embezzling funds from two of his largest clients, rich socialite widows who'd been romanced by G. Markham into giving him power of attorney.

"What's wrong, son? Did you flunk the English test you were so worried about?"

It took Mark a few seconds to realize his grandfather had settled into his recliner in front of the windows and was speaking to him.

"Nah, more like aced it. Kelly Hollister pounded those stupid grammar rules into me so good I was repeating 'em in my sleep."

His grandfather glanced down at the drink in his hands, a strange look on his face. "Sounds like she takes after her aunt."

Mark snorted. "That wacko? Not hardly."

Granddad's head came up with a snap, and his narrowed gaze lanced into Mark's. "Hear me, and hear me well, son. No one uses words like that in my house—or anywhere else—in reference to Miss Dottie Hollister. Is that clear?"

Though the doctor hadn't raised his voice, Mark felt the frigid warning all the way to the bone, and though he managed to keep from cringing, he had to take another deep breath to settle the fear in his gut.

"Yeah, sure, Granddad," he said in the same placating tone he always used with adults to get himself out of a jam. "I was just kidding, you know. I didn't mean any harm."

To Mark's relief the cold tension in his grandfather's face eased off, though it didn't disappear entirely. "I know you didn't, son. Let's forget it, okay?"

"Works for me." Working to control his sudden panic, Mark returned his gaze to the game and congratulated himself for dodging some serious grief. In the future, he planned to be a lot more careful about shooting from the hip around his grandfather. The last thing he needed was to be shipped back to Chicago, especially now that he was just starting to make some progress with Kelly. His sweet angel girl. Mark loved her with all of his heart and soul. She was his. Even discussing her with his grandfather seemed wrong somehow. Like a desecration.

On the thirty-five-inch screen the no-brainer commercial faded into the action on the diamond. Mark released the mute button just in time to hear the announcer making some dumb remark about the pitcher's slow curve.

Watching the game he'd never taken the time to learn, Grey Krebs relaxed his grip on the snifter and willed his racing heart to slow. It had been years since he'd gone off like that over a random reference to Dottie Hollister. A sure sign that he'd been working too hard these past months. Slowly he brought the glass to his mouth for a sip. The mellow brandy suddenly tasted as sour as cough medicine and burned the tender membranes of his throat all the way down.

Shifting his gaze to the spectacular view of the Wenatchee River beyond the thermal glass, he let his mind trace the path of the river southward where it ran past the Hollister property. He knew every twist and bend, every ripple and fall between here and there. The canoe he'd once used to run the river was still stored in the garage rafters, no doubt serving as cushy lodgings for a family of field mice.

He'd been sixteen when he'd coaxed Dottie into coming with him for a calm Sunday afternoon ride to the Peshastin Bridge. She'd just turned thirteen that summer and was as sweet as a freshly ripened peach. It had come to him in church that morning that he wanted nothing more in life than to taste every inch of that warm flesh. He'd been in agony when he'd asked her for a date in the vestibule after church. When she'd accepted, he'd wanted to tap-dance down the church steps. Later, walking up to the front door of Big Malcolm's house to pick her up, he'd been so nervous he would have been hard-pressed to come up with enough spit to lick a stamp.

It hadn't helped that her big brother, Ray, had been hanging around, smarting off about his sister's little tits and her skinny ass. Grey stared into his glass and remembered the battle he'd had with himself to keep from shutting Ray's mouth with his knuckles.

The river had been higher than he'd thought. Dottie had insisted on helping with the paddling, although she'd done a lot more talking than paddling most of the time. The play of expression over that small, heart-shaped face had entranced him to the point where he'd been watching her more than he'd been watching the river and they'd spilled while running Indian Rapids. Wet as a sleek little seal, she'd come up sputtering and calling him names between gales of laughter. While he was trying to get her back into the canoe, she was trying to drown him by climbing on his shoulders. Sometimes, in his dreams, he still felt those small, sweet breasts pressed against his face. He figured he'd fallen in love with her then. Stupidly, wildly in love.

Five years later she left him at the altar. Polite to the end, she'd left a note. A pathetic excuse for an explanation saying she wasn't ready for marriage. She'd gone off to Vegas to follow a dream and hoped he wouldn't hate her. Feeling as though his heart had been torn from his chest, he'd ripped the note apart and thrown it in the river along with the wedding band he'd planned to slip onto her finger.

"I'll get it," Mark called, and it took Grey a second or two to realize the boy meant the phone, which rang once more before Mark snatched up the portable from the end table.

"Hey, how's it going?" The voice that had started out as a macho growl swiftly softened, reminding Grey of his own voice when he was dealing with a shy patient or a frightened child—or, on rare occasions since he'd become a widower five years ago, a lover.

Idly swirling the contents of his glass in one lean hand, Grey watched Mark get up quickly and disappear into the other part of the house, still talking. Going to his room to flirt in private, Grey figured, an indulgent smile playing over his mouth. Though Mark rarely mentioned the girl's name, he gathered from the flush on the boy's face that his grandson was in the throes of a whopping crush.

Not that he blamed the boy, he thought, sipping thoughtfully. Brody's daughter had always been a cute little tyke, all shy smiles and dimples and big blue eyes identical in color and shape to her great-aunt's. The last time he'd seen Kelly had been just after New Year's Day, right after Mark had come to live with him. He'd been showing the boy around town one snowy Saturday afternoon when they'd run into Kelly and some of her friends outside Gerske's Chocolate Factory.

Mark had instantly gone into swagger mode, sending the other two girls into coy giggles while Kelly had stood silently aloof, a solemn fascination sparkling in her eyes. Later, when Grey had made a casual remark to Brody about his daughter's transformation from a sweet, wide-eyed little girl to a potential heartbreaker, he'd been amused to see the normally unflappable chief of police growl like a rogue wolf with his teeth bared. Grey sympathized. The man had had enough trouble in his life without the added burden of protecting his only child from sex-crazed teenage lotharios.

The sudden roar of the crowd on the TV interrupted his thoughts. Grateful for the intrusion, he left his chair and turned it off. It was past nine-thirty, and he had a staff meeting at six A.M. tomorrow.

Working with the fast, efficient skill of a man accustomed to living alone, he washed the snifter in the sink built into the bar, dried it, and returned it to the shelf. Turning out lights as he went, he made his way to the master bathroom, where he planned to take two ibuprofens, strip to the buff, and try to soak out his rotten mood in the big tub with the Jacuzzi jets. He would not, however, allow himself to think about Dottie Hollister.

Twenty minutes later he shut off the jets and pulled the plug. Instead of the peace he'd sought, the headache that had only been nagging him before was now a thudding agony in his right temple, and his sour mood was worse than ever. After a quick swipe with a towel, he walked naked into the darkness of his bedroom and drew open the drapes covering the sliding door to the large upstairs terrace. Though the view to the west was far more spectacular, especially at sunset, the house's two terraces were situated on the north side, a bone of contention with both the architect and his wife, Sarah.

Sweet Sarah who loved the kindergarten kids she taught as much as she loved Markham. He missed her so much. Theirs had been a steady, calm sort of love, as steady and calm as Sarah herself had been. Nothing like the almost savage feeling he'd once had for Dottie.

Feeling every one of his sixty-four years and then some, he shifted his gaze to the jagged slice between the two tallest of the northern peaks. Below and slightly to the east stood the Hollister homestead. Like so many of the original houses in the area, it was a derelict now. A pile of priceless crosscut redwood and lousy memories that had stood empty since Brody had insisted Dottie let him build her a smaller, more modern place. Grey had never been in the house where she lived now. If invited, which fell into the category of fat chance, he would refuse to go.

Squeezing his eyes shut, he banished the image of the young woman who'd broken his heart and instead pictured the woman who'd healed him. His sweet Sarah. Smiling up at him on their wedding day. Holding their son in her arms and cooing over his ugly little monkey face. Hiding the pain of her increasingly laboring heart beneath a soft laugh at a corny joke he'd told a half-dozen times before.

The two of them had built something solid and enduring during the thirty-two years they'd had together. Consciously relaxing his rigid jaw, Grey turned away from the view and returned to the bathroom.

CHAPTER 7

Brody rubbed his hand over his belly and listened to the phone ringing in his ear. It was a little past nine. The meeting upstairs had lasted until eight forty-five. The coffee he'd drunk had given him a sour stomach, and his head hurt from a night of listening to politicians' bickering.

"Hello?" The woman's voice on the other end was cultured and flavored with sadness.

"Mrs. Oates?" His throat tightened, and he drew in air in an attempt to relax the muscles.

"Yes?"

"Uh, this is Brody Hollister from Osuma. I—I was w-wondering how Trent is . . . is making out."

"Oh, Chief Hollister! I didn't recognize your voice."

Brody took a deep breath and prayed. He'd known when he picked up the phone he would have trouble getting out the words. It was always that way when his frigging emotions got the better of him.

"It's kind of you to call," she went on, weariness now clearly audible in her tone. "Trent has mentioned you several times. He said you promised him ice cream."

Brody closed his eyes at the reminder. In all the confusion, he'd forgotten the promise he'd made to the boy. "Guess we never g-got around to it. T-tell him I'm s-s-sorry, okay?"

There was a long pause. He could almost feel her shock coming through the wire. Sometimes he thought it would be better if

107

he wore a sign around his neck announcing his handicap so people would be prepared.

"Yes. Yes, of course, I'll do that." He heard the pity she was trying hard to hide and wanted to slam down the phone, saving them both embarrassment. But he'd made the call for a reason, and he couldn't escape until he got it said. He took a breath and felt the knot in his belly cramp tighter.

"I, uh, was wondering if you—you planned to t-take him to s-s-see a therapist."

"Yes, a woman right here in Kirkland who specializes in dealing with children who've undergone trauma. Our parish priest has worked with her before, and he recommended her highly. I've spoken with her several times on the phone, and she's been very helpful in making suggestions." She paused, and he heard the sound of a rapidly indrawn breath as Mrs. Oates fought to keep from breaking down. "She recommended I not take Trent to his father's funeral on Sunday."

Brody remembered the day of Megan's funeral. Seeing him dressed in a suit and tie, Kelly had thought it was time for church and had run to get the little red purse Megan had bought for their daughter to hold her Sunday school money. He hadn't been able to make Kel understand why she had to stay with a baby-sitter while her daddy and her grandparents went away all dressed up. In the end, he'd relented and allowed her to go along. He still wondered if he'd made a terrible mistake, exposing her to the sights and sounds of grief.

"Chief Hollister? Are you still there? Did you hear me?"

"I—I'mmm . . . h-here." The words came out like high-velocity shells, shaming him. He forced himself to finish. "G-give him a h-h-hug from m-m-me."

There was another pause, shorter this time. "I will. And thank you for caring enough to call."

Brody sagged with relief. He'd found out what he needed to know. "W-welcome," he managed before allowing himself to hang up.

*   *   *

Because of Kelly's sullen mood Summer had suggested that they postpone their dinner out. Dottie had agreed and they'd dined on leftover pot roast. Between bites, Dottie had downed at least four fingers of Wild Turkey, growing happier with each sip. Beaming at her audience, she told stories about her past adventures as the town's most flamboyant eccentric. But not even her tall tales had won more than a few morose smiles from her greatniece, who'd done a good job of pouting for most of the meal and then excused herself after the dishes were done to go to her room.

Brody had called twice during the evening to check on his daughter. Thinking it was a contractor returning her call, Summer had answered both times. And both times she'd been unable to convince Kelly to speak with her dad.

Now it was a few minutes before ten and Dottie was taking a shower. Brody hadn't yet returned from his meeting in town. Kelly had been on the phone in her bedroom when Summer had come upstairs to work on the brochure. She'd just settled down at the desk and booted up the laptop when Kelly wandered in through the open door, looking like a sad little waif in baggy jeans and a sloppy shirt.

"I couldn't tell him. Mark, I mean." She flopped onto Summer's bed and glared at the ceiling. "He still thinks we have a date for Friday night."

Summer turned off the computer and leaned back. Remember, you're just a guest here, she reminded herself even as she prepared to listen. "Sounds to me like you have a fairly major conflict here, kiddo."

Kelly huffed out air. "Mark says his dad never cared diddlysquat about what he did. He says I should be glad Dad cares enough to be strict."

"Mark sounds like a very mature young man."

Kelly's face lit up, and she sat up, looking bright-eyed and alive again. "Oh, he is! See, Summer, that's just the point. Mark *respects* me. He'd never do anything to hurt me."

It pained Summer to see the rapturous look she'd once seen

on her own face whenever she'd thought about Kyle. Silly ninny that she'd been, she'd adored the man. Literally worshiped at his feet, even when he'd been plotting to twist her love into his own perverted advantage. For fifteen years she'd worked to forget how she'd cherished even the briefest touch, memorized each honeyed word. A fierce need to protect Kelly from even a small measure of the disillusionment she'd endured swept through her, but the experience she'd acquired over the years warned her to tread softly. Teenagers hated advice almost as much as they hated zits. God knows, she'd sloughed off more than her share of well-meaning words.

"Kelly, honey, respect between a man and a woman is absolutely essential, I admit."

Kelly bobbed her head, her eyes still shining. Summer took a breath and tried to figure out the best way through the minefield she saw looming. Straight ahead and pray her training held, she decided, taking another, deeper breath. "But in this case you and Mark don't really know each other all that well. It might be a good idea to go slowly."

"Yeah, sure," Kelly tossed off with an impatient wave of one hand. "I mean, we have to, don't we? Dad won't let me do anything else."

"I think that's a fair assessment, yes."

Silence settled into the cozy room, broken only by the strains of "There's Nothing Like a Dame" belted out off-key drifting through the closed bathroom door. "Auntie's a terrible singer," Kelly said, giggling.

Summer grinned as she glanced toward the hall. The woman was also half-plowed. "She is . . . loud, though."

The song broke off suddenly, then Dottie's voice soared into a shrill version of "Eleanor Rigby." Kelly rolled her eyes, then sobered. "Auntie's friend, Miss Steinberg, said Auntie was in all the musicals in high school, but whenever she sang, everyone else just sang louder because they didn't want to hurt her feelings."

"Sounds like she was as popular in school as she was at the Ashram."

Kelly nodded. "Way more popular than me," she said glumly.

"I doubt that, honey. And anyway, there are all kinds of definitions of popularity."

"I suppose you had lots of dates and all when you were my age."

Careful, Summer reminded herself. Her past history was too complex to be revealed in one short conversation. Besides, it was irrelevant, she assured herself in an attempt to quiet the conscience that was jabbing at her. She was a different person now. "When I was in high school, we mostly had parties on the beach instead of actual dates."

"Cool!" Kelly regarded her with what looked suspiciously like envy. "Was it like in *Jaws*? You know, where that girl who later got eaten by the shark and the guy who used to live on the island are drinking beer together, looking all dreamy-eyed and sexy, and then go off to skinny dip?"

"In a way. One boy tried to surf drunk and ended up a paraplegic. Two of my friends ended up pregnant because they had too much pot to remember to say no. One was only a little older than you are now."

Kelly pulled a face. "Bummer."

"Yes, exactly."

"Did your parents get mad at you when a boy brought you home?" Kelly persisted after a moment.

"No, they trusted me." Trust she'd betrayed, to her everlasting regret.

"My friend Tiffany's parents are like that, too. I mean, trusting her and all. Debbie—that's her stepmom—even stands up for her when her dad gets all protective and threatens to ground her for the rest of her natural life."

"Kelly, the fact that a parent is determined to keep his child safe is almost always a sign of love."

"Yeah. I guess." Kelly's gaze fell to the rag rug. "Tiff's mother died when Tiff was six. Debbie helped her make this album with pictures of her and her mom. Tiff said Debbie was feeling real maternal 'cause she's going to have a baby. It's a girl and Debbie wants to name her after Tiff's mom. I think that's totally cool, don't you?"

"Totally." Summer felt an all-too-familiar depression clawing for a hold. She hated talking about other people's babies almost as much as she hated remembering her own. Both invariably led to a recurrence of the nightmare she dreaded.

"I wish my mother hadn't died," Kelly burst out after a short, tense silence. "It's not fair!"

Just like that, one of the mines Summer had seen looming exploded, and her heart bled a little for the motherless girl. More than anything, she wanted to hold Kelly in her arms and keep her safe, but that wouldn't be a good idea for either of them. Kelly was too needy right now, too eager to find a mother substitute. And that Summer could not be.

"I'm sure your father feels the same way, honey," she said over the wavering notes of Dottie's song.

"Oh yeah? How come he won't talk about her, then?"

Since Summer had no answer to give, she resorted to the therapist's tried-and-true method of answering a question with a question. "Have you asked him about her?"

"All the time! At least I used to." Kelly's eyes flashed with bewilderment. "He'd get this trapped look on his face and then make some lame excuse about having work to do."

"Maybe it hurts him too much to talk about your mom," she suggested, keeping her tone deliberately offhand. She was rewarded by a thoughtful frown that quickly turned mutinous.

"Grandma Mary said he never cried when my mom died, not even at the funeral or anything."

"People react to grief in different ways, Kelly. Men especially tend to hold in their feelings."

"Grandma says Dad doesn't have any." Kelly tossed her head, sending her dark hair swirling. "Grandma says he only keeps me with him to spite her, 'cause she wanted me to come live with her after my mom died. See, she and Grandpa have this great condo in Newport Beach. I can see the ocean from my room and she said she'd buy me a car for my sixteenth birthday."

The old witch! Summer thought sourly before catching hold of her rising indignation. In all fairness, she didn't know the lady—or her motivations. "Do you *want* to live with your grandmother?"

"Dad wouldn't care if I did." Buried in the look of defiance was something very like hurt.

Summer thought about the tenderness in a young father's eyes. And the worry in a world-weary man's face. "He cares, Kelly. Maybe he doesn't show it in ways you like or even recognize, but he cares."

"If he cares so much, how come the only time he talks to me is when I mess up?"

Summer had had the same feelings about her own father. Monty Laurence had favored benign neglect as a parenting style, which had worked beautifully with her eager-to-please big brother. On the other hand, she'd come into the world wired to rebel against the slightest whisper of parental restraint. Little Miss Hellfire, Phillip had teased when she'd been serving out yet another sentence in her room.

It had been little things at first. Pushing her curfew, filching cigarettes from her mother's purse. Later it had meant getting high on the excitement of sneaking her first joint rather than the pot itself. Like most of the fathers in her social set, her dad had turned a blind eye to a little experimentation. Hell, he'd been a flower child. He'd dropped a little acid, smoked his share of dope. It would pass.

When her life had spun out of control, however, he'd become explosively angry. Experimentation was one thing. Embarrassing the family was quite another. The thick plaster walls of her room had vibrated from the screaming matches. Little had she realized how much worse it would be when her dad had refused to talk to her at all. Fortunately, Kelly's transgressions were fairly benign. So far.

"What about the tea parties you and your dad used to have in the little house outside?" she prodded with a gentle smile.

Kelly darted a startled look in Summer's direction. "Aunt Dottie told you, right?"

Summer nodded. "He must have talked to you then."

Kelly's gaze slid away, and she fidgeted. "Just about dumb stuff like my dolls and my friends. Mostly he asked questions."

"And listened to the answers?"

Kelly shrugged, looking terribly young and vulnerable. "Sometimes," she admitted grudgingly.

"Some fathers never even care enough to ask questions, sweetie."

"Yeah, well, the last time I wanted to have a tea party he had some dumb meeting to go to. Lately he always has something else to do when I—oh, forget it." Looking terribly hurt, the girl leaped off the bed in a burst of angry energy and began to prowl. Once again Summer fought off the need to pull the suffering girl into her arms.

"Kelly, I think you're being unfair. Your dad made it a point to call twice tonight to make sure you were all right. If that's not caring, I don't know what is."

"He was just checking up on me, is all. Like he checks up on all his prisoners."

Kelly stopped in front of the dresser and poked at the makeup kit Summer had left open. Though Kelly picked up the eyeliner and tested the color against her wrist, her expression remained troubled.

"I have this dream sometimes where I'm this little girl, you know? And my mom is sitting on this white couch and I'm like, curling up in her lap and she's telling me to talk to my baby brother in her tummy."

She absolutely would not cry, Summer told herself firmly. Not in front of this child. Not when she was alone. She'd cried enough over lost children to last two lifetimes. "That sounds like a nice dream," she said with a smile that might have wobbled a little.

Kelly's lashes flickered. She tossed down the liner, then picked up a mascara wand, pulled off the top, and made a determined show of nonchalance as she inspected the spiral bristles. "It's like I try and try to see her face, but there's this dark shadow. I know she's smiling at me. You know, like in the picture on the wall? But I look and look and . . ." Her voice faltered, then surged. "Oh Summer, it was so awful!"

"Dreams can be like that, sweetheart," Summer said as she left her chair to go to Kelly's side. Her hand was steady as she smoothed back the girl's hair. "It's part of nature's way to help us deal with feelings that are too threatening in the daylight."

The girl shook her head. "It wasn't the dream. It . . . there was an accident on Highway 2 yesterday. I was down in the ER waiting for Dad when the ambulance came in." She dropped the mascara and hugged herself as though against a sudden chill.

"What happened?" Summer asked softly.

"This couple . . . the man was already dead. And . . . and she . . . the lady was going to have a baby. Just like my mom." Kelly's mouth trembled, and she bit her lip. "The paramedic said she was having a miscarriage and . . . they took her up to the delivery room." Before she lowered her gaze, Summer caught the sheen of tears.

"It's all right to cry," Summer murmured as she gathered the girl into her arms. Kelly sagged against her for a moment before stiffening. Misery shone in her blue eyes, but her chin was high as she edged away.

"Don't tell Dad, okay?"

"Don't tell Dad what?" Though Hollister's voice was edged with weariness, it still rang with a cop's inborn suspicion.

Summer glanced over her shoulder to find him on the threshold, his Stetson pushed to the back of his head and the gun belt she hated slung again over one broad shoulder. He looked whipped.

"Good evening, Chief." She smiled, hoping to give Kelly time to compose herself.

"Ma'am," he said, looking at his daughter. "Kel, I asked you a question. What don't you want me to know?"

Kelly quickly brushed a tear away before she turned to face him. "Nothing. Me and Summer were just talking." She flicked a beseeching glance Summer's way. "Right, Summer?"

"I got that part, Kel," Hollister cut in before Summer could open her mouth.

"Actually, I was about to offer to show Kelly some makeup tricks," Summer said coolly. To prove her point, she picked up the mascara Kelly had tossed aside and held it up. Just like Cleve Norvell had once held up the satchel of dope. *Exhibit A, Your Honor.*

The look on Hollister's face was every bit as disapproving as Judge Ramirez's. More so, given the man's size and aura of danger. Ramirez was bound by the rules of procedure. In this house at least, Hollister made his own rules.

"Damn it, Kel, how many times have I told you, no makeup until you're sixteen." His voice was harsh, his expression surly.

"Dad, it's no big deal! Everyone else—"

"No makeup." His voice was clipped, his expression hard. Summer managed to suppress a shiver. Kelly didn't.

"You're hateful and mean, just like Grandma says," she cried, her voice thick with hurt. "I don't want to live with you anymore."

He froze, the shock on his face painful to see. "That may be, but until you're eighteen you don't have a choice."

"I do so," Kelly shouted in a strangled voice. "I can run away."

"I'll bring you back. You won't like the consequences."

"I hate you!" the girl choked out before bolting toward him. Instead of moving, he stood like a bulwark, and she slammed into him hard. His arms closed in a hug.

"Kel, baby—"

"I'm not a baby!" she shouted before twisting free. When she spoke again, her tone was more controlled. "Your mother was only three years older than I am when she had you."

Summer caught the flicker of Hollister's lashes, the only sign of emotion in that weary and harsh face. "She was also dead by the time she was forty."

Kelly's face turned red. "See what I mean, Summer," she declared angrily over her shoulder. "He never listens to anything I say."

Before Summer could respond, Kelly bolted. This time Hollister let her go. The shock of the slamming door in the adjoining room had the windowpanes rattling against the frames.

"Shit!" Hollister grated, his jaw tight as he turned to follow his daughter, his intent to have it out with her stamped plainly on his harsh features.

Summer darted across the room to catch his arm. "Brody, wait. I—"

Startled, he swung around so fast she nearly lost her footing before he slipped an arm around her waist to catch her. Somehow she ended up smashed against his side before she jerked free.

"Sorry," he muttered, scowling.

"No problem." She ran her hand up her arm to the spot where it had collided with his rib cage. She couldn't remember the last time she'd felt the strength of a man's arm supporting her when she stumbled. Perhaps never.

"I wanted to talk to you before you went charging after her," she said, forcing herself to focus on Kelly. "She's dealing with a lot more than wanting to wear makeup. Or even puppy love."

He winced. "It's not love, damn it. She barely knows the kid."

"Yes, of course, but that doesn't negate the fact that she's very vulnerable right now. Adolescence is never easy, particularly when one is as sensitive as Kelly."

"Yeah, well let me tell you something, Laurence. One of my officers spotted Krebs speeding down a road that's notched up four fatalities in the last two years." His face hardened. "A few more rides like that and my daughter might end up being sensitive and *dead*."

The words came at her hard, like bullets. Summer reminded herself that she was an experienced professional who had dealt capably with frustrated parents for more than ten years. In all that time she hadn't once lost her temper, and she didn't intend to allow Brody Hollister to push her over the line. Just in case, she took an extra breath before asking calmly, "Did you explain that to her when you stopped the car, or did you just haul her out in front of all her friends?"

His gaze flickered. "What's the bottom line here, Doctor? You trolling for clients?"

"I'm not even going to dignify that with an answer," she said quietly.

He narrowed his gaze. "That's it, isn't it? You want to dig and probe into a little girl's head until she bleeds. Then you can play hero and put her back together again."

"I'm *trying* to help—"

"Back off, Laurence. I'll handle my daughter my way."

"*Your way* has her tied in knots that will slowly choke the emotional life out of her."

He flinched. "That's . . . enough."

"Oh no, Hollister. It's not nearly enough," she shot back, her patience at an end. "I just told you that in my professional as well as personal opinion, your daughter might be heading toward a serious problem and you're fluffing me off like a pesky fly."

He glared at her, his jaw tight, but said nothing. A menacing, sullen brute who could break her in two with no more effort than a sneeze. Well, maybe that steel-edged threat intimidated brawling bikers and speeders, but she'd faced down worse and survived. Drawing herself up to her full height, she did some shifting of her own until they were toe-to-toe.

"Haven't you been listening to me? Kelly needs you to talk to her—"

"You talk to her, then, since you got all the answers!" Without another word he stalked across the hall into his own room—and slammed the door.

An hour later Summer sat propped against the pillows reading the newspaper she'd bought on her trip into town. According to the headline, the accident Kelly had mentioned had occurred on the main highway leading from Seattle.

A three-column colored picture of Brody Hollister was on the front page, walking toward the camera—eyes shielded by the dark lenses, teeth bared as though warning the photographer to get out of the way or be trampled. In his brawny arms he cradled a small boy against his shoulder. One of two survivors, according to the caption beneath the picture. His father had been killed instantly while his mother remained in critical condition after miscarrying. His solemn little face, still round with baby fat, was nestled against a piece of cloth under Brody's chin. The little one's security blanket, she realized, blinking back hot tears.

There was another photo as well, of a stunned young man staring with glazed eyes at the camera. *Joseph Finley, arrested at the scene for criminal negligent homicide, taken as he left the county jail after being released on bail posted by his father, prominent real estate developer Anson Finley, of Bellevue.*

In a statement released by the suspect's attorney, Melvin Bailey, the teenager is said to be utterly grief-stricken and distraught. "Joe is a fine young man who's never been in trouble before," Bailey told this reporter on Sunday evening when contacted at his Bellevue office. "In fact, his doctor has sedated him to prevent him from harming himself because of his terrible remorse."

Summer felt a wrench of pain as the memories of her own arrest came flooding back. The shame, the disbelief, the desperate longing to make it all go away. At least young Finley wasn't alone. Over the years since her release, she'd tried to contact her father several times, but he'd always refused her calls, and her letters had been returned unopened.

Summer let the paper drop to her knees and leaned back, her head resting against the headboard. Horrific as the story was, she'd heard it all before. No one came out the winner when there were drugs involved. Except the dealers, she reminded herself.

The worst kind of carrion. In that, at least, she and Brody were in perfect agreement.

Brody lay with his hands folded beneath his head and his gaze fixed on the ceiling. Outside, the wind was licking at the branches in the big cedar beneath his bedroom window. He'd blown it. Dumped a load of pent-up anger on a woman who didn't deserve it, all because she reminded him of the lady shrink who'd treated him after Megan's death.

He'd been raw inside after the funeral. Bleeding silently from wounds that no one could understand. Seething with a scalding hatred of the man who'd taken his revenge on an innocent woman and unborn child. The same hatred he'd felt for himself.

Meggie's friends had tried to help, but he'd frozen them out. His partner had put up with his rudeness and his sudden bursts of fury for months before backing him up against the wall with an ultimatum. Get help or get a new partner.

Ashamed of himself, he'd gone to the department shrink who kept hacking at him to talk through the pain that consumed him. Eighty bucks an hour and the woman couldn't understand that the rage was the only thing that had kept him sane—that and the vow he'd made to track down Williams and make him pay.

It had taken him five months of following every lead, no matter how off-the-wall, before he'd found the bastard in a filthy crack house in Riverside. Williams had gone to jail without a mark on him. Brody had let the Riverside cops cuff the bastard. He'd been afraid to put his hands on the man.

After the trial and the conviction, he found himself with too much time on his hands. Too many hours to brood. Living in the house Meggie had chosen and decorated only served to remind him of all he'd lost. Being around people she'd known and loved had been the worst kind of pain. Paradoxically, accepting his mother-in-law's scorn had given him a perverse kind of comfort. But when he realized that Mary Cathleen was deliberately trying to poison Kelly's mind against him, he'd pulled himself together and taken a good long look at the self-pitying jerk he'd become.

He'd sold the house, put Meggie's things in storage for Kelly, and moved back home. Which, to him, meant wherever his aunt was. She'd been more of a mother to him than his own. And when—

Brody froze, his hand already slipping beneath his pillow for his weapon, his mind shutting down to a single sharp focus. Though the house was silent now, he'd heard something, he was sure of it. Like a muffled cry for help.

Kelly, he thought, tossing off the covers. Seconds later, dressed only in the jeans he'd discarded earlier, he cracked open the door and swept the space beyond with a narrowed gaze. In the span of a breath he saw the empty hallway, the closed doors, the glow from the small lamp on the table set against the wall between the guest room and Kelly's. The house was silent. He was about to go back to bed when he heard it again, a low, muffled sob from the room where their guest was sleeping.

This was turning out to be one lousy night, he thought as he moved along the hall. Outside her door, he stopped again, wracked with indecision. Was she ill? Hurt? Feeling like a prized jackass, he pressed his ear against the door and listened. The sound was faint, but recognizable. She was crying. Sobbing, the kind of sobbing that started in the depths of a person's soul and tore from the throat until it was raw. Stepping back, he ran a hand over his stubbled jaw and considered waking his aunt, then thought better of it. A person had a right to handle her pain in private.

He'd done enough crying in the middle of the night when he was a kid to know how embarrassed Laurence would be if she got caught. Yeah, better to let her work it out on her own, whatever it was. A broken romance, maybe. Some guy dumped her and broke her heart. None of his damned business. He was halfway to his own room when he heard her cry out as though pleading with someone.

Hell, he thought again, turning back. What if there was some perverted asshole in there with her. It was far-fetched, but possible. Men had died or been maimed for discounting the unlikely. Eyes riveted on the door, he thumbed off the safety on the Smith & Wesson. Standing to one side of the frame, he reached across his body with his left hand and slowly turned the knob. The latch clicked, and he froze, waiting.

Nothing. He ticked off a half-dozen seconds before the cry came again. Jaw set, he eased inside. The room was bathed in moonlight, leeching the color from the walls and turning the bright coverlet to drab variations of gray. Moving only his eyes, his weapon ready, he searched for anything out of the ordinary.

Laurence was tucked up into the bed, curled into herself, her arms wrapped around the pillow. The covers were bunched and twisted around her, as was the oversized shirt she was wearing. One slender shoulder had been uncovered, and her skin glowed like the milky, translucent inner layer of a shell he'd once found at the beach.

Her eyes were closed, her lashes flickering as a bad dream played out in her head. Thickened by tears and muffled by the pillow pressed to the length of her, her words were garbled and hoarse. He made out a few words, nothing that made sense.

Grimly he flicked on the forty-five's safety before tucking it into his jeans at the small of his back. As quietly as he could, he moved to the side of the bed where she lay. Reluctant to touch her, he leaned closer.

"Wake up, Dr. Laurence," he whispered gruffly, his gaze trained on her tearstained cheeks. "It's only a d-dream."

She whimpered, then rubbed her cheek against the pillow like a lost little girl, grabbing his heart.

"Dr. Laurence? S-S-Summer? Wake up. It's okay, honey. It's okay."

Slowly, with each breath she dragged into her lungs, the nightmare images faded, slipping behind a pane of shimmering, melting color. She sighed, grateful.

"That's it, come back."

Summer opened her damp eyes, at once disoriented and

shocked. Someone was there, looming over her, a dark, massive shape silhouetted against the moonlight streaming through the window. A man. She gave a little squeak and groped for the covers, only to find them all but welded to her body. "No . . . get away—" She broke off, her gaze searching frantically for a weapon, only to be jerked back to reality by a low chuckle.

"Not the lamp. It's one of Auntie's favorites."

She blinked, trying to focus. "Brody? Is something wrong? Is Kelly all right?"

"You were having a bad dream, that's all."

"I . . . yes," she managed, still half caught in the horrible grief that never failed to leave her depressed for days afterward. "It's been a long time. I thought—hoped—it was gone." She tried to sit up, but something was pinning her to the mattress. Unable to move, she felt the panic take hold. Somehow she fought it off.

"Hold on," he muttered, working to free the knotted end of the top sheet. "Lift up."

She tried, but the covers vised around her like a boa constrictor. The very thought had her shuddering. "I can't. I'm caught."

He glanced past her, sighed, then frowned. "Roll over. No, damn it, the other way."

"Excuse me," she muttered, turning to her right, only to be stopped by the pillow she must have been hugging in her sleep. Horrible as her nightmare had been, the aftermath wasn't turning out to be all that much better.

She tried to shove the oversized pillow aside, only to realize she had one leg hooked over the plump contours. Frowning, she tried to squirm backward.

"Jesus, Laurence," he grated. Before she could form a suitably tart reply, he reached down and jerked the pillow free. She felt a tug, followed by a ripping sound.

"Hell!"

"I think one of us is in big trouble," she muttered, staring up at him. Silently he held up the pillow with one hand to show her the dangling lace. "Don't worry, I'll take the blame," she promised, busy trying to wedge her hand beneath the sheet.

A sense of doom settled over Brody as he watched her wiggling upward toward a sitting position. If he didn't come up with a plan to short-circuit the powerful attraction already hacking its way through his strongest defenses, he was going to fall for her. He could feel his resolve to remain aloof softening more every time she looked at him with those big, sad eyes.

On the other hand, his body had started getting hard along about the time he'd figured out she was okay. His erection was already jammed against his fly, and blood was still pumping. Grateful for the semidarkness, he spread his legs wider to lessen the pressure and bent down to tug the rest of the covers free. At the same time, she gave a pull of her own, and they ended up in a tug-of-war. He let go first, and she jerked backward. The neck of the big shirt shifted, displaying a goodly portion of her chest. One glimpse of the sweet shadow between her surprisingly full breasts and his control took a nosedive. Feeling like a clod, a voyeur, and a man stretching slowly on the rack, he took a step backward.

"Okay now?"

Summer heard the impatience in his voice and nodded. "Thanks for waking me up."

"No problem." He took another step backward, then stopped. Moonlight bathed his bare chest and dipped his dark hair in silver. "Uh, if you want to talk about it, I mean, now or later, I'm a pretty g-good listener."

Yes, he was, she thought. Listening with silent patience to little girls at pretend tea parties, lonely maiden ladies, and distraught women fighting ghosts. A man trapped by his inability to speak easily, who understood the unspoken pain of others. It took a moment to steady her voice. "I appreciate the offer, but I know exactly why I have this particular dream and what it means. Mostly it leaves me alone. When it doesn't, I just tough it out."

An expression crossed his face that said he understood. "Well, good night, then."

"Good night, Brody. And thanks again."

He nodded once, gave her a quick half smile, and left, closing the door very softly behind him.

CHAPTER 8

Brody was standing at the sink, filling his thermos when Laurence walked in, looking sleepy and just a little grumpy. Her hair wasn't quite perfect, her skin pale. She was wearing jeans, and a sweater the color of peaches. The sweater was soft and fuzzy, the jeans looser than a guy liked to see. Nevertheless, there was just something about the wear-softened denim curving over a world-class bottom that just naturally turned him into an idiot.

"Please tell me there'll be at least one cup left for a desperate woman," she pleaded as she came to stand next to him. Her scent was light. Something cheerful, like sunshine after a rain. It made him want to walk barefoot through thick, cool grass.

"Guess I could manage that." The coffee mugs were in the cupboard overhead. Careful to keep from brushing against her, he reached up to snag the biggest one. He'd already had two cups, gulped down scalding hot as he stood by the sink, trying not to think about the apology he owed her for exploding at her last night. Just his bad luck he'd never once managed to say "I'm sorry" without stuttering like a damned jackass.

"You, uh, you're up early," he said as he poured.

"The curse of a workaholic nature. My mind won't let me sleep in, no matter what my body says. Besides, I want to get pictures of the barn in the morning light." Though shadowed and dulled with too little sleep, her green eyes were fixed with greedy eagerness on the coffee sloshing into the cup.

"You're really serious about this relocation thing?"

"You thought I wasn't?"

"I figured maybe you were just humoring my aunt." He palmed the mug, and handed it to her.

"Thank you," she murmured fervently before lifting the coffee to her lips. The expression on her face was pure bliss. He barely managed not to groan.

"For what it's worth, Hollister, I don't' 'humor' people." Her voice had a slight edge.

"Okay."

Her gaze shifted to a spot over his left shoulder, and the hands holding the mug seemed to grip a little tighter. "I read about Sunday's accident," she murmured. Her chest rose and fell beneath the sweater. "The little boy, Trent, do you know if he has other family?"

He masked his surprise at her question with a frown. "A grandmother. Why?"

"I was wondering if she plans to take him for grief counseling."

For all the good it would do. Still, it was better than letting the boy scream night after night alone. "Said she was. Someone local."

"Good. That's good." She took a sip, then wiped her lower lip with her tongue to catch a stray drop.

"Uh, Laurence—"

"Hollister—"

Summer laughed as they exchanged self-conscious looks. Mornings were not prime time for her.

"After you," Hollister said, looking oddly relieved.

"About Kelly, it wasn't your forbidding her to wear makeup that had her so upset last night."

"Could've fooled me."

Summer heard the sound of frustration in his graveled voice and sympathized. "Sunday, at the hospital, she happened to be down in the ER waiting for you to pick her up when they brought in Mr. and Mrs. Oates. She . . . saw Mrs. Oates and it reminded her of her mom."

"Damn," he bit out, pain exploding in his eyes.

She sipped coffee to give his emotions—and hers—a chance to settle. When she had herself under firm control again, she set the mug on the counter and braced herself. "This has brought up a lot of issues dealing with her mother's death. Feelings I doubt she herself understands."

His ebony lashes flickered. "Kelly was three years old. Her pediatrician said she'd adjust."

"Some children do. But I deal with children Kelly's age every day and a lot of them are in acute pain because of things that happened when they were younger. Things they only vaguely remember—or don't remember at all. That's why they come to me, to make sense of the pain that drives them to behave in ways that are dangerous to themselves and sometimes others as well."

Unlike last night, he was really listening, and she hastened to press the advantage. "Kelly needs you to tell her it's okay to feel sad because she lost her mother. That it's okay to cry when it hurts."

His jaw flexed, stretching the skin white over the hard muscle. He plowed stiff fingers through his hair, then formed a fist with the same hand and rested it on the counter as he stared down at the two feet of floor between them. "I'm . . . that kind of thing, t-talking . . . It's not . . . easy for me."

Summer took a quick breath and kept her gaze steady on his. "Dottie told me about your stuttering."

"I figured."

"Is that why you haven't talked to her about her mother? Because it's difficult?"

"D-difficult, hell. It's damn near impossible." A hard flush took over his cheeks. "Besides, my . . . it . . . b-bothers her."

Summer hid her empathy behind a neutral nod. "I wouldn't suggest it if I didn't think it would help," she said softly. "Just about everything she knows about her mother has come from her grandmother and Dottie. Naturally, their perspective is different from yours. Which means that Kelly's picture of her mom is incomplete. One-sided, if you will."

He rubbed his hand down his cheek, his thoughts turned inward. Then his gaze found hers. She read sadness there, and a quiet strength. "You know what, Doc? You would have made a great district attorney."

Summer grimaced. "I don't consider that a compliment, Hollister."

Curiosity glinted in his eyes for a moment before fading under the resurgence of concern. "I'd rather walk bare-assed naked into S-Sarge's Place on a Saturday night, but if you think it'll help, I'll talk to her."

Summer wanted to hug him. She smiled instead. "If you don't mind a little more advice?"

He gave her a half smile. "Might as well get it all out, Doc."

"Give her permission to use makeup since that seems so important to her. Just a little. Nothing too bright, of course," she hastened to add when he started to glower. "A small concession to show you acknowledge she's no longer a child."

He winced. "Guess I'm behaving like a Neanderthal, huh?"

"More like a daddy who hates to let go of his little girl."

"Guess it'll happen sooner or later, no matter what I do. I'm hoping for later." He rubbed one big hand over his heart as though it hurt. Catching her eye, he dropped his hand to his side.

"She's a neat kid, Brody. Her instincts are good. When she calms down, she'll realize you're only trying to protect her."

"You think so?" The sudden hopeful note in his darkly dangerous voice both amused and touched her.

"Yes, I do. I've spent years working with adolescents in crisis. Many of their . . . problems could be traced to a lack of parental discipline." She drew a breath. "Even though they would cut off their tongues before admitting it, children—and especially teens—need boundaries. It makes them feel safe, even as they're testing them for all their worth."

"I'll remember that the next time Kel slams the bejesus out of her bedroom door."

Summer laughed. "I hate to tell you this, Hollister, but you do a pretty fair job of slamming doors yourself."

He gave her the same sheepish look she'd noticed outside the ranch house when Dottie had been scolding him about his manners. "You think it's catching?"

"If it is, you'd better stock up on door hinges."

He grinned, and the bottom seemed to drop out of her stomach. Coffee, she thought, reaching for her cup. It was nearly empty, and she picked up the pot to refill it.

"Summer?"

She returned the pot to the burner, then turned back around. She felt a sizzle of sexual interest in her chest, and a heat in her fingertips. Pure chemistry, she reminded herself as she folded her fingers more firmly around the handle of her cup.

"Uh, I figure I can carve out some time around eleven-thirty," he said, all business now. "Meet me in town, and I'll give you the VIP tour."

She looked up quickly from the cup she'd been bringing to her lips. "Really, that's not necessary."

"Consider it a favor, then."

Curiosity had always gotten her into trouble. Giving in to it now would most likely be a mistake. Somehow she couldn't help herself. "Why, exactly, would agreeing to take a tour with you be a favor?"

His cheek folded into the half smile she was beginning to like too much. "I drive better than I talk. Be easier to apologize behind the wheel."

"Apologize for what?"

His smile faded, leaving his strong features still. "The things I said last night. I was out of line."

Summer didn't deny it. "It's obvious you dislike psychotherapists."

He shifted, planting his boots a little wider. A gunfighter's stance. "About as much as you like cops, I reckon. Or is it just me who's got your back up?"

He was giving her an out. A woman with a strong self-protective streak would grab it and hang on for dear life. A woman who was beginning to come alive again might not. "No, it's not you," she admitted before taking a quick sip. The coffee had grown bitter.

His grin flashed, sending a ripple of reaction down her spine. "Then we don't have a problem." He picked up his thermos and strode toward the door. "If I'm not in my office, have Max page me."

"Brody, wait!"

"City Hall's on Main, real close to the flagpole. Big white building with cop cars parked out front. Can't miss it."

"But . . ."

"Eleven-thirty. Don't be late."

Summer found City Hall on the first try. As Brody had said, it was big and white and sat on a slight rise on the right-hand side of the main thoroughfare, directly between a Safeway store and a McDonald's, both of which were pseudo-alpine in design. Golden arches and Tyrolean gingerbread, she marveled, shaking her head. Was anything in this town normal?

Even the city building looked like it had come directly from a travel guide to the Alps. Its two full stories of gabled windows, deep overhangs, and window boxes were only marginally less ornate than the rest of the business district. As far as she could see when she pulled into the lot surrounding the building, there were only four visitors' slots in the front, all of which were occupied.

Summer sighed and circled the building at a snail's pace, thinking there might be more parking in the rear. Most of the spaces were either filled or reserved.

Sure enough, Brody's white Blazer was parked dead center between his designated lines. Her heart gave a little flutter as she drove toward the front again. She was being as giddy as Kelly, she thought, disgusted with herself.

A white patrol car with the mountain-and-pine-tree logo on the side pulled in just as she rounded the corner, and she braked, waiting for him to go right or left. The driver was large, with a bull neck. As he drove slowly past, panic raced through her, sending adrenaline jolting into her bloodstream. The man behind the wheel looked like Jessop, the prison guard who'd terrorized her on her way to court.

Jaw clenched, she realized the car was stopped and her foot was jammed against the brake pedal. She took a deep breath, then another. Gradually the scene beyond the dusty windshield took on clarity again, and the panic eased. The policeman in the patrol car was a stranger.

She inhaled slowly, visualizing a peaceful beach. Phoenix House was bigger than her fears or phobias, more important than self-preservation or her mixed-up feelings about a man she'd just met. No, it was about a vow she'd made in a prison chapel, a vow to turn around her life and make it count for something. Hadn't she sworn to wrestle the devil himself to keep that vow?

Darn right she had—although she hadn't taken into the account that he might end up to be six-four with a terribly bruised and battered soul and irresistible purple eyes that had forgotten how to smile. Or the fact that in spite of all the years she'd spent avoiding men like him, she was terribly in danger of succumbing to the pull of those sad eyes.

A shaky laugh escaped her tight throat, and she sat up straighter. Brody Hollister was bound to become her enemy sooner or later. Becoming emotionally tangled with him would be dumber than dumb.

"Mel Bailey's pushing for a hearing in juvenile court. With his media clout, he just might have the juice to do it."

Leaning back in his chair, his boots planted firmly on his paper-piled desk, Brody heard the frustration in the assistant DA's voice and knew it wasn't half of what was coursing through him at the moment.

"Christ, Labeck," he snarled into the receiver clamped between his ear and his shoulder. "At the most, that'll get the little crud a few years in reform school."

"They call 'em 'youth authority facilities' these days, Chief."

"I don't give a rat's ass what they call them. They're nothing but a free ride for a bunch of assholes who belong in a real prison."

"Not all of them, Brody," the DA returned with a hint of steel in his tone.

His temper sizzling, Brody dropped his feet with a thud and sat up. At the same time, he saw a flash of cinnamon and jerked his gaze toward the door he hadn't bothered to close. She was wearing an orange jacket over her jeans and sweater. An orange-and-blue knitted cap was pulled over her ears. She looked warm and cozy and as bright as Christmas morning.

"Hold on a minute, Ted. Got someone here to see me."

"You're tied up," she said, taking a step backward. "We can do this another time."

"No problem. Have a seat." He waved her toward the up-holstered visitor's chair that Max had made him haul up from the storage room downstairs. Said his office needed something to balance the testosterone overload.

"Two minutes," he promised, hauling out a smile that felt rusty as hell.

"If you're sure."

"Count on it."

"All right. Two minutes." As though to reinforce her point, she glanced at her watch before sitting down. Her expression was de-termined and a little pained. Like she was facing a damned root canal.

"You got a date for the arraignment?" he said into the re-ceiver, watching with half-closed eyes as she gave his office a swift once-over.

"Yeah, hang on," Labeck muttered, paper rustling. "May seven, ten A.M."

Brody flipped his calendar to the seventh, grabbed a pen, and made a note. "Got it."

"Who's testifying about the arrest? You?"

"No, Officer Keegan. He was first on the scene and found the drug paraphernalia."

"The kid that took a knee in the family jewels?"

"Yeah. He's still getting flack for that."

"But you're the one who brought Finley down when he tried to run, right?"

Brody knew where Labeck was going in his careful way and tried to head him off. "Keegan had it handled. I was purely an observer."

"It would make a stronger case if you took the stand."

"No can do, Ted. It's Keegan's collar, Keegan's responsibility. Court says so."

That, at least, was true. Even if it weren't, he wouldn't testify. He was too emotionally involved, which was always dangerous for a cop. It was especially so for a man with a disability like his. The last time he'd had to testify in a case where a child had been injured, it had taken him four tries to get his name out, and that'd been the easy part. In the end the members of the grand jury had been too embarrassed to look at him and the DA had hustled him off the stand as though he'd suddenly developed symptoms of the plague. The grand jury had voted not to indict.

"For a man who's dedicated to keeping scum like Joseph Finley out of this town, you're not making things easy, Hollister."

"When the court makes it easy on me, I'll make it easy on you."

Labeck snorted, then apparently resigned, said he'd be in touch, and hung up. As Brody replaced the receiver, he realized he could smell her. A hint of roses, a touch of spice. Sunshine. He allowed himself a moment to enjoy the pleasurable buzz it gave him before asking briskly, "Any trouble finding the place?"

"Not a bit." She glanced around more slowly now, a little wary, a little curious. It was the same reaction he usually got from people coming into a police station for the first time, yet something about the tension in that elegant high-boned face and the rigid way she gripped her purse had his cop's intuition scanning for reasons.

"Interesting," she murmured, trailing her gaze over the bulging bookcases and scarred filing cabinets. Her eyes softened while she studied the framed artwork Kelly had done in grammar school. Her eyebrows wagged a little at the sight of the Playboy calendar pinned to the wall at eye level. Miss April was wearing a bunch of daffodils and a Come-to-mama grin. He felt heat spreading over his cheeks and knew he was blushing. Damned if the woman across from him didn't grin.

"It was a gift," he all but growled. "From my officers. For Christmas."

"Ah."

"I didn't want to offend them by sticking it in a drawer."

"Naturally not. Besides, it goes well with the rest of your office. Very nineteen-forties film noir."

Thanks to a film-buff master chief at the SP office in Long Beach, he knew what that meant. "My predecessor had the office where the computer p-people work now. It was too quiet s-so I had a guy I know b-build this."

"Hmm. The windows are so you can keep an eye on your men, I gather."

"Men and women. We might look like rednecked hicks, but we're m-making p-progress."

"I'm impressed."

"It's not exactly 'NYPD Blue,' but we do our best."

"Your basic craggy cast of lovable but tortured characters, I imagine," she commented, smiling just enough to whet his appetite for more.

"Guess we have a s-sergeant who's about as craggy as they come and a r-rookie who's feeling fairly tortured long about now."

Her gaze was cool, the kind that challenged a man to turn up the heat until those eyes glowed with fire. "Let me guess. You're the designated strong-but-silent type."

He winced. "Now that hurt."

"Sorry. It wasn't meant to."

He got to his feet and snagged his hat. "Ready for the tour, Doctor?"

* * *

Summer offered to drive. Brody insisted on taking the Blazer, claiming it was easier to find parking spots in an official vehicle. She didn't believe him for a minute. It had been her experience that a man always wanted to drive when he was with a woman. In her own world she wouldn't tolerate such behavior for an instant, but somehow Brody had an ability to squash her more aggressive instincts.

"Cold?" he asked, glancing her way.

"Actually, it's a little warm." She glanced toward the door. "Would you mind if I opened the window?"

"Feel free."

It didn't help. Even with the window wide-open, the air seemed stuffy. Almost smothering.

"How's the hand? Any blisters?"

Summer realized Brody was looking at her lap where the hand she'd burned was curled tightly around the edge of her seat belt and forced herself to reply pleasantly, "Fine. It hardly hurts at all."

"Good." His gaze flickered to her face before returning to the road. He was wearing sunglasses again, and the sexy Stetson was pulled low, hiding his expression. She suspected it was done deliberately. To intimidate the innocent and guilty alike. Even though she understood the dynamics, she couldn't quite shake off the effect.

"Something wrong?"

"No, why?"

He compressed his lips, and the slashing dimple in his cheek winked at her. "You seem tense."

She made a conscious effort to relax. "I'm not in the least, I assure you."

His gaze flickered her way again. "I'm a safe driver, if that's what's worrying you. Never had an accident since the first one."

"The first one?"

"When I was thirteen. Ran my old man's pickup into a ditch to keep from hitting a deer. Totaled that old Chevy and got myself tossed out on my can. It was damned embarrassing."

"You were driving at thirteen?"

"Only on the back roads."

"Were you hurt?"

"Busted two ribs and split open my shoulder pretty good when I went through the windshield."

He slowed to navigate a turn, and Summer saw a young couple walking along the sidewalk holding hands. With his free hand, the man was pushing a baby stroller. As she watched, he leaned toward the woman to steal a kiss. Summer quickly averted her gaze before envy could take hold. "Your father must have been upset when he found out."

"You might say that, yeah. He loved that old truck." One side of his mouth made a stab at a smile. "Made me work a solid year on one of his logging crews to pay for a new one."

"At thirteen?"

"I was big for my age."

He checked the mirror, then pulled out to pass a slower car. Summer felt the surge of the engine's power and sucked in. The big hands on the wheel seemed perfectly relaxed. No reason to be afraid.

If only he hadn't insisted on taking the police vehicle, she thought, drawing in another measured breath. The muted chatter on the radio and the lethal-looking shotgun clipped barrel-up to the dash had her stomach clenching. She remembered staring at the dulled surface of a similar barrel through the grid separating prisoner from captor, tears streaming down her face, and her arms folded over her belly as she'd bent forward, trying not to be sick.

"You sure you're okay?" Once again she was subjected to the sharp scrutiny of a cop's eyes. "You, uh, haven't said more than a couple of words since we left the office."

"I'm absorbing the ambience."

His mouth kicked up at one corner. "A twelve-dollar word meaning schmaltz?"

She couldn't help it. She grinned. "Something like that, yes."

He signaled a turn and drove down a narrow alleyway designed to look like a cozy village street in Bavaria. Flowers were painted on the walls and each door was a different color. Quaint streetlamps straight from Hansel and Gretel stood on painted poles.

"Any second now I expect to see Heidi come skipping down those stairs," she said, pointing to green steps with carved sides. Moisture was pearling on her skin and collecting in the hollow between her breasts. Paradoxically, her throat seemed parched, and it hurt to swallow.

"Place used to be a dry cleaners. Went out of business when I was in high school." He stopped at the intersection of the street and waved a group of middle-aged tourists across in front of him. Summer saw the tension in his jaw and wondered if he ever relaxed.

"It must have been exciting, seeing the town come alive again."

"Guess so. I wasn't here." He pulled out and turned left.

"Dottie said your grandfather held on to his mill for a long time until he was close to bankruptcy."

"That's what they tell me." He lifted a hand and waved at a man wearing lederhosen and carrying an accordion. The man waved back.

"You weren't here for that either?"

He shook his head. "I was in boot camp. Aunt Dottie wrote me."

There was a metallic taste in her mouth, and she ran her tongue over her teeth, trying to wipe it away. "Must have been a big change when you came home on leave."

"I didn't."

Respecting his obvious reluctance to talk about his past, she searched for a neutral topic. "Where was it? The mill?"

"Out a ways, by the river. We can drive by if you want." He glanced at her again. She felt herself warming inside, but her skin was still clammy. She edged closer to the window and let the fresh air blow directly in her face.

"I've never seen a sawmill before."

"Don't expect much. All the equipment was sold off years ago, and the rats have been at everything else."

He drove slowly through the pretty little streets with the bright buildings and clean sidewalks, pointing out the chamber of commerce, the main fire station, the library. "Looks new," she murmured, following the upper balcony of the large two-story stucco-and-wood structure with her gaze.

"It is. Aunt Dottie bullied the city commissioners into putting a bond issue on the ballot, then went door-to-door to get it passed. Rumor has it she wasn't above blackmailing old school friends to get a donation. Seems she ran with a bunch of hell-raisers when she was a kid."

"Your aunt is an unusual lady."

"Guess you noticed that, huh?"

"The first time I saw her she had the retreat coordinator backed up against the wall and was shaking her finger at him because the wires of the sound system were crossed and the chanters in one room were interrupting the meditators in another."

He grinned. Enchanting her all over again. Nature's way of wooing an unattached female into a virile male's web.

"Hospital's down that way," he said, jerking his chin toward a narrow street angling off to the right. "Just added a wing. Doctors' offices next door."

"Is that where Dr. Krebs has his office?"

"Yeah, why? You feeling sick?"

Swallowing, she shook her head. "Dottie mentioned him, that's all."

"Yeah? She doesn't usually."

"She was telling me about the area. She suggested I contact him with any questions I might have about the medical community."

"Doc's an internist, not a shrink."

"Sometimes psychologists need to refer a patient." *Her* referrals were almost always related to the damage to young bodies done by drugs.

As he slowed, then turned right onto the main highway, she

wondered how he would react if she told him about Phoenix House. With anger, she suspected. An icy, narrow-eyed fury.

They were on their way out of town now, and the Blazer picked up speed. Her stomach lurched, and she concentrated on the center stripe. "That's the Wenatchee," he said, nodding toward the river shimmering like a vein of silver alongside the road. "Runs along the north end of Hollister property."

Summer nodded. She'd already seen Dottie's report with the map attached. "I suppose it snows here in the winter," she ventured, glancing at the passing landscape. The signs of a recent thaw were everywhere—patches of dirty slush in shaded hollows of the steeply sloping hillsides—pockmarked roads littered with gravel from the winter sanding, snow-capped peaks reaching into a still-pale sky.

"Usually starts around Halloween. In a good year the last snow melts around the end of March."

Soon they were passing open fields, many of which sloped gently upward toward the rocky peaks, all planted with row after row of small, barren trees. "Pears," he said when he saw her looking. "Just starting to bud."

"What are those things stacked against the trees on the end?" She pointed toward a row on his side.

"Props for the branches when the fruit becomes heavy."

With a sudden burst of static, the radio came alive. The female dispatcher spoke in a kind of shorthand—numbers and acronyms. Sunlight glinted off the dark lenses screening his eyes as he listened to the equally terse reply of one of his officers. Fascinated and yet repelled, she stared at the red light that oscillated with the highs and lows of speech. Next to the receiver, the monstrous shotgun seemed to mock her.

She saw Brody's hand reach out to adjust the volume. Such a big hand. Jessop's hands had left painful welts where they'd pinched her nipples.

Relax, babycakes. Where you're going you'll be spending a lot of time wishing for a man's hand on those world-class tits.

Her mouth went dry. Memories rushed at her. Ugly, sickening

images. The cold, hard steel of the cuffs cutting into her wrists. The rude, grasping hands skimming her breasts and hips, sliding along her thighs, pushing up between her legs, lingering.

Frantic now, she gasped for air. Instead of easing the tightness in her chest, it only seemed to make it worse. Beneath the knotted muscles her stomach roiled, and she tasted bile.

"Stop!" she managed to gasp, before clamping a hand over her mouth.

CHAPTER 9

"Jesus, Laurence!"

The Blazer lurched to the side and stopped. Dimly she was aware of Brody jerking open his door and vaulting out. She was still fumbling with the door handle when the passenger door flew outward and Brody slid one arm behind her, the other under her knees. Before she could draw another breath he'd swung her out of the seat and placed her on her knees on the weed-choked berm. Kneeling behind her, he hooked a hand around her middle to support her while he used his other hand to press her head down over the sharply sloping hillside.

"Take slow, deep breaths," he ordered. "That's it, in and out."

She gulped, fought, then realizing she had no control, lurched as far forward over the slope as she could and retched until she was empty. Profoundly embarrassed, she hung her head and wished for a miraculous *Star Trek* zap to somewhere else. Preferably where no one had ever heard of Summer Laurence.

"Better now?" Hollister's voice was a gruff rumble next to her ear, so close his breath warmed her skin.

She managed to nod, still too embarrassed to look at him. Of all the people on the planet, Brody Hollister would have to have been the one to witness her neurotic breakdown.

"Kelly used to get car sick. I've held her head a few times at the side of the road, too." A folded handkerchief appeared in her range of vision, held in deeply tanned, blunted fingers with short clean nails. Grateful, she took it from him and methodically

142

wiped her mouth. The hanky smelled like starch and soap—clean, bracing scents. She pressed the snowy cotton to her nose and inhaled deeply. It took several breaths, but gradually the cloying taste of sickness and shame receded a little. But not enough.

"You should have let me drive," she muttered through a thick red haze of chagrin. "Drivers don't get car sick."

He rewarded her with a chuckle that was surprisingly infectious. "Is that opinion or fact, Dr. Laurence?"

"Fact, of course." She swallowed, then nearly gagged at the sour taste. She would kill for a drink of water. "It's . . ." She had to pause to clear her throat. "It's a survival thing. The mind realizes the danger of sudden distraction and therefore sends signals to the stomach to behave." And a woman fighting demons from her past spouts nonsense to keep from screaming.

"No offense, Doc, but my mind was sending a few survival signals, too." His tone was wry, his voice cowboy lazy. "One of which said that letting a city woman from California drive me around on these roads was the fastest way to some major grief."

She choked out a laugh, surprising herself. Maybe it was the mountain air that made her do ridiculous things. Or some kind of rare jet lag caused by driving over Alp-high peaks. Because it certainly couldn't be the man kneeling at her back, cradling her against his rock-hard chest, who had turned her world topsy-turvy. After all, he was a cop. And she hated cops. Well, most of them, anyway.

Too embarrassed to return a soiled hanky, she wadded it into a ball and shoved it into her jacket pocket. "I'm fine now," she murmured, praying that she wouldn't disgrace herself by falling flat on her face when she tried to stand on jellied legs.

His arms tightened. "Take a minute for your tummy to settle down. We've got plenty of time."

The clean scent of soap on his skin that she'd noticed earlier this morning was fainter now and mingled with the smells of wind and something she suspected was uniquely Brody. A simmering, provocative hint of musk that seemed to swirl down deep inside her and tug at buried longings. Absolutely, unequivocally, she could not afford to like this man. Unfortunately it was becoming increasingly difficult not to. And that made her extremely uncomfortable. So she did what she always did when she found her equilibrium threatened; she started talking.

"This is certainly above and beyond your duty as a tour guide, Chief Hollister." Somehow it was easier to keep her gaze fixed on the craggy peak on the other side of the river gorge while she talked. Perhaps because the threat it posed was safely distant while the man comforting her was much too close. "Perhaps you can put in for overtime or hazardous-duty pay. Or, I know what! I'll take you to lunch. You haven't eaten, I hope, because—"

"Laurence?" Though quiet, his voice was laced with just enough steel to cut through her bluster.

Reluctantly she twisted around to look at him—and saw herself reflected in the dark lenses of his glasses. Her breath caught. The tough-and-together shrink who wore power suits and scheduled her life in fifteen-minute chunks had been replaced by a waif with too-pale cheeks and frighteningly vulnerable eyes.

"It's okay," he told her quietly. "You don't have to keep the bad guys away all by yourself."

She blinked. "I don't know what you mean. What bad guys?"

"The ones you seem set on talkin' to death." Something in his face told her he knew a bit about holding off demons himself.

Summer took a breath. Maybe he didn't have an elitist string of letters behind his name, but she had a strong feeling Brody Hollister would blow the top off an IQ scale. Certainly he had her figured out down to a gnat's eyebrow, which was a feat a goodly number of Ph.D.s of her acquaintance had never managed. As speculation, it was damned scary. As truth, it was downright terrifying.

"Look around, Hollister. The only 'guy' here is you."

"What?" he asked quietly.

She realized she was staring at his mouth. His lower lip was a whisper fuller than the top, and appeared infinitely softer. There was the tiniest indentation in the exact center. She would feel that subtle imperfection if he kissed her.

"I'm sure there's some appropriately witty remark I could make at this moment that would make all this seem like one of those amusing stories people toss out at cocktail parties, but I admit to being fresh out."

His eyes crinkled behind the dark glasses. "Trust me, it'll come to you in the middle of the night."

A gust of wind tugged at their clothes and rustled the dried straw grass that was just beginning to turn green. Slowly he lifted his hand to brush a lock of hair that had been tossed across her cheek. "You have sunshine in your hair." His voice was very low and halting next to her ear.

She felt a dozen different emotions, none of them comfortable. But then he'd been making her uncomfortable from the moment they'd met. "Don't," she said, preparing to stand. It was then that she was suddenly conscious of the distinctly suggestive bulge pressed against her hip. She froze.

"Yeah, I know." One side of his mouth turned down. "Awkward as hell, isn't it?"

She told herself he meant the way they were sitting. Not the disturbing flow of sizzling attraction between them. Or maybe it was just her, she thought with a sudden jolt. She drew a slow breath, only to freeze again when a car speeded by. And tooted.

Brody felt her stiffen and bit off a groan. He'd figured to ease her off his lap a good five minutes earlier, but she'd felt so good snuggled up against him, with her guard down and the chip on her shoulder wobbling.

"Who was that?" she demanded, scrambling to her feet. The chip, he noticed, was now firmly cemented again.

"Just a guess, but I reckon it's someone who knows one of us personally." Next time he saw Junior Fellowes he was going to rip him a new one. Didn't the sorry son of a gun know it was rude to honk at people minding their own business?

He got up slowly, cursing himself six ways to Sunday. For a man who'd already lived half his life, he was sure acting like a kid who wasn't even green broke. He didn't touch her, but it cost him as he followed her to the Blazer. Habit had had him jerking the keys from the ignition before he'd exited, just as it had had him slamming the driver's door. Hers stood open, and her cute ski cap had fallen to the ground.

"I'll get that," he said, but she was already bending to retrieve it. The movement pulled the seat of her jeans taut against her lush backside. He allowed himself a hot two seconds to enjoy the view before he stalked to the back of the Blazer and unlocked the rear door. Reaching inside, he opened the lid to the large black survival kit and hauled out a sealed liter of bottled water. Laurence was already in her seat and buckling her seat belt when he returned to the Blazer's side and handed her the water.

"Figured you might want to rinse your mouth."

"Yes. Thank you." She accepted the water without really looking at him. And when she unscrewed the bottle's lid, she was so stiff she all but crackled. Brody had to fast-talk himself out of hauling her into his arms to stroke away the wash of pink on her cheeks. On his personal scale of embarrassing moments, tossing her cookies scarcely registered, but he had a feeling she wouldn't agree. Just as he had a feeling she couldn't wait to be rid of him and his clumsy ways.

"All set?"

When she nodded, he made sure her arms and legs were safely tucked inside, then slammed the passenger door. On the way to his side he locked the kit again and closed the back. She was lowering the bottle from her lips when he climbed into the driver's seat.

"We need to talk," she said before he could start the engine.

Panic speared him, his usual reaction whenever anyone said that to him. Physical labor he could handle just fine. Long nights, brutal days, no problem. Ramrodding a twenty-five-officer department, no sweat. But the purely simple act of coordinating his brain and his tongue was agony, especially when he cared about the reaction of the person listening.

"You talk, I'll listen." He started the engine, then checked the mirror and pulled out.

"It appears we have a problem."

He spared her a look. "You mean because I don't like shrinks and you don't like cops?"

Summer replaced the cap on the bottle before setting it on the floor at her feet. The Blazer had a stick shift, and he worked through the gears like a pro taking on Indy. Or a man in a hurry. "Actually, I was referring to the, um . . . inconvenient chemistry between us."

He checked the mirror, then zoomed out to pass a dusty pickup. "You mean the fact that I've wanted to take you to bed from the first moment you sneered at me outside my aunt's old house?" he said as he pulled back into the lane. "Or the fact that you think I'm not good enough to put my hands on you?"

For an instant she was speechless. "That's not how I feel at all."

One side of his mouth pushed up. "You *want* my hands on you?"

"No, of course I don't want your hands on me."

His mouth flattened. "That's what I figured."

She drew a breath. "But not because I don't think you're good enough. That is, I'm talking about this physical attraction between us, which is in reality totally impersonal."

"Funny, it felt damn personal to me."

"But that's part of Mother Nature's genius. It's supposed to feel personal. Uh, voluntary, if you will, but it isn't. Not really. Well, actually not at all."

He lifted a brow. "Is that a fact?"

"A well-researched fact," she amplified, relieved to be on more familiar ground. "Erections are purely involuntary, of course, but then I assume you're already aware of that."

He flushed darkly. "I just get 'em, I don't analyze the hell out of 'em," he muttered.

The angry growl of the powerful V-8 under the dusty hood and the muted chatter on the radio were the only sounds for an interminable time before Brody turned to give her an impassive look. "Are you one of those half-assed sex therapists, Laurence?" He sounded offended.

She blinked. "Most therapists who deal with dysfunctions of a sexual nature are not 'half-assed,' Hollister. And no, for your information, my practice is made up exclusively of adolescents."

"Now I get it. A bunch of horny little bastards, right?"

Summer frowned, wet her lips, and told herself he was deliberately being obnoxiously obtuse in order to avoid a serious dialogue. It was an old and tired ploy she'd diffused countless times. Her confidence came tumbling back, and some of the tension eased from her spine. "My point, Chief Hollister, is simply this: Since a sexual relationship between us is totally out of the question—"

"Now that is depressing news, considering my recent level of . . . involuntary erection."

Summer reminded herself of the years she'd put in learning to step outside her emotions. "Let me put it another way, then. Even if I were so, um, inclined—which I want to emphasize very strongly I most definitely am not—it would be an abuse of your aunt's hospitality, and—"

The sound he made was more like a snort, and then it turned into a laugh. Rusty at first, it soon turned into a full-throated rumble that was annoyingly infectious. She found herself grinning before she stopped herself. She hated it when the tough lines of his face relaxed and his eyes crinkled at the corners behind the gold frames and dark lenses.

It occurred to her then that she was no longer feeling panicked inside a police vehicle. And that he might just be the reason. Something about sparring with the man about sex had written over old tapes until they no longer had the power to hurt her. A deep gratitude warred with her need to protect herself. Emotional safety won out. She suspected it would always take precedence.

"That wasn't intended to be funny," she informed him stiffly when he finally got hold of himself again.

"Honey, my aunt would like nothing better than for the two of us to end up in bed together."

"Don't be ridiculous."

"Why do you think I'm spending my downtime chauffeuring you around when I've got a duty roster to finesse and a nasty old budget to wrestle into shape?"

Summer felt an odd tightening in her chest. "You volunteered, remember? This morning, in the kitchen."

"After Aunt Dottie strong-armed me into it."

The hurt sprang up before she could control it. It was ridiculous, of course. Why should she be upset because he'd been coerced into spending time with her? After all, she herself had certainly been reluctant to spend time with him.

More old tapes, she reminded herself. Written during the days after her release from prison when her family made it clear she was no longer welcome—or loved. She'd been raw for a long time after that. As she'd reminded countless patients over the years, payback was a bitch.

"I'll be sure to let her know you did your duty admirably," she said in a neutral tone.

He shot her a look that was pure masculine impatience. "Damn, I hurt your feelings."

"Of course you didn't."

"Honey, your lower lip's stuck out far enough to catch a 757."

"It most certainly is not. And stop calling me 'honey.' My name's Summer."

He slipped on the signal for a left turn and slowed, allowing an oncoming pickup to pass before swinging the Blazer into a litter-strewn driveway. Beyond a high chain-link fence was a ruined parking lot and a half-dozen or so ramshackle buildings, the largest of which appeared big enough to house a dozen of those 757s, with room to spare. Fifty feet or so ahead, a large gate chained shut and heavily padlocked blocked their way. Every ten feet a NO TRESPASSING sign had been affixed to the links.

Brody shifted to neutral and let the Blazer idle as he gazed through the windshield. This section of town was vastly different than the prettied-up blocks near City Hall. Instead of flower boxes and gingerbread trim, the windows here were cracked or covered with plywood, and the streets were riddled with potholes. Even the air seemed to have lost its sparkle.

"Granddad would bust a gut if he saw this place now."

Summer followed the direction of his gaze toward the largest of the buildings. A badly faded sign painted on the concrete blocks proclaimed HOLLISTER AND SON LUMBER. A feeling like sorrow passed through her, though she had no idea why. Perhaps because she hated to see anyone's dreams destroyed.

"I didn't realize your father was part owner," she said when he showed no sign of speaking.

"Family tradition. Hollister and Son started with my grandfather's old man, the first Brody Hollister. He was an illiterate trapper from Ohio who married a psalm-singing, churchgoing widow with four kids and a section of useless s-scrub land. Her name was Mehetabel and she used to hit him with a shovel every time he came home drunk. He finally took to sleeping outside and found a deep vein of s-silver one night after he'd passed out next to a rock slide."

"Really?"

He sent her a guarded look and nodded. "Took the pledge the next day. Claimed the good Lord had been trying for years to show him the error of his ways but he refused to pay attention until the bastard sweetened the pot."

Summer laughed. "You're making that up."

"No ma'am."

"And the sawmill?"

"Granddad started it in the twenties when a crushed femur kept him out of the woods. Sunk the last of his father's money into the equipment and borrowed on Grandma's engagement ring to meet his first payroll."

Summer returned her gaze to the ruined complex. "It must have been impressive."

She caught the faint shrug of those enormous shoulders. "Noisy, anyway. Most old-timers ended up deaf."

"Your father worked there?"

His jaw flexed, and she felt a chill fill the Blazer's interior. "He wasn't much for routine. Mostly he ran the logging crews."

"So you worked for him?"

Behind the shield of the opaque lenses, his eyes narrowed. "Him or one of the other bull buckers."

"Bull bucker?"

"Crew bosses. My old m-man was the 'bull of the woods.' The . . . superintendent."

Summer made a mental note to get a book on the history of logging in the Northwest. "Did you like chopping down trees?"

"Hated it, but the pay was good."

"Was it difficult working for your father?"

"No worse than working for anyone else." She heard the hard edge to his voice and recognized the warning. Back off. Because she had barriers of her own, she respected his.

She extended her legs and shifted to a more comfortable position. A rusted pickup rattled past, spewing blue smoke. An automatic ticket in San Diego, but Hollister didn't seem to notice. "Dottie mentioned that your father was killed in the woods a few years before you moved back to town," she said when he showed no sign of breaking the silence.

"Yeah." On a burst of static, the radio crackled to life again. She felt his attention sharpen, even as his expression remained unchanged. After listening to a few exchanges between dispatcher and patrolman about a traffic stop, he reached out to turn down the volume.

Summer hesitated. She was wildly curious about this man. About the experiences that had forged the impressive strength she envied, the gentleness she hadn't expected, the sheer grit of a boy fighting some really nasty odds to become an impressive man. Even as an undergraduate taking Psych 101, she'd been fascinated by case studies.

"How was your father killed?" she asked softly.

"Widow-maker got him."

She frowned at the unfamiliar term—and the utter lack of emotion in the graveled voice that uttered it. "Another logging word?"

He nodded. "A widow-maker's a branch that's fallen only partway from the top of the tree and ends up balanced overhead."

"And one of those branches fell on your father?"

"Went right through his skull like an iron spear. Doc Krebs said he would have pulled through if he'd been wearing his hard hat, but he hated them. Thought they were for wimps or government bureaucrats. Smashed mine beneath 'dozer treads when he caught me wearing it."

Summer tried not to think about the image evoked by his words—and failed. At least her own father was alive and well. The last she'd heard, he and her brother had just won the Commodore's Cup at the yacht club.

"I know this sounds, well, odd, but everything here feels alien to me," she said, watching a big tawny bird circling over the mill. A hawk perhaps? Or an eagle? She'd never seen one in the wild before, and she found herself leaning forward for a better look.

"It's a red-tailed hawk," he said, watching her instead of the bird gliding so gracefully on the wind.

"Beautiful."

"Yeah."

Leaning back, she looked at the world beyond the tinted windows. Hollister's world. Breathtaking scenery, pickup trucks with guns racked across the back window driven by whiskered giants in work boots and plaid. In the three days since her arrival she hadn't seen one male in a suit. "Talk about culture shock," she mused, more to herself than to the man opposite.

"That's what I felt when I ended up in San Diego for recruit training. All that sunshine and water, cars with surfboards on top and spindly looking palm trees everywhere." One side of his mouth edged upward. "Not to mention the ladies in these shiny little shorts with slits up the side."

"Dolphin shorts," she supplied. She and her friends had deliberately bought theirs a size too small.

"God bless dolphins," he said fervently as he shoved the lever into reverse and swung the Blazer around. They drove in silence for several miles, giving her plenty of time to study the terrain. After four or five minutes of orchards and rocks and towering green mountains on all sides, she realized they seemed to be heading away from town, not toward it.

"Where are we going?"

"Wenatchee."

The nearest large town, she recalled. And the closest airport. She'd considered flying in from Seattle, then decided she wanted to drive in order to decompress from the conference. "Where, exactly, are we going?"

"Guy I knew in the navy has a restaurant there. Best barbecued ribs in the west. No VIP tour'd be complete without a taste of his sauce." He flicked her a quick glance. "If you think your tummy can handle it."

Summer was torn between better judgment and a bone-deep passion for barbecued ribs. "These ribs, are they Kansas City style or your usual Texas plain?"

His mouth twitched. "K.C. all the way."

Summer sighed. She would think of all the reasons why this was a bad idea later. "In that case, Chief Hollister," she said with a quick burst of excitement, "my tummy and I are honored to accept your offer."

"Nobody noticed that the punch was spiked until the principal ended up pie-eyed and tripped over his own feet when he started up the steps to the stage to announce the Homecoming King and Queen. Ended up skidding into the bass drum, nose first." Dottie stopped to tip her glass for a sip. A scant half inch remained of the two fingers of Wild Turkey she'd poured herself while Summer and Kelly cleared away the supper dishes.

Up to her elbows in soapsuds and cooking pots, Kelly cast an awestruck look in her aunt's direction. "Really?"

"Really." The tiny silver bells dangling from Dottie's ears tinkled merrily as she slipped a gravy-spattered stove burner into the hot water. "Mr. Griswold was what one might politely term portly, and in his black business suit he looked exactly like a beached whale, flopping around trying to extricate his head from that big old drum."

Summer and Kelly exchanged looks. Kelly had been in her room when Summer had returned around four, her CD player pumping out grunge full blast. Brody had called at five to tell his aunt he'd gotten tied up and not to wait for him, so dinner had been strictly a female gathering. While they'd eaten, Dottie had regaled them with stories of her teenage years when she and three of her friends had been the Fearsome Foursome of Osuma High.

"Did he find out you were the one who put the vodka in the Hawaiian Punch?" Summer asked as she returned a skillet to the cupboard.

"Unfortunately, yes. Flossie, the rat, couldn't stop giggling. She'd been the official punch sampler, you see, to make sure the taste of vodka wasn't too strong and had taken her position quite seriously."

"Flossie?" Kelly exclaimed, her voice squeaking. "You mean Ms. *Fortier*? The same Ms. Fortier who's principal now?"

"The very same." Dottie hiccuped. "Why do you think there hasn't been an incidence of spiked punch at any of the dances since 1978, when she became principal?"

"How come this is the first I ever heard of this?" Kelly demanded, looking mortally offended.

"It happened a long time ago. I doubt anyone even remembers."

Clearly bemused, Kelly rinsed a serving platter before handing it over to Summer to dry. "I can't wait to find out who the other members of this Fearsome Foursome are."

Dottie gave the place mats one more halfhearted swipe with her dishrag before shoving them back into the drawer so haphazardly Summer winced. "Lucy Steinberg and Mandy Winfield. Well, Mandy Lentel now."

Kelly twisted around to stare at her aunt. "Miss Steinberg, I can understand. I mean, what with her talking to her plants like they were her kids and giving them names and all. And not selling them to anyone she doesn't trust to take care of them, but Mrs. Lentel is married to the pastor of our church!"

"Yes dear." Dottie took another sip, glanced at the glass, then shrugged and downed the rest in one long, satisfying swallow.

"Does Dad know about this?" Kelly asked when her aunt was finished.

"I doubt it. He was only two at the time."

Kelly rinsed the burner and unplugged the sink. "What about your dates? Didn't they protest?"

"Of course. We ignored them." Dottie picked up the bottle of Wild Turkey, glanced at her niece, and then, with a long-suffering sigh, carried it to the pie safe.

Finished with drying duty, Summer draped the damp towel over the counter while Dottie added her now empty glass to the dishwasher and set it to running. "Why don't we go into the living room and let our dinner settle," she said brightly, leading the way in a flurry of skirts and energy.

"Just who *was* your date?" Kelly asked as she and Summer followed.

"Why, Grey Krebs, of course. It was the night I accepted his proposal of marriage."

Kelly stopped dead and gaped at her aunt. "Dr. Krebs? Mark's *grandfather*?"

Dottie paused to look back at her niece. "The very same."

"You were married to Dr. Krebs?"

Dottie didn't know whether to laugh or cry at the utter shock in the girl's voice. As though the very idea was beyond belief. "No, I was only engaged to him."

"How come you never married him?"

"He wouldn't leave Osuma and I couldn't stay." She smiled briefly at the memory of the melodramatic scenes they'd had. "Osuma was even smaller when I was a girl, and more . . . restrictive. I hated it. Girls then had three choices. They could be teachers or nurses or somebody's wife. But I could dance and I wanted bright lights and champagne. Grey wanted to settle down and have babies. I begged him to let us live in Seattle or maybe San Francisco after he finished his internship, but he was determined to come back here and take over his father's practice."

Kelly pulled a face. "Bummer," she muttered.

Dottie realized this was the first time she had told this story. It felt good to get it out, she realized. And yet, in a way, it was almost like letting go of the last lingering connection to the only man she'd ever truly loved.

"So what happened?" Kelly prodded when Dottie would have ended the tale. With a sigh, she decided to finish it.

"Papa and my aunt Naomi planned an enormous wedding. Even had my grandfather's old buggy refurbished so Papa could drive me to the church in what he called 'grand style.' "

"Then what?" Kelly asked, clearly fascinated by this new side of her spinster aunt.

"I got dressed in my wedding finery, then, while Papa was hitching the horses to the buggy, I stole his car and drove to Seattle. From there I took the train to Las Vegas. The second day there I got the job as a showgirl at the Sands. Remember, I told you about the revue I was in when I met Frank Sinatra and Dean Martin?"

Kelly nodded. "It must have been a real trip, walking around in gorgeous clothes and having drinks with movies stars and everything."

"Not to mention mobsters," Summer threw in, a teasing glint in her eye.

"Them, too," she acknowledged with a laugh. "Especially them."

"So why'd you quit?" Kelly wanted to know.

"I got tired of feeing like a prized chicken in a butcher-shop window. So I came home, ate a little crow, and went to college to become a librarian. After that I lived with your grandparents and your dad, too, until he joined the navy. It wasn't long before your grandmother died and your grandfather and I had this huge fight about his drinking. Since Big Malcolm was gone by then, Lucy and I shared her house until you and your father came back to live in Osuma."

"Why didn't you marry Dr. Krebs then? When you came back here, I mean?"

"Because, my darling romantic child, he was already married to someone else. A lovely woman he met while he was in medical school down in Portland. A teacher." Sarah.

"Is that why you're an . . . I mean, you never, like, got married? Because Mark's grandfather broke your heart?"

Dottie lifted her left hand and looked down at the silver and turquoise rings on every finger but the third. She'd never worn anything on that finger since she'd removed the small diamond engagement ring Grey had given her.

"No dear," she said quietly, dropping her hand. "He didn't break my heart. I accomplished that all by myself." She took a deep breath, the pain in her chest almost overpowering. But the pain would pass, just as it always did. Lifting her chin, she gave Kelly a grin. "So, who's up for a rousing game of rummy?"

"My dad's aunt and your grandfather, is that weird or what?" Kelly flipped over onto her back and let her legs dangle over the side of her pink-and-white bed. On the other end of the phone, Mark had grown real quiet all of sudden, and she felt a stab of panic. Maybe she should have waited for him to call her at eleven like he'd promised, but she'd been bursting to tell him about Aunt Dottie. When Dr. Krebs had answered the phone, she'd had to pinch her tummy in tight to keep from giggling.

"No wonder you were about to bust a gut when you called," Mark said finally. He sounded like he was smiling, and she relaxed a little. Mark had a killer smile. Even Tiff said he was buff, and Tiff was really picky about guys. Her boyfriend, Brett Carlyle, was the school stud.

"It's like, me and you might have been related, you know?"

she said, feeling shy and bold at the same time. "Like me and my cousin Patrick."

"Yeah." She heard an odd noise, like he was clearing his throat. "Uh, I was just wondering, did you talk to your dad yet about me maybe coming over to your place some night? You know, to just hang out, maybe crank some tunes?"

Kelly felt some of her happiness evaporate. "He's not home." She turned her head toward the table by the bed and frowned at the photograph of her dad and her at her sixth-grade graduation. Her dad was wearing a suit and tie, one of the few times she remembered ever seeing him so dressed up. It surprised her a lot how good he looked. Kinda hunky actually, even if he wasn't really handsome. Not like Leonardo or Matt Damon. Still, she'd overheard two of the teachers talking about how sexy he was in a scary sort of way. Ms. Garcia had said it was too bad he was so shy, because she sure would like to get her hands on that primo ass of his. Later, when Kelly had told her dad, he'd turned bright red and mumbled something about washing Ms. Garcia's mouth out with soap. She and Tiff had giggled a lot about that.

"A buddy from Chicago's going to send me a bootleg video of an old Pearl Jam concert and I figure me and you could maybe watch it together." Mark's voice went real scratchylike and Kelly's heart leaped right up into her throat. "Like maybe tomorrow night? If your dad says it's okay?"

Kelly felt so giddy she could barely breathe. "Killer," she exclaimed in what she hoped was a suitably sophisticated tone. Play it cool, but not *too* cool Tiff always said. "Only he's probably going to say no, it being a school night and all." Her conscience gave her a hard kick. Dad was going to say no, all right. "He's real strict about homework," she added, just in case Mark thought she wasn't interested.

Mark laughed, and she nearly sighed into the phone from happiness. "Like you have to study, little miss straight As."

"I do so have to study," she protested. "I'm having an awful time with Spanish this year." It wasn't a lie, exactly. More like an exaggeration. Besides, she probably *would* have trouble before the year was out, and Tiff kept saying guys hated girls who were smarter than they were.

There was a pause, and Kelly scrambled to find something interesting to say. Mark saved her by asking, "What time do you think your dad'll be home? So you can ask him about tomorrow?"

Kelly glanced at her clock radio. It was almost eight. "I'm not sure. Soon probably." She took a breath. "Remember that friend of my aunt's from San Diego I told you about?"

"The lady shrink, right?"

"Uh huh. Summer. They went to lunch today. Her and my dad. Dad *never* takes a woman to lunch, so I figure he must really like her. I asked her if they had a good time, because I thought that if they did, he'd be in a real mellow mood, and then I'd ask him about letting me off restriction."

"So what'd she say?"

"Not much. Something about it being mostly business, Dad showing her around town so she could see if she liked it, stuff like that."

"You sound disappointed, angel."

Her heart soared. *Angel.* He'd called her angel, like Brett called Tiff doll face. She decided she liked angel a whole lot better. It was more respectful, somehow.

"I guess I am a little disappointed, yeah. I mean, I really like Summer and all. She's super nice and she listens when you talk to her, like she's actually thinking about what you're telling her. You know, like it's important and not just dumb teenager stuff." She kicked her bare feet up in the air and looked at her toes. Her feet were huge, not tiny like her aunt's and Summer's. She hated her feet almost as much as she hated the way her ears stuck out and her nose sort of angled to one side. "She's really pretty, too. Sort of like Candice Bergen, only younger."

Mark gave a low whistle, like guys do when they see a sexy girl. "Since she's taken a pass on your dad, maybe I ought to come over tonight and check her out myself."

Kelly felt strange, like a giant hand had just squashed all the air out of her lungs. It made her hurt inside. She knew it had been too good to last. Like she told Tiff, why would a great-looking guy like Mark want anything to do with a big-footed geek who couldn't even wear eye makeup or short skirts?

"Angel?"

She wanted to crawl under the bed and cry, the way she used to sometimes when her dad scolded her. "What?" Her voice came out all funny, like it did when she was trying not to cry.

He groaned. "Oh God, you thought I was serious?"

She blinked. "You're not?"

"God, no! Honey, you're the only girl I'm interested in. I told you that yesterday in the car before your dad got all heavy and hauled you home."

"Oh."

She heard the drone of the Blazer's engine as her dad pulled into the garage, and frowned. Thanks to him she'd spent most of the day hiding out in the girls' bathroom and crying because of the teasing. "Daddy's little girl" had been one of the mildest taunts. The ones that hurt most, though, were about her dad's stuttering. Like Janine diCarlo saying it wasn't safe to have a wimp like him for police chief because he couldn't talk well enough to arrest anyone. If it hadn't been for Mark making it a point to sit with her at lunch and walk her to the bus after school, she would have just died of shame.

"Wait until Friday night and I'll show you just how much I want you for my girl."

Kelly closed her eyes. Knowing she had to break the date had been dragging her down all day. But she couldn't. She just *couldn't*. No matter what Summer said, he was bound to think she was a dork. A dork who couldn't even ride home in a car with a guy, no matter how nice he was.

"I . . . I want to be your girl," she whispered, a tremor in her voice. "But—"

She was interrupted by a knock on her door. "Kel? Are you awake?"

She nearly groaned. "I gotta go, Mark. My dad just got home and . . . and he wants to talk to me."

"Killer! Ask him about tomorrow night, okay angel?"

"Okay. I mean, if he gives me a chance, only—"

"Kelly, I know you're in there." Her dad was sounding really mad now. She thought about not answering, but he would just open the door to check on her. He almost always did anyway before he went to bed. Even when it was summer he always pulled the covers up to her chin, then kissed her on the forehead. Sometimes after that he just stood by the bed and looked at her. When she was a little girl, she used to watch him through tiny little slits in her eyes, but she stopped because it hurt her to see him so sad.

"I'll . . . I'll talk to you tomorrow," she told Mark quickly before hanging up.

She had just managed to hide the portable receiver under her pillow when her dad walked in. He was still dressed in his cop clothes, without the black-leather gun belt that used to scare her so much as a little kid. She'd never figured out why, exactly, she'd hated it, only that somehow she had associated his gun with bad things. Just as she'd always associated the smell of strong coffee and lemon drops with her dad's bear hugs. Sometimes, when she was just a little girl, she'd pretend to fall down and bump her head just so she could fling herself in his arms and have him snuggle her against that big old hard chest. She'd felt warm and sleepy and safe whenever her daddy held her. But that was before, when she was still dumb enough to think he had to love her just because he was her father.

To show him she didn't care what he said or did anymore, she sat up and scooted toward the head of her bed, where her American history book was laying upside down on her pillow, still open to the assignment she'd started before dinner. Deliberately ignoring him, she picked up the book and propped it against her bent knees. Only then did she look at him standing just inside her door, his hands on his hips and a funny, tight look on his face.

"See, Dad," she said, holding up her book. "I'm doing my homework like a good little girl."

Instead of ragging on her the way she'd expected, he just nodded before turning around to close the door. Her heart sank when she realized he wasn't leaving. Had he found out about her date on Friday night? she wondered as panic jolted the breath from her body.

"Sounds like you're pretty upset with your old dad, baby."

He was only pretending to be sad like that to make her feel bad, she told herself as she shrugged one shoulder. She wished he would go away and leave her alone. "What do you care, as long as you get to make the rules around here?"

He walked to the bed and sat down. The mattress dipped dangerously low, forcing her to dig in her heels and brace her back against the headboard to keep from tumbling against him. "Kelly, I didn't come in here to argue with you."

"Yeah, well, that's a first." She knew she was being snotty, but she couldn't seem to help herself. But when his face got tight, her chest started feeling funny, like it always did when she knew she'd hurt someone's feelings. If she *had* hurt him, it was his fault, she told herself fiercely. *He* didn't have to sit in class and listen to people she'd thought were her friends laughing behind her back.

"Kel, give it a rest, okay? I came in here to talk to you about—"

"Order me around is more like it."

He closed his eyes and took a deep breath. He looked different, somehow. Kind of, well, *scared* was the only word she could think of that fit. Only her dad wasn't supposed to be scared of anything. Only wimps got scared. And her dad couldn't be a wimp like Janine said.

"Damn it, Kel, it t-tears me up when you look at m-me like that."

Kelly felt that awful sick feeling start in her stomach. She hated it when her dad yelled at her, but it was worse when he stuttered. It make her feel so helpless. Her aunt said she felt the same way sometimes, only she'd had a lot longer to get used to it. Maybe so, but that didn't help Kelly deal with now. "Dad—"

"It was the s-same with your . . . your m-mom. She—" He

broke off to take a deep breath. Kelly held hers, praying he wouldn't have one of those awful blocks. "It wasn't like we fought a lot. H-hardly ever. B-but when we did, she'd get that same stubborn look in her eyes. And her chin would jerk up, just l-like yours."

Kelly let out her breath slowly. She couldn't believe it. He was talking about her mom. Really talking. Telling her stuff she'd never heard before. Summer must have put him up to it. A part of her wanted to be mad at Summer for breaking a confidence, only Summer hadn't really promised not to say anything. She hadn't had a chance, what with her dad interrupting them and all.

"Grandma said she had an Irish temper," she found herself saying, " 'Cause she was a redhead and all."

"A temper as hot as a f-firecracker." His smile was different than she'd ever seen before. Sort of soft around the edges, she realized after a moment's thought. It made her want to smile back, but it also made her want to cry. "F-first time I ticked her off she damn near had me diving under the couch."

Kelly giggled. "Really?"

"True story. She threw a l-lamp at me once. Big sucker. Would have knocked me cold if I hadn't ducked."

Kelly stared at him, trying to imagine the tiny woman in the photographs heaving things at her big, strong dad. "Why? What did you do?"

"Tripped over the laundry b-basket on my way to the can in the dark and woke you up."

Kelly pictured her dad sprawled flat on his belly and grinned. Big as he was, he was always banging into something. According to Aunt Dottie, Grandfather Hollister had wanted her dad to play football, but the coach said he was too uncoordinated.

"How old was I then?" she asked, eager to hear even the tiniest little thing about the woman who was only real in her imagination.

He thought a minute. "Six, seven months. You had colic and used to scream for hours at a time. The only way you'd stop is when you were being held, or sometimes it helped if I rubbed your tummy while your mom sang to you." His voice was gruff and so low she had to lean forward to keep from missing even a single word. "Anyway, we'd just gotten you to s-sleep, and your m-mom was p-pretty tired. During the d-day, she was like this little d-dynamo, always fussing around. And then when . . . when you were born, she carried you around in this sling next to her . . . her heart."

Kelly tried to imagine the lady in the picture holding her, maybe singing a lullaby. Just thinking about it caused a warm feeling in her chest. "Is colic like being sick or something?"

"The doctor said it was more like a bad tummy ache. But your m-mom was so s-sure it was s-something serious. Darn near wore me out trying to reassure her. She was like this mama she-wolf, all claws and teeth when it c-came to keeping you s-safe."

Kelly wanted to hug his words to her heart. "She really yelled at you?"

"Big time." He grinned, but his eyes were so awfully sad she felt kind of guilty. "But once she blew, she was pretty much done being m-mad."

"Like you."

He lifted his eyebrows in that way he had that made him look really cute. "I don't have a temper, sweetheart."

"Aunt Dottie says you do. She says she's only seen you explode a few times, but it was really awesome. Like last winter when you caught that guy who manages the trailer park out by the old mill hitting his son with a bullwhip. Auntie said the whole trailer park heard you cussing that guy out. She said you yelled because you couldn't hit him."

"She's right about that," he said, shifting. "Bas—man deserved to have that whip used on him."

"Is that why you yelled at me yesterday? Because you wanted to hit me?"

He went white. "Think a minute, Kel. Have I ever l-laid a hand on you?"

She shook her head, feeling more and more miserable by the

second. It was *his* fault she was feeling so awful, she reminded herself. He was the one who'd acted like a jerk. "All the kids heard," she muttered, not looking at him. "I wanted to die."

Her dad reached over to take her hand in his. She wanted to jerk free, but she couldn't make herself move. "B-baby, I'm s-ss—" He broke off, that awful look on his face. He closed his eyes and took a deep breath. "When Sargeant Hingle t-told me about M-Mark speeding, all I could think about was keeping you safe."

"He wasn't speeding," she said indignantly.

"Wasn't he?"

Kelly hated it when her dad's voice got all quiet and patient. Like he was giving her a chance to say the right thing. "Everyone knows the cops give you ten miles over the limit," she grumbled almost under her breath.

"Not this cop."

"Auntie always drives way over the limit and you never give *her* a ticket!"

"No, but my men do." He rubbed a hand over his jaw. "Last I heard, the fines she's paid have bought the town two parking meters on Alpine."

Kelly knew that was true, because she'd heard her aunt teasing about putting a plaque in her honor on each one. "So how come you'll let me ride with her but not Mark?"

"Because Aunt Dottie can drive these roads in her sleep. She knows where all the dangerous spots are and she slows down. Mark's not used to back roads and mountain curves."

"You could have waited until we got home to yell."

Damn, this was hard, Brody thought, rubbing his hand over the painful knot that had formed in his chest. Tension, the speech pathologist had told him. Caused by a fear of the father who was still in his thoughts, still calling him names, even though the mean son of a bitch had been dead for years. Not enough years to suit his only son, however.

"You're right. I should have kept it p-private," he finally managed to get out. "I know kids can say things that hurt, but just remember, honey, the fact that your dad talks like Porky Pig sometimes doesn't have anything to do with you. You're a great kid. The b-best."

He dropped his gaze to their entwined hands. Hers had always seemed so impossibly fragile to him. There had been an instant when she'd wanted to pull away. He'd seen the thought in her eyes. It meant a lot that she had left her hand in his. His daughter. His heart. God, how he loved her. He wanted to tell her just how much, but words were beyond him. So instead, he lifted her hand to his mouth and kissed it before letting her go.

She looked a little startled as she stared at him. "Does that mean you're not mad anymore?"

"No, I'm not mad."

"Does that mean I can get off restriction?"

The kid was a crafty little devil, he'd give her that. Just like her mom. He wanted to say yes more than anything, but over the years he'd read darn near every book on child rearing in the Osuma Library and every single one had stressed the need for discipline and limits.

"Sorry, baby. I wouldn't be doing my job if I let you off." The disappointment in her eyes nearly did him in. Damn, he hated saying no to her. "But I . . . uh, about that eye makeup stuff—"

"Mascara."

"Yeah. I don't think you need it, but if that's what you want—"

She launched herself at his chest, all arms and legs and flying hair. He caught her in his arms and held on tight as she buried her face in his neck the way she used to before she went off on her independent teenager kick.

"But not too much of that stuff," he warned when she drew back to grin at him. His chest damn near burst when he realized the sullen look that always tore him apart was gone. It seemed he owed Dr. Laurence another lunch.

CHAPTER 10

Amos Gooding propped one booted foot on the bumper of his company pickup and cast another squinty-eyed look at the roof-line. Clucking his tongue, he wetted the end of a stubby pencil with his tongue, then jotted down another figure on the form affixed to a battered clipboard.

He was a large, spectacularly homely man with a thatch of faded red hair falling farm-boy fashion over a broad forehead. Unlike the last contractor, who'd turned out to have the disposition of a dried prune, Mr. Gooding radiated good humor, along with a reassuring measure of competence. Summer wanted to beg him to come in with an estimate she could accept.

"Yep, I think we can shine her up real good for you, little lady," he said, dropping his foot and turning to face her. "Me and my boys, we like us a rip-roaring challenge like this ever' once in a while."

Summer's heart sank. It had been her experience that repair people and that ilk always mentioned the word *challenge* before coming out with an amount that was at least twice as much as her most conservative estimate.

"Any idea of how much it would cost to do the things we talked about? Keeping in mind my anemic budget."

The contractor cocked his head and considered her thoughtfully with eyes that were neither blue nor brown, but some indescribable color in between. "Now, that's a good question. Yep, good question." He slipped off the battered cap that had been perched atop his thick forelock and gave his head a hard scratch before resetting the cap at precisely the same angle. "What kind of a place did you say you're aiming to turn this old darling into?"

"A residential treatment center."

"Is that a fact?" Gooding took another look at the second story, frowned, and turned back to her. "Like one of them glorified dude ranches for stressed-out bankers and stockbrokers bent on exploring their 'inner selves' I been reading about lately?"

"No, for troubled adolescents. And it will be a real working ranch when I can afford to buy cattle and fix the barn."

"What kind of troubles would those adolescents be bringing with them, Dr. Laurence?"

The first hurdle, Summer thought, and took a deep breath. "Mostly problems with substance abuse."

His gaze sharpened. "Are we talking drugs?"

"And alcohol," she added, trying to read the thoughts behind those cagey eyes. But Amos Gooding was giving nothing away. "Does that make a difference in the amount of your bid?" she asked when he remained silent.

He let the silence play out a little longer, then nodded. "Guess it does at that."

So much for first impressions. "I'm sorry to hear that," she said without bothering to hide her disappointment.

"Hold on there, ma'am. I don't think you're reading me right." He chuckled. "I'll do it for cost of materials and wages for my men. I'll throw in my own labor for free, and I'll include the painting and plumbing work, too, although you'll have to get an electrical contractor to do the wiring. I'm not licensed for that."

Summer realized her jaw had popped open and she shut it with a snap. It took her another moment to get it to work properly. "That's very generous, Mr. Gooding, and now I have a good question for you. Why, exactly, is it so generous?"

Instead of answering, he glanced toward the west. Clouds obscured the white peak of the tallest mountain, but the snow was still there, like a generous coating of marshmallow cream.

"Two years ago come November, my only daughter died of a drug overdose when she was in college down in Portland. Nineteen years old, and bright as a new penny. Going to be a kindergarten teacher." His lips trembled before he pressed them together hard. "If there'd been a place here . . ." He glanced over his shoulder at the sagging porch and boarded-up windows. "Maybe you couldn't have saved her. Maybe no one could, but at least I would have had the comfort of knowing I'd done all I could."

It was familiar story, one she'd heard with variations for years now. But each time she faced a distraught parent across a desk or in a hospital waiting room or, in the worst case, a morgue, she felt the pain as if it were the first time.

"What was your daughter's name?" she asked quietly.

"Jasmine."

Summer smiled. "What a lovely name."

He lifted one shoulder. "We were going to call her Hannah, after my mother, but when we saw her for the first time, Ellen— she's my wife—Ellen said she was too pretty for a plain name like that." A smile crossed his weathered face. "She had red hair, like her old man. And her mama's dimples." His smile faltered and died. "I still miss her."

Summer felt the sting of tears behind her eyes and looked down at the gladiolas, with their pregnant buds. One had cracked open, revealing a delicate white petal still curled and waiting. It seemed so terribly fragile, like a young life.

"Well, enough of my meanderings," Mr. Gooding said as he pulled open the door to his truck and tossed the clipboard onto the seat. "I'll work up some firm figures and drop them by Miss Dottie's place by the end of the week—unless you need them sooner."

"That will be fine." Summer extended her hand. "It was a pleasure meeting you, Mr. Gooding. And thank you."

"Well, you're sure welcome, Dr. Laurence," he said, shaking

her hand so heartily she felt her wrist snap. "Can't say I've done much more than walk around for a couple of hours poking into dusty corners with a pretty little lady for company, but I surely did enjoy it."

Summer smiled. She was a feminist from her eyelashes to her toenails. Two days ago she would have frozen any man who dared call her a "pretty little lady." But Amos Gooding meant no offense, so she took none.

"And I enjoyed spending time with you," she said, meaning it sincerely. "When I came up here, Phoenix House was still an idea in my head. Now I have a hunch it's going to rise."

"Is that where you're from? Phoenix?"

"No, San Diego. The Phoenix is a bird that was supposedly sacred to the sun god in ancient Egypt. According to the myth, it lived for five hundred years before building its own funeral pyre. Then it laid down and died, and out of the ashes a new phoenix was born."

Gooding looked at her with disbelief. "The hell you say."

Summer grinned. "According to a Greek writer, Herodotus, the Egyptians saw this whole process as symbolic of the rising and setting of the sun. Over the years it's become a metaphor for a new start."

He considered that for a moment, then glanced toward one of the towering pine trees behind the barn. "That's what Hannah and me were hoping to give Jasmine."

Summer felt a tug inside as she thanked Gooding for coming. "I hope we can work together," she said with a smile.

He gave a courtly tug on his cap, his face seamed with kindness. "Don't you worry none, little lady. We'll make this work. I guarantee it." His eyes grew somber. "Between the two of us, we'll have this phoenix bird of yours shining like new in no time." He took a breath. "I gotta believe Jasmine would have liked you."

Impulsively Summer reached out to touch his hand. "I wish I'd known her. With you as her father, she had to have been very special."

Surprise darkened his face as he looked down at her. Tears glazed his eyes before he blinked them away. "She was always a daddy's girl."

"At least you had her for nineteen years. Some parents aren't that lucky."

"Yeah." He cleared his throat, then hitched his frayed khaki work pants a little higher over his impressive girth. "Well, I'd best be letting you get on with your day. I'll talk to you tomorrow late, or maybe Friday. Soon as I have the numbers fixed."

She stepped away from the open driver's door to allow him to climb into the seat. "You have Miss Hollister's number, right?"

Gooding patted the pocket of his heavy twill jacket. "Got it right here."

Moments later, watching the big white truck plume out exhaust like a vapor trail as it sped back toward town, Summer realized that she had just made up her mind. Dottie was right. This was where she belonged.

Slouched in the back row of advanced geometry, Mark was impatient for the class to end. It was the last period of the day and Kelly had promised to wait for him at her locker so that he could walk her to the bus. Curbing his impatience, he glanced at his watch, then at the nerdy instructor passing out the graded midterms. What a wimp.

Mark could count on one hand the men he'd met in his sixteen years who merited his respect. His grandfather, certainly, an assistant football coach at New Trier High School who'd helped him lose his baby fat and taught him to throw a perfect spiral, a priest who'd talked to him after his father's death. Kelly's dad, too. Now there was one tough dude. Straight-arrow all the way. Not someone he wanted to cross, which was why he was taking it real slow with Kelly.

Tuning out Mr. Phelps and his pathetic attempts at banter, he eased open his notebook and took another look at the picture she'd given him just this morning. She'd been wearing the yellow blouse with the flowers on the collar, and her hair was all fluffy around her neck, the way he liked it best.

He could scarcely believe she was really his girl. His love. She was perfection. A dream come true. Nothing like the plastic sweethearts he'd grown up with. Little bitches in training, his old man had called them with a cynical laugh. Ready to grab a man's balls and squeeze till he was bled dry.

Kelly was different. Whenever her big innocent blue eyes smiled into his, his heart grabbed an extra beat. And at night, when he was sacked out in his bed, he imagined their wedding night. Her sweet sighs of pleasure as he worshiped her, the glow of wonder in her eyes when he made her his in every way. Sometimes he wanted her so much he ached with it, but he revered her purity too much to defile it.

Not that he wasn't one horny dude. It got real rank sometimes, the way he got a hard-on just thinking about her. Last night while he and his granddad were grabbing a hamburger, he'd started talking about her and got stiff as a poker. Granddad, he'd been real cool and all. Pretending to believe him when he said he wanted to borrow the old man's trench coat because he was cold.

It was embarrassing, but he could stand it. He could stand anything for his angel girl. She belonged to him. Only to him, he reminded himself as he slanted a look at that dumb-ass jock Chuck Sawyer in the second row.

Twice he'd caught Sawyer hitting on Kel in study hall. Sitting real close and making her giggle. Old Chuckie didn't know it yet, but he was in for a heavy-duty ass-kicking one of these days. No one flirted with his angel girl and got away with it. It was a matter of pride.

"Good job, Krebs," Johnson Phelps wheezed in his fussy voice as he took Mark's midterm from the stack in his hand to place on the desk in front of him. "Keep it up and you'll be on the short list for every quality college in the country by your senior year."

"Thank you, sir," Mark replied in the earnest tone teachers invariably lapped up like the fools they were. "I'm hoping to get into Stanford. Where my granddad went."

"Very good, very good," the biology teacher replied before passing on to the pimply faced girl who had the desk in front of Mark's.

Behind him, Mark heard a snicker and added fat Drew Watkins to his list of enemies. Beneath the desk, his fingers closed into a fist and he felt his blood begin to pound in his temples. He could hardly wait for payback time.

Alone in the kitchen, Brody shoveled the last bite of pie into his mouth and allowed himself to sink into the taste of rich chocolate before washing it down with cold milk.

It was past eleven, and the house was bedded down for the night. Facing an early start again tomorrow, he hadn't intended to do more than snag a glass of milk before heading upstairs to bed, but the baking pan on the counter had changed his mind. There'd been two pieces left. He'd scarfed down one like a starving dog and was now giving some thought to polishing off the last.

Since he couldn't think of a single reason against it, he was lifting the plastic wrap when he heard the creak of the warped floorboard in the hall. He jerked his hand back, then shook his head. Forty-five years old and he still felt guilty about sneaking an extra dessert. Expecting Aunt Dottie, he was surprised when Summer walked in. A dark sweet feeling of pleasure ran through him as he took in the tidy shape bundled in that fuzzy yellow robe he was beginning to like a lot.

"Did you come down to raid the icebox or were you planning to take on a prowler in your bare feet?" he asked after returning her greeting.

She glanced down, then wiggled toes painted a bright pink. "To tell you the truth, if I thought I'd run into a prowler, I'd already be back upstairs hiding under the bed."

"Smart woman."

She came closer, bringing the scent of soap with her. Nothing special, just clean and light, yet he found himself wanting to bury his face in the hollow of her throat and draw it in. He started to scowl before he stopped himself.

"Do you think it would be a serious breach of guest etiquette if I ate that last piece of pie?"

"In this house the only mistake a guest can make is to leave anything on her plate," he told her with perfect sincerity.

Her golden eyes narrowed in mock suspicion. "You wouldn't be trying to get me into trouble, would you?"

"No, ma'am." Not the kind she had in mind, anyway.

"Good." Greedy anticipation stamped on her face, she bustled around like an eager little housekeeper until she had a plate, fork, and napkin in front of her. Brody shifted, a little annoyed to find himself turned on by the subtle movements. If he had any sense at all, he'd take himself off to bed before he got into serious trouble. Instead, he found himself politely pushing the pie plate closer to her side of the table.

"I'm not really hungry, you realize," she said as she sat down. "I already had two pieces for dinner. Big ones. Heaven knows I've eaten more today than I usually eat in a week at home." Looking as eager as a kid on Christmas morning, she slipped the last piece onto her plate and picked up her fork.

She took a bite, then closed her eyes halfway and savored the taste the way some women savor the touch of a man's hand, with her face soft and dreamy—except for the two tiny lines of fierce concentration between her eyebrows. He could almost hear her purring. It was one of the most erotic sights he'd ever seen. His body certainly thought so.

"I don't know how Dottie does it," she said with a sigh as she forked up another small bite. Rationing her pleasures, he realized, the way he'd always had to ration his words. "She got home a little after four and by six she'd whipped up this incredible pork roast, with chocolate pie for dessert." Pausing with fork poised, she smiled across the table, more relaxed now. Maybe that's why guys instinctively asked a woman they wanted to hustle into bed out to dinner first, he thought. Like gentling a nervous filly with sugar. It was an interesting notion.

"Auntie likes to cook. She's got this theory that if Eve had been a better cook, all that stuff with the snake never would have happened."

Summer chuckled. "My Bible-study days are pretty far back, but it seems to me Eve was the one who took that fatal bite of the apple."

"Yeah, well, Auntie has a way of bending things to suit her."

"I've noticed." She took another bite. "She could make a fortune as a chef."

Brody felt the tug of long-forgotten memory. "I don't ever remember my mother cooking anything more complicated than oatmeal. Auntie did all the good stuff."

"Did she always live with you?" she asked, fork still poised, her lips slightly parted. Brody had to work to stifle a groan.

"Long as I can remember."

To distract himself, Brody turned his glass around and studied the image of the Empire State Building. Dottie's souvenir of an American Library Association convention in New York City. He glanced up in time to watch the tip of Summer's dainty pink tongue wiping chocolate from the corner of her mouth.

"What happened to your hand?" she asked brightly when she caught him watching her.

"My hand?"

She dropped her gaze. "Your left hand. The Band-Aid?"

He jerked his attention from her mouth to the strip of adhesive. "Pig bite," he said, dismissing the stupid wound with an embarrassed shrug.

Her gaze flew to his face, her brows drawn in disbelief. "Did you say *pig*?"

His back teeth ground together. "It's a long story," he muttered.

"I'm a shrink, remember? I like long stories."

Brody shifted in his seat. He could hear the hum of the refrigerator and the scrape of his boot heels on the floor as he stretched out his legs. Tired as he was, he was still wired from the long day. In times past he'd sometimes sat with Meggie in their tidy kitchen talking over their respective days. If neither was too tired, they'd go into their bedroom and tumble into bed. It was a pleasant, comforting life, one that had brought him a rare kind of peace. Summer Laurence wasn't peaceful. And she intimidated the hell out of him, with her quick mind and classy looks, but like Big Malcolm always said, a man ought to have a little vinegar with his greens now and then to keep him sharp.

"Well?" Her grin challenged him to share. To tell her his long story. To goddamned chat with her. Well, hell, he thought as he watched her eyes sparkle in anticipation. He'd give it a shot. His pride had taken enough hits to withstand one more.

"It was an ugly little bastard. Had this big potbelly on him and beady little eyes. The guy that owned it was staying at the Yodeler."

Her mouth popped open, and she blinked. He thought she was flat-out adorable. "They allow pigs in motel rooms here?"

"Most do, yeah. It's a tourist town, remember? There's a lot of competition for those dollars."

Her mouth curved down into a little pout as she considered that. He wondered what it would feel like to kiss her.

"Cats and dogs, maybe. Well, smallish dogs. But I'd definitely draw the line at a pig," she said finally, then frowned more deeply as a thought occurred to her. "Didn't it smell?"

Brody felt an urge to grin. "Yeah, like Old Spice."

She blinked. "You mean the aftershave?"

He nodded. "The owner claimed Cuddles liked to watch him shave."

She blinked again, giving him another look at those butterscotch lashes. "Cuddles?"

"Cuddles."

"Good heavens."

Brody realized he was enjoying himself, and damned if she didn't look like she was, too. At least he thought that was a smile in her eyes. It made him a little dizzy. "Cuddles was a vicious little hunk of rancid bacon. Got ticked off because his owner left him in his van while he went to have dinner. The pig wiggled his little fat butt out of the window the guy'd left open for ventilation."

"Poor thing. I hope it didn't hurt itself."

Brody snorted. "Aggie May at the Brat Haus called it in. Claimed the little beast had her cook cornered in the pantry and threatened to blow off its little pointed ears with the twelve gauge she keeps in the office if we didn't get a man over there pronto." He paused for breath, and let himself enjoy the look of rapt interest on her pixie face. It was a heady experience, having a beautiful, sexy woman hanging on his words. "I lost the toss. Everyone else was on patrol."

"You didn't shoot it?"

"No, but I should have. Damn thing got loose from . . . from the kitchen by the time I got there and was running all over the place. People were . . . were bailing out right and left, and one lady had climbed on top of a table."

Her hand went to her mouth and her eyes shone with laughter. "Oh my lord, what in the world did you do?"

"What could I do? I got down on my hands and knees and played pig. Finally got it trapped in a corner booth. The same one that had the lady on the table."

"Oh dear."

"By the time I got my belt looped through the damn thing's collar, it'd taken a chunk out of my hand and the lady on the table had whacked the hell out of my shoulder because she thought I was trying to look up her skirt."

"And were you?" she asked, biting back laughter.

"Hell no, I was too damn busy. Besides, she had fat ankles."

She giggled, charming him right down to his ten-year-old boots. He felt his mouth twitch, and then he was laughing with her.

"I love it," she said, struggling to control herself. "Where is Cuddles now?"

"If there's a God in heaven, in s-some other poor s-s-sucker's t-t-town." As soon as the words were out, he wanted to recall them. She'd gotten him so tangled up in his emotions he'd let down his guard. He felt heat scald his cheeks and wanted to bolt. Instead, he made himself wait out the next few moments of humiliation.

Summer smiled as she got to her feet and gathered the dishes. "You have had a tetanus shot within the last ten years, haven't you?"

"Yes, ma'am," he said, relaxing. Just for tonight, for a few more minutes, he would pretend it was all right to need someone. "Department regs. Like drug testing every quarter and an HIV screening every six months."

He helped her rinse the dishes and stowed them in the dishwasher before walking her upstairs, turning out lights as they went until only a small lamp on the library table at the head of the stairs remained burning. In the dim light her hair was a dark shiny gold, a soft halo around her face, like an angel he'd seen in a painting once.

"Thanks for sharing your pie with me," Summer said when they reached her room. She hadn't thought to close the door when she'd gone downstairs for a snack, and the evidence of her research was spread out on the table next to her laptop.

"Looks like you've been working."

"Inputting the bids from the electrical contractors."

"Does that mean you're serious about relocating?"

"I'm serious about exploring my options, yes."

Light from within the room fell across his face, giving her a close-up view. The therapist in her registered strength and reserve and a subtle cynicism. But it was the eyes that riveted her. So gentle and . . . lonely.

He leaned a shoulder against the doorjamb and looked down at her. As he'd spun out his story, he'd forgotten about being controlled and watchful. Little by little he'd relaxed until his face had lost its austere harshness. Now, in the subdued light, he was almost handsome. "Uh, just so you know, I talked to Kel."

"Yes, she told me." Her lips curved in a smile. "I don't know which pleased her more—your promise to tell her about her mother or permission to wear eye makeup."

He grunted, but his mouth was soft at the corners. "Damned mascara."

"And a darker lipstick. To match her coloring."

"That's . . . important, is it?"

"Oh absolutely. As important as having the right shells for your pistol."

"Bullets. Shotguns and artillery have shells." His mouth slanted, even as his gaze dipped to hers. A tingle of anticipation ran through her. He was so tough and self-contained, this giant. A hard man with a blue-steel gun slung over his shoulder and a heart as big as the sky.

"It's late," she whispered, a soft, sweet, slippery feeling deep inside.

"Is it?" He moved closer to brace one hand against the wall next to her head, crowding her. He was so tall his badge was at eye level, gleaming as gold as the shield Kyle had waved at her when he'd threatened to arrest her the first time they'd met.

"Brody," she began, then stopped, took a breath, and started over. "Do you think this is wise?"

"Probably not." He lifted his free hand and traced the line of her jaw with his fingertip. She fought the urge to lean into his touch. "Three days, and you've t-turned m-my house upside down."

Her *life* was in serious danger of being turned upside down, all because of an inconvenient attraction. "I'll be gone in four more days."

"You think we should leave it at that?"

"There are things you don't know, things about me you should know."

His gaze lingered on her mouth while her pulse stumbled. She couldn't seem to catch a proper breath. "I know I want you," he said, his voice as rough as winter wool.

She felt the heat of him. And the need he kept so carefully locked behind those surly scowls. "We're virtual strangers."

"Are we?"

"I won't sleep with you. Not while I'm a guest in your aunt's house. Maybe not ever."

"But you want to. It's in your eyes."

She didn't love the man, this dark and dangerous alpha wolf. But since she had no intention of acting on her feeling, she saw no harm in admitting that she was wildly attracted to him. "It would be a mistake."

His hand flattened along her neck, his thumb gently stroking the delicate bones framing the hollow of her throat. What should have been threatening was intensely pleasurable. "K-kiss me."

A polite refusal was trembling on her lips even as she brought up both hands to rest on the wide shelf of his shoulders. Just one kiss, she promised herself as she went up on her toes and pressed her mouth lightly against his. Sensations jolted through her. Surprise at her own boldness, desire, a promise of something wonderful.

He groaned, his mouth coaxing. She swayed, and his arms braced her. Protected her. She felt herself pressing closer, felt the need rising. More . . . she wanted more. Frowning, she tilted her head to fit her mouth better to his. Their noses bumped, and she jerked back.

"I'm no good at this," she muttered, her face flaming. She tried to pull away, but he flattened one huge hand against the curve of her back, holding her.

His eyes smiled. "You're perfect. It's the p-place that's wrong."

Reaching past her, he pushed the door wider, then urged her inside. "I know, you won't s-sleep with me in my aunt's house," he murmured when she uttered a protest.

"I won't."

He eased the door closed until it clicked. Her heart gave a leap, then raced. Behind her was the bed. The big, beautiful, sexy bed. "Tell me you don't want me to kiss you again, and I'll leave."

Say it, Summer, a desperate voice urged. Do it! Do it now before you want him too much. Before you forget.

"I don't believe this," she muttered, nerves and excitement making her voice quiver. "I know this is foolish in the extreme. But I can't say it."

He smiled a split second before he bent his head and brought his mouth to hers. She arched upward, trying to get closer. At first he merely tasted, exploring her mouth slowly, thoroughly with his. Perhaps she could have withstood a demanding kiss, but the sweet persuasion of his surprisingly gentle mouth was more difficult to resist.

She swayed, suddenly unsteady on her feet. His arms were powerful and strong, supporting her. Needing to touch him more intimately, she skimmed her palms up his arms to link behind his neck. His powerful frame shuddered, as though it had been a long time since he'd been caressed.

Groaning, he pulled her closer. His mouth grew hungry, tasting hers over and over, taking her deeper, and her fingers clutched at his hair. His mouth controlled hers, lifted, returned with greater pressure.

His lips were insistent, his body hard, but she thought only of the pleasure he was drawing from some hidden place inside her. Of how he was making her feel. Of the desire building in her.

His tongue moistened her lips, sending slow waves of the sweetest sensation spiraling through her. Her legs went watery, she clung to him, her fingers pushing against the lean, hard muscle of his neck. Her pulse was roaring in her ears, and fire flickered low and deep inside her.

Brody felt the heat in her, and his body swelled to full arousal. He had known desire for other women, but not since Megan had he felt the need to take and take and take until he was filled. The taste of her mouth, the warmth of her skin. The almost virginal sweetness that delighted as much as it surprised.

Summer. He even loved her name. Summer, he whispered in his mind, his tongue tracing the line of her mouth until it trembled for him.

Summer felt his body rock against hers. Hard, insistent. Distinctly male. Very male, she realized as her body stirred, eager to open for him. Small darts of need shot through her, and she moaned.

Brody heard the small, helpless sound, and knew he was sliding close to the line between choice and demand. In another few seconds it would be too late. Reluctantly, he lifted his mouth from hers and drew back far enough to stop himself from plunging his tongue between her parted lips.

Summer whimpered, her eyes opening to gaze up at him in drowsy confusion. "Brody?"

He took a breath—and a risk. "I've got two men out battling the flu so I'm not going to have much free time this week, but even a cop gets to eat. Meet me at the bandstand on Main, Saturday night at seven. I'll buy you dinner."

Without giving her a chance to reply, he pulled her to him for another hard kiss that drove the breath from her body and the sense from her head. While she was still pulling herself together, he was gone.

Summer couldn't sleep. No matter how she tried to get comfortable or how many times she went through her never-failed-yet relaxing routine, she kept feeling Brody Hollister's mouth settling over hers. Determined to ignore the jittery feeling of sexual arousal that was part of the reason for her insomnia, she shifted to her back.

It shouldn't have felt so good. A mouth that hard shouldn't have been so gentle. It had undone her then. It was torturing her now. The firm texture, the surprising sweetness, the electric moment when he'd turned hungry. She'd sensed some powerful need in him, held under a control so tight she'd felt the subtle vibration deep in those heavily roped muscles as his arms urged her body to mold to his. It had been a need to rival her own. A need that still pulsed in her like a desperate punishing tension.

"No," she said, shifting to her side and drawing up her knees. "I don't want him. I refuse to want him."

No matter what kind of torture her body put her through, the risk was too great. Kyle had seduced her with a kiss. By the time it had ended, she'd had sand in her bikini bottoms and stars in her eyes. After that, sixteen-year-old Summer Laurence had belonged to twenty-eight-year-old Kyle Bogan, body and soul. Even after he'd betrayed her, she'd been so lost in love it had taken a hard-faced judge pronouncing sentence on her to make her believe it.

Something had died in her then. An ability to trust wholly, unconditionally. An innocence that had nothing to do with virginity. It had taken her years after her release from prison to accept a date with a man. He'd been a fellow graduate student, a nice guy. She'd frozen in his arms, crushing his ego and leaving her feeling miserably guilty for hurting him. The next time had been a little better. The man was older and far more patient. After months of dating she'd finally let him past her bedroom door. The humiliating debacle that had ensued still had her stomach seizing up. After that, she'd written off the dating scene. Now and then, the ladies of her support group prodded her to work on her "intimacy" issues. She considered it a waste of valuable time. Though she'd long ago worked through her rage, she wasn't about to open herself up to another man. Especially this man. No, tomorrow she'd simply have to find a tactful way of breaking their date for Saturday night.

Confident that she had made the right decision, she adjusted the covers, gave her pillow a little thump, and closed her eyes. All it took was careful thought and rational reasoning to release tension and relax muscles. Two hours later she was still staring at the wall.

CHAPTER 11

The lunch crowd had thinned when Summer walked into the basement café with the dress she'd purchased from a little shop in the Market Platz in a plastic bag folded over one arm. The restaurant was busy and smelled of sausage spice and sauerkraut. While she waited by the entrance for the hostess to finish seating a young couple with a toddler, she glanced around, absorbing the feeling of the place. Bright spring flowers decorated each surface—pansies, primroses, begonias in bright clay pots. Like every other establishment she'd visited in Osuma, this one had a holiday air about it. Though the flavor was decidedly European instead of Mexican, the festival atmosphere reminded her of Old Town San Diego. Maifest instead of Cinco de Mayo. Polka music instead of mariachi brass and guitars.

She could hardly wait to settle in permanently, she realized as the hostess bustled up. Middle-aged, dressed in the ubiquitous dirndl and an embroidered blouse, the woman was short and plump, with apple cheeks, and a thick blond braid wound around her head.

"Table for one, miss?" Her smile was pleasant, if a bit worn at the edges.

"I'm looking for Dottie Hollister," Summer explained, returning the smile. "Her assistant said I'd find her here."

"She is indeed! Follow me, please."

The hostess grabbed a menu from the stack on a table behind her before leading the way through a long narrow room right out of a Tyrolean storybook, complete with smiling gnomes and beer steins. Alpine scenes had been painted on the rough white walls, and an old-fashioned pair of skis had been hung from one of the rafters.

Fewer than half of the tables were still occupied, though many showed signs of recent occupancy. Most of the diners appeared to be enjoying themselves—all but a serious-looking group of business types seated at a large table near the rear, the men in dark suits, the women in conservative garb. Brody was there, too, sitting with his chair tipped back against the wall, his thumbs hooked into his belt loops and his shirt stretched snug across his wide chest. She was used to the badge now, she realized, as well as the air of absolute command of the man wearing it.

He didn't move, but his gaze was suddenly on her. The slippery feeling inside was suddenly back, like a silent yearning as she offered him a friendly smile, which he returned with a lift of one eyebrow and a barely perceptible nod. She thought about her resolve to break their date and felt herself wavering.

"Looks like an important meeting," she murmured to the hostess when they were safely past the table.

The woman gave a low laugh as she led Summer through an arched passageway in the rear. "The city council. Mayor Kurtz's cousin owns this place. The council holds one of their weekly meetings here every month.

The area in the back was smaller, with the cozy air of a family dining room. Dottie glanced up from a corner table as Summer and the hostess approached, her pixie face lighting. "Summer, dear! What a wonderful surprise!"

Today Dottie was wearing a purple blouse with puffed sleeves and silver rick-rack at the neck and wrists, and red palazzo pants. A wild paisley scarf was wrapped around her waist, tying the two together. Summer found herself grinning. Dottie was as bright as a spring garden.

The woman with her was spare and lanky, with close-cropped hair the color of hand-rubbed mahogany. She had an austere face, world-class cheekbones, and a sharp, measuring gaze that had Summer instinctively sucking in her stomach and straightening her posture. Dressed in a mossy green coverall, she reminded Summer of a string bean with an attitude. One of the Fearsome Foursome, Summer surmised, a guess that was soon proven correct when Dottie tossed off with a smile, "Summer, meet Lucy. Lucy meet Summer."

The two of them exchanged smiles.

"How did you find me, dear?" Dottie asked as Summer draped the clear garment bag over an empty chair, before taking a seat. "Not that I'm not thrilled that you did, of course."

"I went to the library first," Summer explained as a busboy appeared at her elbow with water and a place setting. "Your assistant gave me directions."

Dottie beamed. "Dear Gregory is such an accommodating boy."

Lucy rolled her eyes. "Dear Gregory has to be thirty-five if he's a day. You spoil him rotten because he's hung like a horse."

Dottie caught Summer's eye over the bouquet of wildflowers on the table. "You have to excuse Lucille today," she said with exaggerated patience. "She's in a royal snit because the potted daffodils she ordered for next weekend's Maifest are stuck on a railroad siding between Portland and Seattle."

"You'd be in a snit, too, Dottie Hollister, if you had a six-thousand-dollar investment wilting in a stuffy railroad car."

Hiding a smile, Summer spread her napkin on her lap and took a sip of the water. "I can see how that could put you in a bad mood," she told Lucy somberly.

"Thank you, dear. At least someone understands."

The waitress arrived, pad and pencil in hand and a harried look on her face. "Just coffee and a dinner salad, Roquefort dressing on the side," Summer told her with a smile.

"Been shopping?" Dottie asked when the waitress departed.

Summer glanced at her new dress. "I couldn't resist. The embroidery hooked me."

"Lovely," Dottie exclaimed. "Where'd you find it?"

"The Edelweiss. I went in to look at a pair of sunglasses on one of the mannequins." The soft rose color had caught her eye first, but it was the way the long, flowing skirt flirted with her ankles when she'd tried it on that had sold her. Fashioned of soft jersey cotton, the dress had felt wonderfully sensuous against her skin. "The embroidery's hand done," she added as Lucy and Dottie exchanged looks.

"Hand done, meaning someone shoved the material under a machine," Lucy muttered before shooting Summer a look of apology. "Dottie's right. I'm a real grouch today. I hate inefficiency."

The waitress arrived then with Summer's salad and coffee. Both Lucy and Dottie watched as she spooned a dollop of dressing onto the greens.

"Did you hear from Amos?" Dottie said, reaching for her own coffee.

Summer speared a lettuce leaf, then grinned. "Yes, this morning at ten, and I can afford him!"

Dottie gave a little cry of pleasure, her pink crystal earrings clattering wildly against her neck. "Does that mean you've made up your mind?"

Summer drew a breath. "No, not until I've talked with Brody." She glanced up to find Dottie watching her with eyes that were suddenly sharply focused. "I thought we'd agreed not to tell him until it was a done deal."

"I can't do that, Dottie. It's not fair to him."

"Nonsense, dear," Dottie declared with a wave of her hand. "Men hate change. Big Malcolm ate the same Sunday dinner every week of his adult life."

"It's not quite the same thing," Lucy said quietly.

"Of course it is, Luce. No matter what the stimulus, a male's first instinct is to resist. You just have to wait out the explosion."

Summer put down her fork and stared at the greens for a moment. A hearty male laugh rang out in the other room. The busboy rattled dishes as he cleared the table near the door. During it all an oompah band pounded out one polka after another.

"No, Lucy's right. This is too important to play mind games with a good man who's had enough pain in his life."

"But what if he protests?"

"*If?*" Lucy interjected.

"Shut up, Luce," Dottie snapped, sounding very much like an angry little terrier. "This is serious."

Summer couldn't help grinning. "Don't get me wrong, ladies. I intend to argue hard and long for the cause. But if I can't convince Brody to accept Phoenix House on its own merits, that's it. I'll start looking for someplace else."

Dottie looked from one of her friends to the other, sulking. "Where's that waitress got to?" she muttered, craning her neck to look around. "I need a drink."

Brody had been in Lucy's Alpine Garden exactly twice in his life: once to pick up a bunch of carnations and frilly yellow things to take to his aunt in the hospital when she'd had her appendix out four years ago, and once to buy a potted violet for Hingle's wife when she'd given birth to twin daughters last spring.

Setting his jaw, he slapped his palm against the bright green door and shoved it open. The bell overhead jangled loudly, doing the same to his nerves. It was cooler inside, and the air had a damp, sweet smell that made him want to sneeze. A quick glance told him the front part of the shop was empty. Apparently four-fifteen on Thursday afternoon was a slow time in the flower business.

Jamming his clumsy hands in his pockets to keep from knocking anything over, he carefully navigated his way between a half-dozen or so display tables filled with fancy vases and cutesy figurines. Just as he'd made it past the last table, Lucy burst through the beads separating the front from her potting area in the back. At the sight of him, the welcoming smile froze on her face.

"Is it Dottie?" she asked in a rush. "Something's happened?

Tell me, what? An accident. I knew it. The woman drives likes a kamikaze."

"Auntie's fine," he jumped in to assure her when she was forced to stop for breath. "I came in to buy some flowers."

Her jaw dropped. "Flowers?"

He shifted his feet and shot her a belligerent look. "Yeah, flowers. Roses."

She narrowed her gaze and inspected him with the same suspicion he'd been known to direct at a stranger in a back alley at three A.M. "Did you say *roses*?"

He lowered his chin and gave her his best stare. "You want my business or are you gonna talk it to death?"

She cleared her throat and wet her lips. "How many?" she said blandly, her expression carefully blank. He'd pay for this later, he decided grimly. No way was his aunt going to let this pass. But he was committed now. Might as well tough it out. "What's normal?"

"Who's it for?"

"A f-friend."

"And the occasion?"

Brody wondered how much jail time he'd get for strangling a nosy florist in her own shop. "Don't push it, Lucy," he warned in his scariest voice.

Her lips twitched. "Hmm, yes, well, for a *friend*, a dozen long-stems is customary."

He let out a sigh of relief. "Okay, go with that."

"And the color?"

Shit! "Whatever you got."

"I've got *everything*. The question is, what message do you want to send?"

"No card. I'll deliver them myself."

"No, the message of the flowers. Traditionally, each color has a meaning. For example, white is for love."

He felt his stomach twist into about a hundred separate knots. His throat tightened, and he had to grab a couple of quick gulps of air to loosen it. "Forget white."

"Red, perhaps?"

He eyed her warily. "Uh, what does red stand for?"

"Seduction."

His mind went straight to an image of Summer stretched out on the fancy sheets in the guest room bed, draped in that sexy nightshirt with a smile that was just for him. "Forget red," he muttered. Summer was a bright lady. He figured it was just possible she knew all about this color thing, and he didn't want her thinking he was only interested in getting her into bed—even if it was true.

Lucy's stone-gray eyes had a way of calling a man a liar, even when she was smiling. "Yellow, then. For friendship."

"Yeah. Good."

She arched one skinny eyebrow. "You know, of course, that Dot is going to find out about this, although, I, myself, am extremely good at keeping secrets—for a price, of course."

"Damn it, Lucy—" He clenched his jaw so hard his back teeth creaked. Lucy bit her lip, then burst out laughing.

"Sorry, but you looked so fierce there for a minute. Twelve long-stemmed yellow roses to go. I'll have to get them from the back." Still chuckling, she disappeared behind the screen of beads, setting them swinging wildly in her wake.

Brody pulled one hand free to rub the back of his neck. If he hurried, he could get home and slip the roses to Summer before his aunt showed up. He felt a stir in his groin in anticipation of the kiss he'd figured he'd steal while Summer was busy being bowled over with shock. Maybe she might even kiss him back the way she did last night. Be worth another restless night fighting with his pillow, to feel her arms around his neck and those perfect little breasts flirting with his chest.

"Here we go," Lucy boomed as she emerged again, this time with a long cone of flowers wrapped in pale-blue tissue paper. A frilly silver ribbon was tied in the middle. "That'll be forty-five dollars, tax included."

Brody did a double take, then sighed heavily as he hauled his wallet out of his back pocket. "I usually arrest highway robbers," he muttered, pulling out five tens.

Lucy harrumphed as she took the money. "If I'd known I was going to be insulted in my own shop, I wouldn't have given you a ten-percent discount."

"Forty-five bucks for a bunch of s-stems and buds is the real insult," he groused under his breath.

"Five dollars is your change," she said brightly, handing him the bill. "Thank you and come again."

"Not unless the city gives me a raise," he told her as he returned his wallet to his pocket, then grabbed the flowers. Shoulders hunched to keep from knocking over stuff on the taller display racks, he made his way through the minefield to the door.

"Oh Brody, one more thing," Lucy called as he pulled it open.

"Yeah?" he said when the jangling ceased.

"I like the shorter hairstyle. Where'd you have it done, My Lady's Image?"

Strangling was definitely too kind. Maybe a two-by-four between the eyes. "It was Sam's Barber Shop like always, and if I hear one more word out of you, I'm going to haul you in for extortion."

Her hoot of laughter damn near followed him all the way down the street to his office.

The Olds wasn't in the drive, but the Neon was. The last time he'd bought roses for a woman she'd just had his baby. Tiny pink buds in a pink bootie. Meggie hadn't needed words to know how he felt about her.

Grim-faced, he rid himself of his Stetson and hung it on the barrel of the shotgun, took off his shades and hooked them over the mirror, then ran his hand through his hair. Not that it did much good. His hair pretty much did what it wanted. And what it wanted was usually pretty scruffy. At least it was clean. His neck felt naked where Sam had snipped off a good inch. Cut, not styled, damn it. He snorted, thinking about Lucy's jibe. Like he'd ever set foot in one of those places where the stylists wore pink smocks and shot hair spray on everything that didn't have sense enough to get out of the way.

Figuring he'd stalled as long as he could, he grabbed the flowers, jerked open the door, and got out. The air had cooled some since early afternoon. Mid-sixties would be his guess. Someone had a fire. He could smell the smoke. The grass had started growing and was getting longer, he noticed as he cut across the lawn and headed for the back door. The snow level on the peaks had been climbing for a couple of weeks, and road maintenance supervisors were laying off winter workers. Spring was settling in nicely.

One of these days he'd have to replace the storm door with screen, he thought as he pulled it open. He stepped inside and was instantly enveloped in the bitter smell of burned chocolate.

Bent over something buried in a mound of soapsuds in the sink, Summer whipped around at the sound of his entry, her expression fierce. Wisps of pale hair had come loose from that sleek twist at the back of her head to curl against her neck, and her cheeks were pink. Her tawny eyes blazed into his, as fierce as the tiger eyes they resembled.

"Do *not* say a word, Brody Hollister," she warned in a low throaty growl that had his blood heating. "Not . . . one . . . word."

That suited him. At the moment he sure as heck didn't have a clue what to say. Instead he turned his back, closed the door, arranged his expression into a polite look of inquiry, and turned back to face her.

Looking hot and harried, she had a towel clutched to her midriff and her golden eyebrows were drawn into a painful-looking knot over her nose. "It was supposed to be a surprise for Dottie," she said, all but shooting the words at him. "She was talking last night about how she loved fudge and never seemed to find time to make any."

He figured a nod was safe enough and took another step. She'd changed out of the slacks and sweater she'd been wearing earlier into a comfortable-looking sweatshirt and those butt-hugging jeans. He wondered if he would burn in hell for wanting to see her naked just one time before he died.

"I followed the recipe *exactly*," she said heatedly while directing a murderous look at the thick volume lying open on the counter. When she glanced back to him, he played it safe and gave her another nod.

"I kept stirring and testing, waiting for the soft ball stage, but the stupid stuff just kept bubbling. My wrist was getting tired so I switched hands and kept stirring." She paused for breath, drawing his attention to the soft contours of her breasts under the pale-green sweatshirt. "A sensible, logical person would assume that the flame wasn't hot enough, right?" She glared at him, obviously waiting.

"Works for me."

She nodded. Satisfied. "So, I just nudged it up a little. The next thing I knew the stupid stuff was all dried out and sticking to the bottom of the pan." She stabbed an accusing finger at the cookbook. "That recipe is *wrong*. Obviously the author left out an important step. No doubt it's a man whose real intent is to drive women berserk."

He nearly choked on that but managed to keep a straight face, fairly sure she was finished but unwilling to make any sudden moves. During her tirade a lock of hair had flopped over her brow and she blew it away from her eyes. For all her ranting, he had a feeling she was enjoying herself. And the subtle peeks she kept sending his way made him wonder if she wasn't doing this to make him laugh. Maybe because she'd noticed he'd been damn near bored out of his mind at the council meeting.

It was her way, he realized suddenly. Listening, watching, figuring out what each one needed, and then doing her damnedest to give it. Like the way she puzzled out what had Kelly so sad and mopey, then slapped him around a little until he realized he was being an insensitive jerk. And like the way she asked his aunt slyly clever questions so that Dottie could take center stage.

"Well, say something," she said when the silence lengthened, glaring at him.

He thought about reminding her that she'd told him not to say a word, then took the cowardly way out instead. "No doubt about it. Book's wrong."

She held his gaze for three beats then burst out laughing. He liked the sound. It made him feel like strutting because he'd drawn it out of her.

"Thank you for that," she said when she sobered. "I'm afraid you picked the absolute worst time to come through that door."

"Dairy Dell on Alpine has pretty good fudge," he said because he knew she would puff up like an irate little cat. "Slap it on a plate and Auntie'll never know."

"*Now* you tell me." Summer pretended to be annoyed as she turned to hang up the towel. Facing him again, she smiled. That edgy, not sure he was welcome look was gone from his eyes, and unless her eyesight was failing her, there was even a hint of a grin playing around the corners of that stern mouth.

"Don't mind me," she said with an exaggerated sigh. "I'm just treating myself to a bout of the sulks. I do that every now and then to remind myself of the teenage mind-set. It helps me relate to my patients."

"Must be why you're s-so good with Kelly." He'd brought the flavor of the wind in with him. And in spite of the almost-grin, a palpable tension. The easy companionship of last night seemed to have ended with the dawn. She realized she missed it.

"I almost forgot. About Kelly. She called earlier to say she was at the library and would catch a ride home with Dottie. Apparently she has this big research paper due on Monday."

He nodded, his face unreadable. "She say anything about her friend Tiffany being in on that project?"

She thought back. "I don't think so. No, definitely not. Why?"

His mouth slanted, folding that beguiling crease into his bronzed cheek. "Caught a glimpse of Tiff and a couple of Kel's other friends heading that way after school. Probably a coincidence."

Summer laughed. His humor was as sneaky as the unpracticed charm that had a way of easing through her defenses when she least expected it. "Poor Kelly. Busted again. Does that mean the library will be off-limits, too?"

His eyes softened. "Figure I'll let her slide on this one."

Summer wanted to hug him. "You're a good dad. Someday she'll know just how good."

He wasn't a man used to compliments, she realized, watching him shift uneasily on those long legs. He looked different today, she thought, as she took a drink of the now cold coffee she'd poured before attempting to chisel hardened chocolate from the bottom of the pan.

"Saw you'd been shopping," he said as she sipped.

Apparently so had he. In the flower shop. "A few things," she said as she slipped the empty mug into the soapy water. "Gifts, mostly. My grad-student intern collects T-shirts. I got her one with edelweiss on it. You know, those little whitish flowers."

"Yeah." He looked startled, then dropped his gaze to the bouquet in his big fist. "Damn," he muttered before stepping forward. "Uh, they're not edelweiss, but I heard you tell Auntie you like roses, and I saw these." Sounding a little desperate, he shoved them at her. "Here."

Summer felt a surge of pleasure as she carefully extricated the slightly battered bundle from his grasp. Her fingers trembled slightly as she pealed back the tissue paper and buried her face in the velvety buds. Her lashes dropped as she drew in magic. Roses, she thought in a kind of wonder. Brody was courting her. A feeling so fragile she was afraid to breathe stole over her.

"Thank you," she said, lifting her gaze to his. "No one has ever given me roses before."

Surprise shimmered in his poet's eyes before his gaze dropped to the bright blossoms. "Actually they're a bribe."

"They are?"

When he brought his gaze back to her face, the surprise was gone, replaced by a heat that had her nerves humming. She took a breath, let it out slowly. She had that breathless feeling she got once when she'd reached the top of that first big hill on a roller-coaster ride an instant before the car hurtled downward.

"Guys in the movies always get kissed when they bring flowers." He sounded belligerent.

Battling nerves, she gave him a smile. "What happens if they don't?"

His eyes flared heat. "You don't want to know." Moving quickly, he plucked the bouquet from her arms and plopped it, paper and all, into the soapy water. Before she could do more than squeak out a protest, he hooked one hand around her neck, tilted her head with the other, and brought his mouth down on hers.

It was a hungry kiss, tasting of wind and restraint and a strong man's helplessness. She responded willingly, for once letting her feelings run. As though aware of her years of caution, her lack of sexual expertise, he was offering her gentleness. Grateful and unbearably touched, she slid her fingers along the slope of his shoulders, feeling the little ripples of reaction from a man who disciplined every breath, reveling in the hard-packed strength. His very size made her feel dainty and fragile and very cherished. Love, she thought in a haze. She was tumbling into love right here in his arms. Shaken, she broke the kiss and buried her face in his shoulder.

He drew back, his dark gaze searching her face. "Am I p-pushing too hard?"

"No, it's me. I'm . . . scared." The admission was out before she thought.

He lifted his hand and brushed his knuckles along her cheekbone. "I know I'm too b-big and m-mostly clumsy, but I won't hurt you." His voice was husky, his expression fierce. "I p-promise."

"I know. It's . . . not you. It's me. Old . . . tapes, as we say in my business."

His brows drew together. "Did s-someone touch you wrong? Is that it?"

"Yes, someone touched me wrong. But you . . ." Her voice

broke and she drew a breath. "Touch me, Brody. Please." Heal me, she added in a silent plea straight from the depths of her soul.

He answered her plea, bringing his mouth to hers again, softly, then more insistently until his kiss was deep and greedy, pleasure spinning giddily in her head.

Brody heard the urgent little whimper in her throat and need slammed into him with the force of a high-velocity slug. He'd been celibate too long, and he wanted her too much. Every nerve in his body was screaming. Desperation clawed at the walls of his belly. His muscles strained with the urge to go slowly, to let her get used to his size, the feel of his big, rough hands on her soft skin. Even as he disciplined his movements, the need tore at his control.

Still, he made himself wait, savoring the glorious feel of her in his arms. His hands trembled as he skimmed his palms over her back, tracing the bumpy length of her spine, the sexy curve at the small of her back, the contours of her bottom beneath the soft denim. The pressure drove him harder, needing the blessed gift of release. Close to the line between will and insanity, he drew back, his breathing out of control.

Whimpering, Summer let her head fall back, exposing her throat. On a groan, he bent to trace the elegant line. Opening his mouth, he breathed on the silky skin and felt the moan ripple through her throat. Her fingers dug into his shoulders as she swayed, clung. He tightened his arms, letting her know without the words that invariably failed him that he would never touch her wrong, never let her fall.

She moaned again, clung, her small body molding to his. Her hands were everywhere. On his shoulders, his neck, fisting in his hair. She begged him with the rake of her fingers over his scalp, the frenzy of her kiss. The arching of that slender body to bring her pelvis against his. His control wavered, broke. With a groan, he yanked up her sweatshirt, and fumbled to unfasten her jeans. She gasped and grabbed his wrists. Her eyes were bright with passion, her lashes sleepy and quivering. "No, wait," she said, her voice bordering on desperate.

"What?" His mind was sluggish, his blood hot. Waiting was the last thing on his mind.

Her eyes were passion-glazed, her cheeks pink as she stepped back, away from him. Her sweatshirt was pulled over one shoulder, revealing smooth skin tanned to a golden glow. That glorious butterscotch hair was tumbled around her face. He wanted her desperately.

"Do you . . . ?" She stopped to run her tongue over lips still rosy from his kiss. "I don't believe in unprotected sex."

Oh God. "If you need to see a blood t-test, I have a s-stack of 'em."

"Me, too," she admitted before inhaling deeply. "I try to be an example for my patients."

"Well, okay, then." He started to reach for her, but she held him off with a hand pressed to his chest.

"Now what?"

"I'm not on the pill, and I don't have a condom. Do you?"

"No. Haven't needed one." He wanted to kick something. "Guess you wouldn't want to take a fast trip to the drugstore with me, huh?"

Her laugh was shaky. "I don't think that's a good idea." When she stepped back, he let her go. He was just insecure enough to be a little glad she was flustered.

"Maybe this, uh, um, glitch is for the best," she said as she staggered to a chair and sat down.

"Glitch, is it?"

Her grin was self-conscious, making him wonder if she, too, was feeling less than confident. Or was that just wishful thinking?

"I need a minute to recover." A small, nervous laugh escaped her. "Your aunt was right. You are formidable."

He was pretty sure that was a compliment, but he didn't trust his control enough to ask. Instead, he walked to the double sink, turned on the cold tap full blast and dunked his head under the violent stream.

Summer pressed her fingers to her lips and watched him

shake his head like a big old bear, then grab a clean towel from one of the drawers to wipe through the dripping strands of ebony. She laughed when he looked up, his expression rueful.

"Why is it that men dunk their heads when it's really another part of their anatomy that needs cooling off?" she asked.

"Hell if I know," he said, smiling at her with his eyes as well as his lips.

Her heart gave a little leap. She knew enough about men to know that he was a lot more uncomfortable at this moment than she was. At least physically. She wasn't sure anyone could be more chagrined. And yes, disappointed.

"I'm sorry, Brody. I didn't see this coming, or I never would have . . ." She broke off, feeling confused and uncertain. How was a woman supposed to think rationally when her lips were still throbbing from his kiss and her insides felt all melted and warm?

Smiling a little at the thought, she glanced up to find herself facing the same remote man who'd confronted her outside the ranch house. The change was so sudden and so total it had her inhaling sharply before trying again. "I mean, I've always prided myself on being straightforward—"

Impatience hardened his jaw. "I got the message the first time, Doc. Hands off." His voice was surly. He was protecting himself again.

She rose and went to him. The man was as volatile as a teenager. And maybe as unsure of himself? The thought made her want to wrap her arms around him and hold on tight. "That's not what I'm saying at all."

"Maybe you'd better spell it out." Though his eyes were still guarded, one side of his mouth inched upward. "In words of one syllable for this ignorant country boy."

He *was* feeling insecure. "All I'm saying is that I'd like to go a little more slowly. Get to know you and let you know me before we take this to the next level."

He wiped water from the counter, then rehung the towel before looking at her with brooding eyes. "Damn, I should have known a shrink would be hung up on that intimacy thing." The smile was back in his eyes.

"I can't help it. It's in the manual."

"Department regs, huh?" His eyes turned a dark, warm purple as he reached up to cup her cheek with his huge, callused hand. Bemused, she nuzzled his palm, loving the warm strength she felt there.

"Honey, don't look at me like that, or this pile of good intentions I'm standing on here is gonna bury us both." As though to emphasize his point, he shifted his hips so that she felt the hard ridge of his arousal against her belly.

"Saturday night," he said, his voice graveled. "We'll have dinner. Start on this knowing each other business."

CHAPTER 12

Arranging an appointment with Dr. Krebs had been easier than Summer had anticipated. She'd called on Tuesday afternoon and arranged to see him at three on Friday. His office was on the ground floor of the hospital, a plain, three-story, square, cinder-block building located on the eastern end of the village proper. As was her habit, she arrived ten minutes early. The doctor was late. Tied up in a staff meeting, his middle-aged, stylishly dressed receptionist had explained before offering Summer coffee.

Now, twenty minutes later, Summer was seated in a cushy leather chair across from his desk in his office, sipping Vienna roast and trying to get a clearer read on the man who customarily sat behind the desk.

It was a starkly masculine office. Lots of brass, dark wood, and muted colors, predominantly burgundy and navy. The scents of leather, beeswax, and old books blended together in a way that was both virile and homey. Framed diplomas and a myriad of professional credentials covered one wall. Summer knew enough about the pecking order of medical institutions to be impressed.

As befitted a man of his status, the desk was large with spare lines and a gleaming surface. A photograph in a silver frame sat to the right of the phone. His wife? she wondered. The woman who'd consoled him after Dottie had rejected him. Summer fought a fast and furious battle with herself—and lost. After glancing over her shoulder to make sure the door was still firmly shut, she leaned forward to turn the frame toward her. She had a quick impression of a woman with a dark cap of curly hair, kind brown eyes, and piquant freckles before the door opened behind her.

Greydon Krebs was as impressive and upscale as his office, a nice-looking man of medium height, solidly built, with wide shoulders, silver hair framing a square lived-in face, and a twinkle in his eyes. "That's a picture of my wife, Sarah, on our twenty-fifth wedding anniversary. It's one of my favorites."

"She's lovely." Somehow Summer managed to get to her feet without spilling coffee all over her peach skirt. "And I was being nosy. I apologize."

His smile invited confidences. "No need, Dr. Laurence. My receptionist told me you're a psychotherapist. It's been my experience that you folks are generally curious critters."

"It's both a curse and gift," she said, extending her hand. "And, please, call me Summer."

"Only if you call me Grey." His handshake was firm, but without the crushing pressure some men thought was necessary to prove their virility.

"It's a deal." Summer felt herself relaxing. Dr. Krebs exuded integrity and a certain sweetness of temper, but with hints of steely strength.

The doctor walked behind the desk. He was wearing gray flannel trousers to match the suit coat hanging from a brass hook on the wall, a pale-blue oxford-cloth shirt, and a surprisingly bright red-and-gold silk tie with tiny golf clubs sprinkled here and there. A memory of Dottie's comparison of masculine neckwear to the medieval codpiece popped into her mind and she wondered what kind he would have chosen. Something whimsical, she suspected.

"I'm sorry to keep you waiting," he said as he sat down. "Things get a little hectic around here at the end of every month. That's when we do staff evaluations."

Summer made a face. "I empathize totally. I'm only responsible for evaluating one intern, but I agonize for days over my remarks."

He acknowledged that with a congenial smile, one colleague to another. She suspected he would make a strong ally. *If* she could win him over. "So what brings you to Osuma? Or more specifically, to me?"

She primed herself with caffeine, then set the cup and saucer on the desk and sat forward, her back straight, her gaze steady on his. "The reason I'm here, Grey, is to tell you about Phoenix House."

Twenty minutes later she stopped talking and waited. Grey sat in thoughtful silence, his hands steepled over a surprisingly flat midriff. "As you said, the concept is similar to other inpatient facilities currently in operation," he said at last. "When I was still in private practice, I referred several of my patients to one near Portland that's had fair success." A sad look crossed his face and Summer wondered if Jasmine Gooding had been one of those patients. "I like the idea of requiring the patients to participate in the upkeep of the property, although I have a feeling that mixing city kids and country livestock is going to provide you with some interesting moments."

Summer laughed. "I'm a city kid myself, and I totally agree. Just the thought of getting near a horse is enough to bring on a major case of hives."

His grin lit his face and crinkled his eyes. He had perfectly aligned and very white teeth, with just a hint of a gap between the front incisors. "How many horses did you say you've been offered?"

"Six. The gentleman rancher who's promised to donate them swears they're all very docile, and more important, used to inexperienced riders. Not a bad-tempered one in the lot. I may make him sign a blood oath to that effect, however."

He leaned forward and rested both forearms on his desk. He had nice hands. Very clean, with clipped nails. And strong wrists. The latent strength she saw there reminded her of Brody's huge hands and forearms, though the doctor's skin was not nearly as

tanned. Unlike Brody's plain silver watch with a no-nonsense
leather band, Dr. Krebs's timepiece was wafer-thin gold, and
very expensive. And yet he wore his success with an impressive
modesty. "It's been a long time since I've been out to the Hollister ranch. What kind of shape is it in?"

"Fairly good, actually." Encouraged by his interest, she went
on to briefly describe the renovations that had to be made before
she would be ready to receive patients. "I'm already working on
a brochure. All I need is a provisional license, a date when I can
start accepting patients, a schedule of fees, and of course, a telephone number."

"Have you a staff?"

"Two firm commitments at the moment. Both former interns
who've received their licenses and are working temporary posi-
tions in San Diego. Of course, we'll all have to become licensed
in Washington, but I've already filled out my application and
picked up several more to take home with me. Frankly, I don't
anticipate problems."

In response to his tactfully probing questions, she went on to
tell him a little about her own educational and professional
background as well as the credentials of the other two graduate
psychologists, Charlotte Jackson and Mansur Rashid. "Manny's
a fanatic for skiing, so I'm thinking of paying a portion of his
salary in lift tickets."

He chuckled and started to reply when the intercom on the
phone buzzed. "Yes, Jill?"

"Sorry to disturb you, Doctor, but Mark's here and wants to
know if you can spare him a few minutes."

Grey glanced across the desk. "Mark's my grandson. Would
you mind?"

"Not at all," Summer said with a smile. In fact, she was more
than eager to meet Kelly's friend.

"Send him in, please."

Summer swiveled in her seat in time to see the door open.
Mark Krebs was stocky and solid like his grandfather, with the
same square face, brown eyes, and thick golden hair blessed

with just enough curl to give it interesting highlights. Deepen his tan, exchange the faded jeans and Cubs sweatshirt for baggies and a surfboard, and he'd be perfectly at home in Ocean Beach. And, she suspected, an instant hit with girls who hung around the lifeguard stations in string bikinis and Ray-Bans.

"Dr. Laurence, I'd like you to meet my grandson, Mark." His voice was edged with pride and his eyes had gone soft. Clearly he adored the boy.

"Hi," Mark offered with a dimpled grin as he took the hand she'd offered. His fingers pressed a little too tightly, he shook a little too long, but the look in his eyes was almost puppy-dog engaging.

Her first impression was a disturbing one. Please like me, his expression pleaded, while her instinct told her there was another, darker message hidden in those guileless eyes. It took her a moment to realize why she had instinctively withdrawn the moment she and the boy had made eye contact. Though she told herself she was being paranoid, she saw Kyle in this boy's lopsided smile. A shiver ran down her spine, and her protective instincts flared. If Kelly were her daughter, she'd be seriously thinking of discouraging her from spending time with this junior Adonis. Still, she believed in giving everyone the benefit of the doubt, so she offered him a smile as she reclaimed her hand.

"Hello, Mark. It's nice to meet you."

"You're staying at Kelly's place, right?" His voice was deeper than she'd expected, more like a man's than a boy's, and the rather harsh accent was one she'd always associated with the Midwest.

"Right." She smiled. "Kelly's mentioned you several times. I'm glad to have the chance to put a face to the name."

"Yeah, me, too." His grin blazed again as he added, "She said you looked a lot like Murphy Brown. You know, Candice Bergen? Only . . . a whole lot prettier."

Summer cooled her expression. "That was sweet of Kelly."

His gaze narrowed almost imperceptibly before he turned back to his grandfather. "Actually it's Kelly I wanted to talk to you about, Granddad. See, we—Kelly and me—got to talking after school on Monday and she missed the bus. Like, see, she said she'd call her aunt, only she really hated to bother her, and her old—her *father*—is really hard to reach, you know, so I said I'd take her home. I mean, no big deal, right?" Like a born salesman, he paused to wait for his grandfather's agreement. It was a technique she sometimes used. Get the patient to agree to small, inconsequential tasks, then lead him gently into tackling the more difficult ones.

"What's your point, son?" Grey asked pleasantly. The old fox, she thought, looking down at her hands in order to hide a smile.

"Well, the thing is, before we got to her place, her dad showed up. Man, he was really pissed—" He caught himself and sent a look of apology in Summer's direction. "Sorry, ma'am."

"I've heard worse," she assured him.

He hunched his shoulders, then sidled closer to the desk. He had the look of a wrestler about him, she decided. Or maybe a football player. "The thing is, Kelly and I were supposed to have a date tonight, but her dad grounded her, 'cause of the car thing and all. See, she's not supposed to ride in a car with a guy unless her dad checks him out first."

Grey gave a little shrug. "That's Chief Hollister's way, son, and I can't say I totally disagree. Guess you'll have to make an appointment for a driving test if you want to date his daughter."

"Yeah, right. Okay, but in the meantime, I thought you could, like, call him yourself. Sort of vouch for me, you know? I mean, you know I'm a safe driver, right?"

"I'm not the one who needs to be convinced."

"C'mon, Granddad. I plan to let him check me out, but in the meantime, I thought you could fix things so me and Kelly could still go out."

Summer saw that the doctor was tempted. Mark was tenacious, with a strong will. An only child, Dottie had said. Perhaps a little overindulged. She drew a breath and hoped Dr. Krebs would hold firm. Both Kelly and Mark needed to accept the consequences of their actions. It was better to learn that now, when the stakes weren't so high. Still, she knew from her years working with both parents and grandparents of her clients that it was hard to say no sometimes. Tough love wasn't easy.

"No, Mark," he said finally, shaking his head. "Kelly's dad is a good friend. It wouldn't be fair to put that kind of pressure on him."

A vein throbbed in Mark's temple and his hands clenched briefly before he shoved them in the pockets of his windbreaker. He glared at his grandfather for a long silent moment, his frustration all but palpable. "I gotta split," he muttered finally. "I got baseball practice at four."

"Take care, Mark," Summer said when he would have walked away without bidding her good-bye.

"Whatever," he mumbled before going out the door.

Grey sighed and rubbed one hand down the side of his face in a gesture of parental exasperation that Summer suspected had begun with Adam and Eve, no doubt when Cain turned thirteen.

"Poor kid's had a rough time of it," he said by way of explanation. Or perhaps apology. "His father killed himself and Mark found the body. His mother is assuaging her pain with one affair after another. He's been moody and volatile ever since."

"I assume he's had counseling?"

"Intensive. In fact, it was his therapist who recommended he come to stay with me. It was amazing how fast his mother got him on a plane." His smile was both sad and pleased. "Having him around has certainly put more pep into my life."

"Not to mention a few headaches, I would imagine."

He laughed. "Too true." His amusement fading, he drew a breath. "But enough of my parental angst. About Phoenix House, what can I do to help?"

Standing dead center in a sickly patch of sunlight streaming through the broken patio doors, Detective Harvey McVey shifted the toothpick from one side of his mouth to the other and hitched his trousers a little higher on his paunch. It was a little past five, and the seasoned pro and his partner were on overtime.

"Way I figure it, Chief, the guy'd been casing the place for a day or two, watching when the doc came and went."

Brody acknowledged that with a nod before turning his attention to Paulette Tong, McVey's partner, who was dusting the den's doorjamb for prints. A transplanted Californian on the run from overcrowding and a failed marriage, she was a recent hire and already one of his best detectives.

"Anything?" he asked Tong.

"Lots of clear prints mixed with partials and smudges. The doctor's already given us a sample of his. We'll have to get a set from the grandson and the woman who comes in to clean once a week."

Brody shifted his attention to the man silently sipping Scotch and staring out the bank of windows overlooking the river. Grey had said virtually nothing since greeting Brody at the ruined patio door twenty minutes earlier.

Brody'd heard the call on the scanner in his office and as soon as he'd caught Doc's name, he'd jumped for a chance to escape his office for an hour or two. "Anyone else we need to print for comparison, Grey?"

The doctor turned from his study of the view, his face drawn and tired. "I had a man in to fix the furnace a few weeks back, but he wasn't in my office."

"You sure about that, Doc?" McVey asked, his pencil poised over the small notebook cupped in his hand.

"Positive. I was working in my study the entire time. When he was finished, I came out and paid him."

The detective made a note. "How about friends of your grandson?"

Grey thought a moment, then shook his head. "Mark's only been living with me since the first of the year. He's been slow to settle in, hasn't made too many close friends, although now that he's on the baseball team, I'm certain that will change."

McVey made another note, then ambled off toward the study

again. Grey watched until the detective disappeared, then offered Brody a smile. "I understand you and my grandson met recently."

Brody removed his Stetson and combed the flatness out of his hair with his fingers. "We met."

Grey turned to lean against the wall separating one window from another. "Don't be too hard on the kids, Brody. They're young and impulsive."

Brody resettled the Stetson. "That's what I'm worried about."

Grey saluted that with his drink. It was a graceful gesture, one Brody couldn't manage in his lifetime. "Mark's had a rough time, but he's come through remarkably well. His therapist said that he is an extremely resilient young man. Markham's death was a horrible blow for all of us, but it seems to have given Mark a sense of what's important, like family."

"Yours, not mine."

Grey laughed. "I admit he's a bit intense about Kelly, but everything seems intense to a boy of sixteen." He lifted a fatherly eyebrow. "You were pretty intense yourself at that age if you'll recall."

"I recall being pounded on by a drill instructor trying to marry my backbone with my belly," he muttered, his rough tone designed to discourage further trips down memory lane.

Grey's amusement faded. "I'd forgotten you were so young when you joined up."

"I didn't stay young long." Brody heard a car pull up outside and flicked a gaze toward the patio.

"That'll be Mark," Grey said, striding to the ruined door.

Brody heard the back gate open, and then Mark Krebs's voice barking out an obscenity as he encountered the yellow tape stretched across the patio. "Granddad?" he called when he spotted his grandfather through the glass door. "What's going on?"

"It's okay, son," Grey assured him, before asking Brody, "Should I have him go around to the front door?"

"Tong, you done out back?"

"Yes sir," she said without looking up.

Brody nodded to the doctor, who called, "It's okay, Mark. Come on in."

Frowning, the boy closed the gate carefully behind him before crossing the patio with quick, athletic strides. He was wearing faded navy sweats and a bulky Chicago Bulls warm-up jacket. A pair of dirty cleats were slung over his shoulder. His face was flushed, and he looked tired and sweaty.

"I saw the cop cars and nearly busted a gut," he said as he approached the door. "I was afraid—" He broke off, his expression tortured.

Brody felt himself softening toward the kid. Much as he'd hated his own father, he would've been pretty torn up if he'd walked in one day and found him dead.

"We've been robbed," Grey said, stepping back to let the boy enter. Mark's gaze flickered Brody's way and his eyes narrowed for an instant before his handsome face became stiffly respectful.

"Hello, Chief."

Brody responded with a nod. "Looks like the coach worked you pretty hard," he said for want of something better.

Mark pulled a face. "Wind sprints and drills mostly. Guys are still out of shape from the winter, so we broke up early." He lifted his eyebrows. "Do you play ball, sir?"

"Tried it once, when Kelly was learning softball. Tripped over my feet mostly."

"I didn't know Kelly played. Maybe me and her could practice together."

"Maybe." Brody put just enough grit in his voice to raise a flush on the boy's cheeks.

"So, somebody broke in, or what?" he said, glancing at the glass and dirt strewn over the tile at their feet.

"Looks that way."

Mark transferred his attention to his grandfather. "Did they take a lot of stuff?"

"The usual, according to Detective McVey. Both VCRs and my camera."

Mark's gaze flickered to the entertainment center taking up one wall. Wires were hanging free and two of the shelves were now empty. The living room was a mess. "Guess it's a good thing the TV is so big," he muttered.

Grey sighed, and a look of pained anger crossed his face. "The bastard took your grandmother's cameo."

Mark's expression clouded. "Jeez, that's heavy, Granddad. But maybe they'll, like, get it back." He shifted his attention Brody's way. "Right, Chief?"

"Possible. Not likely, though. Too easy to fence."

"The detective will want your fingerprints," Grey interjected.

Mark blinked and looked worried for a moment before understanding dawned. "Oh yeah, like on TV." He glanced toward Tong, who was now preparing to take photos of the crime scene.

"It'll be a few minutes before I'm ready," the detective said, smiling at the boy.

"Cool." He dropped his shoes by a worn leather recliner and shrugged free of his jacket. Brody noticed that the boy was more well built than he'd thought, with the bulky chest and upper arms of a weight lifter. The thought of those strong arms closing around his daughter's fragile body twisted his gut.

Suddenly restless and edgy, Brody walked to the door of the study and looked inside. Tong stood to the right of the desk, angling her body one way and another as she snapped off pictures. McVey was on his hands and knees with his big butt in the air, sifting the rug with his fingers. Satisfaction ran through Brody at the sight. The entire Osuma PD was smaller than one division of the LAPD, but it ran like clockwork and everyone on the payroll put out quality work—or they didn't stay on the payroll. Himself included, he thought, resigned to returning to his desk and the stack of papers he'd left behind.

"You guys good here?" he asked.

"Got it handled," McVey said, sparing him a quick glance over one shoulder.

Tong lowered her camera to cast a thoughtful look around.

"My instincts tell me we're dealing with more than a fast in-and-out burglary here."

Brody's attention sharpened. "Why?"

"Look at all the ruined books. Must be hundreds, most of them leather-bound. Either the guy we're looking for hates good literature or he's got some kind of vicious hate case going against the doctor. My money would be on the latter."

Brody let his gaze rest on the pile of torn pages and destroyed bindings. "You think the robbery is a cover?"

"Maybe, although the question is why take the risk of being caught just to mess up a guy's house?"

McVey sat back on his considerable haunches and offered Brody a sly grin. "You gotta excuse my partner, Chief. Her being down in Lalaland for so many years working with nutsos and acid heads, she sees crazy everywhere."

Tong's grunt was good-natured. "More cases have been solved with intuition and open-mindedness than plodding through procedure like a trained bear."

McVey snorted. "Maybe the guy was having a bad hair day and wanted to vent." He grinned. "That's big in Hollywood, ain't it, Paulie? Venting?"

Tong frowned. "How about I borrow the chief's baton and do a little creative venting on your hard head, McVey?"

McVey sent Brody a pleading look. "See what I gotta put up with for eight hours, five days a week?"

Brody grinned. "I have to agree with Tong on this one, Detective. Check it out."

McVey groaned with great feeling, and Tong shot Brody a triumphant look. Congratulating himself for putting together a damn good combination in those two, he turned back to the living room to find the doc pouring himself another hefty drink at the wet bar while Mark stood nearby with a soda in his hand. As soon as he had Brody's attention, the boy came to attention.

"Problem?" Brody asked, lifting one brow.

"No sir, I mean, yes sir." His gaze shot away, then came back slowly. "About me and Kelly. I know you had to punish her and all, but it really wasn't her fault. It was mine. I messed up."

Brody felt a tug of admiration. Admitting a mistake was never easy. For him it had been doubly difficult. The few times he'd been called on the carpet had turned into an agony of humiliation that he'd never forgotten. For that reason he tried never to screw up.

"Yeah, you messed up, but you weren't the only one. Kel knew the rule about accepting rides."

"Yeah, but, see, it was 'cause of me she missed the bus," Mark said earnestly.

Brody figured he was being worked, but Mark was good enough to make him want to play it through, just to check out the kid's moves. "How do you figure?"

The boy's eyes lit from within for the barest instant, like a Vegas hustler angling for a sucker. "I got this problem with an English paper I got to write, and I was trying to talk Kelly into saving my a—my butt." Mark's grin flashed, revealing twin dimples and even, white teeth that had probably cost his parents a bundle in orthodontia. "Like, you know, she's a whiz at grammar and sh—stuff like that."

Brody had been good at English, too, although his grades had indicated the opposite. He still loved the written word in all its forms—especially poetry, although not even his aunt knew that about him. The books he checked out of the library were mostly nonfiction and mysteries. The poetry books he bought in Wenatchee, where no one knew him. "I admire you for admitting that, Mark, but it doesn't change anything."

"Right, sure. But, I was thinking—" He stopped, looked down at his Coke, hunched his shoulders, then straightened them as though determined to face his punishment like a man. "Is there, like, any way Kelly could get off restriction tonight? Just for a little while."

"Why tonight?"

The teenager brightened. "I thought me and her could go out for pizza."

Brody wondered if all fathers of teenage daughters went cold inside at the thought of letting go, then decided he didn't give a shit what anyone else did. He'd lost half his family because he'd let a smooth-talking con-artist play on his sympathies. He didn't intend to risk losing his daughter, too, just so he could be a hero for a few hours. "Kelly's not allowed to date."

"Actually, it's not a date, sir. I mean, she's already planning to do research in the library tonight, and I figured it wouldn't hurt me to get in more book time. Like study hall, you know? Only it'll just be me and her. And she has to eat, right?"

The kid was a good negotiator, Brody would grant him that. And he liked the way Mark tried to take the heat for Kelly. From the corner of his eye Brody saw Grey turn and grin. Vouching for his grandson, Brody realized.

"I'll think about it," he conceded grudgingly. Trying to do the right thing by his daughter was the toughest job he'd ever tackled.

"Yeah, but—"

"Take my advice and don't push it," Grey said as he ambled closer, drink in hand. "Chief Hollister has been known to dig in when he's being backed into a corner."

Indecision crossed the boy's face before he shrugged and flashed an expensive grin. "It's cool."

Brody glanced around, saw that there was nothing more for him to handle. "Sorry about all this, Grey," he said as the doctor, too, surveyed the signs of violation. "Can't promise we'll get the guy that did it, but McVey and Tong are the best we have."

Grey nodded. "I appreciate your stopping by, Brody. I know this is a busy time."

Brody moved his shoulders. "It's . . . cool," he said, glancing Mark's way. The teenager looked befuddled, then grinned.

"Okay if I grab a shower now, Granddad?"

Grey looked at Brody. "Do you need him for anything else?"

"Check with the detectives," Brody said. "Tong should be ready for those prints."

"Yes sir." Mark surprised him by extending his hand.

Brody liked the kid's manners and the firm strength in his handshake. "Take it easy, Mark."

"You, too."

The kid was okay, he decided as he watched Mark edge carefully into the study. A nice, clean-cut young man. Maybe it wouldn't hurt to cut Kelly and Mark some slack. But just pizza, he reminded himself as he straightened his shoulders. As long as they walked to Mario's.

"It's hell being a dad, isn't it?" Grey said, his eyes sad in spite of his smile.

"I figure I'll be lucky to get out alive."

Grey laughed. "You're doing fine, Brody. Kelly's a special young lady."

Brody felt emotion move through him. "A lot of the credit goes to Aunt Dottie. She's been the only m-mother Kel's ever known."

Nodding, Grey dropped his gaze to his glass. "I ran into her at lunch last week. She appears . . . well."

"Seems to be, yeah," he said, moving toward the back patio. Always the perfect host, Grey walked with him.

"I met your houseguest this afternoon," he said as they both slipped under the yellow tape. "Nice lady. Very impressive credentials, too. I have high hopes for that Phoenix House of hers. It sounds as though she's come up with an effective combination of treatment methods. I especially like the idea of an obstacle course and Outward Bound training. I made a tentative agreement to act as consulting physician."

At the gate, Brody paused to ask tightly, "Consulting on what?"

"Detox procedures, mostly, though I'll have to do my homework on the new designer drugs before she gets the place up and running." Grey frowned. "I expect there'll be a few protests from the more narrow-minded of our citizens when the word gets out that there's a drug rehab facility only fifteen minutes from town, but it'll help the cause a lot, knowing you and Dorothea are supporting it."

Brody had taken a knee to the groin once when he'd been working waterfront dives as an SP officer. He'd felt the numb iciness of shock first, before the pain had taken him to his knees. This was worse. It was all he could do to force air in and out of his lungs. Somehow, though, he managed to nod to Grey, jerk open the gate, and walk out.

Summer carefully lifted the leathery leaves of the pretty blue primrose out of the way and pressed her fingers into the cool, crumbly soil until it was nice and firm. Overhead, the breeze sang through the budding branches, and the low-riding sun cast elongated shadows over the lawn. Littered around her on the porch floor were two-dozen black-plastic plant containers, now empty. Pony packs, Lucy had called them. Little bassinets for newborn baby plants.

After wiping a hand across her sweaty brow, she let out a pleased sigh and sat back on her heels to survey the result of a good hour's hard work. Twenty-four bedding plants were now firmly settled in their new home. Healthy-looking primroses and pansies in a rainbow array packed into the biggest Mexican clay pot Lucy had had in her shop. As a thank-you gift, it seemed woefully inadequate, but Lucy had assured her that Dottie would love it.

"Such sweet, darling babies, you're all going to grow big and strong and beautiful," Summer crooned as she reached for the watering can.

Humming tunelessly, she headed for the spigot on the side of the house. She'd just finished filling the sprinkling can when the sound of an approaching car drew her attention. Expecting Dottie, she was surprised to see the Blazer pull in next to the Neon. Her heart speeded as she put down the can and brushed the worst of the planting mix from her hands.

For the first time in her stay Brody was home early. Had he been as eager to see her as she'd been to see him? she wondered as she watched him climb out and head her way, his long strides eating up the distance. Bareheaded and in shirtsleeves in spite of the definite chill in the air, he seemed oblivious to the mountain wind that whipped at his clothes and tossed his hair. Just the sight of him had her going soft and eager inside.

Somehow he'd bulled his way through the solid wall of defenses no other man since Kyle had ever scratched. She hadn't felt so vulnerable since she'd walked out of prison virtually penniless and without a single friend, to face the rest of her life. The fear she'd felt then was nothing compared to the terror she felt at opening herself up to this man, however. And yet, she couldn't seem to stop herself. Her feelings for him were so fragile, like those tender blossoms. But Brody wouldn't hurt her, she reminded herself as he approached.

She was expecting a hug, hoping for a kiss, but he stopped before he reached her, his shadow a long dark sword on the ground. Lord, but the man was bashful. Tenderness washed over her.

She started to smile, then froze. Something was terribly wrong. It wasn't shyness she was seeing, but fury. The last of the sunlight glinted off his badge, and she was acutely conscious of the gun on his hip and the big brutal hands fisted at his sides. This was the lethal, steely-eyed cop she'd known lived behind the shy smile and the poet's eyes. The man who could kill. Fear shot through her, and she took a stumbling step backward before she caught herself.

"What is it?" she managed to get out calmly.

"Phoenix-fucking-House, that's what, Doctor." The words came at her like bullets, with no hint of his characteristic hesitation. He wasn't wearing his dark glasses, and his beautiful eyes were nearly black.

She felt nausea explode in her throat. Her chest felt squeezed. "How—"

"Doc Krebs."

"I see." She inhaled slowly, drawing in the scent of fertilizer and damp earth. "I was going to tell you tomorrow night at dinner."

He nodded. "And my aunt? When were you going to clue *her* in on your real plans for her property?"

Summer hesitated, then decided Dottie had hoisted herself on her own petard. "She knows. She's always known. But make no mistake, it was my decision not to tell you. If you need to blame someone, blame me."

He looked staggered, but recovered quickly. "Is my daughter in on this, too?"

"No, of course not. And stop talking like it's some kind of conspiracy against you, because it isn't. Dottie told me how you feel about addicts and why. Neither of us wanted to upset you until we knew how things would work out."

"Upset me." His expression turned coldly mocking. "Yeah, guess it could be upsetting for a man whose wife was butchered by a junkie fresh out of *treatment*."

She felt a surge of compassion. "I give you my word I won't admit anyone to Phoenix House who has a prison record. It's not that kind of facility. The idea is to reach them before they get into the system."

He lashed her with a disbelieving look. "Williams didn't have a record either. Had the whole courtroom damn near in tears by the time he finished pleading for mercy. Did his six weeks in a hospital room with color TV and gourmet food. He wasn't on the street more than a week before he went looking for revenge. Only I-I wasn't there and—" He turned away, his chest heaving, to stare at the mountains. His back was straight, those strong shoulders braced. She raised a hand to touch him, then let it drop. He would only shake her off.

"I'm so sorry," she whispered.

"Yeah, everyone's always sorry. The prosecutor, the judge, even the lady shrink who'd convinced the judge the lying bastard was a prime candidate for rehab." When he turned around to face her again, a terrible weariness seemed etched into the stark lines of his face. "Call it off, Summer," he urged in a rough tone. "Don't waste your time trying to save a bunch of frigging junkies who're just conning you for a free ride."

"Please don't use that word. I hate that word."

"What would you prefer? Scumbags?"

Summer flinched only in her mind. Words could only hurt if given the power. "I'm not saying drug abuse isn't evil. Or that there aren't evil people who deserve to be punished, because there are! Calvin Williams is one of them. I hope they never let him out of prison. All I'm saying is that addiction is a disease. A terrible, insidious, seductive disease that destroys lives and ravages families. And like all diseases, it needs to be treated."

"Don't give me that crap about druggies being the same as diabetics. I've heard it before. It was a stupid analogy then and it ain't changed."

"Okay, alcoholics, then. We don't lock *them* up simply because they drink. If we did, darn near all the boardrooms and office buildings and country clubs in this country would be half-empty. According to the statistics, there's even a high incidence of alcoholism among cops."

She saw that register and linger. "Booze is legal."

Summer repressed an urge to shake him. He didn't want to listen. All he wanted to do was attack. Because she understood that anger was his way of dealing with the pain of his wife's death, she kept her own on a tight leash. "It's also a drug, though, heaven knows, no one wants to admit it."

"Last time I checked, bartenders weren't shooting each other in the streets."

"No, but bootleggers were massacring each other right and left during prohibition. Just like the rival cartels today."

"There wouldn't be cartels if sob sisters like you would give us the money and the authority to blast them out of business instead of using it to coddle criminals."

"Some of my patients are younger than Kelly," she said quietly. "One little boy was only nine. His father turned him on to pot because he wanted company getting high. Should I throw him in with hardened cons, too?"

His gaze flickered, then tightened. "What about that bastard, Finley, who wiped out half a little boy's family on Sunday? Don't tell me Finley's some helpless victim, because lady, I don't buy it. Nobody tied him up and forced him to inhale that shit."

"Did you ever stop to think that if someone had gotten to him last week or the week before and put him in a treatment center, Mr. Oates and the baby would still be alive?"

"Bullshit. Half the people in those centers are still using."

"Not in the one where I work now, and not in the one I intend to run."

"Oh yeah, how are you going to manage that, Dr. Laurence?" he challenged, each syllable bit off and jagged.

"It's not all that hard to know when someone is using, Chief Hollister. All you need is a little training and experience."

"Lady, the kind of experience I've had you don't want." His eyes flashed hot, but buried in the fury was a stark pain that tore at her. He wasn't the only one who'd suffered a terrible loss, she reminded herself as she forced air into her suddenly starved lungs.

"In my opinion, you should be going after the pusher, not their victims. Yeah, okay, maybe your prejudice is understandable, but it's still prejudice."

"I hate to break that p-pretty pink balloon of yours, Doctor, but victims kill each other the same as pushers. Only they do it for a nickel bag instead of a boatload."

"But don't you see, that's what I'm trying to prevent!"

"By coddling their little asses?" He shifted his big, dangerous body impatiently. "It's time you climbed down off that pedestal of idealistic crap you piled up and get a dose of the real world."

"I live in the real world," she told him with a growing sense of the inevitable. "I have for a long time."

"W-wrong! The real world isn't s-s-some clean office with nice c-cushy chairs and a box of Kleenex handy to catch the crocodile t-tears." Despite the stammer he couldn't quite master, his words were hard and cold. There was a terrible fury, an even more terrible pain. It hurt her to listen, but she did because she cared. "It's kids getting wh-whacked in a crossfire and babies born screaming from the heebie-jeebies and . . . and a woman drowning in her own b-blood because her only crime was being married to a cop."

She wanted to cry. She wanted to heal him. Most of all she wanted to love this strong, solitary man who hurt so terribly. Though their time together was short, she'd seen so much in him to admire. His courage, his resilience. His decency. The last thing she wanted to do was hurt him.

Her own courage shaky, she took a quick breath and forced out the words she had to say. "The real world is also me, Brody. I'm an addict, although I'm not using. A junkie. One of those worthless scumbags you want to lock up for good. Except that they let me out on parole."

He flinched, and his deep tan went white. "You were in prison?"

She nodded. She'd told her story countless times. In Narcotics Anonymous meetings and support groups. Even to charitable organizations in order to stir up support. She'd taken her share of hits, and even cried a few tears over the most cutting remarks. But because she might just love him, Brody had the power to really wound. "I served thirty months of a five-year sentence for possession and . . ." Something snagged in her throat, forcing her to stop and clear it. "And conspiracy to sell."

Revulsion exploded in his eyes. "Jesus! You were a goddamned p-pusher?"

It hurt. It hurt so much she could scarcely breathe. "I was innocent. Framed by a man I thought I loved." She drew a breath. "I was also only seventeen years old, tossed into a women's prison with hardened criminals. When I say it was hell, I'm understating."

He stared at her, his gaze narrowed before he turned his back to her. Standing motionless, every line of his body rejecting her, he stared up at the sky, one big hand resting on the butt of his weapon. As symbolism it was perfect, she decided. While they'd been talking, the sun had disappeared into a thick gray cloud bank coming from the west, and the air seemed colder now. Even the flowers had lost some of their gaiety.

"If it's any consolation, I've paid for my mistakes every day since," she said to that broad, stiff barrier he'd put between them.

Instead of answering he stood frozen, staring at the angry thunderheads forming over the peaks slicing at the sky. "But I guess that's not enough, is it?" she asked quietly, willing him to turn around and open his arms. To accept her imperfections the same way she'd accepted his.

"Why didn't you tell me this before I . . ." he broke off, his shoulders rigid.

"I hoped that once you got to know me it wouldn't matter."

He said nothing. The small hope that had kindled inside her went out. "I think perhaps you understand now why I wasn't eager to lay out my entire past for you the moment I met you."

Sick inside, where no one could see, she walked to the porch steps and bent to gather the little plant containers together, one inside the other. When she stood again, he had turned to face her. His expression was remote, his eyes narrowed. "I can't control my aunt, though God knows someone should, but I can damn well keep you away from my daughter. If you won't leave, she will."

She thought she'd never be hurt more than she'd been hurt in that courtroom. But this was worse. Much, much worse. "I'll leave tonight."

A muscle jerked in his jaw. "Storm's coming up. Wait till morning."

It was her turn to offer a cynical smile. "You almost had me groveling," she said, her hands tight around the containers. "I admit it. I spent most of this week feeling miserable because I was keeping a secret from you. But now I realize I lost all that sleep for nothing."

He didn't say anything, just watched her.

"It must be nice to be perfect," she said in a conversational tone that hid the sick hurt and anger she felt. "To know you've never made a mistake, or done something you've regretted. How nice never to wake up nights sweating because you're afraid you might slip and make those same mistakes again. I really envy you, never lying awake night after night, praying that someone will give you another chance to make things right."

His eyes went blank, and then something harsh surfaced. "This isn't about me, damn it."

"I think it is. For a man who professes to hate his father for his bigoted cruelty, Brody, you've done a very good job of becoming just like him."

CHAPTER 13

Brody stood completely still, his boots rooted to the ground and his hands hanging at his sides as he watched her disappear behind the house. He couldn't make himself move. He'd used his rage before as a weapon, but always on someone who deserved it. He'd prided himself on never losing control, never shooting from the hip—until now.

Damn, she'd looked stricken, her eyes frozen in her white face—right before she jerked up her chin and walked away. Slowly he dropped his gaze to the big clay pot where the flowers huddled together liked scared little children, holding on to one another to keep the bad guys away. Slowly he reached out a hand to touch one of the blossoms. It felt cool and delicate. And as fragile as trust.

Half his life had been spent proving his old man wrong. That he wasn't stupid or weak or a crybaby. Now he realized the mean son of a bitch had been right all along. He *was* stupid. Worse, he was a blind fool. Dumb ass that he was, he'd been had big time. Sucker punched and damn near down for the count before he'd even known what hit him. And his darling, eccentric aunt—the one person in his life besides Meggie he'd trusted not to hurt him—had been a willing participant.

The hurt staggered him. Once, when he'd been a snot-nosed kid who prayed every night to be normal so his parents would love him, he would have slunk off to the tool shed to bawl his eyes out. Now he intended to fight back the same way he'd been attacked, no holds barred.

224

Slowly he curled his hand into a fist and thought about smashing it into the four-by-four holding up the porch roof. At the same time he heard his aunt's car barreling down the driveway. She tooted when she spied him by the porch. Kelly was with her.

Jaw tight, he squared his shoulders and walked toward the carport.

"Well, hello dear, how lovely to see you home so early," Aunt Dottie trilled as she emerged from the car in a flurry of chartreuse and lavender.

Kelly came around the back of the car, a stack of books in her arms. "Don't look so cross, Dad. I went straight to the library after school and I was there the whole time. You can ask Aunt Dottie if you don't believe me."

"I believe you."

A puzzled look came over Kelly's face. "Then why are you looking at me like you're really, really mad about something."

"N-not at you, b-baby. M-myself."

"Brody, what's wrong?" his aunt asked with a little catch of worry in her voice. "You look . . . pale."

He nearly laughed in her face. Dumb-fuck Brody Hollister who'd only told one lie in his life had been suckered in good on this one. Played for a fool by two females no bigger than the spruce sapling he'd planted at Easter.

"I owe you a lot, Auntie," he said in the respectful tone he'd always reserved for her. "Which is why I'm going to do my damnedest to forgive you."

She offered him one of her impatient looks. "Brody, I wish you'd get over this nonsense about my matchmaking." She tossed her head, making her earrings dangle wildly. "Truly, dearest, I've forgotten all about it."

Pain was beginning to bleed through his control. "Like you forgot to tell me about Phoenix House?"

His words came out with a bitter edge. Her eyes widened in alarm before she shot a fast glance at the house. "Is Summer all right?"

"How the hell do I know? Go ask her if you're so concerned."

* * *

The last time Brody had been in Sarge's Place all hell had just broken loose. The three troublemakers he and Fitzpatrick had hauled off to the slammer last Sunday had done a job on the main barroom, smashing furniture and breaking glasses—as well as a few heads. Tonight was relatively calm, however. Seated alone at the end of the bar with his boot heels hooked over the dented brass foot rail and his Stetson shoved to the back of his head, Brody slammed down his second double shot of Kentucky bourbon and signaled the bartender for a refill.

Nodding, the barkeep reached for the bottle. On the far side of fifty, the man was around Brody's height, with grizzled orange hair and the ruddy, wind-scoured complexion of a logger. Like a football lineman long past his prime, his muscles had gone to fat. Habit had Brody searching his memory for the guy's name, but he came up blank. When the brawl had started on Sunday, Sarge himself had been behind the bar, serving up shooters and brews with his usual biting sarcasm as a chaser.

"Ain't seen you around here before, cowboy," the man commented as he poured out a double shot into the glass Brody had just emptied. "You workin' one of the crews over on Lemon Ridge?"

"Nope." Brody rarely drank, but when he did, he preferred Scotch. Tonight, however, he was drinking Wild Turkey in honor of his loving and loyal aunt. This one's for you, Auntie, he saluted, with a bitter smile for the ugly son of a bitch with a too-familiar face glaring back at him from the mirror behind the bar. The one-hundred-one proof poison damn near burned through his gullet before it hit bottom. Just his luck the knot in his gut was still untouched. Scowling, he tapped the glass with two fingers, and the barkeep obliged.

"Ever work with Stanhope's crew outta Vancouver?"

"Nope." The lethal bourbon went down easier this time, sloshing into his belly with a welcome bite.

"Thing is, I got me this feeling I know you," the barman persisted as he poured again. "Been eatin' at me since I seen you come in."

Brody kept his gaze fixed on his drink. A heavy fatigue layered his mind as well as his body, and he was in no mood to put out the effort even minimal conversation required. From the corner of his eye he caught the bartender's shrug, then the sound of a booze-soaked voice from the center of the bar calling for a refill.

"Fuckin' bikers," the barkeep muttered as he left to draw more drafts for the four middle-aged road toughs in black leather and chains who'd come in a few minutes after Brody. He'd sized them up as a fight waiting to happen, pegged the beefy guy with the greasy ponytail and the dirtiest Harley shirt as the most likely to throw the first punch, and filed away the fact that the man was left-handed.

Eyes narrowed against the sting of the smoke, Brody withdrew into himself and stared at his drink. One clean glass to a customer was the rule at Sarge's Place. No fancy napkins ever graced the scarred bar, and the beer was U.S. made, served on draft or in cans. Bottlenecks were too easy to smash when a man needed an edge. His kind of place, he decided, swirling the bourbon enough to catch the light. Not a frigging cuckoo clock in sight, and the selection on the jukebox was low-down shit-kickin' country all the way. Nothing like the prettied up beer gardens across town, where the tourists sipped microbrews from chilled pilsners and munched on party mix while comparing stock tips. Summer's kind of ambience.

Shit. He'd promised himself he wasn't going to think about her. The hurt was too raw. The slice she'd taken out of him was still bleeding. Christ, he'd fallen hard. Brought her frigging roses.

At first, he'd been afraid to touch her. Afraid he'd forgotten how to gentle the brutal strength he knew he carried in his big Hollister hands, but he hadn't been able to keep from reaching out. He could still hear the little sound she'd made in her throat right before he'd kissed her the first time. A sweet, urgent needy sound that he'd taken into his mouth and savored. A sound that filled some of the emptiness in his life.

He'd come home with Doc's words still twisting in his brain to find her with a smudge of dirt on her chin and her cheeks pink from the wind. God help him, she'd looked like every man's dream. Sexy and innocent at the same time. Emotion coiled and seethed inside him as he remembered the way her eyes had lit up at the sight of him. A man could handle a lot of ugliness in his day if he had a smile like that waiting for him when he got home.

He muttered a savage curse under his breath before tossing back the whiskey. How many was that now? he wondered idly. Two, three? A half-dozen. Whatever the number, it wasn't enough. Not nearly enough. Along with his size and the frigging purple eyes he hated, he'd inherited his old man's head for booze.

From the corner of his eye he saw the bartender glance his way. He lifted two fingers from the glass, and the man nodded. At the same time he saw ex–Marine Staff Sergeant Gunnar Stenner, the Sarge of Sarge's Place, emerge from the private room in the rear. Cocky as hell, he swaggered toward the bar, fielding rude remarks and tossing back a few of his own. Even as a kid Gunnar had been quick with words, especially when they were directed against someone smaller and weaker.

"Hey, Sarge, how 'bout some service over here for a friggin' change?" someone called through the blue haze.

"Tie a knot in it, and shove it up your ass, Whacker," Sarge shot back to the accompaniment of catcalls and ripe insults.

A female voice called out a suggestive comment, and Sarge blew her a kiss. One of the bikers bellied up to the bar, nudging the bleary-eyed brute next to him. "Check out the chick with the boobs in the corner. Ain't had a mouthful of so much sweetness since my old lady split."

"Blow me another one, Jocko, your old lady had tits like walnuts."

It occurred to Brody that it had been a long time since he'd been in at the start of the brawl instead of the finish. Since he'd been a seaman apprentice, he decided, thinking back. He'd ended up in the brig with a half-dozen stitches in the back of his head and his ears ringing from the blow he'd taken from a shore patrolman's baton. It was that indignity that had made him decide to be the guy holding the baton instead.

But sometimes a man just naturally had to blow off steam. With his fists, if there wasn't any other way, especially if the bastard on the other end of a quick left jab deserved a clip on the jaw. His spirits perked up a notch. He was off duty, wasn't he? And even the chief was entitled to have himself a good time. Hell, maybe that was why he'd decided to do his drinking at Sarge's instead of Mulrooney's, where cops and firefighters usually hung out at the end of their shifts.

"You gents over from Seattle?" Sarge asked, positioning himself directly behind the biggest of the bikers.

"Nah. Wenatchee," the cleanest of the group volunteered before letting out a belch. "Jocko here's got him a sister in these parts."

"Yeah, what's her name? Maybe I know her?"

Jocko reeled a little as he leaned back to squint into Sarge's face. "Arlene Rasmussen. Barmaid at a place called The Brewery."

Sarge pursed his thin lips thoughtfully. "Can't say I've had the pleasure," he said with what sounded like genuine regret.

"We woulda done our drinking there, only the place don't serve booze. Just that local microcrap."

"Well, you're welcome to drink your fill here, gents," Sarge offered with a chuckle. "Ask anyone, he'll tell you Sarge serves a full measure for a fair price." He slapped Jocko on the back and nodded at the others who were already turning back to their drinks. Brody felt a pang of disappointment when old Jocko did the same. Well, hell.

Trouble averted, Sarge slipped behind the bar to draw himself a cold one. The glass was halfway to his mouth when he caught sight of Brody. A muscle jumped in his heavy jaw as he walked to the end of the bar. His expression hooded, he dragged out a stool and settled his flat ass onto the padded seat.

Brody noted they were equal in height now, if not in weight. He figured Sarge had a good thirty pounds on him and a longer reach.

"You got some reason to be here I don't know about, Hollister?" Sarge asked after allowing himself a long drink of brew.

"Can't think of a one."

Eyes narrowed, Sarge took another sip, then set the beer on the bar and wiped his mouth with his sleeve. "Not that I mind taking your money, but if you're looking to bust me for something, you're wasting your time. Ain't nobody here under twenty-one, and everyone's drinking real peaceful-like."

Brody let his gaze wander around the room for a beat longer than necessary. "Gives a man a real good feeling, knowing he can drink in peace."

"You're telling me you're not on duty?"

Brody looked down at the flannel shirt he'd pulled out of his locker at the station when he'd decided that going home with his gut still tied in knots would be a bad mistake. "You see a badge pinned to this shirt?"

"You might be undercover. Pulling some kind of raid."

Brody allowed himself a tight smile. "According to you there's nothing going on here that would make it worth the effort." He took his time lifting the shot glass to his mouth. He sipped this time, his gaze locked on Sarge's. "No poker game going on in the backroom, for example."

"Last I heard, playing poker for money's illegal in this county."

Brody admired the bastard's cool. Only a flicker of an eyelid showed Brody he'd guessed right. "Last I heard, too." Brody glanced around, skimming faces, and shrugged. "Doesn't seem fair, though. Man works hard for his money and wants to relax, play a few hands with a few friends. He ought to have a place where he can go."

Sarge shifted. To the casual observer he appeared relaxed. "How much do you want?"

Brody lifted one eyebrow. "You offering me a bribe, Gunnar?"

"Call it a token of friendship from one old friend to another."

Brody finished his drink and flicked a glance at the bartender who was already bringing the bottle. He waited until his glass was filled and the barkeep had returned to the cash register to mark his tab before saying softly, "We were never friends."

An angry gleam came into Sarge's muddy brown eyes. "Is that what this is about, Hollister? Some kind of scam to pay me back for all the times I beat the shit out of you when we were kids?"

Enjoying himself, Brody let the moment play out. It was easier to keep the stuttering under control when he was half-drunk. He'd damn near become an alcoholic in his early twenties before he'd figured out he was only trading one problem for another. "Busting you for illegal gambling on the premises would be payback. Having a drink is having a drink."

"All right, I get the point. How much is it going to cost me?"

Brody toyed with his drink before taking a sip. "One apology. Now. Nice and public."

Sarge's face turned red. "Fuck you."

Brody sighed. "Now that just upped the ante, Gunnar." He nodded toward the center of the bar, where Jocko was shooting dice with the bartender for the next round. "I'd like you to stand on the bar when you tell me you're sorry. Right in front of old Jocko there."

"Eat shit, Hollister. The only thing you're getting from me is a fist in that stuttering mouth of yours."

"Well, hell, S-S-Sarge," he taunted, relaxing his control. "That s-s-sure s-s-sounds s-scary to me."

Sarge narrowed his gaze until his eyes were brown gashes in the gouged landscape of his face. "You'd like me to throw the first punch, wouldn't you, Hollister. Make it real easy for you to toss my ass in jail for assault."

Brody felt a jolt of adrenaline. The old hatred of Gunnar ran strong and clean and deep. Simple emotions for a simple man. Nothing that tore at him in ways he hadn't anticipated and so hadn't thought to protect.

"No badge, no jail. Just you and me, outside, without witnesses. Loser pays my tab and buys a round for the house."

Sarge curled his lips into a feral smile. "You're on. But don't say I didn't warn you."

CHAPTER 14

Of course it was raining, Dottie thought philosophically as she walked downstairs a few minutes before seven. It always rained at pivotal moments of one's life. Hadn't it been pouring buckets when the train had pulled out of Wenatchee on her wedding day? In fact, as she recalled, the clouds had started gathering overhead as soon as she'd opened her eyes and made her final decision to leave Grey at the altar. But, she reminded herself firmly, even the hardest rain cleared the air of all kinds of nasty little poisons, and the sun invariably came out again. The trick was to keep from drowning until it did.

The house was deathly still. The slapping of her mule heels on the risers and the steady drumming of the rain were the only signs of life. For once, the usual morning chatter of the birds was silent, as though they were sleeping in.

Kelly and Summer were still asleep. Brody's door had been open when she passed it on her way to the bathroom, his quilt jerked over the tumbled covers as though he'd been too rushed to make his bed in that neat military way of his. He hadn't been home when she'd gone to bed, and she'd been asleep when he'd come in. Though she hadn't heard the Blazer, she imagined he'd already left for town. Osuma PD invariably geared up early on weekends.

She herself had been awake since dawn, plotting strategy. Summer and Brody belonged together, and that was that. The trick was making them realize it. Unfortunately, she seemed devoid of clever ideas to make that happen. Still, she was a patient woman. Something would come to her. Even if she had a plan, however, Summer was too bruised at the moment for any kind of gentle nudging to be effective. Though she'd hidden it well, Brody's bullheaded reaction had hurt her deeply. Though regrettable, Dottie considered that a good sign. Only those we care about have the power to inflict more than momentary pain.

Yawning, her movements still sluggish, she traipsed into the living room to open the drapes. The day was awash in gloom. Gray skies, gray rain, even the normal vibrancy of the newly sprouted grass seemed dulled.

As she suspected, Brody was already gone. And had been for some time, she realized when she noted that the gravel in the spot where the Blazer would have been parked was rain-soaked and soggy. He'd made coffee, however, because she'd caught a whiff of it coming down the stairs. A man of burned-in habits and steely convictions, that was her nephew, she grumbled silently as she made her way to the kitchen. With a protective shell around his heart as tough as aged hickory, more's the pity.

Thinking only of coffee, she was already across the threshold when she realized she'd been wrong. He hadn't left, though he was fully dressed, with that awful gun strapped to his hip. The rest of his uniform—the Stetson that gave him such a dangerous look and the old leather jacket he refused to replace on pain of death—were on the counter, along with his oversized thermos. Hands braced on the counter, he was standing with his back to her, looking out at the rain. His back was rigid, his shoulders stiff.

"I thought you'd already left," she said coolly by way of greeting.

He remained silent and brooding. So that's the way it was going to be, she thought, reaching for a mug.

"Where's the Blazer?" she asked, reaching for the pot.

"In town." His voice sounded clipped and a little hoarse.

She poured, inhaling the delicious aroma. Zimbabwe dark, she guessed. It was a new blend she'd bought on a whim. It had a dense, biting taste, with the caffeine kick of a particularly ill-tempered jackass. A perfect choice for this morning, she decided, though she suspected Brody had simply reached into the cupboard and picked one of the half-dozen bags at random. To him, coffee was coffee, served scalding hot and thick enough to chew.

"Did you have engine trouble?" she asked.

"I was too drunk to drive. Hingle brought me home." He turned to face her. At the sight of his battered and swollen face, an icy shock jolted through her.

"Oh my goodness! You poor baby." She put down her cup and hurried toward him. She reached out to touch his bruised jaw, and he jerked away.

"Don't fuss," he muttered, a dark flush racing over his battered features.

"Where did it happen?" she demanded, studying the truly awesome shiner he sported around one eye.

"Sarge's." He shot an impatient look at the wall clock, then scowled.

Dottie narrowed her gaze before running it carefully over his body. When she caught sight of the bruised knuckles on his right hand, she winced. "Who else was involved?"

A muscle worked beneath the discolored skin of his jaw. "Sarge."

"You were in a fight with Sarge Stenner?"

"Isn't that what I just s-said?"

"The same Sarge Stenner whose given name is Gunnar?"

"Give it a rest, Auntie. You know who Sarge is."

Ah yes, she thought. Hollister men invariably turned to violence to relieve their pain. When Big Malcolm had lost Mama he'd gone looking for the biggest, meanest bullwhacker he could find and picked a fight. Ray had done the same every time Odessa had delivered a stillborn child—except when he'd been laid up with one of his frequent injuries. Then he'd taken out his hurt on his son.

"Was this brawl in the line of duty?" she inquired innocently while taking stock of the bruised jaw, gashed eyebrow, and cut lip.

Something flashed in his eyes. Chagrin, she decided, with a hefty element of disgusting male satisfaction. "No."

"Ah." Satisfied that he wasn't seriously hurt, she retrieved her coffee and sipped. "Who won?"

"That's under dispute." He shifted, then winced and flattened his hand against his side.

"Cracked a rib, did he?"

His scowl was truly a sight to behold. "No more questions. I'm not in the mood."

"Fine. If you don't want to talk, you can listen." She slammed her mug down on the counter and squared her shoulders. "I never thought I'd say this to you, Brody Hollister, but I'm ashamed of you."

His shoulders jerked, and the dusky flush that had started to recede deepened. "It was just a bar fight," he muttered. "No one else was there but Sarge and Hingle, though God knows Slate will rag me about it enough for a damned crowd."

"That's not what I'm talking about. You insulted and abused a dear friend, and I wouldn't blame her if she never spoke to you again. Personally, I think she should have kneed you in the groin, but she's too much of a lady."

His face tightened, stretching bruised flesh. "Lady, hell. She . . . she's a convicted felon. And she's trying to bring filth into this town. But then you know that because you're dead set on helping her."

"I certainly am! In fact, I'm proud to be a small part of Phoenix House."

His mouth flattened. "You're lucky I didn't cram her little ass in the Neon and shove you in behind."

Dottie felt her ire rising. "That's enough, Brody Hollister! More than enough. You're behaving like a jerk."

Anger exploded in his eyes, and his chest heaved with the force of his indrawn breath. "Back off, Auntie."

"No, you back off. You're wrong about Summer. About as wrong as you can be."

His gaze pinned her hard. "How do you know what I think of her?"

"Did you or did you not order her to leave?"

"Hell yes! The woman's a junkie. I don't want her anywhere near the people I . . . near you and Kelly."

She advanced on him, fury making her small body vibrate. "She's a former junkie, and don't ever use that word in my presence again!" she declared, jabbing her finger hard into his chest. "As to her past, everyone makes mistakes—even you. God knows, she's paid for hers."

His eyes turned icy, and Dottie knew she'd pushed him toward a dangerous line. "Careful, Auntie. I'm not real happy with you either. The two of you set me up, and then sat back and watched me take the bait."

"Aha! So that's it. Your ego is hurt."

"Bullshit."

"It's true. You're just so wrapped up in leftover hatred you can't see it."

His big hand shoved through his hair, his expression tortured. "Damn it, Auntie, this isn't about m-me. She . . . she . . . that Phoenix House of hers is nothing but a frigging breeding ground for t-t-trouble."

"It's a treatment center for lost souls, Brody. Like you were once, only you had to fight your battles alone. And heaven knows I'm proud of you. But not everyone has your strength, dear heart. Some need a helping hand to heal."

"Heal, my ass. Calvin Williams was—"

"A gang member and a criminal. Using drugs was only a fraction of his evil."

"Read the goddamned headlines for a change instead of the horoscope. Watch the nightly news. Most of the damned stories are related to drug abuse in one way or another."

"Exactly, which is why we desperately need places like Summer's to help young people before they turn to crime."

"What we need are more jails."

Dottie let out a snort. "I have a better idea. Why don't we just round up everyone who's ever experimented with drugs and shoot them." She took an angry breath. "And you might as well know, I'd be one of those lined up against that wall myself."

Shock settled into his eyes, which were now the color of glittering amethysts, and she rushed to press her advantage. "During my time in Vegas I used to smoke marijuana on a regular basis. In fact, I quite liked it."

He absorbed that like a blow, then shook it off, much as she suspected he'd shaken off one of Gunnar Stenner's powerhouse fists. "You're not going to back off on this, are you?"

"No."

"It doesn't bother you to have a bunch of addicts living next to your niece?"

"Not at all. As a matter of fact, I think it'll be good for Kelly to be around young people who are in the process of turning their lives around."

"She can't be around them if she's living someplace else." The threat came out low and silky and deadly.

Dottie felt a violent crushing sensation in her chest. "You don't mean that," she cried, her hand clutching the lapels of her old flannel robe.

A look that might have been guilt raced over his face before it was wiped away. "Ask me anything else, and it's yours. But I won't risk my d-d-daughter's s-safety. Not for you, not for anyone."

"He's right, Dottie." Summer's voice cut into the tension like a skinning blade.

Dottie spun around to see her friend standing pale but composed in the doorway, her briefcase in one hand and her laptop case over one shoulder. She was dressed for traveling, in jeans and a sweater, and her hair had been pulled back into a French braid. To Dottie's eye, she looked tired and fragile and far too young to be carrying so many burdens.

"I won't have you punished because you have a big heart and a generous soul," Summer added before setting her cases by the back door.

"My feelings have nothing to do with this. Even if they did, I refuse to give in to blackmail."

"It's not your decision to make, Dottie. It's mine, and it ends here. No more discussion. I'll find another place for Phoenix House." A determined light shone from her shadowed eyes, and her jaw was set as she took a cup from the cupboard and filled it.

"Summer, Brody doesn't mean it. He would never be that cruel." Dottie turned to look at him. "Would you?"

"Oh, I think he would," Summer said before lifting her coffee to her mouth for a sip. Her lovely face was closed, the vibrancy of her green eyes replaced by a stony wariness that tore at Dottie's heart.

"Then he'll just have to do what he thinks best, because we have a verbal contract, you and I, which according to my attorney, whom I called last night when we returned home, is as binding as anything on paper. Five years at a thousand dollars a month." Which she intended to give back as her donation to Phoenix House, though Summer didn't know that. "If you want to break it, that's fine with me. Hand over sixty thousand dollars and we're even."

Summer frowned. "Dottie, don't," she said quietly. "It's not worth it."

"Fighting for what's right is always worth it," Dottie countered, leveling a glance in Brody's direction.

His face darkened. "I can't fucking believe this. You care more about some half-assed project that's most likely nothing more than a scam to make money than you do your niece?" And me. Dottie heard the words he would never utter.

"Brody, listen to me," she implored, moving to his side. "I adore my niece and I love you dearly. The two of you are my life." Lifting a hand that trembled at the terrible risk she was taking, she touched his arm. Though his muscles went rigid beneath her fingertips, she was relieved when he didn't shake her off. "Please believe me when I tell you I would never do anything to harm either of you."

He started to speak, then bit down hard, and she realized he couldn't get out the words. Even as her heart went out to him, she felt a momentary surge of hope. Something she'd said had touched him in that fiercely protected place where he hid his tender side. Whatever feelings she'd drawn from him had his throat closing.

"Brody—"

The blare of a horn interrupted her plea. She glanced through the window to see one of the department's patrol cars outside.

"Sergeant Hingle," she said, stepping back.

He slipped into his jacket and his hat, automatically tugging it lower over his forehead. He grabbed his thermos and strode to the door. After jerking it open, he turned to level a stare in Summer's direction, then her own. "This . . . isn't over," he warned before he stepped out in the hard cold rain and slammed the storm door behind him.

"One of these days that boy is going to learn he doesn't have to do everything the hard way," Dottie muttered, tightening the belt of her robe.

Summer continued to regard her coffee for a tension-filled moment before lifting her head to look at Dottie. "I'm so sorry. This is all my fault."

"It most certainly is not." Dottie walked to the refrigerator and pulled it open. Summer watched while she took out bread and a carton of eggs, unsure where to begin.

"I hope you like French toast," Dottie said with surprising cheerfulness over the muted crunch of tires on the wet gravel outside.

"We have to talk."

"Of course, dear, but while we talk would you mind setting out the butter and the syrup? And the bacon, too, please. You'll need something substantial in your tummy for that long drive back to the city."

Summer glanced at the clock. It was barely seven. Too early to call Mr. Gooding at his office, and she hated to bother him at home so early.

"Dottie, I appreciate what you're trying to do more than I

can say, but there's no sense in your trying to change my mind, because—"

"Later, dear. I'm afraid I can't concentrate on more than one thing at a time. And right now, I'm making breakfast."

Knowing it was futile to argue, Summer braced herself with another greedy sip of the strong, bitter coffee before obeying. Side by side they worked to create breakfast while the rain spattered the window and bacon sizzled in the skillet. It tore at her to think this was the last morning she would spend in Dottie's home.

"Two places or three?" she asked, opening the place mat drawer.

Dottie looked up, then cast her gaze overhead. "Two, I think. No sense waking Kelly so early, especially since it's such a great morning to sleep in."

"Exactly my thought when I opened my eyes."

Dottie turned off the burner and forked bacon onto a paper towel. "Lucy said it was going to be a wet spring. Something about the number of caterpillars she was seeing in the greenhouse." She frowned. "Or was it ladybugs?" She heaved a noisy sigh. "I can never keep Lucy's omens straight."

Unconvinced, but grateful for the effort Dottie was making to lighten the mood, Summer glanced out at the leaden sky. "Maybe it'll clear up later. Spring showers do that sometimes."

Between sips of her second cup of coffee, Summer set out silverware and poured juice. Dottie carried the food to the table and sat down. Summer took the chair opposite and tried to ignore the hard tangle of conflicting emotions in her stomach.

"It smells wonderful," she said, helping herself to enough toast and bacon to be polite.

"It's my grandmother's recipe. She used a pinch of cinnamon and a splash of the syrup in the eggs." Dottie spread butter and poured syrup. "In the winter she would add a touch of brandy. Personally, I prefer a smidgen of bourbon."

Summer managed two bites before her stomach warned her against the third. Hoping Dottie wouldn't notice, she put down her fork and reached for her juice, then thought better of it and returned the glass to the table.

"As soon as we've finished eating, I'm calling Mr. Gooding and canceling the renovations," she said, meeting Dottie's gaze over the centerpiece.

With a small sigh, Dottie, too, put down her fork and pushed her plate away. "That's your choice, dear, but I think you should know that I meant what I said about holding you to your contract."

Summer couldn't believe her ears. "Let me get this straight," she said carefully. "You'd actually make me pay you rent even if I never step foot in that house again?"

"Without a moment's hesitation."

"Even if that meant I wouldn't be able to establish Phoenix House somewhere else?"

"I would hate that, but yes."

Summer rubbed at the spot on her temple that had begun throbbing the moment she'd walked into the kitchen and heard Dottie quarreling with Brody.

"But why?" she asked, her bewilderment plainly audible in her tone.

Dottie lifted one of her flapper-thin eyebrows. "I believe you'd call it tough love," she said with a wealth of kindness in her voice. "And you need more coffee," she added as she rose to fetch the pot.

Summer forced herself to be patient. Unfortunately, her therapist's cool always seemed to disappear around anyone named Hollister. Except for Kelly, she reminded herself hastily.

"Tough love implies the need to enforce discipline," she enunciated carefully as Dottie refilled both cups.

"I prefer to think of it as preventing a serious mistake." Dottie set the pot on her napkin before resuming her seat. "In other words, I'm trying to keep you from doing something you'll spend the rest of your life regretting."

"Which is?"

"Running away from a fight. One, I might add, that badly needs fighting."

Summer glared at her, her heart slamming in her chest in response to a sudden spurt of outrage. "I am not running away."

"That's my girl!" Dottie broke into a bright-eyed grin and reached for her juice. "Well, now that that's settled, eat your breakfast and tell me what I can do to keep things moving on this end while you wrap up your affairs in San Diego."

Summer felt as though a cotton-candy cloud had just closed in around her and gave her head a little shake to clear it. "When I said I wasn't running away, I meant that I was making a rational decision, based on well-considered facts, to cancel my plans to rent your property. There are too many negatives and too few positives."

"Too many obstacles, you mean?"

"Exactly!" she exclaimed, relieved to be on solid footing again.

"Like the wrong zoning?"

"No, the zoning's correct."

"Inadequate water supply? A septic system that's too small?"

Summer gritted her teeth. "All right, I get the point. There's only one obstacle. One very prejudiced, determined obstacle who has it in his power to hurt you. I can't allow that to happen."

"Isn't that my risk to take, Summer? Or do you think I'm incompetent as well as eccentric?"

"Of course not! I think you're anything but incompetent."

"Then please allow me to make my own decisions and deal with whatever consequences might result."

Summer opened her mouth to respond, then shut it again. Pain pounded in her head, echoing the hard drumming of the rain. "You're right," she admitted softly. Reluctantly. "I truly don't want to see you hurt, but the coward in me seized on that as a great excuse for doing what I really wanted to do—run."

"Self-honesty is a bitch, isn't it?" Dottie said with grin.

"So my patients tell me, yes."

Summer slumped back in her chair and stared at her orange juice. "You should have been a shrink, Dottie. You're a natural at spotting self-deception."

"Oh no, I'm just an old woman who ran away once herself and lived to regret it."

Curiosity moved in Summer, and she held a fast debate with herself before giving in to it. "You're referring to Dr. Krebs, aren't you?" she guessed.

Dottie nodded. "Grey wanted children, you see. At least three. I'd watched both my mother and my sister-in-law wear themselves into an early grave trying to give the men they loved sons. And I was afraid." She manufactured a smile, but it took effort. "I know now that I should have shared my fears with Grey, but 'sharing' wasn't a concept we understood in those days. I convinced myself I was being coerced into a boring marriage to a man I didn't love so that I wouldn't feel guilty, and I ran. By the time I came to my senses and came running back to tell him how much I loved him, he was married to someone else." She gave a little laugh and reached for her juice glass. "Here's to self-honesty, the good fight, and Phoenix House."

Summer sat up and reached for her own glass. "And to tough love and dear friends."

They clinked glasses and drank. As she put down her glass, Summer didn't know whether to laugh or cry. She solved the dilemma by picking up her fork and digging in.

It was nearly eight-thirty by the time she and Dottie finished eating and had stowed the luggage in the Neon's trunk. The rain had eased off to a halfhearted drizzle, which spattered the top of the umbrella Dottie was holding over their heads as they stood next to the driver's door, saying their good-byes.

"It looks lighter in the west," Summer decided, studying the sky over the peaks. "I think I see a little glimmer of sun."

"Be careful going over the passes. It's always colder at the higher altitudes and it's not uncommon to run into ice."

"I will." Summer glanced toward the house. "Tell Kelly I said good-bye, and that I'll write."

"I'll do that." Dottie smiled. "Keep me posted, okay?"

Summer nodded. "First thing tomorrow I'm going to list my

condo for sale and then break the bad news to my supervisor that I'm leaving. My contract stipulates two weeks' notice but I'll give him three. I'll need at least a week after I stop working to pack and wind things up." She drew a breath that tasted of rain and pine. "I have a trust fund from my grandmother that's supposed to come to me next January. My father's the trustee. I'm going to ask him to release it to me early."

"That seems reasonable, given it's for a good cause. I can't imagine he'd object."

"You don't know my father." She felt a stab of pain at the thought of approaching him again.

Dottie reached out to rub her palm up and down Summer's arm in silent support. Summer felt her throat constrict.

"I'll keep my eye on the house," Dottie said, glancing down the driveway in the direction of the Hollister homestead. "I'll enjoy spending time with Amos. He has a fondness for corny jokes and loves to spring them on the unwary."

Summer laughed. "He's promised to call frequently." She cleared her throat. "I don't know how to thank you."

"Your coming back is thanks enough," she said as they exchanged an awkward hug around the handle of the umbrella.

Summer turned toward the car, then changed her mind. It was simply her cursed curiosity prodding her, she assured herself as she cleared her throat and arranged her features in a look of casual interest.

"Not that I care," she said with an offhand smile, "but what happened to Brody's face?"

Dottie's lips twitched. "From what I understand, he and Gunnar Stenner had a fight. You know, the boy who used to beat him up before Brody got big enough to defend himself."

"Are you talking about a barroom brawl?"

"Knowing Brody, I'd say it was a private fight. And, I suspect, something he had to do in order to slay a few ghosts."

Summer felt a totally illogical burst of satisfaction. She hated bullies. "Maybe it's just me, but it seems fairly impolitic for the chief of police to be fighting."

Dottie chuckled. "Brody makes his own rules."

Summer's face tightened. "I've noticed."

"Don't judge him too harshly, Summer. He doesn't handle emotional trauma very well." She bit her lip, then added earnestly, "He's a fair man under all the anger. Once he calms down, he'll accept Phoenix House." Her grin was quick and rueful. "He'll also watch you like a hawk for a while, just to make sure his worst fears aren't realized."

"I don't mind public scrutiny. In fact, I'd welcome it." It was the thought of seeing Brody Hollister frequently that had her stomach all riled up again. When she'd opened her eyes that morning, the first thing she'd seen were the bright yellow roses on the desk. Even the air was perfumed with their scent. Angry and hurt as she was, she realized she still cared for the soul-scarred man with the desperate need to be loved who'd given them to her. It was the other man—the hard-eyed, implacable judge and jury she abhorred.

Summer shifted her gaze toward the town. The clouds hovered like dark gray shadows on the face of the towering mountains, cloaking the jagged peaks in a deceptive softness. But the bone-chilling snow was still there, as thick and deadly to the unwary as ever.

Shivering, she zipped her jacket closer to her neck and pulled open the door. She had a long drive and things to do. It was time she got started.

Over the years Summer had found that noise helped combat the claustrophobia she invariably felt when trapped in a car for more than a five-minute trip to the dry cleaners or a quick run to the grocery store. She preferred educational tapes and always kept a supply of new ones in her briefcase. But since the Neon wasn't equipped with a tape player, she used the radio instead, cranking the sound of country to a mind-soothing volume. She'd been singing along with vintage Patsy Cline when she suddenly realized her mirror was reflecting a flashing red light.

The desperate hope that it was a fire truck behind her was

dashed when she spied the white Blazer. A quick glance at the speedometer had her heart sinking. Unless Washington had miraculously raised the limit on state roads from fifty-five to sixty-seven miles per hour, she was in trouble. With a sense of impending doom she applied the brakes and pulled to a stop on a wide section of shoulder, the Blazer hugging her bumper all the way. It was too much to hope that the Osuma PD owned two dusty white Blazers, she thought as she turned off the ignition and riveted her gaze to the rearview mirror.

Brody climbed out slowly, checking both east and west lanes for traffic as he did. The dark scowl on his face told her he was anything but pleased. Gritting her teeth, she rolled down the window and watched him in the side mirror.

"Would you get out of the car, please?" he asked politely, even as he pulled open the door.

"Why?" she asked warily.

His jaw flexed. Twice. "Because I have a badge and a gun and I'm bigger than you," he said with that same distinctively flavored tone he'd used the first time he'd dealt with her in an official capacity.

Allowing herself to sigh heavily, she unlatched her seat belt and reached for her purse. "Leave it," he ordered.

When he'd seen her speeding, why couldn't he have just looked the other way? she asked herself with something close to emotional overload as she swung her legs out of the car and stood up. "I realize I was going a little too fast," she admitted. Anything to get this over with as quickly as possible. "It's in the nature of a bad habit I'm trying to break."

He raised one eyebrow above the rim of his glasses. It was the one bisected by a painful-looking gash. "Up here we call it s-speeding, Dr. Laurence. It's in the nature of a misdemeanor."

"Okay, you've made your point, Chief," she said with a fairly decent stab at flippancy. Cars were speeding by, polluting the wonderful mountain air with carbon monoxide and generating a chilly wind that sent little shivers over her skin. Far above the looming Cascades, twin vapor trails paralleled one another like wavy railroad tracks. "Are you going to run me in or can I send the city a check?"

"I ought to throw your cute little fanny in the county lockup for insulting a police officer who's trying to do you a favor."

"If that's a threat, it's wasted. I'm a hardened con, remember. Cages don't frighten me."

His jaw flexed. "I pulled your record. Thirty months is a long time."

"According to the prosecutor, it wasn't nearly long enough for an amoral purveyor of death." She swallowed against the sick taste of memory. "I'm paraphrasing, but that was the gist."

He shook his head. "You . . . wouldn't. It's not in you."

For an instant she was certain she'd misunderstood. Surely Brody wasn't absolving her of guilt. "You saw the record. I was convicted and punished."

"The . . . woman who . . . indulges an old lady's whims and . . . fights to protect a confused teenager is not a criminal." Though halting, his voice was steely with conviction.

She couldn't seem to catch her breath. Finally she managed to draw air into her lungs. "Thank you for that," she said in a voice she couldn't keep steady.

He lifted a hand to brush a lock of windblown hair from her cheeks. His fingertips were rough, and wonderfully gentle. "Tell me."

"Why?"

"So . . . we . . . I can p-put this behind me."

She drew a shaky breath. "You hurt me, Brody."

He nodded. "You were r-right about me. My old man is s-still in my head. I'm s-sorry."

Something told her that the admission hadn't come easy. But he'd made it. Perhaps it was a start. "I'm sorry, too."

His mouth slanted as he shifted. "Tell me," he said again.

She took a breath and braced herself. "I was fifteen when I really started using heavily. Crystal meth mostly. Uppers. I stole from my parents and they threw me out, so I came up with another scheme." Talking quietly, she went on to tell him the story of Summer Laurence's life as an almost-prostitute.

"I was sixteen when I met Kyle. He was an undercover cop, working the beach where I hung out, only I didn't know it. We smoked some dope together, and then he threatened to arrest me unless I became an informant."

Something dangerous flashed in his eyes. "You took the deal?"

Summer nodded. "We became lovers not long after that. That's when I found the courage to quit using." She heard a car approaching and waited until it passed. The wind kicked up dust, and he led her farther onto the shoulder. "The war on drugs was just getting started. His bosses were pushing hard for results in order to impress the politicians who were screaming for blood."

She paused, and Brody nodded. "Yeah, same with L.A. As soon as the dope moved out of the inner city, it was suddenly crunch time."

Another car passed, and Brody watched it speeding toward the mountains. When it disappeared around a bend, he returned his gaze to hers. Every time he was with her, he found himself wanting to wrap her in his protection and snarl at any son of a bitch who dared try to hurt her. Until yesterday, he corrected bitterly. He'd been the one attacking her then. Flat out, no holds barred, with a vicious need to draw blood. After Dottie had ripped a piece off his hide, he'd finally figured it out. It was like the stuttering. As long as he was angry, he was safe. When he was lashing out, no one could hurt him.

"He married the deputy commissioner's daughter soon after my trial," she continued, her voice calm, even casual. Nothing like the fierce tones she'd used when she'd been defending her patients—or his own daughter. "When I was in prison, I heard that he'd been given some kind of award by the mayor. My roommate had to restrain me from throwing a chair at the TV." She smiled at that, and he tried to smile back. He wasn't sure he succeeded. "Last I read, he was deputy chief of the metro division." Finished, she waited for his reaction, her green eyes as clear and steady as the spill of the river in the sunlight.

"About this place," he said, feeling his way through the dangerous minefield of emotion. "It goes against all my instincts."

"I understand, believe me I do. But I honestly believe with all my heart that Phoenix House needs to be here for some reason I don't really understand. I just know that as soon as I saw that magnificent old house, I felt a sense of rightness, as though this was truly a place of healing. I suspect you feel it, too, which is why you brought your daughter back here."

His jaw flexed. "You're wrong. My mother died in that house, t-trying to push out another premature baby. Bastard made her try five times after he discovered I wasn't good enough to carry on the Hollister name. Made her life a living hell, called her a failure and a weakling. I tried to get my aunt to s-sell it years ago, but she loves that old place."

"Maybe it just needs laughter and love," she countered softly, touching the hand he'd raised to his chest.

"Not in that cold place."

"There are no guarantees. But my staff and I will take all precautions."

Summer saw him struggle to accept that. "How? With locks? Guards?"

"No, but the patients will be restricted to the grounds unless accompanied by a staff member."

"But no fences?"

She shook her head. "I believe in the honor system. And a healthy dollop of peer pressure."

A look that questioned her sanity came over his stark features. "Peer pressure is what lures kids into trying that shit in the first place."

"Sadly, that's true. But a negative force can also be a positive one, which is the basis of my entire modality. Use the patients who want to stay clean to pressure the others who don't."

"Yeah, well, it's the ones who don't I'm worried about."

She had to resist the urge to wrap her arms around that strong body and press her lips to that wounded heart beating steadily in his magnificent chest. "What if we could arrange a compromise?" she proposed finally. "Some middle ground where we'd both be comfortable."

He shifted, his eyes narrowing. The gash over his eye made him look even more like the street-tough she'd envisioned. "I'm listening."

The first step, she thought. And for Brody, a major concession. Emotion moved in her. Pride, she realized. In him.

"I don't think a fence would be feasible, but I would agree to locks on the doors and downstairs windows. We'd keep the keys to the vehicles locked up as well and, much as I'd hate it, have regular bed checks."

He looked unconvinced. "Someone determined to leave could find a way." A bitter look crossed his face, and his jaw hardened, throwing the purple bruise into stark relief.

"The way you did?" she guessed quietly.

He ignored the question. "These aren't babies you're dealing with. An addict looking for a fix is little better than a rabid animal!" The muscle in his jaw ticked, as though he'd suddenly realized what he'd said. Because he was trying, she forgave him. She had a feeling she would always want to forgive him, and that was dangerous.

"Then tell me what you suggest? And don't say forget the whole thing."

"What do you think the people of this town would want me to say?" he countered impatiently. "Go ahead and bring the p-possibility of crime to the valley? Add Phoenix House to the list of t-tourist attractions?" He scowled at her darkly. "When I pinned on this badge I made a promise to do everything in my power to keep the people who pay me s-safe."

"Give me six months, Brody. Six months to show you that I can make it work. Please!"

Brody looked into her eyes and saw the gentle compassion of a woman without rancor. A woman who truly believed the things she'd told him. A feeling of terrible yearning ran through him, a need to crush her into his arms and bury himself in her light.

"I was like you, once. When LAPD formed a juvenile anti-drug task force, I fought to sign up. Guys in the squad figured I was crazy, said I was tanking my career trying to rescue a bunch of punks who weren't worth the hassle. Even Megan . . ." He stopped, his jaw tight. She waited while he fought the constriction, wanting to hold him so much it hurt. "Meggie tried to t-talk me out of it, but dumb me, I had this idea I could make a difference." He rubbed his hand over the sudden ache in his chest. Get it said, Hollister. She deserves to hear it all. "When that little punk Williams swore on his grandmother's life to stay clean, I believed him. I even supported the DA when he asked for rehab instead of prison time." His mouth twisted. "Damn near broke down right there in the judge's chambers while the consulting psychologist was describing poor Calvin's lousy childhood. The abusive father, the alcoholic mother." He'd felt it all—a lonely, scared boy's confusion and pain, and he'd seen himself in that boy. "Meggie paid a terrible price for my mistake, Summer. I don't want you to . . . to get hurt."

The smile that curved her lips was like an unexpected gift. "You're a very special man, Brody. I hope you realize that."

Something hard and mean loosened inside him. It had been a long time since he'd reached out for a little piece of happiness. "What I am is outnumbered by two strong-willed females," he grated as he reached into his pants pocket. "Here," he said as he grabbed her hand with battered fingers and slapped something hard and cold into her palm. Startled, she almost jerked away, only to freeze when she saw the silver key he'd given her.

"What's this?" she asked, her heart already racing.

"You know what it is," he said in an irritable tone as he let her go. "You want six months to show your stuff, you've got it."

"You've changed your mind?"

"Let's say I'm trying to be fair and compassionate. But if one of your people so much as jaywalks, I'm closing you down. No negotiation."

Summer stared at the key and then at him while the tears she'd fought half the night seeped into her eyes.

"I accept," she said in a husky voice she couldn't quite force past a whisper. For good measure she closed her fingers over the precious key.

"Damn straight you will," he said, jerking off his hat to slap it onto the top of the Neon. The sunglasses went into the crown of the hat an instant before he reached for her. Her arms were already lifting toward his strong sun-burnished neck when he pulled her hard against him. She had a sensation of rough, prowling need barely kept in check before his mouth crushed down on hers. She arched hard against him, feeling pleasure and desire pulsing with each wild beat of her heart. He was strong and lean and all the things a man should be, and for this moment, he was hers.

She linked her fingers and burrowed against him, his heavy belt buckle punishing her midriff. His kisses became hot, insistent, and she met his hungry demand with a heat of her own. His restless hands roamed her back, the hollow of her spine, moved urgently to cup her buttocks and bring her closer. She rotated her hips, and he groaned, his mouth greedy and clever. His shoulders jerked under her hands, and his muscles rippled.

He shifted, widening his stance, and pulled her tighter to him. His wide chest crushed her breasts, and she felt a half-forgotten ache in her nipples. Moaning, she opened her mouth to him. His tongue slipped inside, tentatively at first, and then when she welcomed him with her own, more urgently. She was hot, eager—and suddenly whimpering as he drew back.

His features were taut, his eyes dark as midnight and tortured as he gulped air and fought for control. She felt the same wild, angry pressure inside to mate. Nature's way, she told herself, barely resisting the need to scream in frustration.

"You certainly have a way of keeping a woman off guard,"

she muttered as she eased backward until her body was no longer welded to his.

"Give . . . me a minute, okay?"

Lashes fluttering, she glanced up to find him standing with his eyes closed, breathing hard. The cut on his lip had opened, and there was a smear of blood in the corner of his mouth.

"Give me your handkerchief," she ordered, her voice shaky.

His eyes snapped open, and he looked at her with slightly dazed eyes. "What?"

"Your hanky. You're bleeding."

"Hell," he muttered before reaching into his back pocket for a folded handkerchief.

"Hold still," she ordered as he instinctively drew back from the hand she raised toward his face. Finished tending his hurts, she stuffed the hanky into her jeans pocket, along with the key.

Scowling again, he plowed his hand through his hair before putting on his glasses. It struck her then that the sun wasn't shining. Professional armor, she surmised. Hiding gentle eyes.

"I meant what I said," he warned as he reached for his hat. "Just because I want to sleep with you doesn't mean I'll cut you any slack if one of your test cases screws up."

"I understand." Because she needed to touch him again, she reached up to adjust his collar. His face softened for an instant before he put on the Stetson and opened the door for her.

"Keep to the limit," he ordered as she slipped into the car and reached for her seat belt. "There are a lot of blind curves on this road. Hit one going too fast and you're over the edge."

She smiled as she turned the ignition. "I've already figured that out," she told him as he shut the door. "And I'll be careful."

CHAPTER 15

Brody was at his desk trying to decide if he dared put in for a replacement vehicle for a four-year-old Chevy that badly needed another ring job when Rich Keegan rapped on the door to his office. The preliminary hearing to decide if Joseph Finley should be tried as an adult had been held at three that afternoon in the county courthouse in Wenatchee. Keegan was still in the suit and tie he'd worn to testify. To Brody's jaded eye he looked even younger in his civies. A greenhorn kid trying to measure up. Brody knew the feeling.

"Make me a happy man, Keegan," he said after returning the rookie's greeting. "Tell me the judge fried the bastard's ass."

Keegan's Howdy Doody features contorted. "No such luck, sir. Judge Starnes refused the DA's petition. Finley goes before the juvenile court in two weeks."

Brody sat back and motioned Keegan to a chair. "Starnes always was a bleeding heart," he told Keegan with a cynical smile. "She and Mel Bailey probably belong to the same country club."

Keegan settled himself, then reached up to loosen his tie. "I have to admit Bailey damn near had *me* close to tears a couple of times, talking about Finley's remorse, and crap like that. But mostly it was Finley himself. Bailey put him on the stand and the asshole broke down and cried like a baby. Swore on his mother's life he'd never use drugs again."

Brody curled his hand into a fist and beat it softly against the arm of his chair while the old anger clawed at his gut. When he had it handled, he allowed himself a small, bitter smile. "Geneva Starnes has a son about Finley's age."

Keegan was still green enough to be surprised. "And they say the justice system doesn't need reform?"

"I hear you, son, but it's all we got, so you'd better learn to deal with days like these."

Keegan's face contorted. "If it was up to me, I'd throw the murdering bastard into the meanest lockup with the roughest cons I could find and toss away the key."

Brody winced. Keegan was using the same words he'd thrown in Summer's face. "Yeah, well, we've been trying that, Rich, and so far it hasn't worked worth shit." He'd done a lot of reading in the seven days since Summer had gone back to San Diego. About solutions that had failed and those that looked promising, though unproven. He was a long way from accepting Summer's contention that jail time didn't work as a deterrent, but his research had left him far less certain.

Keegan glanced down at his spit-shined dress shoes. Brody waited. "Do you ever get used to it, Chief?" he said finally. "I mean, kids shooting each other, families getting wiped out because some asshole was off in his own world?"

Never. "Some do. Some don't. I'm not sure which is best."

Keegan drew a heavy breath. "They warned us, at the academy, but . . ." He shrugged one shoulder self-consciously.

"But it's not the same."

"No sir."

Brody glanced at the photograph of Kelly on his desk. Because she and her mom shared a passion for chocolate, he'd brought home two pieces of cake from Sergeant Petty's retirement bash. Hating to leave Meggie alone when she was feeling queasy, he'd come home early, only a little after ten. Like always, he'd parked next to her new red Civic hatchback, tucked the laundry basket full of clothes she'd left on the dryer under one arm, and walked into the kitchen, anticipating the pleasure of her face when he surprised her with the cake. Instead, he'd stepped straight into hell.

Brody felt his throat closing and snagged air. He willed himself to relax. Realizing that Keegan was watching him uneasily, he manufactured a smile. "You did your job, Rich. That's all anyone can ask," he said, getting to his feet. Suddenly restless, he needed to work off some energy.

Keegan leaped to his feet as Brody grabbed his hat. "Yes sir, but this one really sucks."

"Don't take this home with you, son," Brody said as he followed the rookie into the dayroom and pulled the door closed behind him. But Keegan would. And the frustration would eat at him for as long as the kid wore a badge.

To keep the edge he needed to survive, he'd find a way to live with the frustration and the disgust and then, finally, the constant, simmering rage. Gradually, month by month, year by year, he would stop asking questions, stop believing in absolutes like good and evil—and justice. But because Rich Keegan was a good and decent man, he would never stop caring. And that was the most frustrating thing of all.

Standing at the kitchen counter with packing materials taking up most of the available space, Summer clamped the portable phone more securely between her shoulder and her ear and reached into the cupboard for another bowl. It was the third time in five minutes her father had put her on hold to take another call.

Between interruptions she'd managed to ask him to release the money from her trust fund now instead of next January as stipulated in her grandmother's will. Before he could give her an answer, however, he'd left her hanging on hold. Though it rankled to be such a low priority to her own father, she was grateful he hadn't banged down the phone the instant she'd identified herself the way he'd done countless times before.

"A positive omen, don't you think, Snowy?" she called to the fluffy white cat who was presently toying with a Mylar balloon left over from the farewell party her fellow counselors had given her last night at the Mexican deli near the hospital. Surprised and touched at the tributes they'd piled on her, she'd cried and laughed and made everyone promise to visit the ranch. Several of the junior counselors had cautiously felt her out about jobs. When she'd left the deli with her balloon clutched in one hand and a bag full of silly presents and cards in the other, she'd felt as though she'd closed the door on another phase of her life and opened the door to an entirely new set of challenges.

"Are you as scared as I am?" she asked the cat who paused with paw raised to direct a reproachful look her way.

"Sorry," Summer said with a grin. "Please forgive me for interrupting the king of the jungle at play."

There was a click in her ear, and her father's impatient voice replaced the canned music. "How do I know this Phoenix House isn't just a con to get me to release your money early?"

Montgomery Laurence hadn't changed, she realized. Always quick to assume the worst in her. But then, he had good reason, she reminded herself.

"If you'd feel more comfortable, I'll fax you copies of my lease and the license from the state of Washington to operate a nonprofit care facility. I can also send you copies of the grant proposals I've submitted and the business plan for the bank loan, which has been approved, by the way."

She felt a sweet rush of pride that her meticulous planning and extensive research had paid off. The last major hurdle was insurance accreditation.

"If you have the loan, why do you need your grandmother's money?" Though his tone was still antagonistic and cold, Summer thought she detected a reluctant note of curiosity as well. It gave her hope.

"First of all, it's my money," she said, careful to keep her tone from becoming confrontational. "Second, I can get the ranch up and running without it." Barely, a little voice reminded her as she took a breath, and only if Mr. Gooding managed to keep down expenses. "But I want it as a cushion in case I have to use the money from donations and grants I've set aside for payroll and expenses. Isn't that what you always tell your clients when they consider buying a fixer-upper? Expect to pay more for renovations and improvements than anticipated?"

There was a pause. "When is the contractor going to start work?" he asked.

"He started three weeks ago. The kitchen is almost finished, and his men are partitioning the bedrooms. The roofers are supposed to start on Monday."

"Good God, girl," he exploded in her ear. "You mean you're letting some podunk yahoo work on your place without supervision?" He gave an all-too-familiar snort of derision. "I thought you might have actually learned something in all those college courses you took, but I see now I was wrong. You're just as gullible as you always were."

Summer took a deep breath and reminded herself of all the reasons why she had to make Phoenix House work. "Dad, do you really care what I do with the money, or is this just another attempt to punish me for something I did sixteen years ago?"

The pause was longer this time. "I don't care to discuss the past, even with you." The icy rejection had returned to his tone, chilling her.

"What else do you want me to do? I've tried to prove to you and Mother and Phillip that I'm not that same selfish, stupid girl who destroyed your trust." Her voice wavered, surprising her, and she took a breath. "I love you all. I miss being part of a family. I'll do anything you say to mend this rift, but you won't even give me a chance."

"You call it love when you list your condo for sale with a competitor?"

Summer blinked, knocked off guard by the unexpected shift in conversation. "But you only handle commercial real estate."

"Did you think I wouldn't find out?" he went on as though she hadn't spoken, his tone angry now. "Or did you list with Beach Cities just to piss me off?"

"I . . . no, of course not. Velma Peters at Beach Cities handled the sale when I bought this place, so naturally—"

"Velma Peters is an incompetent bumbler." He sounded

personally affronted, which surprised her into nearly dropping the bowl she'd been wrapping in newspaper.

"Dad, if it hadn't been for Velma, I never would have been able to buy this place. After every lender in town turned me down because of my prison record, she managed to talk a private investor into taking a chance on me."

"Velma didn't do squat. She would have blown the deal if I hadn't stepped in."

"You?"

"Hell, yes, me."

"But . . . how—"

"Velma's been in Ocean Beach a long time, Summer. She knew exactly who you were and how we were related. She called me as soon as the deal started to fall apart."

Shaken, Summer hooked a chair leg with one sneaker and pulled the chair close enough to catch her as she sat down with a hard thump. Velma had let her think she'd gotten mortgage money from a rich retiree and his wife. Summer sent her payments to an account number at a local savings and loan.

"You're M and D Associates?" The sudden pressure in her chest made it difficult to speak.

"Your mother and I, yes."

"You . . . lent me money?"

"Didn't I just say that?" His tone was impatient.

"But you wouldn't even take my calls," she said, staring at the open drawers and packing boxes.

Her father cleared his throat. In the background she heard the intercom announcing another call for him and she prepared herself for more sugary music. Instead he ordered his secretary to hold his calls.

"Bill Crenshaw's son was one of your patients," he said to Summer. "Bill swore you saved the boy's life."

She remembered the Crenshaws from the parents' support group. A rather intense, obviously sophisticated couple who clearly adored their youngest child. "I didn't know Billy's dad worked for you," she murmured, as much to herself as to her father.

"One of my best salesmen."

"He never said anything."

"I told him not to. I wasn't sure how you'd feel if you knew."

"Dad—"

"Then your mother heard you were scrounging for money for this project of yours," he went on quickly, as was his habit. "Some women's group she belongs to contributed."

She thought about all the luncheon meetings she'd attended and the hands she'd shaken during the five years she'd been working toward her goal. Given her family's social prominence, she'd always thought it was possible she might have run into one of them. But she never had.

"All . . . contributions are greatly appreciated," she murmured, still dazed.

She heard the sound of a drawer opening, then her father's mumbling voice, "Can never find a pen when I need it." He cleared his throat. "All right, where should I send my check?"

Stunned and still a little wary, she gave him the number of the trust account she'd set up for donations, and the name of the bank. Though he was generous with his money, he never wasted it on causes he considered frivolous.

"I . . ." She paused to clear the sudden tightness in her voice. "I'll use it wisely," she said, because she thought that would please him.

"Damn straight you will, young lady. And make no mistake, I intend to keep an eye on my . . . my money."

She smiled at Snowy through a film of tears. "You'll have to come up to Osuma to do that. I'm leaving in two weeks whether my place sells or not."

"What's wrong with the offer on the table?"

"What offer?"

An explosive curse ran down the wire. "Can't that Peters woman do anything right?" he muttered, his voice sounding oddly muffled.

"Dad, what exactly are you trying to tell me?"

There was a brief silence, during which Snowy trotted over to her and leaped onto her lap, as though sensing her need for support. Summer immediately curled her fingers into the cat's thick white fur, and the sound of purring filled the kitchen, soothing her.

"One of my clients has been looking to buy a place near the water," he said gruffly. "He made an offer on your place this morning."

Summer glanced at the wall clock, then realized she'd packed it already. "What time is it now?"

"Nearly two. Peters should have been there hours ago. That woman ought to be drummed out of the Realtors' Association for blatant incompetence."

Summer heard the growl in his voice and felt a smile starting inside. Her father was taking care of his little girl again. It was almost more than she could handle. "Is it a good offer?" she managed to ask lightly.

"A fair one. Five thousand less than asking, a clean cash deal and a short escrow. And don't be thinking you can hold out for more, because the price was already inflated ten thousand."

"Fifteen," she corrected without thinking, then bit her tongue.

"The hell you say!"

"It's worth it. Besides, I need all the money I can get."

Her father snorted. "Guess there's more of your old man in you than I thought."

Summer drew in a careful breath and let it out slowly. Tears spilled from her brimming eyes and rolled down her cheeks to plop on Snowy's head. The cat offered up a sympathetic look from wise green eyes before licking her hand.

"Daddy, I'm sorry. I'm so sorry I—"

"There now, none of that!" His tone carried the same panic that she remembered from her childhood whenever he'd been pushed too close to an emotional edge.

"Then could we talk about Grandma's trust fund instead?"

Her father choked a laugh. "If you ever decide to change careers, you'd make a hell of a good salesman, Sunshine."

It had been so long since she'd heard her father's pet name for her. Years and years of longing to hear it just one more time. Closing her eyes, she curved her lips into a trembling smile. "That's high praise indeed."

"Yes, well . . ." He cleared his throat. "About your money, I . . . why don't you come by the house sometime next week and pick up your check. Might as well make it for dinner. You know how your mother likes to entertain. She'll probably want to invite Phillip and Jenny and the twins." He cleared his throat again. "Sissy and Miranda are almost eight. It's time they met their aunt."

"I'd like that," she managed in spite of the huge ball of tears in her throat. "Any night you say."

He muttered something about checking his schedule, and Summer heard the sound of paper rustling. She pictured him at his desk overlooking La Jolla Cove, flipping pages in his leather-bound, gilt-engraved calendar. "Thursday looks clear. I'll check with your mother and get back to you."

"I'll be waiting."

"Do you want this marked 'bedroom' or 'bathroom'?" Rowena Fuentes asked, her magic marker poised over the large cardboard box she'd just packed with things from the linen closet.

Seated cross-legged on the floor by her bed, Summer glanced up from the tape gizmo she was struggling to load with a new roll. "Mark it 'bedroom, storage.' That way I'll know to tell the movers to put it in the shed until I build my cottage."

The plump young counselor grimaced as she printed. "I can't believe you're really going to live in a trailer."

"It's an RV really. One of those big ones. My contractor bought it for me. And it's only until I can afford to build a little place of my own."

"What about the other counselors?" Rowena shoved the box aside and opened an empty one. "Where are they going to live?"

"Manny is going to stay in the staff bedroom in the house. Char's already called on several rentals in Osuma, but she's waiting for her angels to give her the final okay."

Rowena glanced up, a pile of sheets in her arms, to roll her liquid brown eyes. "When she was working at the clinic, she had me trying to establish communication with my guardian angel, but so far, he's refused to answer. Guess he's the stubborn sort."

"Mine has purple eyes and wears a cowboy hat."

"Pardon?"

"He's a reluctant sort of angel."

"Have you gotten your insurance accreditation yet?" Rowena asked, her head submerged in the box she was packing.

"Not yet. The woman handling the application warned me it could take a month to process the paperwork. I should know next week sometime."

"Sounds like things are really falling into place."

"I know. That's what scares me. I keep waiting for this huge crisis to hit and—"

She was interrupted by the ringing of her phone. It was ten o'clock, Monday night. The time when Brody had taken to calling her. To fill her in on the progress of the renovations, he'd told her the first time he'd called. As though he needed an excuse they could both handle. Her heart was already racing as she scooped Snowball into her arms and headed for the door.

"I'll take it in the other room," she said when Rowena glanced at the extension by the bed.

After snapping on the light, she snagged the portable receiver and tucked it against her ear. "Hello?"

"You busy?" It was Brody's standard greeting, and the sound of his gruff voice sent a flurry of warm pleasure running through her.

"Not at the moment. Rowena's here. She's helping Snowy and me pack. But please don't hang up or I'll have to go back to it. What's happening up your way?"

"Amos finished the porch today. Wanted me to ask if you're gong to buy the paint or should he do it?"

"I'll buy it. I don't trust his color sense. Unless *you* want to pick it out?"

"No way. Kel says I'm color-blind. Way she said it, I figure the kindest thing I could do for humanity is put a bullet in my head." She heard a rustle of clothing as he shifted position, and pictured him leaning back in his chair in his den with those huge feet propped on his desk. She smiled as she settled into the corner of her sofa and pulled up her legs.

"How is she?"

"Mostly set on t-turning her father gray before his time. I never should have let the two of you talk me into letting her date."

Summer chuckled as she repositioned Snowball in her lap. "Is she still infatuated with Mark?"

"Totally," he drawled, and she burst out laughing. "Not funny, Laurence. This boyfriend thing's about to drive me into an early grave."

Summer heard the subtle note of fear in his deep voice and her heart turned over. He was letting his little girl test her wings, and it was scaring him to death. He'd given Mark a driving test, then laid down the law on curfews. She could almost hear him putting the fear of God in the boy, especially when it came to kissing in the backseat.

"You said yourself Mark was a careful driver. And Kelly's a sensible girl."

"He's sixteen and horny," he grumbled. "Every time he comes to the house I want to check his wallet for rubbers."

Summer pictured him glowering at the phone and smiled. "Be patient with her, Brody. A girl in the throes of her first love is very fragile emotionally."

There was another silence, longer this time. "Guess you'd know that from your work, huh?"

"And from experience."

"Yeah, I guess. The bastard who broke your heart." She heard the harsh note in his voice and shivered a little.

"So, uh, how's Dottie?"

"Ordering Amos around like a drill s-sergeant. Last I heard he'd threatened to toss her off the property on her fanny if she d-didn't let up on him and his crew."

"Oh no." Summer shifted, jarring the sleepy-eyed cat who twitched his tail irately in silent protest.

"She's relentless. Had me running all over with her, looking at RVs. She had the salesman so dizzy with questions he was all but begging her to take the thing off his hands."

Summer giggled before she remembered that Ph.D.s never giggled. "Before I forget, I need to ask you about the horses."

"What horses?"

"The ones donated by the father of a former patient. He called yesterday to ask me the name of my vet so he could have their records faxed up there. I was wondering if you could recommend a good, uh, horse doctor."

"My grandfather used Dr. Shorter, but last I heard, he was thinking of retiring. Let me do some checking and I'll get back to you."

"Thanks. I'd appreciate that."

She fell silent, and so did he. In the bedroom, Rowena was belting out salsa in a terrible, off-key voice. A jet just lifting off from nearby Lindbergh Field roared overhead, rattling the windows. "How can you stand living under all that racket?" Brody asked when the sound faded a little.

"It's the price one pays for living near the beach."

"Guess you'll miss it, huh? The beach."

"Probably, but I'm rapidly developing a fondness for the mountains." And a certain mountain man who had charmed her right down to her beloved deck shoes in spite of all the reasons why she should have been impervious.

"Uh, guess I'll let you get back to your packing." He cleared his throat. "Kel said to remind you about the T-shirts you promised to bring her. Seems to think it'll impress her friends to have genuine California shirts."

"That's the first item on my list." She leaned down and rubbed her cheek against Snowy's fuzzy head. "I might even bring you one. I was thinking something in pink or baby blue. Size extra large, right?"

"Don't push it, Laurence." She heard laughter in his voice and felt a burst of happiness.

"On second thought, how about purple to match your eyes?"

"Only if you model it for me—with nothing but that great tan of yours underneath." The husky suggestion sent heat spiraling deep inside her.

"I . . . that could be arranged," she murmured, her body softening. "In fact, I'm going to insist on it—although I might dab on a little perfume in strategic spots."

He groaned, and she tightened her fingers around the hand receiver, wishing it were warm, resilient muscle beneath her fingertips. "Cotton collects body heat, you know. It'll be all nice and warm when I slip it off. It'll feel really good against your skin when you model it for me. With only that lovely bronzed skin underneath of course."

She heard the sharp intake of his breath and felt her own catch. Beneath Snowy's warm weight, the mound between her legs ached to be stroked. "When?" he demanded, his voice ragged.

"As soon as you can arrange it," she murmured into the phone. "If all goes well, I'll be arriving a week from next Friday, around six."

"Plan on dinner at s-seven-thirty. And, Summer, wear the shirt." He hung up before she could think of a suitably clever remark.

"But Kel, you have to come! Everybody will be here, and I rented tons of videos and Marnie's bringing her Green Day CDs. She even has the first album they ever made, before they got famous and all."

Kelly shrugged the phone against her ear and scrunched closer to the foot she'd propped on the edge of her desk. The smell of nail polish made her nose tickle. "I really, really want to, Tiff, but Mark says his grandfather went to a lot of trouble to get tickets to the game."

"You hate baseball!"

Kelly winced at the shrill note in her friend's voice. "Not anymore." Kelly closed one eye and concentrated on painting the nail of her big toe.

"I'm beginning to think you're obsessed. You spend all your time with him and I never see you."

Kelly frowned. "Yeah, right! Like we don't have two classes together."

"I meant after school, Kel. We used to hang out a lot before he showed up."

Kelly bit her lip, her hand poised over the new bottle of frosty blue polish. Of course she wanted to be with Mark. He was her boyfriend and she loved him more than anything else in the world. But it was also true she hadn't been spending much time with Tiff lately. Or any of her other friends. She had to admit she missed them a lot, especially now when so much was happening at the end of the school year. Besides, sleepovers at Tiff's house were always a riot, especially after her parents went to bed and Tiff brought out the *Playgirl*s she'd filched from the bottom of her mother's cedar chest.

"Maybe I could come late? Like after the game or whatever."

"Killer!" The excitement in Tiff's voice made Kelly smile inside. "Only you have to promise not to let Mark talk you out of it like he did the last time you were supposed to sleep over."

"I told you, Tiff, he was upset 'cause his mom has this new boyfriend who's really dorky and all, and she and Mark got into this big fight on the phone." Kelly dropped her foot, careful to keep from smearing the polish, and stood up. "He was like really, really crying. I couldn't just leave him alone. He needs me."

"Get real, Kelly," Tiffany sneered. "Who wants a crybaby?"

"He's *not* a crybaby. He . . . he's just going through a bad time."

"I can't talk to you," Tiff grumbled. "You're not rational when it comes to that control freak."

"He's not a control freak! He loves me. He just wants to be with me, is all."

"You know what, Kel. You used to be a lot of fun before you started going out with that creep. Now you're a real drag!" Tiffany banged down the phone in Kelly's ear.

Summer had just walked in the back door with another roll of packing tape in one hand and a large pepperoni-and-mushroom pizza in the other when the phone rang.

"Don't hang up," she yelled at the phone as she kicked the door closed behind her. Heart thumping, she hurried toward the kitchen, dodging stacks of boxes as she went. Along the way, she set the pizza down, freeing one hand to snatch up the receiver and gasp out a nearly breathless hello.

"Dr. Laurence?"

Disappointment speared her when she realized it wasn't Brody. Though the masculine voice was unfamiliar, the note of authority it contained caught her attention immediately.

"Yes, this is Dr. Laurence. Who's calling, please?"

"This is Judge Arthur Mandeville. We met last April at the conference of juvenile court justices, in Seattle."

"Yes, of course. I remember you very well. As a matter of fact, I recently sent you a letter announcing the opening of Phoenix House." Her heart was thudding so hard she could scarcely breathe.

"That's correct. Is this a good time to discuss a referral?"

CHAPTER 16

Brody considered Harley Kurtz a donkey's ass, but he'd learned to get along with him over the last six years, since the man's election to mayor. Still, there were times he wanted to throttle Kurtz with his own sissy necktie. Three o'clock on the first Friday in June was one of those times.

"Be reasonable, Hollister," Kurtz whined, his gold pen clutched in one plump hand. "Other towns our size get along with a smaller force."

"Other towns don't have to deal with tourists up the wazoo damn near every weekend."

"Our crime rate isn't high enough to warrant twenty-four officers."

Brody narrowed his gaze. Instead of taking the chair Kurtz had offered, he'd remained standing. Since verbal negotiations weren't one of his strong points, he counted on the sheer force of his size to even the field. "Our crime rate is low *because* we have so many officers."

"There's nothing I can do. The money only spreads so thin, and there are more pressing priorities."

Out of patience, Brody braced both palms on the mayor's desk with its fussy bunch of daisies on one corner and a photo of Kurtz shaking hands with Bill Clinton on the other, and stared the man straight in his lying eyes.

"I don't give a rat's ass about the leaky plumbing in the second-floor men's room, Kurtz," he declared slowly and dis-

270

tinctly, making every word count double. *"Not a single one of my officers gets laid off."*

Kurtz went goggle-eyed before sputtering something unintelligible.

"I'm taking that as agreement, Kurtz." Fed up with bureaucrats and the never-ending problems of dealing with them, he slammed out of the mayor's fancy corner office more furious than he'd been going in and headed down the back stairs to his own cluttered cubicle. On the way he stopped to drop seventy-five cents into the pop machine. When nothing came out, he jammed the heel of his hand against a couple of buttons, earning himself a startled look from the day receptionist, a newly hired part-time college student who had a way of dropping things whenever he was around.

Max had warned him to go easy on the girl until she settled in, and he'd damn near bent over backward trying, keeping his voice down, smiling at the bespectacled young woman whenever he caught himself frowning at one of her many mistakes. "Make a note for whoever fills this miserable thing that it owes me seventy-five cents," he ordered with a truly noble effort at gentling his tone.

"Y-yes sir," she said, reaching for a pen. In her haste, she knocked over the can of soda she'd somehow managed to get out of the damned machine, sending Pepsi spraying all over the desk. The clerk let out a gasp, then burst into tears and bolted for the ladies' room. At the same time, the phone rang. Teeth gritted, he reached over the counter and snatched up the receiver, only to have Pepsi drip onto his shirt from the drenched handset.

"Osuma PD." And you'd better have a damn good reason to be calling, he added silently.

"Brody, it's Summer."

Heart slamming wildly, he jerked his gaze toward the wall clock. Twenty past three. "You're . . . early."

"I know. The movers finished sooner than I expected yesterday, so I got an earlier start." He heard her inhale quickly.

"Well, anyway, I just got to the ranch and the horses are already here! The man with the trailer says he has to leave and I don't have any hay or whatever it is horses eat and . . . help!"

"C'mon, darlin', you're gonna like it here." Brody led the pretty little gray into the stall and signaled Summer to latch the gate. The rest of the mares were all safely tucked into their new homes.

The horse let out a plaintive whinny and skittered sideways. One of her "sisters" answered with a snuffling snort. Another rubbed her rear against the wall of her stall and gave Summer a dirty look. After witnessing the lethal power of the mare's hooves a few minutes earlier, when the unhappy animal had tried to kick down the side of her stall, Summer was careful to keep out of her way.

"Are horses always so . . . temperamental?"

"Nah, these pretty ladies are just skittish from being in a trailer. They'll settle in."

Summer hadn't realized just how big horses really were until the driver of the van had led them one by one down the ramp— huge, hulking beasts that exuded heat and a pungent scent. Every darn one of them knew she was scared, too—and had immediately set about tormenting her. One had tried to butt her in the back when she wasn't looking, another the color of cream silk had tried to eat her hair. All of them had taken great pleasure in relieving themselves in the nice clean straw she'd spread so carefully on the floor, adding the steamy aroma of manure to the earthy mix of alfalfa, dust, and horseflesh.

"Why do I have this truly depressing feeling that the bedding has to be changed every day?"

"You'll get used to it." Brody knuckled the gray's nose, before slipping off her halter and tossing it Summer's way. She reached out to grab it, and missed.

"Not me," she declared firmly, picking up the halter. "Hiring a wrangler or . . . whatever has just become my number-one priority."

"Vet might know who's looking for work." The gray snuffled a little as he ran his hands over her shiny coat, caressing, stroking. Gentling the animal right into an equine puddle of adoration. Summer saw it happen, and suffered an acute pang of envy.

During the last few hours of the trip she'd been thinking a lot about those big, rough hands, imagining how they'd feel sliding over her bare skin. By the time she'd pulled into the driveway, her stomach had been filled with butterflies and her pulse had been skittering all over the place—and then she'd seen that blasted horse trailer. That had been three trying, fun-filled hours ago.

The only highlight had been the hard, impatient kiss Brody had given her the instant he'd stepped from the Blazer. He hadn't even said hello before crushing her against him. As though, he, too, had been waiting impatiently. Her cheeks had been hot and her legs wobbly when he'd released her—with satisfying reluctance, thank heavens—and ordered her to get the pitchfork from the shed. He'd been fully aroused at the time, and she'd marveled at his self-control. She herself had been dizzy. Under other circumstances she might have found the pent-up sexual frustration amusing.

"I should have asked Amos to get someone to clean this place out," she said in an effort to lessen her frustration. "My plan was to have the patients do it, as part of the process of building self-esteem, but then, I also thought the horses were coming the first week of July instead of June."

Heaving a sigh, she glanced around at all the things that needed to be done. Mostly cleanup projects that required little more than elbow grease. The floor swept, odds and ends sorted through, lights hanging from the rafters repaired. Several of the windows had been boarded over and needed replacing. The structure itself was right out of a cowboy movie, with rough-hewn beams, huge pillars, and an uneven cement floor. The front section was empty, but, according to Brody, had once been used to store equipment. The horse stalls were in the back, two rows of four each, separated by a wide aisle.

It was cooler inside and a little clammy, like a cave she'd been in once. Dust motes and bits of straw darted and spun in the shaft of light streaming through the open double doors. Though it was dirty and neglected, it had a solid feel that reassured her. It also seemed much smaller to her now that it contained six very large horses.

"The black one's named Mabel." Summer glanced up from the typewritten list in her hand to study the large inky horse with the funny squiggle on its forehead. "I think she's much too pretty to have such a pedantic name," she muttered, staring into the liquid brown eyes that stared back with what appeared to be malicious intent.

"Don't know about pretty, but she's got a sore leg." Brody stood up and handed her the bundle of cotton wrappings he'd just removed.

"Sore? Are you sure?"

"Probably injured her metatarsal during the trip up from California," he said as he stepped out of the stall and hooked the gate behind him. Since he'd arrived with bales of straw and hay in the back of the Blazer, he'd been working steadily. First he'd cleaned out the stalls filled with cobwebs and dust and cast-off equipment. Then, while Summer filled each stall with straw, he'd repaired a couple of the gates. According to his instructions, Summer had filled the water buckets he'd brought with him, certain that she was about to be crushed at any moment by one of those huge, warm bodies. As it was, she'd been backed against the side of the stall twice and had to shove her way free.

"Do you think she's in pain?" Summer asked, studying the horse warily.

"Only when she puts weight on it," he said, brushing straw from the front of his shirt. "Vet'll likely give you some liniment to rub on her."

Panic speared her. Today was the first time in her life she'd ever touched a horse, and only with great reluctance. "Oh. Yes. Well, sure. I guess."

Brody's smile was indulgent and just a little cocky. He looked wonderfully mussed, with bits of straw in his thick black hair and sweat dampening the back of his filthy uniform shirt. He smelled of hard work and horse. Somehow he seemed more at home in the barn than in his police cruiser. Perhaps because she was more comfortable with the image of cowboy than cop.

"You really don't know anything about horses, do you?" he asked in a husky voice.

"Not a thing," she admitted. "I'd planned to study up on them before they arrived." The pinto in the nearest stall nickered, and Summer shot it a nervous look. "I think that one hates me."

"She's curious," he said, slipping his arm around Summer's waist and aiming her toward the double doors. "Like all females."

Summer harrumphed, but slipped her arm around his waist. He was as solid as a tree trunk. Side by side, they walked from the gloom into the soft light of early evening. The twilight chorus of the nesting birds had begun while they were in the barn, and the sun was completing its journey toward the peaks, casting long, gentle shadows on the newly shorn grass.

The ranch house seemed larger to Summer. More stately and welcoming, with its new green-metal roof, sparkling white paint, and repaired porch. She'd been so busy she hadn't even had time to take a quick tour.

The black-and-gray travel trailer was parked in the shelter of a huge gnarled oak twenty yards or so from the back door. The van she'd bought last week was parked nearby, the sliding doors still gaping open. The inside was crammed full of the necessities. The moving van would arrive on Wednesday with the rest of her things. Thanks to Dottie, however, the trailer appeared to be remarkably well equipped. The bed had been neatly made and towels hung in the bathroom. There were dishes in the cupboards and a bouquet of daisies on the counter next to the sink.

"I'd forgotten how still it is here," she said as they walked toward the trailer. "And how fresh the air is."

Brody chuckled. "Give it a day or two, honey. Now that your stock is here, it'll get to smelling like a ranch, real quick."

"Don't say that," she begged as they stopped by the trailer's only door. "I'm not ready to be a den mother to a horse herd."

Brody glanced around, as though remembering the years spent growing up on this land. She sensed a coiled stillness in him, saw the sudden tension take over his rugged features. "Guess maybe you're out of the mood for dinner," he said, bringing his gaze back to her face.

"Actually, I'm starving," she said, smiling. "But I need to clean off some of this barn dust. I wouldn't want to offend the other customers."

Something very like relief gleamed in his eyes before he blinked them clear again. "Couldn't happen," he declared gruffly. "Even mussed up and smelling like horse, you're b-b-beautiful." He flattened one hand against her neck and used his thumb to rub at a spot on her cheek. "I . . . missed you," he got out with more difficulty than usual.

"I missed you, too," she whispered, her body starting to quiver. His ebony hair was wind tossed, his bronzed features taut, his huge body radiating a lethal power that had once sent panic racing down her spine.

"Did you b-bring the T-shirt?"

"It's in my suitcase," she said, slipping her arms around his waist. She started to smile, then uttered a little cry as his mouth came down on hers. It was a hard, deep kiss that had weakness traveling in a rush all the way to her toes. He drew back before she was ready to let him go, and she frowned a little as he brought up a hand to smooth a lock of hair away from her hot cheek.

"Keep that thought," he said, his face tight. "I'll be back to pick you up at s-seven-thirty."

"All right." She waited for him to move. Instead, he started rubbing the fingers of one hand in small, provocative circles in the small of her back. She sighed. Surrendered. Let her lashes droop.

"Long drive?" His voice was husky, like rich dark chocolate flowing from a spoon.

"Endless." He widened the circle, finding the kinked knots and working them loose with blunt fingers that could so easily make a punishing fist, yet were so sweetly gentle. She dropped her head and rested her forehead against his shoulder. He flattened his hand and urged her closer. It seemed so natural to melt against him, her cheek pressed against his chest, just above the shiny gold badge. His hand came up to rub her shoulder, and she nuzzled her cheek against him.

"You feel so good," she murmured. "Safe."

His groan was ragged and heartfelt. "Honey?"

"Hmm?"

"This is definitely *not* s-safe."

She opened her eyes and drew back far enough to look up at his face. His eyes glittered with sexual heat as his gaze meshed with hers, and his face was taut, as though he were in acute pain. To prove his point, he drew her closer, letting his heavy erection speak for him. Excitement thrummed the length of her, setting up restless pulses in her womb. At sixteen, she'd had the fine art of seduction down to a science. But her heart had been utterly detached, her mind tortured by guilt. Now, when she wanted a man with all of her heart, she seemed at a loss for words. "Brody, would you mind terribly if we had dinner after?"

He went so still it frightened her. "After . . . what?"

She tried to take a calm breath, but she was shaking inside and the air seemed to whoosh into her lungs, then out again. For so long she'd considered every action, measured each decision against a rigorous standard of ethics. After those miserable attempts at a relationship in graduate school, she'd realized she wanted more. Her heart told her she would find that with Brody. In spite of their differences, in spite of her past shame and a growing certainty that he'd buried his heart with Megan, she loved him. Wholly, unconditionally, with all the pent-up longings of so many lonely, disciplined years. She was tired of putting off her personal needs. For this moment there was only

Brody's dark, sad eyes. Brody's hard mouth. Brody's bone-deep need to be cherished.

"Make love to me, Brody," she whispered over the thundering of her heart. "I've been waiting so long, and—"

Without giving her time to think, he had the door open, and then his hands were at her waist, lifting her over the step and into the trailer. Before she could take a breath, he'd climbed in behind her and closed the door.

"Wait, the shirt!"

"Next time," he muttered as he yanked her into his arms. His mouth was hot over hers, his hands cupping her buttocks as he pulled her closer. Sensation shot through her, driving her to open her mouth under his. To touch his lower lip with her tongue, inviting the hard thrust of his. With a groan he complied, sending a shock through her. Her moan filled his mouth. She felt him draw back. With a groan, he yanked up her shirt, slipped the button on her Levis, and jerked down the zipper.

Brody's blood was singing in his head and pounding in his loins as he drew back and used both hands to slip the jeans over her hips. She moaned and clutched at his shoulders, trembling, urging him on. Brody wanted to be gentle, but the feel of her lips against his was maddening. Hand trembling, he skimmed his palm over the wiry curls between her legs, then slipped one finger inside her. She was wet for him. As ready as he was. The last of his sense fled and he had to have her. Here, now. He'd die if he couldn't.

Summer felt his body shaking, and pressed closer, absorbing the terrible trembling of those hard, rigid muscles. Her hands dug into those magnificent shoulders and she arched. He shifted, drew back. She whimpered and opened her eyes. His face was taut, his eyes dark violet, his lower lip clamped between his teeth as he jerked his wallet from his back pocket and took out a condom. His fingers trembled as he tore open the packet. She blinked, her mind fogged. Her fingers clutched at his shirt, her lower body heavy and hot and needing. So long, she thought in a haze, and never like this. Never wild and desperate and slicked with sweat.

"Let me," she ordered, needing to touch him.

Startled, he looked at her as she took the flat disk of latex from his hand. His eyes closed and his teeth bared as she took him in her hand. He was hot and hard, silk over heated marble. He groaned and jerked when she began sheathing him. She was awkward and slow. He threw back his head, breathing hard, the tendons in his neck distended. The muscles in his stomach convulsed, his breathing a terrible rasp of need.

He was large, much larger than Kyle, and thick. Part of her marveled and part feared. He could hurt her, yet he wouldn't. He would be gentle. When she was finished and he was ready, his arms went around her. He kissed her hard, lifted her, and moved. She felt something unyielding against her back. Dimly she realized it was the refrigerator, even as he jerked her panties down her thighs. She trembled inside, so ready she ached.

"P-put your legs around m-me," he ordered, and she did, her arms around his neck, supporting her. With one hand he opened her, then pushed gently into her, letting her body adjust. Sensation gathered inside, then built and bunched until she cried out from the sheer aching explosion. She felt heat spreading in her like a starburst. He groaned, then pushed deeper, his body shuddering and his breath hot on her neck.

She felt his damp skin, heard his harsh breathing as he plunged. She gasped, tried to move, but he was holding her still. "Not . . . yet," he grated, his expression taut.

She wriggled, desperate. He was deep inside, her body soft, quivering, so terribly ready. "Now," she demanded, digging her nails into his shoulders. "It has to be now."

He drew back, thrust again, and she shattered. Reality dimmed, and there was only Brody, his thick engorged body driving into hers, his need a savage thing, a bond they shared as his body became part of hers.

The shudder that took him was wild and primitive, beyond

even his steely control. She felt him come apart as her own climax spun and spiraled. He groaned again and the muscles of his arms went rigid, granite beneath bronze. And then all that marvelous strength seeped away and he dropped his head to her shoulder, his breathing labored. She clung to him, reveling in the tiny little shivers of the afterglow. The fingers that had clawed at him now wanted to play with the thick black hair that was damp from the labors of their lovemaking. The musk of love surrounded them, as exotic as the scent of the roses she still carried in her heart.

"My wonderful wild stallion," she whispered against his neck and felt him smile.

"Whipped s-stallion," he muttered against her shoulder, and she laughed.

He lifted his head, dusky color in his face. His was smiling, but his eyes were nearly black and intense. "You're . . ." His jaw clenched, and he took a breath. "Mine. You're mine now. No one else t-touches you."

"No one ever has," she whispered. "Not the way it counts. Not until you."

Summer was deep in a lovely dream when something woke her. Frowning, she batted Snowy's tail out of her face and reached for the alarm clock, only to realize it wasn't buzzing. Focusing with difficulty on the little red numbers, she discovered it was only a little past five-thirty. In the morning. She groaned, and closed her eyes.

"Go back to sleep, Snowy," she muttered, snuggling her cheek against the pillow. She was just hovering on the edge of sleep when a large fist hit the door, sending her heart rate into overdrive. Bleary-eyed, she stumbled to the window and looked out. Brody's Blazer was parked next to her van. The driver's seat was empty. No doubt it had been his arrival that had wakened her.

Already smiling, she fumbled open the door. A rugged cowboy in frayed jeans, a worn blue work shirt, and the devil's own grin stood there holding a familiar thermos. His eyes darkened at the sight of the purple T-shirt she'd thrown on after they'd returned from dinner, around nine. Though he had declined her invitation to come in for cappuccino, he'd given her a good-night kiss that had melted her into a warm puddle.

"Tell me there's black coffee inside that thermos and I will personally nominate you for the Nobel prize," she pleaded as she unlatched the screen door.

His eyes crinkled, and she wondered how she could have ever thought him cold and unfeeling. "It was black when I brewed it."

She stepped back to give him room. At the same moment she felt Snowy brush past her bare calf. "Snowball, stop this minute!" By the time she was down the steps, the little hellion was streaking toward the barn. A pang of fear shot through her at the thought of her ten-pound cat tangling with those huge beasts.

"Do you think it's safe?" she asked anxiously, clutching the edge of the doorway.

"Honey, it's a cat."

"He's my baby, and he's never even seen a horse before," she explained as Snowy vaulted into the window Brody had left open yesterday for ventilation and disappeared.

Brody's sigh was heavy. "Hell," he muttered as he handed her the thermos.

"Don't scare him, okay? He's not used to cowboys."

He made a rude noise. "Yeah, while I'm pampering your damn baby, you'd best put something on besides that s-sexy little shirt, Dr. Laurence, 'cause this old cowboy is g-going to show you how to shovel a little shit."

When they were finished in the barn, she slipped her arm around his waist and walked him back to the Blazer. The sun was splashing light across the northern slopes, and the air was warming fast. So far, June was setting up to be a gorgeous month in the mountains.

"Auntie'll likely stop by this morning on her way to work. She wants you to come to dinner tonight."

"Are we having pot roast?" she asked eagerly, winning a grin.

"Probably. Auntie likes to s-spoil people she loves."

Summer felt a warm glow. "I love her, too. She's the closest thing I've had to a mother in years."

He leaned down to kiss her. "She's g-good at that. Should've had a houseful of kids."

"It's not too late. Kelly's bound to have children."

He looked horrified. "In ten, fifteen years, maybe."

Summer laughed before turning her attention to the unpainted porch. She had paint to buy and work to do before the furniture arrived. Manny and Char officially went on the payroll on Monday. Char was already in town, settling into an apartment she'd described as "mountain funk." Though Manny had been visiting his parents in San Francisco, he had left a message on her machine to expect him on Sunday.

When they reached the Blazer, Brody dug into his pocket and pulled out his wallet. "Almost forgot," he said, handing her his business card. "The number for the vet is on the back."

"Kathy Sills," she read before tucking the card into the back pocket of her jeans. "Can she really handle those monsters?"

"You haven't seen Kathy," he said as he replaced his wallet.

"I'll call her first thing." Dottie had arranged to have phones installed and hooked up in both the RV and the ranch house. She'd even had the cable hooked up.

"Kel's last day of school is Friday," he said, glancing at his watch. "Guess when you talked on the phone she told you she's got this part-time job at Mario's."

"Three times, actually." She grinned. "I think we're all going to be eating a lot of pizza."

"Me, I hate the s-stuff almost as much as bratwurst and kraut." He pulled open the door, then turned to kiss her. Reluctantly, her heart pounding, she placed both hands on his chest, stopping him.

"Before you go, there's one more thing I need to tell you." She took a breath and reminded herself that he'd promised her six months. "Our first patient is arriving Monday."

He closed up. "You work fast."

She had to take another breath. "It's Joseph Finley."

CHAPTER 17

Brody was about to leave for the day when his phone buzzed. With a weary sigh, he reached for the receiver. "Hollister."

"Chief Hollister, this is Blanche Oates."

Brody sat up straighter. He hadn't spoken to Trent's grandmother since the day after the arraignment. "Yes, ma'am. How's Trent doing?"

"Much better, although he still cries for his dad." She paused. "Thank you for the book you sent him. He asks me to read it to him often."

He took a slow breath. "My daughter was always p-partial to Dr. Seuss."

There was another pause, longer this time. "I just heard from my attorney that the person who killed Marty is being sent to a treatment center in your town. Some new place called Phoenix House. Have you heard of it?"

Brody stared at the empty chair across from his desk. He didn't want to have this conversation. But at least, this time, he was prepared, thanks to Summer. "Yes, ma'am, I've heard of it."

"My attorney warned me that this might happen. What with all the money Anson Finley was paying that horrible Bailey person." She paused for air, then went on. "Joseph Finley belongs in prison, not some dude ranch. He's a vicious, amoral criminal who shouldn't be allowed to walk the streets one more minute."

Brody drew in a careful breath. "Mrs. Oates, I . . . I understand your f-frustration, but—"

"Chief, my grandson wakes up screaming night after night. He stands at the window hugging his blanket and waits for his daddy to come home. No matter how many different ways his mother and I explain to him that his daddy is in heaven, he won't believe us." As she paused to draw in a breath, Brody tried without success to keep from thinking about the months and months that Kelly had spent crying for her mother.

"But before this moment, I was able to console myself that Finley would pay for what he did," Trent's grandmother continued in a barely controlled tone. "Now I find out he's getting little more than a slap on his hand. Six weeks of so-called drug rehabilitation and he's free. Or have I misunderstood?"

Brody rubbed his hand over his chest. "No ma'am, you didn't misunderstand."

"I want you to know I consider that an outrage and an insult to my son and his dead baby."

He bit down hard. "Sometimes the s-system fails, Mrs. Oates. In this case, it was the judge's decision."

"But it's so unfair! Finley is still alive and my son is dead."

The sound of a muffled sob tore at him. "I . . . understand how you feel, b-but—"

"Do you?" Her voice was suddenly sharp and cold, startling him. "Then why have you allowed that . . . that refuge for murderers to locate in your town?"

Because I gave my word. He took a slow breath, blew it out. "M-Mrs. Oates—"

"Please don't contact me or my grandson again. Find some other way to soothe your conscience." The phone banged down in his ear.

"Was Brody upset when you told him about that Finley boy?" Dottie rinsed the potato she'd just peeled and started cutting it into quarters.

Summer glanced up from the salad she was creating and grimaced. "He looked at me as though he wanted to take me apart, and then just got into the Blazer and left. I have no idea what he's thinking."

"He does that sometimes when he knows he's going to have trouble getting out the words." Dottie dropped the potato quarters into the Dutch oven. "It's ironic, though, that this Finley boy is the first. Almost as though fate has a sense of the dramatic."

Summer frowned a little. Her shoulders were sore from wielding a paintbrush for nearly five hours without a break, and her back ached. "To tell you the truth, I would have preferred a less dramatic beginning."

"Of course you would, dear. On the other hand, it does seem fitting, somehow."

Finished with the potatoes, Dottie started on the carrots, looking very festive in a lime-green skirt and a camp shirt spattered with brilliant yellow daisies. A brooch in the shape of a bumblebee was pinned to one lapel. Summer felt positively dowdy in her scoop-necked ivory T-shirt and short navy skirt. A little brown moth next to a glorious butterfly.

"I've talked with Joe's father several times on the phone since Judge Mandeville called," she said as she tore romaine into bite-sized bits. "Apparently Joe is devastated. When he's not in school, he just sits in his room and stares. Mr. and Mrs. Finley are terribly worried about him."

"It was a tragedy, no doubt about it. For everyone." Dottie dropped chopped carrots into the pot. "There does seem to be a certain synchronicity to it, though, doesn't there?"

"I'm a little worried about taking on such a complicated case before the staff has a chance to shake out the start-up bugs. Even though Manny and Char are experienced clinicians, they're not used to working together. Or working directly with me." She sighed, then blew a lock of hair out of her eyes.

Dottie popped a slice of carrot into her mouth. "I admit I feel a certain amount of sympathy for the boy," she said when she'd swallowed.

Summer reached for a towel and wiped her hands. "So do I. But he also has to take responsibility for what he did, and accept the fact that he'll spend the rest of his life living with guilt. The key is to turn the pain he feels into a positive motivation to make the rest of his life count for something good."

Dottie clanged the lid onto the pot and pulled open the oven door. "When is he due to arrive?"

Summer heard the low growling rumble of the Blazer's engine and smiled. "A week from Monday. Until then he's under house arrest."

"With one of those electronic gizmos strapped to his arm?" Dottie walked to the counter for the Dutch oven.

"It's attached to his leg, actually." Summer filched an olive from the salad and chewed. "Judge Mandeville made that a condition of his being allowed to finish school instead of remaining in juvenile hall."

Dottie closed the oven door as Kelly came breezing into the kitchen, her earphones around her neck. In the six weeks since they'd parted at the end of April the girl seemed to have shot up two inches, and her waist had slimmed. Summer suspected Kelly was going to have her father's height, but the fine bones and delicate features were her mom's. She hoped Megan knew what a lovely child she'd borne. Ignoring the heavy weight that settled in the vicinity of her heart whenever she thought of her own lost child, Summer turned to accept the girl's exuberant hug.

"Summer, you won't *believe* the neat eyeshadow Tiff lent me," Kelly exclaimed with all the verve of a healthy, happy teenager. "It's called misty mauve, and it's totally perfect with the surfer shirt you brought me."

"You'll have to show it to me after dinner," Summer told her before grabbing another olive. She couldn't help darting a glance through the window over the sink. Brody was just sitting out there. He had to know she was here. But surely he wouldn't refuse to come inside simply because he was angry about Joe?

"Hey, you cut your hair!" Kelly walked around Summer, her fingers fluffing the layered strands curling over her neck. "It's totally rad. Way sexy."

"It's supposed to be wash and wear, but I'll accept rad." And sexy, too, although a part of her was still nervous about indulging the more frivolous side of Summer Laurence.

Eyes sparkling, Kelly grinned ear to ear. "Bet Dad was bowled over, huh?"

"Actually, I don't think he noticed." Other things, maybe. Like the way her thighs had quivered beneath those big rough hands. Or the shudders that had taken her when she'd climaxed.

"Guys are so dense sometimes." Kelly sighed and rolled her eyes. "Like Chuck thinking Mark slashed his tires on account of Chuck asking me out."

Summer caught the startled look Dottie sent her niece and felt the same surprise. "Did you accept?"

"Nuh uh. I'm Mark's girl." Kelly reached for a glass in the cupboard.

"Why would Mark be jealous, then, dear?" Dottie asked as Kelly took a pitcher of juice from the fridge.

"I told him I thought Chuck was cool." Kelly's dimples flashed. "Tiff says you have to do stuff like that to keep a guy from taking you for granted."

"And you always do what Tiff suggests, do you?" Summer asked, tempering the question with a smile. The last thing Kelly would accept was a lecture on interpersonal ethics.

"Sometimes. Tiff's got way more experience with guys. Jenelle and Marcia and me are sorta like her pupils."

"Sounds like one of the classes she's teaching is Manipulation 101."

Kelly swallowed juice, swiped her tongue over her upper lip. "What's that?"

Dotty handed Summer the bottled dressing she'd just retrieved from the refrigerator, raising her eyebrows as their eyes met. "Kel, no offense to your best friend," Summer said as she opened the bottle, "but playing games with someone else's feelings can backfire in some fairly dangerous ways."

Kelly wrinkled her brow as she took another sip. "Yeah, but Summer, how else are you supposed to keep a guy interested?"

"Lots of ways. Being fun to be with. Really listening when the other person is talking. Showing them you care in special ways, like maybe baking a birthday cake or planning a surprise picnic."

Kelly seemed to consider that carefully before nodding. "That sounds cool." She grinned. "Or like the way Dad helped Mr. Gooding every night after work, maybe."

Summer looked up from the vinaigrette she was pouring, surprised. "Your dad helped with the work on the house?"

"Uh huh." Kelly rinsed her now empty glass before stowing it in the dishwasher. "One of Mr. Gooding's men broke his leg and he couldn't find anyone right away to take his place."

"Amos tried, dear," Dottie interjected while pouring herself a Wild Turkey. "He even called several contractor friends in Seattle to see if they could lend him someone, but this is the absolute worst time to try to get a carpenter." She took a dainty sip, a look of pleasure softening her features as she swallowed. "I didn't even know Brody'd volunteered until he came home with a bloody nose from where he'd stood up too fast and smacked into this beam."

"Dad is kinda clumsy," Kelly said with a grin.

Except when he's making love, Summer thought as she capped the dressing. "He didn't mention it on the phone," she said glancing toward the window again. The sun was still high, though it was well past seven. According to the almanac it stayed light in the Northwest at least a good hour after the sun set in California.

"Well, you know Dad. He doesn't say much about his feelings. Like you said, I guess. He just does nice stuff for the people he loves."

It was so still Summer could hear the faint music of the Wenatchee rippling over the rocks far below the bluff where she and Brody were standing side by side, watching the last rays of the sun slipping below the mountains. Ramrod straight, he had his hands tucked into the back pockets of his jeans and was staring down into the gorge. Now that the weather had turned warm, he'd switched to uniform shirts with short sleeves, revealing arms packed with hard muscle.

He'd been quiet during dinner, but afterward he'd relaxed visibly when Kelly had oohed and aahed over the shirts Summer had brought. That had been an hour ago, and other than the gruff invitation to take a walk, he'd said very little.

"I brought you a shirt, too," she said when he showed no inclination to break the silence. "It's not new, though. I got it at a Padres game last year. Comes down to my knees."

He smiled a little at that. Her heart smiled back. "You like baseball, do you?"

"Are you kidding? I *love* it. How about you?"

"It's okay." He watched a hawk soaring over the river gorge. "Meggie was a Dodgers fan. Knew all the players and their stats. I got her season tickets one year for her birthday. Had to promise to work security free for a year to get 'em." His face softened, giving her a glimpse of that man who was so clearly in love. "She cried, she was so happy."

She didn't begrudge him his memories of a happy marriage. How could she? But still, the part of her that wanted to think she was somehow special to him was hurt. "Sounds like Megan and I had a lot in common." She reached down and plucked a leaf from a bush he'd called a salal. It had a pungent smell that caused her to wrinkle her nose.

He shifted his gaze from the graceful predator to her face. Wariness crept like a flush over his solemn features. "If you're asking me if I've got the two of you mixed up in my mind, I don't."

Summer tossed the leaf to the wind and watched it float downward. "I know that, Brody. I also know that along with the person I am now, a man has to take my past. It's not something I can change, and it's not something I'll deny if asked." She took a breath—and a risk. "I know you're trying hard to accept the work I do, and I salute you for that. Maybe this is the time to ask you if you can accept me, with all my flaws and past sins."

Brody heard the brittle tension beneath the calm words and felt a stab of guilt in his gut. He wondered if she'd asked other men that same question. Wondered how they'd answered. He turned to look at her and the emotions in his belly twisted. Her chin was high, her mouth curved in a smile that was as vulnerable as hell, though he doubted she realized that. But a cop was trained to look for the small details most people miss, like the nearly imperceptible trembling of her lower lip before she brought it under control.

How much honesty could she handle? he wondered. Not the whole truth, he knew. About the dreams that had come shortly after she'd returned to San Diego, dreams from his days on the street when he'd hauled in teenaged hookers high on whatever they could beg, steal, or earn by spreading their tight thighs. Acknowledging that she'd been one of those sad-faced babies tore him apart.

He took a breath. "There's a place I know up in the mountains above the tree line where I used to go s-sometimes. Wasn't much there, just some scrub grass and boulders. But in the spring there were these little gold flowers." He dropped his gaze, kicked at a rock embedded in dirt with the toe of his boot, and felt long-buried feelings wash over him. Damn, he shouldn't have started this, he realized now. But it was too late.

"It sounds lovely," she said, a soft little lilt to her voice. A shrink's trick, telling him she cared about knowing more. Cops had their own tricks to get someone to open up. He liked hers better.

"I, uh, used to talk to those flowers. Not about anything in particular, just . . . talk, where no one could hear me." He felt heat creeping up his neck. He'd never admitted this before to anyone. Not even Meggie. "I didn't even care what I said because it felt so good to talk and not stutter."

He saw the confusion in her eyes and added stiffly, "I d-don't stutter when I'm alone. Only when s-someone is l-listening."

"Fascinating," she murmured, frowning a little.

"More like damned frustrating," he admitted before reaching

up to snap off an alder twig from a low-hanging branch. Words
came easier when he had something in his hands to distract him.
"You're like those flowers, S-Summer. You . . . accept people
who c-can't make themselves p-perfect no matter how hard they
try."

"Oh Brody." Her hand trembled when she laid it against his
cheek. He saw the tears glistening in her eyes and felt himself
freezing up. He hadn't told her the story to end up being frigging
pitied. "You idiot," she said, choking out a laugh. "Stop glaring
at me like you want to rip my head off, and give me a hug." Before he could protest, she wrapped her arms around his waist and
snuggled close. With a sigh, he surrendered and pulled her even
closer.

Brody had just finished changing the oil on the Harley when
Mark brought Kelly home from Mario's. He checked his watch,
then wiped his greasy hands on a rag before walking out to meet
them.

"Hi, Chief," Mark said as he hurried around the Miata to help
Kelly out. Brody frowned when he saw how much of his little
girl's legs showed beneath the short red skirt Mario required his
waitresses to wear.

"Hi, Dad. Fussing with the bike again?" She was growing up,
he realized with a pang as she sashayed across the gravel toward
him. A young lady instead of a child with skinned knees and a
hole in her smile where her two front teeth used to be. Now she
was wearing makeup and her hair was done up in some kind of
new shaggy style—and her body was filling out in all the dangerous places. Just thinking about the randy studs hanging
around Mario's place, all primed and ready, was enough to give
a man permanent worry lines.

"You're a little late, aren't you?" Brody shot a look at the setting sun to make his point.

Before Kelly could answer, Mark stepped forward to take the
heat. Putting himself between his girl and her old man's wrath,
Brody decided with reluctant appreciation for the boy's protec-

tive instincts. He liked the way the kid took care of himself, too. Wearing jeans and a nice polo shirt instead of a sloppy T-shirt and baggy shorts like damn near every teenaged boy he laid eyes on these days.

"It's not Kelly's fault, sir," Mark said in a firm, but respectful tone that some of Brody's younger officers would do well to adopt. "Her replacement didn't show up and she had to cover until Mario could get someone to come in."

Brody shifted his gaze to his daughter, who nodded. "It was cool, though, 'cause I got to work the dinner crowd. That's when you make the killer tips."

"Next time call, okay?"

She wrinkled her nose as she took off the billed cap that covered her hair when she worked. There was a grease spot near the hem of her skirt and something that looked like coffee on her sleeve. She smelled like pizza. "Yeah, okay. I'm sorry, Dad. Mark said I should let you know so you wouldn't worry and all, but I got busy and, you know." She gave him one of those dimpled grins calculated to charm the old guy into letting her slide. Hell, if it didn't usually work, too. "I promise, it won't happen again."

He nodded, then glanced at the house. "Your aunt could use some help with supper."

"Oh, yeah, sure." She glanced at Mark. "Thanks for the ride."

"Sure, no problem. What time should I pick you up tomorrow?"

"Actually, I promised Summer I'd come over after school and help out with the horses." Kelly's gaze slid away, toward the garage. Brody noticed that one hand fiddled with her cap, and his cop's instinct kicked in. Something wasn't quite right. "See, this old guy, Mr. Tidwell, she hired, he can't start until Friday," she continued after taking a quick breath. "It's like, Summer says she's not afraid to handle the mares alone, only every time one of them tries to nuzzle her, she makes this funny yelping noise and leaps practically all the way across the barn."

Brody turned away to hide his grin. He'd seen that leap of Summer's a time or two himself. It was cute as hell, though he doubted she'd appreciate him saying that to her face. For some reason he couldn't figure out, she seemed to think it was some kind of character test to hang in when she was plainly terrified. Him, he'd just as soon test himself against something important. Like working up the nerve to ask her to marry him . . .

"No problem, Kel," Mark said with the easygoing grin he'd inherited from his grandfather. "I'll just come along and help."

Kelly rejected that with a disdainful look that had Brody wincing. "Oh Mark, you're from Chicago. You don't know anything about horses."

"So? I can use a shovel." He sounded hurt and a little defensive— but determined. "Besides, Dr. Laurence would appreciate the help. Right Chief?"

Brody held up both hands. "I'm just a bystander here, son."

Brody had expected Mark's look of disappointment, but when Kelly turned to glare his way, he was mystified. From the disgusted look on her face, he figured he'd somehow said the wrong thing. Hell of it was, he didn't know what she expected. Figuring it wouldn't hurt to take a stab, he fell back on the familiar. "Kel, don't you have homework?"

"Yeah, right." He could have sworn she looked relieved— until she turned to offer one of those long-suffering looks. "I gotta go, Mark."

"Yeah, well. Catch you later, I guess."

"Yeah, catch you later." She waited until Mark was heading back down the driveway before rounding on old dad. "Honestly, Dad. How come you're like this really heavy parent every time but when I really need you?"

Brody blinked. "You want to run that by me again, baby?"

"Weren't you *listening*?"

Brody wondered if the other dads at the father-daughter banquet in school last month had this same recurring urge to regularly bang their heads against the nearest tree. "I thought so, yeah."

Her expression reflected impatience. "Well, obviously you thought wrong, or you would've backed me up."

He got it then. Or thought he did. "You wanted me to tell Mark not to help you with the horses, right?"

"Duh."

"Kel, I'm willing to cut you a lot of slack, but that's one expression I don't expect to hear from you again."

"Whatever." Her mouth drooped into that sullen look he hated.

"Kel—"

"I can't believe how totally I screwed up," she exclaimed, turning in a complete circle, too upset to stand still.

"You mean, by lying to Mark about promising to go to Summer's after school?"

Her face turned crimson. "How did you know?" she mumbled, ducking her head.

"A lot of years listening to more lies than you can count."

"Oh."

"You want to tell your old dad what's going on?"

She jerked her head. The red in her cheeks had faded to a rosy pink. "Summer's been back three whole days, and the only time I've seen her was on Saturday night at dinner. And then the two of you left to take a walk right after we ate."

Brody felt a thud in the vicinity of his belly button. Summer had been right about him. He was about as sensitive to the needs of his little girl as the slug sliming its way along the edge of the driveway. "Guess that wasn't real sensitive of me, taking her away when you two have so much to catch up on."

Her mouth drooped at one corner. "Only the thing is, she's real busy getting stuff ready, and you said you didn't want me going to her place unless you were with me, on account of the druggies that are going to be living there, too."

"Sweetheart, I thought we were clear on why I made that rule."

"Yeah, I know, on account of that guy who killed my mom, only Summer would never let anything happen to me." She gave him a plaintive look that tore at his heart. "It's like I'm being punished, only I didn't do anything wrong."

Brody glanced past the forlorn figure in the red, white, and green uniform, toward the playhouse he'd built with his own hands. He'd tried so hard to make sure Kel never lacked for anything. Hell, he'd even played Barbie with her, looking over his shoulder every few minutes to make sure one of his men didn't come by and see him struggling with the doll's spiky-heeled boots.

"All right, I'll amend the r-rule, but on one condition." The sudden happiness that lit her face shamed him.

"Whatever you say, Dad. Honest."

He drew a breath. "I want your word you will never, under any circumstances, be alone with any of those . . . any of Summer's patients. Male or female."

"I promise."

"I'm dead serious about this, Kel."

"I *know*, Dad. I'm not some dumb two-year-old who can't figure stuff out."

He took a breath. "Okay, t-then."

She launched herself at his chest, and he hugged her tight. Her hair smelled like sunshine and pepperoni, and he felt a pang as she pulled away to grin up at him, Meggie's dimples flashing in her daughter's face. "Don't get me wrong, Dad. I think it's real cool you're spending time with Summer, you two being in love and all."

Brody felt a flare of pure panic. "It's not exactly l-love."

Kelly's grin widened. "It's okay, Dad. I know you wouldn't sleep with someone you didn't love. Aunt Dottie said all Hollister men were like that. I think it's gnarly." She hugged him again, then took off jogging toward the house.

Brody stood motionless, her words clanging in his head. God help him, was that what Summer thought? That because he ended up as hard as rock every time he touched her, he was in love? Jesus, wanting to sleep with Summer was one thing. And yeah, maybe he had been edging up on the idea of marriage, but love?

He admired Summer, and he liked her a lot. In fact, he was coming to think he cared about her very deeply. God knew he wanted her. So damn bad he broke out in a sweat sometimes, just thinking about burying himself in that luscious body again. Knowing her, spending time with her, was the best thing that had come his way since he lost Meggie. But he wasn't sure he was best for her. For all her in-your-face confidence and give-as-good-as-she-got guts, every now and then he caught a quick look of something fragile in her eyes. Something easily trampled, like that pretty little gold flower up in the hills. And everyone knew Brody Hollister was damn clumsy around delicate things.

Not that Summer was delicate, exactly, he amended as he watched a couple of gray squirrels playing tag in the sun-dappled treetops. *Defenseless* was the word that kept running through his mind whenever he thought of her—and he thought of her plenty. Maybe like a junkie thought of a fix. It had occurred to him more than once that he was beginning to crave being with her too much. Damned if he wasn't mooning around like a lovesick calf, storing up little bits of his day to tell her later. Wondering if the corny joke Mr. Klein at the feed store had told him would make her giggle. Buying a new shirt because she'd teased him about looking scruffy when a button fell off his old one.

The question that kept nagging at him was, what could he do for her that would make him special? Other than give her pleasure in bed. He couldn't help her in her work, she didn't need his financial support, and his conversation was pretty much limited to small-town gossip, what current events he could snatch from a quick scan of the morning newspaper and the nightly news.

He moved his shoulders, then turned and walked back to the Harley he'd rebuilt as his own version of therapy. He glanced down at his dirty jeans and grease-spotted sneakers and told himself he was in no fit shape to go calling on a lady. He shoved his hand through his hair, reminded himself Auntie would shoot him if he was late for dinner, then sighed and swung a leg over the wide seat. Summer probably wasn't even home, just like she hadn't been home the last two times he'd stopped to see her. What the hell, he told himself as he kicked the engine into full roar. The old bike needed a drive anyway.

CHAPTER 18

Summer sat back on her heels and wiped the back of her hand across her damp brow. The potting soil she'd worked into the crumbly red dirt had a rich, earthy scent, which mingled with the ripe smell of the fish emulsion Lucy had ordered her to use.

She was wondering if she had time to prune the climbing roses when a flash of white caught her eye. While she'd been working, Snowball had been taking his afternoon siesta under a tomato vine. Now it seemed nap time was over, and the mischievous cat was ready to play.

"Stop it, Snowy, you're traumatizing my new little babies!"

Paw extended, Snowball gave her a disdainful look before batting at the parsley start that had caught his eye. "Bad kitty," Summer scolded as she scooped the cat into her arms and nuzzled his fur. "Mama's just spent two hours planting her kitchen garden, and I don't want you messing with it."

Snowball licked her hand, then closed his eyes to concentrate on his purring. "Yes, Mama loves you, too, you little dickens. But you have to stay away from the plants so they can grow."

Shifting the feline to his favorite spot next to her neck, she climbed to her feet and stretched, wincing a little against the stiffness in her back. Six solid days of nonstop work were taking their toll. But it was worth it, she thought as she directed a proud glance at the neat yard. Most of the landscaping would be done by the patients, with Lucy's advice and planning.

Upstairs in his corner room, Manny was unpacking. Judging from the sound of a jazz trumpet wailing through the open window, hooking up his new speakers had been a priority. Tomorrow would be their first staff meeting. Anson Finley had called earlier to say he and his son would be arriving at ten A.M. on Monday. The clock was ticking, and in less than four days Phoenix House would be officially up and running.

A dream come true.

Her stomach was already a ball of nerves. In response to the brochures she'd sent out, she'd had nibbles from several other parents, from various places in California mostly, but one or two from Washington as well.

"I want this to work so much, Snowy," she whispered against the thick fur still warm from the afternoon sun. "No, it *will* work. Like Davy Crockett always said, 'Make sure you're right, then go ahead.' At least I think it was Davy Crockett, although it could have been Daniel Boone. One of those frontier types anyway."

Snowy opened one eye and stretched. "Oh God, I'm scared," Summer admitted, rubbing the cat with her chin. "The idea of failing terrifies me." A shiver ran over her before she shoved her fears back into their dark cages. "What I need is coffee."

After one last beaming look at her tiny green charges, she turned and walked toward the RV. At the familiar thudding of iron hooves on hard ground, however, she changed direction and headed toward the barn, her heart speeding.

Brody had taken to helping her and Kelly with the horses after work. Since he was the only one other than Dottie within miles who knew how to ride, it had become his job to take one of the mares out while Summer cleaned the stalls and Kelly measured out grain. Today he was exercising the pretty gray horse with the spotted rump. Kelly was riding double, snuggled up against her dad's broad back, her hair flying.

He'd promised to teach both Kelly and Summer to ride after the summer crowd thinned, and Kelly could hardly wait. Summer was more wary, though she had to admit she loved the exhilaration of galloping over the field with the sun overhead and the world whizzing past. There was something primitive and wild about sitting astride a powerful animal with her arms around

Brody's waist, feeling the flex and give of his steely muscles as he controlled all that power and speed.

Kelly was grinning as her dad reined the Appaloosa to a walk near the corral fence now sporting sturdy new railings and posts. "You should have seen us, Summer," she called, forgetting for once her teenaged need to be blasé. "We spooked a deer and raced it to the river."

"Who won?" Summer called, shifting Snowball from one arm to the other over the cat's sleepy protest.

"The deer, but only because she took a shortcut over some bushes."

Summer waited until Brody brought the mare to a stop, then moved closer. She no longer jumped when one of the huge beasts nuzzled her, but she wasn't altogether comfortable around them either.

Turning in the saddle, Brody gave Kelly a hand down, watching to make sure she stepped clear before dismounting himself. He was a picture of the Old West in worn chaps, a faded blue shirt, and the wear-seasoned Stetson, and yet, somehow, he looked utterly natural, even relaxed. And most definitely in charge. In her mind's eye she saw him as a taciturn and tough cattle driver, surrounded by milling cattle and swirling dust, beautiful eyes squinted against the sun, huge body relaxed and easy in the saddle. A cop, a cowboy, and, she thought with a slow, sweet, and very private smile, her lover.

His gaze, when it came to her, sent small prickles of need shivering down her spine. "You have dirt on your chin," he said with quirk of his mouth, which seemed softer every time he smiled at her. Before she could wipe it away, he did it for her, the leather of his gloved hand erotically rough against her skin. "Better," he said, his eyes heating.

She inhaled against the familiar rush. Being head over heels in love with the right man, she had discovered, was better than any drug. "I, uh, bought cookies while I was in town. Chocolate chip with black walnuts, in case you two are interested."

"Got any coffee to go with those cookies?" he asked as he pulled off a glove to reach into his pocket for a sugar cube.

"I was about to make a fresh pot."

"Then I'm interested," he said over the sound of the mare's eager snuffling as she took the sugar from his palm. At his suggestion, Summer bought the little cubes by the gross. She was thinking of investing in sugarcane futures.

"Not me, I gotta go," Kelly said, raking wind tangles from her dark hair with her fingers. "Me and Mark have a date to see the new Brad Pitt flick tonight and I have to wash my hair."

Brody scowled. "Remember—"

"My curfew." Kelly pulled a face. "Dad, you tell me that every time I go out."

He looked so offended that Summer had to bury her face in Snowy's fur to keep from laughing. "Just so you know," he muttered, rubbing his hand over the mare's neck.

"I know, Dad. You're worried about your little girl and I love you for it. Only chill, okay?"

He grunted something indistinct, and Kelly shot Summer a glance. "The seniors are practicing for graduation tomorrow, so the rest of us get out early. I can come at two instead of four if you want."

"I desperately want," Summer said with a grin. "The rest of the furniture is arriving sometime in the morning, and we still have the kitchen to organize."

"I'll be here. You guys behave yourselves while I'm gone," she said with a grin before turning to jog toward the driveway.

"Last one. Better get it while I'm feeling too stuffed to fight." Summer nudged the cookie plate closer to his side of the table.

"If I s-say no, I'll hate myself long about break time," he said with a sigh. The man had a huge appetite, and, she had discovered, a passionate sweet tooth. Since coming inside, he'd devoured a dozen cookies and most of a full pot of coffee. As was his habit, he'd left his chaps hanging on a peg in the barn, along with something called a lunging line he used to exercise the mares in the corral.

"I got a call this morning from someone named Phil Potter at the *Osuma Register*," she said, smiling a little at the look of pleasure on his face as he chewed. "He wants to do a story on Phoenix House."

"Wouldn't doubt it," he said after he'd swallowed. "Word's out."

She toyed with her napkin. "Do you know him?"

"Some. Went to school with his older brother." He leaned back and stretched out his long legs. Ever the opportunist, Snowy left his favorite spot on the built-in sofa and trotted over to leap onto Brody's lap. Though Brody grumbled ceaselessly about "that damn pampered cat," she noticed that he immediately reached down to scratch Snowball behind one tattered ear.

"Will Potter be fair-minded if I give him an interview, do you think?"

When he didn't answer right away, she turned to look at him and saw that he was frowning a little, considering her question from all angles, she suspected, the way a cop would. A good cop, she amended, surprised that she could link those two words in her mind and actually accept them. But Brody *was* a good cop. He really did try his best to protect and serve. He was also fair, though sometimes he forgot that.

"Phil's out for Phil," he said slowly, choosing his words. "Make it worth his while to s-support you and he p-probably will."

"In other words, he's an opportunist?"

He shrugged. "Phil likes to feel important. Guess it s-started in high s-school when he was always wanting to date the prettiest girls. Thought of himself as a real s-stud."

"Is he?"

"Hell if I know." He palmed his coffee mug and took a long swallow. "Man'll probably take one look at your legs and beg you to let him gush about this place."

She laughed. "Does that mean you think I have nice legs?"

His smile started in his eyes but it took time to reach his mouth. When it did, though, it was devastating. "Honey, I get hard just thinking about your legs. I don't even have to see 'em, though that's about as great as it gets."

"Yeah?" She reached out to trail her fingers over his wide forearm. The muscles under the furring of soft hair bunched spasmodically, and she smiled. "I've had some truly spectacular fantasies just thinking of running my hands over that butt of yours. All those hard, bunched muscles. And those thighs." She dug her nails in a little as she ran them along the cablelike sinew. "Did I mention that I'm a sucker for a man's thick, muscular thighs. Yours, Chief Hollister, are prime, quite possibly the best I've ever seen—and I grew up around surfers with great legs."

He inhaled swiftly, his throat turning red above the soft rolled collar. "You like to live d-dangerously, d-don't you, honey?"

"Only when I know it's safe."

His eyes were dark between the black-as-sin lashes, focused intently on hers, a savage need simmering there as he put down his mug, then lifted the cat to the floor. "Up, woman."

"Up?"

He reached down to wrap his hands around her upper arms, lifting her easily to her feet and then, before she could take a breath, into his arms. His mouth was over hers. A glorious feeling of power burst in her at the thought of all that fierce warrior strength answering to her command. Arching closer, she linked her hands at the nape of his neck and used her toes to push herself against him. Sensation shot through her. She dug her fingers into the muscle cushioning his massive shoulders. She felt him jerk, then draw back. Hands clutching at the hem of her T-shirt, he pulled it up and over her head in one fast movement. The air hit her overheated skin, and she gasped.

"S-stop?" he demanded, breathing like a long-distance runner at the end of the race.

"No, no," she managed, reaching for the top button of his shirt. He yanked the tails free, and started at the bottom. They met in the middle, their hands tangling as they each reached for the same button. She laughed, then bit her lip.

Between kisses he stripped her to her bra and panties, then ran a finger over the swell of her breasts above the unadorned cotton. The rasp of his rough finger sent little prickles of excitement spiraling deep. But when his hands went to the waistband of her panties, she grabbed them with her own.

"My turn," she said, forcing a lightness into her voice in spite of the lump of trepidation in her throat. She drew off his shirt, reveling in the wonder of that huge, granite chest as she urged him to lift his arms. He helped, jerking the shirt free to join the other on the floor. His stomach muscles spasmed as her fingers found the tab of his zipper and ran it down.

"Oh my," she whispered as his erection sprang free of the thin boxer shorts.

His face turned a fiery red. "I've got a lot of lovin' saved up," he muttered, looking acutely embarrassed.

"I've always liked a challenge," she said, trying not to stare.

He framed her face with his big rough hands, something very like humor mixed with the hunger in his eyes. "You are the damnedest woman to understand," he grumbled, dropping his gaze to her mouth. She sighed a split second before he kissed her gently, sweetly—and much too briefly. After turning her around, he gave her a little push toward the compact bedroom.

While he got rid of his boots and jeans, she closed the blinds and drew back the covers on the bed. Turning, she found him behind her, clad only in his shorts, his head bent as he removed a telltale foil packet from his wallet. Because she'd only started on the Pill, the doctor recommended she continue taking precautions for the first cycle.

"Damn things come in colors now," he said, looking a little sheepish. Smiling, she slid her palms up his brawny arms to his shoulders. Muscle rippled beneath her fingertips, under her control, not his. Gripping his neck, she pulled his head down and touched her mouth to his lips and heard the harsh gasp of his indrawn breath.

She helped him take off her bra, then went warm and soft at the hunger in his eyes. He filled his hands, his thumbs brushing the tender nipples. Weakness ran through her, and she reached out to clutch at him for support.

His arms went around her and they tumbled onto the bed together. When his mouth came to her she responded eagerly, her body sensitized and alive. Tiny shocks ran through her, one after another as he slipped his fingers beneath the elastic of her panties. She loved the feel of those raspy calluses, the faint trembling of his fingers, the hard masculine impatience held under rigid restraint.

He slipped her panties down her thighs one slow inch at a time while his mouth followed, his tongue leaving a slow, hot trail along her belly, through the tightly curled hair at the juncture of her thighs. Hands resting now on her thighs, he dipped into the cleft there, and she cried out, her fingers gripping at the pillow beneath her head. He blew on her thighs and she whimpered. Swiftly he swept her panties away, then worked his way up her body, his hands gliding, stroking.

She was losing control, her hands clutching at his hair, trying to urge him to hurry, but he seemed absorbed as he nudged her legs apart again to caress her with long, feathery strokes. She shivered, her stomach muscles jerking uncontrollably as the tension built inside. A hot rush of need took her, and she writhed helplessly, a painful ache building inside.

His breathing and hers mingled in harsh, urgent gasps. The sheets felt hot beneath her bare skin, and the air seemed too thin to satisfy her quest for oxygen. Above her head the ivory ceiling seemed to undulate as her eyes went out of focus.

"Please," she said on a moan. "Oh please."

He groaned, moved swiftly to rid himself of his shorts, and then he was kissing her again, his lean, heavy body bathing hers in heat. His hand stroked over her belly, his fingers trailing fire before burrowing gently through the curls. She was sobbing now, needing him. Helplessly, she arched up against his hand. He pressed lightly, then dipped a finger inside. She was wet and ready. He withdrew, pushed two fingers gently back in. Clutching at him, begging, she felt herself tip over the edge into a shattering climax. She cried out, her voice trembling uncontrollably. And yet he demanded more, his fingers kneading the sensitive bud of sexual nerve endings until she crested again and then quickly once more.

She was sobbing and wild for him as he sheathed himself in the thin latex, then positioned his body over her. His gaze on her face, his eyes dark and primitive with the torment of waiting, his forehead glistening with the exertion of control, he drew closer.

With blood pounding in his ears and his muscles screaming from restraint, Brody eased into her, feeling the slick heat lubricate his passage. She was tight, almost as tight as a virgin, and so incredibly sweet.

Her arms were holding him, welcoming him, her small hands running up and down his back. He felt the small shudders take him, and froze, desperate to give her one last orgasm before finding his own. But he'd been thinking about this all day and his body was throbbing to the point of pain. Clenching his jaw, he pushed deeper, exulting in the small, eager moans he was wringing from her. He thrust and she bucked against him. She cried out, her fingers raking his shoulders. He broke then, driving hard into her until he was fully seated. She gasped, then began to move. He withdrew, then thrust harder and harder, driving her with him.

He felt her come and plunged hard—once, twice—then exploded. He groaned, wrapped her in his arms, and rolled her on top of him, keeping them joined. Holding her close, absorbing with his body the tiny tremors of hers. Soothing her with long shaky strokes of his hand.

She murmured something, and he kissed her damp temple. For now, for this unbearably sweet moment, she was his.

Summer surfaced from a deep, satisfying sleep to feel Snowy's paw batting at her ear. It was a game they'd played with countless variations for the past ten years. The next move in the game required Snowy to walk over Summer's chest and snuggle close to her neck, which was currently impossible because Brody had Summer tucked very firmly against him like a blanket. His body exuded heat, and the soft pelt of his chest hair was tickling her nose. They seemed to be entwined, with one of his heavy thighs pinning hers. One of her arms had fallen asleep. She bit her lip and knew she would have to move soon, but she wanted to savor the sheer joy of waking up wrapped in Brody's arms. As though sensing her playmate's preoccupation, Snowball let out an irate meow and climbed over her back. The instant the cat put one paw on Brody's chest, he jerked.

"No, Snowy," Summer whispered, trying to free her hand from Brody's grip, but it was too late. Snowball dug in. Brody jerked again, then reared up, still half asleep, toppling Summer onto the mattress in a warm little heap. His hand shot out, and he tossed Snowy halfway across the small space. The cat landed on his feet and hissed a warning that had Summer giggling and Brody glowering.

"Hell of a way to wake up," he muttered, scooping a hand through his hair. In the half light of fading twilight, he seemed intimidatingly large and powerful.

"Careful, that's my baby you're tossing around," she warned on a laugh.

He turned to look down at her, his black brows drawn together in a fierce frown, but the look in his eyes was so tender she felt her amusement fade. There was a wealth of emotion buried in the dark violet depths, emotion she didn't dare name for fear she was wrong. For fear the longing she had for him to return her love would go unfulfilled and leave her feeling more alone than ever. As though avoiding questions he didn't want to answer, he shifted his gaze away from her face toward the white ball of fur presently walking with regal hauteur over the dark-gray carpeting.

"Animal has it in for me," he muttered, his voice husky.

"On the contrary, he's already bonded. He loves you."

Groaning, he settled on his side, one arm outstretched under his head, the other curving with a lover's possessive intimacy around her waist. His expression was absorbed, his face taut. With the newfound insight of a woman in love, she saw a lonely boy's hunger to belong stamped on his weathered face, as obvious as the burned-in tan and the harsh lines of a life that had been anything but easy. He needed moments like this, she realized. Sweet, lazy interludes when he could allow his gentle side to peek out just a little.

Smiling, she stretched, then shifted until she got a better look at the tattoo of a magnificent green-and-gold dragon curving over the cap of his shoulder. "Awesome," she murmured, running her fingertip along the barbed tail that wound around his biceps.

"A dumb mistake," he muttered, before bending to nuzzle her ear. She shivered, and arched back to give him easier access. "I thought about getting a tattoo once," she said when he drew back. "It was the cutest little thing. A yellow butterfly settling on a red rose."

He smiled a little at that. Her heart smiled back. "Why didn't you?"

"I took one look at the needle and chickened out. I was afraid it would hurt." She reached over to sift her fingers through the thick black hair covering his chest. His muscles jerked, then went hard. "Did it?"

"Probably." One side of his mouth kicked up. "I was pretty plowed at the time."

"How old were you?"

"Eighteen. It was the same night I ended up in the brig for thirty days. Drunk and disorderly. Damn near drove me crazy being locked in." He bunched the pillow into a comfortable position, then arranged her more snuggly in his arms. "How did you stand being locked up for so long?"

"The flip answer is, one day at a time. Sometimes one minute at a time." Needing time to settle the quick rush of bad memories, she leaned forward to kiss the dragon's fierce grin. His skin smelled of soap and healthy sweat. "Prisons are terrible places," she went on when she had herself in control again. "I know they're necessary, but I still hate the idea of anyone—or any living thing for that matter—being locked up." She hesitated, then added softly, "Over the years I've discovered that prisons don't have to have bars and locked doors. Guilt is one of the worst punishments of all because it's self-imposed and it's usually a life sentence."

He nodded, then blew out air before turning his head toward the window. "Getting dark," he said, his voice a little gruff.

"Are you hungry?" she asked, tracing one imperious eyebrow with her fingertip.

"Depends on what you have in mind, honey." He looked wonderfully intense in the thick light as his gaze roamed her flushed face.

"Is that what's commonly known as an indecent proposal?"

"Guess it is."

"Guess I accept."

School was finally out. On Saturday afternoon, to celebrate, Mark took his angel girl to their private place high above the valley and parked in the wide space overlooking the river. Far below, a party of rafters drifted with the current, and a hawk made lazy circles over one of the orchards on the western side. Above the open top of the convertible the leaves of a sugar maple danced on the breeze.

"Okay, close your eyes and hold out your hand," he ordered after shutting off the engine. He loved her best when she looked at him like this, all starry-eyed and happy. It made his heart feel like it was going to burst out of his chest.

With an eager little murmur Kelly released her belt, then flipped her hair over her shoulders and sat back. His hand shook as he dropped his gift into Kelly's outstretched hands. He'd been wired all day, just waiting to see the look on her face at this moment. "You can open your eyes now."

Her heart was beating like a drum beneath the Deadhead shirt he'd given her last week. He'd been promising something wonderful. Now here it was, a small oblong box wrapped in shimmering paper. "I bet it's another charm," she said, holding up her wrist so that the bracelet he'd given her on their first date caught the sunlight.

"How much?" he said with the mischievous grin she loved.

"Oh, no, you don't. I'm saving for a new CD player. No way am I gonna bet with you," she declared as she untied the ribbon and ripped off the paper.

"Oh, Mark, it's beautiful!" Her fingers felt clumsy as she fumbled with the gold chain. "Are you sure you can afford it?" she blurted out. "I mean, a real antique and all?"

"Don't worry, I can afford it," he said, his voice hurt. "Mira has a new boyfriend. Some guy she met in Cancún. She's spending the summer with him in Greece."

"Is she going to bring him with her when she comes to visit next month?"

"She's not coming. She sent me a check instead."

"I'm sorry, Mark."

"Yeah, well, I'm not. It's always a drag when she's around anyway."

In spite of the bored look on his face Kelly knew he was hurt. She knew how awful she would feel if her dad didn't want to come see her. "Oh Mark," she whispered, leaning forward over the gearshift to brace her hand on his shoulder.

"Angel," he choked before he kissed her.

She felt the shivery tight feeling settle between her legs the way it always did when he kissed her—like she wanted to rub herself against him to make the feeling go away. Beneath her shirt her nipples poked against her bra like hard little peas and her breasts felt achy. When he lifted a hand to cup her breast, a feeling like liquid fire shot through her, and she moaned.

"I love you, Kelly," he whispered, his voice thick and strained. "I need you so much." With his free hand, he reached for the bottom of her shirt, and she froze, then jerked back.

"No, Mark, we can't." But she wanted to let him touch her

there and everywhere. "Don't be mad," she pleaded, clutching the hand he wrapped around the steering wheel.

He drew a breath, his gorgeous face all tight and scary. Tiff always said guys got all uptight and funny when girls waited too late to cut them off. Only she didn't want to wait. Not really.

"Mark, please. You know I love you, but Dad trusts me. If he ever found out . . ."

"I won't let things get out of hand, angel, I promise," he said in a jerky voice. "It's just that sometimes I get so hot for you, I . . ."

She rubbed her fingers over his knuckles until she felt him relax. "I get hot for you, too. But it would be wrong."

His face changed, and his eyes darkened, the way she hated. "Don't say that, angel. How can it be wrong if I love you and you love me?"

Feeling all funny inside, she opened her fist and looked down at his present. "Guess you want this back now, huh?"

He looked ashamed. "Oh God, Kel, I'm sorry. I was out of line, okay? I mean it. I was all wrong to push you. I swore I'd wait until we were engaged, and I will. But that's okay because you're still my angel girl, right?"

She nodded.

"Here, let me put that on for you, okay?"

"It's perfect, Mark. The most beautiful thing I've ever seen, only the thing is, I . . . I can't keep it. Dad wouldn't like it."

"But see, angel, that's why I got you a necklace instead of a ring. So you can wear this under your clothes, and he won't have to know."

Kelly bit her lip. She wanted to please Mark more than anything, but she didn't want to hurt her dad. Summer would know what to do, she thought. Summer knew all about making things better.

He leaned toward her, his face so full of emotion it shocked her into forgetting the words already forming on her tongue. "You love me, don't you, angel? You said you did."

Even as she nodded, she was trying to remember what Tiff

had said to do when guys came on too strong, but all she could think about was Mark's mom, and how he'd talked for weeks about the things the three of them would do when she got here.

"You won't leave me, will you, angel? Promise me you'll never leave me." Mark reached around the gearshift lever to grab her arm. Pain shot into her shoulder, and she flinched.

"P-please, you're hurting me," she whimpered, trying to twist away.

His face went white, and his eyes changed. He gentled his hold on her, but he didn't let go, even when she tugged a little against his hand. "Don't be afraid, angel," he said in a hollow voice. "I won't hurt you. I'll never hurt you. I love you. You're mine. Only mine."

CHAPTER 19

The Finleys arrived promptly as promised at ten o'clock on Monday morning. Charlotte Jackson poked her head into one of the private treatment rooms which Summer was using as a private office.

"Whoo-ee, girl, we are in tall cotton now," Char said as she perched on the edge of the desk. "Here we've been pinchin' pennies till they bleed and our first patient shows up in a stretch limo."

"That certainly gets the kid started off right," Summer muttered, her stomach clenching around the nervous jitters that had been with her since her eyes had popped open at dawn. "Is Manny getting Joe checked in?"

Char nodded. Tall and slender, with runner's legs and a perfect café au lait complexion, Char was the least experienced of the three of them—and at twenty-four, the youngest. She was also rock-solid reliable, with a knack for calming the most agitated patient—or the most stressed-out therapist, a function she'd performed for Summer a time or two in the past. The result of being the middle child in a family of twelve growing up in Watts, she'd told Summer during her tenure at the McDonald Center.

"Don't know about the patient gettin' off on the wrong foot, but from what I saw before Manny ushered them into the office, I got me a real strong feeling we're going to have trouble with Dad."

"Did he hassle you?" Summer asked quickly.

"Not me, girlfriend," Char said with a throaty laugh as she swung her foot. "I just have a feeling about patients arriving in limos, that's all." Char bent to sniff the red roses on Summer's desk. A good-luck present from Brody that had warmed Summer's heart. "At least those two downstairs are doing right by their boy."

"That's a start, anyway," Summer said as she tossed down her pen and got to her feet. Before the nervousness built, she strode purposefully to the door, then stopped and braced her hand against the door frame. "God, I'm scared," she said, giving Char a rueful look.

Char appeared none too calm herself suddenly. "Like my daddy always told us kids, no matter what happens, nobody can make you feel like a failure but yourself."

Summer let out a long breath, glad she'd added a large bottle of Pepto-Bismol to the first-aid closet. "He's absolutely right, but just in case, how about a hug for luck?"

They fell into each other's arms like two shaky survivors of a train wreck before drawing apart. "Catch you later," Char said. Summer walked to what Dottie had called the ladies' parlor and, because she wanted a good read on the reactions of the visitors inside, opened the door without knocking.

The office fairly vibrated with tension, slapping at her as she entered. The Finleys were seated on one side of the desk, Manny on the other. As she crossed the threshold, Manny's dark curly head shot up, and she saw the hard line of white around his mouth. Short and wiry, with the chiseled features of his Bedouin ancestors, Mansur Rashid had a placid temperament that masked a fiery temper. At the moment he seemed to be working hard at keeping it under control.

Summer had a strong feeling the imperious-looking man getting slowly to his feet to face her had a great deal to do with that. Anson Finley was well dressed, well shod, with a perfect South Seas tan and thick steel-gray hair razor cut to mold his decidedly patrician head. He and her father could be blood cousins—or at least golfing buddies.

"Good morning," she said, striding forward with her hand extended. "I'm Summer Laurence."

"Dr. Laurence," he said, inclining his head like king to subject as a well-tended hand closed around hers. His fingers were dry, bony, and pressed against hers a little too hard.

"This is my wife, Vondra," he said, indicating the stylishly dressed woman who'd remained seated. "Joe's stepmother."

The woman was Summer's own age or perhaps a few years younger, with a mane of sun-streaked blond hair that looked natural and a tan that rivaled her husband's for perfection. She was also very pregnant.

"Welcome to Phoenix House, Mrs. Finley," she said politely as she and Mrs. Finley shook hands.

"Thanks." The woman offered her a friendly smile, then went back to fiddling with an emerald solitaire the size of a chicken's egg on her marriage finger. The image she presented wasn't particularly uncaring, Summer decided. More like detached, as though she was content to let her husband deal with his own son.

With the formalities out of the way, Summer turned her attention to the silent young man standing with his back to the room, looking out the window. Her first impression, albeit incomplete, was of a taller-than-average, well-built preppy in a blue blazer, tan slacks, and cordovan penny-loafers. The slumped shoulders suggested a very nonconfrontational young man. An image at complete odds with society's usual impression of an addict.

"This must be Joseph," she said, her gaze still fixed on the back of his short blond hair.

Mr. Finley nodded, then frowned when his son did nothing to acknowledge her presence. "Damn it, boy, turn around and act like you give a damn what happens to you."

"Like I do?" the boy muttered to the window.

Scowling, Finley took a step forward, only to halt when Summer touched his sleeve. "Manny, are you finished with the paperwork or do you need a few more minutes?"

Manny glanced down at the open file folder in front of him. A cashier's check lay on top. "I was about to get Mr. Finley's signature as Joseph's legal guardian, but everything else is done."

"Why don't I finish up here while you take Joe upstairs to his room."

"Will do," Manny said, getting to his feet, his attention already focused on the young man at the window. "Joe, you want to come with me?"

Joe turned around, a bored look on his face. "Whatever," he muttered, but Summer caught the quick look of desperation that shot into his eyes before he masked it with a sneer.

"Your parents will be up to say good-bye before they leave," Summer told him as he and Manny walked to the door.

"About the boy's accommodations," Finley said over the sound of retreating footsteps. There was an edge to his voice now and impatience in his eyes. "I realize my son is the only patient at the moment, but Rashid told me he'll have to share a room with another boy if the place fills up."

"That's correct."

"There must be some misunderstanding." It surprised her when his lips curved into an engaging smile. "I'm paying for a private room."

Summer supplied a smile of her own. "There are no private rooms at Phoenix House, Mr. Finley, as I discussed with your accountant. Bonding between patients is crucial to positive group dynamics. For that reason, the patients are required to interact with one another. Private rooms encourage isolation."

Like a lightbulb switching off, the congenial smile disappeared, and his silver brows drew together. "I'm sorry, Doctor, but that's unacceptable. My son is *not* sharing a room with undesirables for six weeks. Not at the price I'm paying."

"Then I'm afraid you've made a wasted trip." Summer was pleased to see that her hand was steady as she picked up his check and held it out to him. "I wish you and your family the best of luck."

His jaw tightened and eyes as hard as sapphires bored into hers. Though her stomach knotted, and her throat constricted, the therapist's cool held firm. He who blinks first loses, she reminded herself as the impasse lengthened.

Finally, when she was sure the muscles of her arm would give out, he blinked. "Tell me, Dr. Laurence, have you ever played poker?"

Summer hid her elation behind a professional smile. "No, but I suspect you have."

"Enough to know when the only smart move is to fold." His expression was rueful as he reached into the pocket of his beautifully tailored suit for his fountain pen.

"Marissa Gladstone's parents are driving her up from Portland on Saturday. We also received the go-ahead from the insurance company to admit the new referral from Judge Mandeville."

"Blessed be his name," Char intoned as Summer put a check mark next to the last item on her list.

"I've made appointments for both with Dr. Krebs for the initial workup." Summer stifled a yawn as she flexed her tired shoulders. She'd stayed up until nearly two with a new admission who was determined to leave. It had taxed every ounce of her ingenuity to talk him into giving them one more week, but it had left her emotionally drained. Instead of conducting the daily staff meeting, she'd wanted to take a nap.

"The referral from the judge, male or female?" Char asked, glancing up from her notes.

"A fourteen-year-old female." Summer looked at her yellow pad. "Susan Stanforth. According to the judge, she's been flirting with gang affiliation and was picked up for possession in a sting operation at the high school. Her parents were ready to declare her an emancipated minor and turn her loose on the streets, but he talked them into giving us a try."

Summer shifted in her chair and tried to ignore the feeling of claustrophobia that threatened to overwhelm her whenever she was shut into the small staff office on the second floor. As soon as they'd started having meetings there, she'd realized she should have had Amos put in a skylight. Or maybe another window.

Manny leaned back against the chair cushion and rubbed his thick waist with a stubby hand. "Too bad that kid from Spokane couldn't get insurance approval."

Char scolded him, "Lighten up, dude. Seven patients in three weeks ain't bad."

"It's the first one I'm still worried about," Summer said with a grimace as she uncurled from the corner of the sofa and got up to file her notes. During her initial interview with Joe, she'd heard his version of the story she'd read in the newspaper. He'd had a fight with his girlfriend about his drug use and had gone for a drive to blow off steam. To spite her, he'd smoked some crack, then drunk a few beers to mellow out the high. His memory of the accident was hazy—but not the aftermath. Summer had made sure of that.

Char glanced up from the notes she was flipping through, her long red fingernails serving as a filing aid. "Twenty-one nights of nightmares has got be some kind of record."

"Not to mention being pretty darn rough on the kid," Manny said before shifting his attention to Summer again. "And every time Finley flips into nightmare land, his roomie ends up losing sleep."

"Who's he bunking with? David?"

Manny nodded. "Poor Davy's got black circles under his eyes. I think we should give some thought to letting Finley have that private room his old man was yammering about."

Finished with her notes, Char tucked them into a red folder. "Me, I think Joey-boy's scammin' us big time."

Manny snorted. "You think everything's a scam. Comes from growing up so close to movie land."

"Yeah, well, you think every junkie you meet is just drippin' remorse and beggin' to be saved."

"Not true. In Finley's case, though, yeah, I think the guy is genuinely suffering."

Char rested her elbow on the filing cabinet and regarded him with calm eyes. Her words, when she spoke, were laced with concern. "In case you haven't gotten the word, the first step in recovery is ownin' up to powerlessness. In this case, against drugs. And so far, I ain't heard Joe admit to anything but being bummed because Summer assigned him to work in the barn."

Summer had been experiencing some of Char's reservations herself. Since Manny was Joe's primary therapist, however, she'd been reluctant to intervene. "Sounds like we have a major disagreement here, guys. You think maybe a third opinion would help clarify things?"

"Sounds good to me," Char said, stretching her arms over her head and bending at the waist to touch her toes. Limbering herself up for the run around the makeshift obstacle course she was to lead the patients on later.

"Couldn't hurt," Manny said, hauling himself to his feet. "When do you want to see him?"

Summer glanced at the schedule posted on the bulletin board. Every minute of the patients' lives was regimented, which meant the therapists followed the same schedule. "When's your next one on one with him?"

"Ten minutes from now. We're going to exercise Mabel and Sweet Sue."

Summer grimaced. "Forget that. How about I meet with him for a chat during the movie tonight."

She met with Joe in his room. Because the memories of the cramped, cheerless cell that had been her home for two and a half months were permanently imprinted on her mind, she'd made every room as bright and distinctive as possible. Dottie had helped her choose different motifs for each one. Consequently, the upstairs was now a riot of vivid, jewel-like color.

In spite of the bright surroundings, however, the mood of the room's tenant was sullen. "Hey, I'm here, aren't I?" His gaze averted, he slouched lower in the desk chair. "What do you want from me?"

"Many things. At the moment, I'll settle for your starting to take an active role in your own recovery."

"I thought that's what I've been doing. Writing in my f—in' journal. Spilling my guts to Manny every day. Mucking out stalls till I smell horse shit in my sleep."

"Yes, and those are all positive things. What you haven't done, however, is admit that you're an addict."

"Yeah, well, that's 'cause I'm not. I just got high a couple of times, is all, because I was bummed out and needed to chill for a while. Everybody's trying to make like that's some kind of major character flaw or something. Hell, even my old man snorted cocaine when he was in college."

Summer stifled a sigh. She'd been with him for nearly fifteen minutes and still he'd managed to staunch her every attempt to break through his wall of denial. She'd tried the carrot, she told herself with a sigh. Now it was time for the stick. Not her favorite part of therapy sessions.

She took a breath and braced herself. "Sit straight and look at me when you speak," she ordered, her voice snapping like a whip into the silence.

His head came up and his eyes blazed defiance, but he obeyed with satisfying speed.

"I'm tired of you moping around here feeling sorry for yourself," she said when she was sure she had his full attention. "If it's sympathy you want, you're not getting it from me or anyone else on these premises. Not until you show us some remorse for what you've done."

His jaw went slack, then snapped shut. "You can't talk to me like that. My dad'll—"

"I run Phoenix House, not your dad. While you're on the premises you follow my rules."

"Fine. Soon as Dad sends the limo, I'm outta here."

She shook her head. "No limos. If you want to leave, you'll do it on foot. Now." She gestured with a nod. "There's the door. It's open."

He eyed her warily, like a trapped rabbit eyeing a swaying

cobra. "Yeah, sure, and as soon as I walk out, you'll be on the phone to Mandeville."

"Yes, of course," she said with deliberate impatience. "I have a responsibility to the court, and unlike you, when I give my word I keep it."

"Hey, that's bogus. I promised to do my time here, and that's what I'm doing."

"I read the transcript, Joe. You begged for mercy, then swore you wanted to get clean and sober and stay that way."

"You'd swear, too, if you were facing prison."

"If you stay, you'll do the work. No more excuses."

Judge Mandeville's ruling had been precise and specific. Joe had been given the maximum sentence allowed for manslaughter, which would be suspended if he successfully completed six weeks of treatment. If not, he was to be taken into immediate custody to began serving his sentence.

"It's not fair," he cried, leaping to his feet and raking his hands through his hair. "I know guys who get high all the time. No one ever gives them any grief."

"Grief? I'll give you grief, Joe. You killed two people." She bored in, her voice sharp and unrelenting. As unrelenting as the addiction that always waited to claim her soul again. "Two innocent people, dead. Dead! One was a baby, for God's sake. And a nice little boy will grow up without a daddy because of you. How's that for unfair?"

His face twisted. "I didn't fucking know it was going to happen, okay? I wasn't even speeding. And then this Jag comes outta *nowhere*."

"Don't give me that. You were on the wrong side of the road."

"Says who? That storm-trooper cop?"

"No, the evidence."

"I . . . it's . . . I . . . oh God, it . . ." He staggered to the chair and sat down, burying his face in his hands. A sob shook him, then another. His shoulders jerked as he fought to regain control. "I can't make it go away," he cried, his voice thin with anguish. "Help me make it go away, please."

"It's all right, Joe," she said, going to kneel in front of him. "I'm here for you. We're all here for you."

When she left his room twenty minutes later he was laying exhausted, but calm on his bed while she was emotionally wrung dry. Char was waiting for her at the end of the hall, a steaming mug of chamomile tea in her hand.

"Here, drink this," she ordered when Summer reached her.

Too whipped to argue, Summer smiled her thanks, then braced herself for the foul taste as she sipped. "I heard his sobs all the way down the hall," Char said when Summer lifted her head. "You think it was a breakthrough or an act?"

Summer inhaled the pungent steam and felt some of the tiredness lift. "In other words, who do I think is the better diagnostician, you or Manny?" she teased gently.

Char looked sheepish. "Busted again," she admitted.

Summer forced several more sips. "I think you're both right. Joe's doing his darnedest to skate through here without doing the hard work—which includes playing on our heartstrings for all he's worth. On the other hand, I think he feels real remorse—and that we can work with."

Char lifted one eyebrow. "Progress, not perfection, right?"

Summer smiled. "Right."

After one full month of operation, Phoenix House was almost to capacity. There were only two beds available. It was the Fourth of July weekend and Manny and Char had taken the patients for a walk along the river.

Summer was helping Dottie get ready for a backyard barbecue. Brody was still on duty. While Dottie was busy whipping up delicious things in the kitchen, Kelly and Summer were washing off the picnic table so they could set out the plates and silverware. So far Kelly had talked virtually nonstop. While Summer scrubbed and Kelly rinsed, they'd discussed Tiffany's new hairdo, which was killer, and the new busboy at Mario's, who was rank. While Summer hosed down the lawn chairs, they'd moved on to rock groups and videos and her father's flat refusal to let her get two more holes put into her earlobes. It seemed that Brody was incapable of understanding why a woman might want to wear four earrings instead of two.

They'd laughed a lot, but Summer had sensed an undercurrent of something somber and disturbing beneath the girl's bright facade. She'd told herself to bide her time. Like Brody, Kelly had a stubborn determination to do things in her own way.

"Summer, there's this sort of . . . thing that's, you know, sort of bothering me." Kelly wiped a towel over the dripping seat of a lounger, the charm bracelet Mark had given her tinkling like little bells whenever she moved her arm.

"What's that, sweetie?" Summer asked as she walked to the spigot to turn off the water.

"It's about Mark and me."

"Problems?" Summer bent to wind up the hose.

"Not really. I mean, I really like Mark and all, only it's like he's always wanting me to spend time with him, you know?"

"And that bothers you?"

"At first I thought it was really neat, but now it's kinda like . . . intense."

Finished with the hose, Summer stood and wiped her wet hands on her shorts. "Intense how?"

Kelly drove her brows together in a dainty version of her father's ferocious frown. "I don't know exactly. Mostly he just talks about how it's going to be when we're married and all."

Summer ran her hands through her hair, careful to keep her expression impassive. But inside an alarm was jangling wildly. "I didn't realize the two of you had talked about marriage," she said as she grabbed another towel.

Kelly cast a worried look toward the spot near the garage where Brody usually parked. "You're not going to tell this to Dad, are you? I mean, this is just between you and me, right?"

"If that's what you want," Summer promised.

Looking a little wilted, Kelly sat down on the redwood bench and regarded her bare toes. "It's just that I don't know what to do. I know Mark's supposed to be my boyfriend and all, but I kinda like Chuck, too."

"Ah, I see."

Kelly's face lit up, and her eyes glowed. "See, Chuck's got this really neat sense of humor. Like at church, you know? Last Sunday Chuck sat with me and Auntie and during the sermon he made these weird faces. I nearly busted a gut laughing."

Summer hid a smile. "Sounds like you're more interested in Chuck than Mark at the moment."

"Yeah, maybe." The animation left her face, and her mouth turned down. "All Mark ever talks about is how much he loves me." She hesitated, then added in a low voice. "It gets kinda scary sometimes."

"Scary how?"

Kelly looked down at the grass. "Yesterday when he brought me home from work, I sorta hinted about how maybe we should, like, maybe date other people."

"That seems reasonable," Summer said when Kelly looked her way, a question on her face.

"That was Tiff's idea. She said guys have these really big egos and they get all bummed if you, like, dump on them all at once." She looked nervous. "I don't want to hurt his feelings, honest."

"I believe you, sweetie." Because she sensed the girl needed an extra dollop of nurturing, Summer reached out to brush back Kelly's hair. "You're a very sensitive young woman."

Kelly seemed reassured enough to go on. "We were still in his car, only parked down by the dead end near the river so Dad wouldn't see. We go there sometimes to make out." Guilt crossed her face. Summer merely nodded.

"His face got all funny, and all of a sudden he reaches under the seat and pulls out this old gun, like you sometimes see in the movies. He said it's exactly like the one his dad used when he, uh, you know, like shot himself and all. It was loaded, he said, and then he put it to his head and threatened to pull the trigger unless I promised to never talk about breaking up again."

Summer went cold. Only her promise of confidentiality kept her from walking to the phone and calling Brody immediately. Instead, she sat down on the bench and put her arm around the girl's shoulders. "Oh sweetie, no wonder you're so upset. If I were in your place, I would have been terrified!"

"It was awful! He was crying and the gun was shaking. I didn't know what to do." Kelly broke into tears and turned into Summer's arms.

"Sweetheart, I totally understand your reluctance to speak to your father about this but—"

Kelly jerked free of Summer's arms, a look of abject panic on her face. "No! You promised not to tell him. You *promised*!"

"And I won't, but I have to tell you, I've very uncomfortable keeping secrets from your dad. The last time I did, it nearly ended our friendship, remember?"

"That was different."

Shortly after her return, she'd told Kelly about her past and the reason her father had been upset about Phoenix House. After a flurry of questions about prison, which Summer had answered honestly, Kelly had simply accepted. "I disagree, sweetie."

Kelly shook her head and jutted her chin. "Nuh uh. You know Dad." She wiped at her eyes with her fingers and the charms jingled musically. "He'll just get mad and say I told you so and never let me go out on a date with a guy again."

"Perhaps he wouldn't go quite that far," Summer said gently.

"Yeah, but he'd be really ticked."

"I suspect you're right." Summer glanced toward the house. Flowers spilled from the window box beneath the kitchen window, and the blood-rousing beat of zydeco pounded through the screen. Dottie was making Cajun.

"Would you like my opinion?" she asked quietly.

Kelly nodded eagerly, relief bright in her eyes.

"First, it sounds to me like Mark has some unresolved issues over his father's death. A phobia about being abandoned being one, which is his problem, not yours. My concern is for you, sweetie, and a relationship with a young man who uses emotional blackmail is not healthy."

Kelly blinked. "Like with the gun, you mean?"

"Exactly. You would have broken up with Mark if he hadn't pulled out that gun, wouldn't you?"

"Yeah, I guess so."

Summer glanced at her watch. It was just past five. "It's my professional opinion that Mark needs some intensive therapy, and with your permission, I'd like to share what you've told me with his grandfather. Privately, of course."

Alarm crossed Kelly's face, and her skin seemed to pale. Summer's own apprehension grew. "What if Mark finds out and gets really mad at me?"

"Kelly, Mark needs professional help. This obsession he has with suicide isn't healthy."

Kelly worried about that for a while, then nodded. "What about Mark and me?"

"This is what I would do." She cleared her throat. "I would ask him to your house when your aunt and your dad are home, so you feel more comfortable. Maybe sit in the porch swing or on the front steps." When Kelly frowned, she went on quietly. "Give him back the bracelet and the other presents he's given you, too. Very calmly tell him you want to be his friend but you can't be his girlfriend anymore. Don't let him get you into an argument or a discussion. Mark's very good at negotiation."

"I can't talk to him, Summer. I just can't! I know he'd talk me out of it."

"Not if you remain firm."

"You do it, okay?" Kelly pleaded, her look beseeching. "You're good with words. He won't argue with you."

"Sweetie—"

"Please, Summer."

Summer took a careful breath. What would a mother do? she wondered. A mother who adored her child and wanted to wrap her up tightly in sweet dreams and brave the demons of hell to keep the nightmares away? She would do her best, Summer thought. With love.

"Mark barely knows me. If I talk with him, he might think I'm trying to drive you two apart and keep pestering you. But he'll have to listen to his grandfather."

"But you'll be the one to talk to Dr. Krebs, right?" When Summer nodded, Kelly slumped with relief. "Soon, okay, Summer? Like maybe—tonight?"

Summer smiled. "If the doctor's available, yes. Why don't you finish up here, and I'll go down and give him a call?"

Grey had been out when Summer had called, forcing her to leave a cryptic message on his machine. He'd returned her call first thing the next morning, and when she'd told him it was urgent that she see him, he'd arranged for her to meet him at his office at nine. She'd arrived early, but he'd been delayed. It was nearly ten when he returned to his office. By the time Summer finished recounting her purpose in coming to see him, his eyes were jagged with pain.

"I had no idea he had that dueling pistol," he said as he slumped back in his desk chair and stared at the shoe box Summer had brought with her. Inside were the gifts Mark had given Kelly over the course of their relationship. Anxious to put this behind her, Kelly had gathered everything together after the cookout. The box was sealed with tape. Grey hadn't opened it.

"I'm sorry, Grey." It was the customary thing to say in times of trouble, and yet she truly felt empathy for both the doctor *and* his grandson. "If there's anything I can do . . ."

"Thank you." He passed a hand over his jaw, then let it drop. "As soon as we're finished here, I'll call Henry Gottlieb and arrange for him to see Mark, ASAP." He glanced across the polished desktop, his struggle to maintain his composure painful to watch. "Have you met Henry yet? The head of our psychiatric unit?"

"I have, yes. He paid Phoenix House a courtesy call shortly after we opened. He's a very impressive man."

Grey acknowledged that with a distracted smile that faded quickly. "I suspect Henry will put Mark on medication immediately." Though Grey was outwardly calm, she sensed a deep anxiety behind the facade.

"I'm sure you can understand why it's best if Mark not contact Kelly again for a while," Summer said as gently as she could.

"What? Oh yes, of course. I'm surprised Brody didn't show up in person to warn the boy off."

"Actually, Brody doesn't know about this. Kelly begged me not to tell him." She smiled when Grey's eyebrows shot up. "I know, it's never wise to keep secrets from a parent, but in this case I have to admit I sympathize with Kelly. She had to lobby long and hard to be able to date at all, and she's terrified he'll rescind her privileges—or as she put it, handcuff her to his wrist for the rest of her natural life."

Grey chuckled, but sobered quickly. "I've seen Brody in protective mode, and the girl has a point. I'll make sure Mark keeps his distance." His sigh was heavy. "I thought it was a simple crush. Puppy love."

"I think we all did. All but Mark, that is."

Summer plucked a stray thread from her linen slacks, then crossed her legs and drew in a careful breath. "You have to understand, Grey, that although I am extremely concerned about Mark's welfare, my primary goal is protecting Kelly. I don't want her hurt in any way."

Dismay raced over his face. "Surely you don't think he would attack her."

"Honestly, no. On the other hand, my experience has taught me to plan for the worst—just in case. Which is why we don't allow strangers on the grounds, and conduct regular bed checks and unexpected room searches. I hate doing it, but I'm not an ostrich either."

Grey accepted that with a sad smile. "How would you suggest I handle telling him that it's over with Kelly?"

"I thought about that, and the best thing I could come up with was to have Kelly write Mark a letter explaining that she really liked him as a friend, but that she didn't want to date him anymore." She leaned down to draw the envelope from her purse. "I wanted to check with you first, though, before she sent it. I would suggest you run it by Dr. Gottlieb before you give it to your grandson, however."

Grey accepted that with another nod. "Mark usually calls Kelly every night. What's going to happen when he calls tonight?"

According to Kelly, Mark called more than once a night, but Summer saw no reason to burden Grey with more bad news. He'd heard enough to convince him to take appropriate action, and that had been her goal. "She's arranged to spend the night with Tiffany. Hopefully by tomorrow night it won't be a problem."

CHAPTER 20

"A refill on the iced tea, Miss Dottie?" Chuck Sawyer asked politely, the pitcher poised to pour.

"Why yes, thank you, Charles." Dottie adjusted the ruffle of her turquoise peasant blouse and beamed up at the earnest young man who'd been hovering around their table from the moment they'd walked in. Kelly, too, had made frequent trips to their table, bringing more bread sticks even though the first basket was still half-full and making her father a larger than usual salad with extra tomatoes and black olives. Just the way he liked it, she'd assured him with a quick, nervous grin. Then she stopped by after he'd scarcely taken more than a couple bites to ask if he wanted more.

"Uh, how about you, Chief?" Chuck asked when he'd filled Dottie's glass to the brim. "Hit you again?"

"Three's my limit, son." Though Brody's tone was polite, Chuck turned scarlet. Summer hid a grin.

"Yes, sir." Clearly nervous, Chuck jerked his gaze Summer's way. She took pity on him and shook her head. Across the table Dottie nibbled on a bread stick, a look of bright speculation in her blue eyes.

Chuck cleared his throat, and Summer noticed that his knuckles were white, no doubt from the death grip he had on the pitcher. "Uh, pizza's almost ready. The special, right? Extra cheese."

Brody tilted his head and regarded the teenager thoughtfully. "Something bothering you, Chuck?"

The boy's Adam's apple bobbed convulsively. "No sir. Uh, yes sir. That is, Kelly said I had to take a driving test."

"How about checking on the pizza?" Summer interjected when she saw Brody's eyebrows draw together.

Relief flooded the boy's eyes as he jerked his head toward the kitchen. "Yeah, right away." He took two steps, then turned back. "Uh, excuse me, please," he said, suddenly remembering his manners.

"So that's why Kelly broke it off with Mark," Dottie said brightly when Chuck had disappeared into the kitchen. After asking Summer's advice, Kelly had told her father and her aunt only that she and Mark had broken up. Brody had seemed a little puzzled, but relieved. Dottie had been philosophical—and a bit sad. Remembering her first love and how it had ended, Summer suspected.

"Hell," Brody muttered in a tone so low it was nearly a groan. "I just got used to that Krebs kid hanging around."

"Charles is a lovely boy," Dottie informed him before carefully lifting her glass to take a sip. "Even though he does prefer swords to plowshares."

Brody's eyes narrowed to slits. "You want to explain that, Auntie?" he ordered in a steely tone that had Summer laughing.

"I'm referring to the story of Joshua, dear heart. And his flaming sword. When I taught Sunday school that story was Charles's favorite."

"So now it's the Sawyer kid I have to worry about." As he lifted a hand to rub his jaw, his expression turned rueful. "Way things are going I'll be gray by fifty."

Dottie reached for another bread stick. "Big Malcolm looked gorgeous with silver hair. Personally, I think he got better-looking the older he got." She crunched the hard bread, then waved the remainder of the stick in Summer's direction. "Remind me to show you a picture, dear."

"You already have," Summer said. "And I agree. Your father was a very handsome man."

Dottie beamed. "Brody favors him, don't you think?"

"Auntie—" The rest of Brody's warning was cut short by a familiar buzzing. Both Summer and Brody reached for their pagers.

"Mine," Summer said, already reaching for her wallet. "I'm on call tonight."

"Oh dear, I do so hate those electronic gizmos," Dottie said as Summer walked to the pay phones in the rear, near the rest rooms.

Brody recognized a diversion when he heard it. After two hellacious weekends of traffic jams, bar fights, and fender benders, he wasn't in the mood to be handled. "Auntie, I thought we had an agreement. No more matchmaking."

His aunt offered him an innocent smile. "But dear, it's perfectly clear to anyone with eyes . . . oh my goodness, Summer's as white as a sheet. Something terrible must have happened."

Brody was already on his feet by the time Summer reached the table.

"Snowball's been hurt," she said in a shaky voice before snatching up her purse.

"Oh my God! What happened?" Dottie cried, leaping to her feet. "Is it bad?"

"Manny and Joe found him in the barn when they got back from their ride. He was in one of the stalls and it looked as though he'd been kicked. Manny's rushing him to the vet's now. Char . . . Char thinks my baby's dying."

Brody leaned back against the headboard of her bed, watching while Summer nervously punched out the number of the vet's office. "Honey, it hasn't been twenty minutes since you called the last time."

"It's okay," she said as she lifted the portable to her ear. "The night tech said she didn't mind."

In the small waiting room, she'd paced and fretted and bitten her lip raw. It had been almost eight by the time they'd gotten to the vet's, close to eleven before Kathy Sills had come out of the OR with the news that the cat had made it through surgery and was resting comfortably.

It had taken all of his persuasive skills and Kathy's to convince Summer that Snowy was going to sleep through the night whether she was there or not. After Brody had gotten her back to her trailer, it had taken him a solid hour of coaxing before he got her to eat some leftover stew he'd found in her fridge, another hour to get her to change into another of those oversized shirts she slept in. This one had a sad-faced basset hound on the front. Now, close to midnight, he figured she had to be exhausted, and yet she couldn't settle.

"Hi, this is Summer Laurence again, calling to check on Snowball." Summer frowned, then rubbed at her temple as she listened intently. "But you'll call if there's any news?" Apparently reassured, she thanked the person on the other end and disconnected.

"No news is good news, right?" she said as she returned the phone to the table by the bed and settled back next to him.

"Absolutely." He reached up to flip her tousled hair over her shoulder.

"Although . . . you know, that sounded like a different tech than the one I spoke to earlier. Maybe he didn't have the latest information. I think I'll just double check."

"Enough," he said, capturing her hand before it reached the phone. "It's time to shut down for a while."

"I can't, Brody. I'm too wired. Maybe I'll . . . I have letters that need answering and . . ." She stopped and started again. "It's late. I know you have to work tomorrow—"

He leaned forward to silence her with a kiss he took pains to keep gentle. He felt her sway, then clutch at his shirt. He noted his body's normal reaction to her scent, the taste of her mouth, the silk of her hair where it brushed his cheek. Though he wanted to hold her, he made himself draw back until he was under control again. Then he reached to cuddle her against his chest.

"P-put your head on my s-shoulder, honey," he said. "Stop being strong long enough to build up a little of that s-strength you keep handing out with both hands to others."

"I'm—"

"Fine. Yeah, I know. That's why you keep clamping your lower lip between your teeth."

Surprise glinted in her eyes. "Busted again," she muttered, blinking a little before she dipped to rub her forehead against his shoulder. "You can't be a cop, Hollister. Not with all that sweetness you keep hidden behind those fierce frowns."

"Keep stalling, and you'll find out how fierce this old boy can be." He figured if he made his voice rough she would stop pouring gratitude all over him long enough for the exhaustion to hit her.

"I want—" She stopped and squeezed her eyes shut. "Oh God."

"What?" he asked harshly, the words constricting in his throat.

She opened her eyes and looked up at him. There were no tears, but her skin was chalk. "I don't want to be alone. Not . . . tonight."

Brody brushed a kiss over her temple. It had been a long time since he'd been needed. "I'm not going anywhere, honey."

It was still dark when Brody jerked himself from sleep. In a flash he was wide awake and braced, only to force himself to relax when he realized he was in Summer's bed and she was crying in her sleep. "Please, please," she muttered, her voice shredded.

He tightened his arm around her and stammered out her name. She pulled away, then cried out, "No!"

"Shh, honey. It's just another b-bad dream." He rubbed her arm with his palm, trying to ease her back to reality. "Come on, honey. Wake up."

She took a shuddering breath then stiffened, her eyes opening. Confusion glittered there before anguish settled in. "Brody?"

"You were dreaming."

She blinked, still drowsy. "My baby," she murmured, trembling. He hugged her closer, letting her find her own way through the tangles holding her.

"He's fine," he assured her. "S-sleeping."

More awake now, Summer drew a breath. Her head still ached, and her eyelids were swollen. "I know it's silly. He's . . . he's just a cat."

"You love him."

Summer shifted, and he turned, settling her so that they were face to face. "The first time I saw him he was crouched under this oleander bush on the San Diego State campus, spitting at this big old black tom, fighting over a piece of hot dog someone had thrown away." She laughed a little as she remembered the furious hissing coming from such a tiny scrap of fur and bone. "His hair was all matted and he was so skinny his skin seemed to hang on him. One ear was already tattered, but that little brave back was up and he was nose to nose with that other cat."

"Good man." He smiled and played with a lock of her hair. His bare shoulders looked huge and powerful against the pale-yellow sheets, yet his gaze was gentle and warm. In his own calm, patient way he was letting her talk it out. And she needed to talk, she realized suddenly, just as he needed to hear.

"It was a bad time for me," she said softly, feeling her way. "One of the worst. I'd just found out this part-time job I'd counted on to get me through to the end of the semester had fallen through. I had a grand total of four dollars and thirty-two cents in the bank, and my rent was due in three days. I didn't know how I could make it through to the end of the semester, and worse, I didn't much care."

He acknowledged that with a rueful grin that warmed her. "I've been there a time or two myself."

She shook her head. "I can't imagine your quitting anything once you'd started. It's not in your nature."

"I quit s-speech therapy more times than I like to admit."

But never for long, she suspected. And not until he'd gotten what he'd wanted. "Snowy bit me when I picked him up. He spat and clawed all the way to the convenience store where I went to buy cat food." She gave a little laugh. "Synchronicity," she murmured. "Dottie mentioned that to me not too long ago."

He frowned. "What do you mean?"

She drew a breath. "There was a HELP WANTED sign in the store window. I got the cat food and the job and Snowy became my best friend and good-luck charm. I can't imagine life without him."

He smoothed her hair again, his expression intense. "You should have kids. You would make a g-great mom."

Summer drew a breath. Her stomach felt hollow, and there was a terrible pressure in her chest. "I *am* a mom," she said very quietly. "I have a daughter."

He went still. Only his eyes showed signs of life. "W-what?"

The pressure in her chest increased. She breathed into it as she'd once breathed into the vicious labor pains that had gone on and on until she'd no longer had strength enough to whimper. "Kyle and I had a child together, although he denied being her father. She's a couple of years older than Kelly."

Brody had killed two men in his life, both in the line of duty. Even though he'd had no choice, he'd had nightmares for months afterward. At the moment, he could willingly pound the bastard who'd hurt her into a bloody pulp and sleep like a baby for the rest of his life. Because he had no words, he tightened his arms around her and kissed her temple. She shivered, then burrowed closer. He waited patiently.

"I was just over seven months along when I went to prison," she resumed after drawing in air. "They put you in chains, you know. Even women. I remember the little rattling sound they made when I pressed my hand against my belly."

He flinched, but took her hand in his and entwined their fingers before pressing a kiss to the wrist that had once worn steel. "In my cell block, there were five us who were pregnant. We supported one another the best way we could. I knew I had to make arrangements for the baby. For temporary custody. I wrote my mother. Begged her. But she refused. I didn't exist for her, for my family, and neither did my child." Grief squeezed her chest until she ran out of breath. Forced to silence, she drew as much air into her lungs as possible. "I wanted to hate them," she said when she could resume more calmly. "I think I did for a while."

Brody had spent enough years with helpless rage burning in his belly to know the kind of pain she'd endured. It made him want to rip and tear into everyone who'd ever hurt her. Instead, he simply held her close.

"They have a special ward at Santa Rita where they lock the newborns in with the moms," she said, her voice rougher now. "For six weeks I held her in my arms as often as they'd let me. Until my muscles went numb and I was afraid I'd drop her if I held her even one second longer. I played mind games so I could stay awake watching her sleep, and every time she let out a peep I put her to my breast so I could feel her breath."

She inhaled the distinctive scent of Brody's skin. She would know him in the dark now. Just as she'd once known her baby. She shifted and looked up at him. His face was taut, his eyes dark. She'd never told this story before. Not even to her therapist. No one but Brody. "Have you heard enough?" she asked with an attempt at lightness.

His mouth moved. Instead of answering he bent his head to kiss her. It was a gentle kiss, without passion. She wanted to cling, but the need was too strong to indulge.

"I remember telling myself that the system was overloaded. That everyone talked about the bureaucracy and how cumbersome it was. Maybe I'd just . . . fall through the cracks. That I'd have a few more days, weeks maybe. And then six weeks to the day, they sent someone from social services to take her."

She went a little crazy then. Fighting, screaming. Begging—until the guard had put her in chains.

"Leon, my attorney, fought them, but in the eyes of the state, I was an unfit mother." She let out a little laugh that felt raw against her throat. "The caseworker was too overworked to be tactful. I was a junkie and a pusher. Pond scum. There wasn't a judge in the state who would find in my favor."

She felt her stomach roil and fought for calm. She talked faster, needing to get it all said. "Of course, there's no shortage of qualified couples looking for healthy infants. My caseworker was kind enough to allow me to choose who would raise my child. I met them once. Nice people, upper middle class, the caseworker said. The woman was blond like me and the man had a sweet smile. They asked me if I wanted to know what they were going to name her. I said no. It was hard enough to give her up. To know I'd spend the rest of my life thinking about her. Trying to imagine her taking her first step, blowing out her birthday candles. They asked me to sign a paper that I would never contact her. They . . . they were afraid she'd find out her mother was a criminal. And they were right."

She stopped, drained, then closed her eyes. She felt naked and exposed. As though sensing her feelings, he reached down and pulled the sheet over them both. Her eyes stung and she pressed her head against his shoulder. Borrowing a little of his unyielding strength.

When she felt stronger, she went on. "After they left, I went back to my cell and cried until I was empty. That night . . . that night I heard her crying. It was so clear, so vivid, and I knew I'd made a mistake. I started screaming, begging them to let me out so I could go to her. She was mine. *My* baby. I couldn't give her up. I just couldn't." A sob took her and she realized she was crying. Her cheeks were drenched, and she could scarcely see through the tears. "They wouldn't let me out." She lifted a hand and scrubbed her cheeks. "That's the dream I have."

She glanced up at him in time to see his face twist with anguish. He started to say something, but nothing came out. His eyes closed, and he reached for her. He held her while she cried, his big hand making slow sweeps of her spine, leaving a trail of warm sensation where the calluses had rubbed. The hair on his chest grew wet from her tears and clung to the bronzed skin in black ringlets. His hand pressed her against his heart, and the steady thudding beneath the warm skin soothed her.

She cried until she had nothing left inside but the ache that never went away, and then lay quietly while his fingers gentled her. Gradually, his touch became more intimate, more seductive, yet she sensed a restraint in him, a need to comfort her the only way he knew how. He pressed a kiss to her temple before rubbing his cheek against her hair. His movements were slow and gentle. Giving her time. Arousing her slowly, sweetly. His kisses were easy, wooing her into demanding from him what he was willing to give.

She pulled her hand free and clung to him, kissing him back, rubbing against him, needing to feel alive again. His hands were reverent as they stroked the breasts that yearned to feel her baby's soft mouth one more time, his mouth warm as he trailed kisses over her throat.

He peeled back the sheet, his mouth seeking first one nipple, then the other. He laved the dusky skin with his tongue. She felt the heat beneath her skin, the small throbbing pulses gathering inside her breasts.

His hand caressed her belly, flattening, then cupping the slight swell. He kissed her with all the reverence of a man who adored his own child. She felt tiny contractions begin in her womb, and a sob escaped her. Of need, not pain, she assured him with her eyes when his dark and intense gaze sought hers.

She clutched his hair and moved her head side to side, floating on a wave of pure pleasure. Very gently, carefully, he eased her thighs apart and kissed her. Fire licked at her loins, and she moaned. His fingers replaced his mouth, fondling her with a sweet skill that had her moaning and bucking.

He slipped a finger into her warmth, and then two, thrusting and retreating until the orgasm shook her. The slick sweat of lovemaking lubricated each little move, arousing her more. She cried out, her hands clutching at his shoulders.

"Please," she whispered in a tortured voice. "Inside me. Please."

He moved over her, her hand already reaching to guide him. He entered slowly, torturing her inch by inch. Sensation ripped through her. He drew back, then thrust again. She cried out, felt him tip over from seducer to seduced. A harsh groan tore from his throat at the moment of release, and she felt the hot rush of his ejaculation.

He collapsed on top of her and let her feel his weight. His spent strength. He buried his face in her shoulder, his breathing still ragged. One hand was loosely curled around her thigh. She smiled against his shoulder, loving the feel of his magnificent body pressing her against the mattress. "Thank you," she murmured before kissing his shoulder. "That was lovely."

He snorted, and slid to one side, his head propped against his hand. His eyes smiled at her, but she saw the tension in him. The concern. The love. "Lovely, my ass. It was damn t-terrific."

"Yes," she said lightly. "It was terrific. And so, my wonderfully sensitive knight in shining armor, are you."

A look of acute discomfort came over his face. "I'm no knight, honey."

"You're right. You're a wonderfully caring, sweet, sensitive man, and I love you dearly."

His gaze wavered, then fell. She felt his wariness. "Honey—"

"Don't look so stricken. I don't expect you to return my love or even accept it, although I hope that you will."

He smiled a little. "Can you give me a little t-time? I n-need to think this through."

"Take all the time you need, big guy. In the meantime, I'll do my best to make sure you're thinking about the right things." She circled his neck with her arms and kissed him. He resisted, his expression tight. Smiling just a little, she rubbed against him and felt the shudder travel the long length of resisting muscle and will.

"You're cheating."

"Yes." She smiled. "I'll stop if you ask me."

"Over my d-dead body," he muttered before covering her mouth with his.

CHAPTER 21

Mark checked the rearview mirror and relaxed a little when he saw that the road behind was clear. He was taking a chance driving on the Hollister Ranch road so often, but he couldn't make himself stay away. Since his granddad usually drove his Mercedes to the hospital, Mark had been able to use the old man's beat-up old pickup most weekdays. Naturally, he was always careful to return the keys to the hook by the back door and keep the gas tank topped off so Granddad wouldn't notice. Being that today was Saturday, however, he was stuck with the Miata.

Old Fishface Gottlieb had helped him see that he'd come on too strong and scared Kelly away. He understood better now. His angel just needed time to get used to the idea that they were destined to be together. His mind buzzing with things he wanted to say to her, he braked, then downshifted for the turn into the road leading to Kelly's house. He'd driven past the driveway to her house three times in the last two weeks, hoping to find her alone. But there'd always been a car in the drive. Her aunt's Olds or the chief's Blazer. He knew she worked nights at Mario's Wednesday through Saturday. He knew she volunteered at the hospital on Sunday. He'd almost worked up the courage to talk to her there, but she'd never stood still long enough.

He was slowing for the wide turn leading past the ranch when he saw the Olds rocketing along the spur road. He slammed on the brakes, then let out a relieved sigh as the old car turned the other way toward the ranch house. Letting the Miata idle behind a stand of brambles, he squinted through his shades to make sure Miss Hollister got out.

Excitement raced through him at the thought of finding Kelly at home by herself. He'd just talk to her first, real easy like. Nothing heavy. Ask her about work, maybe. See if it was okay if he stopped by for a pizza, and then, real casual-like he'd ask her out. Gottlieb was right. He'd come on too strong. This time he'd be more subtle, but sooner or later it was going to happen. They were destined to be together. If not on earth, then in heaven. One way or another, she was his.

Although Kelly wasn't due at Mario's until five, they'd left the house a little past four so that Dottie could stop by the ranch to pick up the list of books Summer wanted her to order.

"Dad's going to ask Summer to marry him." Kelly changed the station, and music blared from the rear speakers, rattling the windows and jangling Dottie's nerves.

"Why's that, dear?" her aunt yelled over the noise.

Giving up in disgust, Kelly sighed and snapped off the radio. The silence was blessed, Dottie decided, relaxing her grip on the wheel.

"Dad bought Summer an engagement ring."

The Olds rocked dangerously as Dottie shot her niece a startled look. "How do you know?"

"I saw it, when I went into his room last night to kiss him good night. It was in this little black velvet box and he was looking at it when I walked in. Soon as he saw me he snapped it shut and shoved it in his sock drawer, but I'm almost sure it was a ring. I mean, what else could it be?"

Dottie's eyes lit up. "We did it, Kelly girl. And Lucy said I was getting senile. Ha!"

Kelly laughed. She'd been stoked all day just thinking about Summer being her mom. "Don't say anything to Summer, okay Auntie? I mean, if she knows and all, it wouldn't be nearly as romantic as if Dad surprises her."

"Well, of course, I won't tell her, dear. Knowing your father it might take him days to work up the nerve to pop the question. Hmm, I wonder where that expression came from? Remind me to look it up when I get to the library, dear." She beamed as she brought the Olds to a shuddering stop next to Summer's van and shoved the lever into park. "Still, it wouldn't hurt to buy the champagne today. Just in case. Big Malcolm always favored Mumm's but I think an occasion like this rates Dom Perignon. No, Cristal!"

"Whatever," Kelly said, slipping free of her seat belt. "Tell Summer I'll be up in a minute, after I check out the horses."

"Kelly, you know your father doesn't want you wandering around the ranch grounds alone," Dottie chided as she opened the door.

"I'm just going to the barn, Auntie. Besides, Mr. Tidwell will be there. How dangerous can that be?"

Brody had been upstairs meeting with the mayor for the better part of the afternoon and had walked into Max's office to filch a handful of her miniature peanut butter cups when she informed him McVey and Tong needed to meet with him ASAP.

About the Krebs breaking and entering, he figured as he headed down the hall to the interview room. It'd been three months without a solid lead. Doc had long since settled with the insurance company and replaced his electronic equipment. But he'd called twice to ask about the cameo. He'd even put up a hefty reward. So far there hadn't been a nibble.

Brody was about to ask about the necklace when he saw the plasticine bag filled with crack on the scarred table. Next to the dope was an evidence bag containing three hundred-dollar bills. The good mood that had started when Summer accepted his invitation to dinner tonight splintered in a cold anger.

Though seated, both detectives came to attention. After nine years his men knew to come right to the point. Still, McVey took a minute to look over his notes while Tong clicked her pen a couple of times, something Brody noticed she did only on those rare occasions when she was unsure of herself.

Hiding his impatience, Brody reached over to pick up the crack. "You find this on one of our citizens or a tourist?" he asked.

McVey and Tong exchanged looks. Apparently McVey lost the mental toss of the coin. "Sawyer and Keegan busted a biker on his way out of town last night," he said as Brody dropped the dope to the table and sat back. "Stopped the guy because he had a taillight out. Failed a sobriety test, *and* gave them enough lip to rate a body search. Turns out the dude was carrying a Beretta with a full clip and one in the barrel, which Sawyer figured was cause to search his saddlebags. Paulie and me have been with him most of the day in the jail. Had to wade through a lot of crap before we finally got something concrete out of him."

Picking up his cue, Tong glanced at her notes. "Guy's name is Stanhope. Two priors for possession, one for B and E five years back in Portland. A liquor store. Served two and change in Oregon. No arrests since."

"Sounds worth following up." Brody saw McVey and Tong exchange resigned looks. Like two kids walking into the principal's office, he decided and braced himself for more bad news.

McVey closed his notebook. "It's probably self-serving bull-shit, Chief, but Stanhope swore he was just doing a favor for a pusher on the coast side, delivering the crack to a regular customer. Claimed the dime bag was his fee."

Brody moved his shoulders, trying to release some of the tension clawing his spine. "You get the name of this customer?"

"Just the location." McVey exchanged another quick look with his partner. "Claims he dropped three dimes' worth at Phoenix House."

The pain was a knife slice in the belly. "How and when?"

Tong fielded this one. "Said he delivered it on his way into town, about an hour before dawn. The connection on the coast told him to park his bike on the road and hike across the field to the barn. He put the dope in an old feed sack shoved under loose straw in an unused stall and removed the C-notes he found there. Slick as you please. Then he spent the day playing pool and drinking beer at Sarge's with some of his biker buddies from this side of the mountain."

After twenty-three years as a cop it was second nature to ice over his emotions. This time it took him longer than it should. He told himself it was because the anger that surged was white hot. He suspected that was only part of it. "You check it out?" he asked, his voice deliberately curt.

McVey smoothed last year's Christmas tie over his substantial belly. "Not yet, Chief. Before we asked for a warrant, we figured we'd best check it out with you first."

Damn, this was going to be a bitch. "Get the warrant," Brody ordered, his voice coming out hard and flat. "When you have it, contact me. I intend to go—"

"Sorry to interrupt, Brody," Max said with controlled urgency as she stepped into the room. One look at her thin, freckled face had Brody bolting out of his chair before she'd even finished. "Nine-one-one just got a call from Phoenix House. Someone's been hurt." Her hesitation was slight, but chilling. "Your aunt called it in."

Brody was already moving past her by the time she said the last few words. "Roll two more units," he ordered, breaking into a run.

Fear was a demon with claws shredding his insides. He knew the limits of the Blazer and his own skill and pushed both over the line. By the time he braked for the turn into the newly graveled lane to the ranch house, his back was slick with sweat and his knuckles ached from the effort to hold the rig tight to the road.

Medevac and the fire truck that was required to roll with it were already on the scene, parked side by side near the open doors to the barn. The rear door of the paramedic unit gaped open. One of the EMTs was running a gurney into the barn.

He saw Dottie's Olds, Summer's van, Mark's Miata, two other vehicles. Oblivious to the rough ground, he drove fast over winter ruts, wincing as the Blazer jolted him hard against the seat belt. In the rearview he saw Sawyer's Taurus pulling in behind him. Another OPD unit stood next to the fire engine, strobes cycling in a familiar pattern.

He braked hard, killed the motor before the rig came to a full stop, and jerked free of the belt. Out of the vehicle, he sprinted toward the door, his boots pounding the ground. Sawyer and Keegan were a half step behind. A group of teenaged residents, male and female, had gathered at the door, milling and peering into the interior.

"They're inside," a young voice called as he neared. He halted a few steps inside the door, frantically scanning for Summer first and then Dottie. Summer's two counselors were standing nearby. The man held a baseball bat in his hand and wore a grim expression. The woman held a towel saturated with blood. Officer Paul Philipetti was already inside the barn, talking to that asshole Finley. Blood covered the scumbag's face and splattered his blue T-shirt. Mark Krebs sat on an upended bucket, his head in his hands. His knuckles were split, his shirt, too, was spotted with blood.

Directly ahead, the EMTs were crouched over someone lying on the ground near one of the massive support pillars. Brody's breath came out in a harsh cry as he saw Summer and his aunt clinging to one another a few yards away. Relief crashed over him and he took a quick step forward, only to freeze when he realized that it was Kelly lying there. She was dressed for work. The little red cap she usually wore was laying a good ten feet away.

The blood drained from his face, and his brain fogged to a sick gray haze before he forced himself to focus. The EMTs were at her side now. Brody knew he would only be in the way, yet it took every ounce of will he possessed to keep from shouldering the medics aside and lifting his baby girl in his arms to kiss it all better, the way he'd done when she'd had a skinned knee or a pinched finger.

He took in a long, slow, bracing breath flavored with fear and the scent of horses and hay as one of the medics slapped a BP cuff on Kelly's arm. Another checked her pupils. The third listened to her heart. She looked so fragile lying there, like a rag doll she'd had as a little girl. His heart tripped, bled as he fought to keep himself calm.

Somehow he got out Summer's name. He must have, he realized when she turned her head and called to him. He was already reaching for her when she flung herself against him. "Oh God, Brody, I'm so glad you're here."

Beyond speech, he crushed her to him. "It's okay," she said through her tears as she felt the hard shudder run through him. "She's alive. Brody, did you hear me? She's alive."

He drew back, his hands running over her shoulders, down her arms. "You . . . okay?" he managed to get out, his gaze roaming her face.

"Yes, I'm fine." She took a breath as Dottie came up to them.

"Oh, Brody," his aunt whispered, her voice breaking. He reached out an arm to draw her close, then rested his head atop hers for a moment.

From the corner of Summer's eye she saw a huge black officer with sergeant's chevrons on his sleeve and controlled authority in his demeanor hurry into the barn, stop short to survey the scene, then make his way to Brody's side.

"I heard the call go out and thought you might need backup," he said as he approached, then frowned when he caught the identity of the victim on the ground. "Jeez, I'm sorry, Brody. Beg pardon, ladies."

"It's all right, Sergeant," Dottie said with a fleeting smile.

The officer's measuring gaze shifted to Summer. He nodded, though he didn't smile, and she sensed curiosity mixed with a cop's innate suspicion. "What happened?" He directed his question to Brody, his voice clipped. A professional police officer speaking to his superior.

Summer saw Brody's jaw clench and rushed to answer. "I don't know for sure," she told both men, her voice thin and shaky. "When Dottie and I arrived, Kelly was on the floor, unconscious and . . . and Mark and Joe were fighting."

As she spoke, the sergeant reached into his back pocket to withdraw a notebook. After flipping to a clean page, he pulled out a pen. In their stalls, the horses whinnied and shifted, stomping their hooves against hard dirt. Voices rose and fell as the policemen demanded answers from Joe and Mark. The EMTs spoke terse medical shorthand.

"Mark and Joe?" the sergeant asked, his pen poised.

Though Brody's gaze was fixed on the medics, she knew that he was taking in every word. "Mark Krebs, Dr. Krebs's grandson, and Joseph Finley, one of our residents." She caught the sergeant's quick frown and knew that he'd recognized the name.

"Go on, ma'am," the sergeant said courteously. She took a breath, painfully aware that Brody seemed to be withdrawing from her. "Well, from what I can gather, Joe had just gone into the barn to feed the mares. Our regular wrangler, Foss Tidwell, has the stomach flu."

Hingle made another note. "What happened then?"

"When I got inside, Mark and Joe were rolling around on the floor. I screamed for them to stop, but they wouldn't." She paused for breath. Brody's gaze was fixed on his daughter, his jaw granite, his eyes tortured. "I was checking on Kelly when Manny and Char and the others arrived. Manny threatened to brain both boys with his bat, and they stopped fighting."

Hingle finished writing, nodded. "Did Kelly say anything?"

Summer felt the bile rising and fought it down. "No, she was unconscious the whole time. I think she hit her head on the post."

"Want me to check out the boys, Chief?" Hingle asked, sympathy bleeding into his voice.

Brody nodded. He heard the senior medic, an ex-navy corpsman named Dalton, contact the hospital, listened numbly as he read off numbers, received instructions. Kelly's face was a sickly gray. Bruises were purpling one side of her face.

His gut twisted. She looked so young and fragile, with her eyelashes resting on her white face. Baby freckles still dotted her skin, and her mouth was relaxed, the way it used to be right after she'd finished nursing at her mother's breast.

God, he couldn't lose her. It would kill him. Needing to move, he walked to Hingle's side.

"We have a difference of opinion, Chief," Hingle said when Brody reached him. "Finley here claims he walked in and saw Krebs knock Kelly into the post."

"That's bullshit and you know it!" Mark shouted as he leapt to his feet. He looked far less battered than Joe, with only a few red scrapes on one cheek. His hands, however, were badly bruised, and one knuckle was swollen. "Kel was already on the ground when I showed up."

"I don't even know her!" Joe protested, anguish in his eyes. "Ask Dr. Laurence. She won't let us mix with nonresidents."

"That's true," Summer put in quickly and felt Brody stiffen.

"Chief?" Hingle asked quietly. "What do you want me to do?"

Brody took a fast breath. He had to go with the odds—and his gut. He told himself it wasn't personal. "Book Finley. Keep him here, not juvie."

"Assault?"

Brody turned to look at his daughter. First Trent Oates and now Kel. Innocent victims. He felt his gut clench. "Attempted murder."

"No, I didn't do it!" Joe exploded, surging past the officers. Sawyer caught him, and twisted his arm behind his back. Finley's face contorted, and he choked out a cry of mingled protest and pain.

Summer grabbed Brody's arm, her fingers digging in. "Brody, it's just one word against the other. When Kelly wakes up, we'll know the truth. Until then it's only fair to consider both boys as suspects."

His face twisted. "I was fair once, S-Summer. That just might have gotten my daughter killed. It might have gotten *you* killed, damn it."

"Brody, listen to me. There's something you should know, something—"

"Ready to roll, Chief," Dalton called as he snapped the lid on the large metal box that held their supplies. Brody swallowed hard, his throat cinched tight, his belly knotted as two of the medics pushed the gurney past him. He reached out, only to close his hand in a fist when he realized he would only be delaying the rush to the hospital. Reaching Brody's side, Dalton stopped to say quietly, "Her pulse is steady and her respiration's good. There's a good chance she's concussed."

"You . . . got room for m-me?"

Dalton nodded. "If you come right now."

Brody caught Hingle's eye and the sergeant nodded. "I'll handle it."

Summer exchanged a quick look with Dottie, who drew a breath, then said quietly to Summer, "I'll follow the ambulance to the hospital. Come when you can."

"I'll be there as soon as possible," she told Brody before giving him a fierce hug.

Willing away the tears took more effort than it should. Somehow he managed as he turned and jogged to the ambulance.

Dottie walked away from the pay phone, her heart heavy. Summer wasn't at the ranch house. That nice boy Manny had explained that she was at the jail with Finley.

Feeling her years and more, she walked slowly back toward the waiting room outside the double doors leading to the operating rooms. During the sixty-some minutes since they'd taken Kelly upstairs for tests, several other people waiting for loved ones had come and gone.

She was nearly to the small waiting room when she heard Grey call her name. He was dressed in shirtsleeves, his silk tie loosened. In one hand he carried a cup and saucer. A tea bag hung over the edge of the cup.

"I thought you could use a bracer," he said with a brief smile. "And machine coffee does unspeakable things to the lining of the stomach."

She huffed out a nervous laugh. "I can imagine," she said as he accompanied her into the room. He waited until she seated herself, then settled into the chair next to her.

"This is wonderfully thoughtful of you, Grey," she murmured as he passed her the cup and saucer. She saw that he no longer wore a wedding ring.

"Still have a sweet tooth, I take it?" he asked as he withdrew two packets of sugar from his shirt pocket.

"Of course." Her eyes filled with tears, and she bit her lip. "Oh Grey, I'm so terribly frightened," she whispered. The cup rattled in the saucer as her hand began to tremble.

"It's going to be all right, Dot," he assured her, taking the cup with one of his big, capable hands. Leaning forward, he placed the saucer on the magazine-strewn table in the center of the small space, then took her trembling hand. Though she fought them, the tears overflowed. She bowed her head and bit her lip but a sob broke through anyway. She felt him shift and then press a folded handkerchief into her hand. Snuffling inelegantly and feeling terribly exposed and helpless, she dabbed at the moisture on her cheeks.

"Why's it taking so long?"

"Dealing with the brain is always a delicate procedure, even when the operation itself is a relatively simply one like removing a blood clot. MacNeil is extremely skilled and he's also careful. He wants to get as much information as possible before he takes Kelly to the OR."

She drew a shaky breath and wadded the handkerchief in her hand. Slowly she turned to look at him. "Brody was opposed to a treatment center, but Summer and I—" Her voice broke, and she swallowed. "If Kelly dies, I'll never forgive myself."

Grey's eyes clouded. "I blamed myself for Markham's suicide for a long time, but I was wrong, Dot. He made the decision to end his existence for reasons that had nothing to do with me."

"I was very sorry when I heard the news."

"I appreciated the card you sent." He filled his chest with air, let it out slowly. "Just as I appreciated the card you sent when Sarah died."

Dottie looked into his eyes. "Oh Grey." She heard the anguish in her voice, years of regret whispering through the silence of the room.

"I know, princess," he whispered. "I know."

He pulled her into his arms and pressed her head against his shoulder. "I still have that canoe," he murmured gruffly. "Maybe, when this is over, you'd like to take it out for a ride?"

"Only if you promise not to dunk me again," she managed to say.

He chuckled. "As I recall, that was the best part."

Dottie drew in a breath. He smelled like laundry starch and aftershave. "Yes," she said, hope trembling in her heart. "That was indeed the best part."

Summer raced down the corridor, her sandals slapping on the shiny white linoleum as she followed the arrows painted on the pale-green wall directing her to the OR waiting room. After Brody and his men had left, she'd taken a few precious moments to reassure the patients before placing a call to Joe's father. Anson Finley was in Japan on a business trip, and she left a message with his assistant. Her next call had been to Melvin Bailey, Joe Finley's lawyer, who had promised to leave his office in San Francisco immediately. If the weather held, his Lear jet would be landing in Wenatchee in another two hours. She'd done all that she could do for Joe at the jail. Now her attention was on Kelly. All the way into town, she'd prayed that she would find her awake and laughing, those bright blue eyes full of mischief.

She'd wasted a few precious moments finding out where they'd taken Kelly. Fear had gripped her stomach when the receptionist had directed her to the surgical wing. The waiting room was tucked into an alcove near a pair of swinging doors plastered with a huge NO ADMITTANCE sign. It was a small room, painted blue. An artificial ficus with dusty leaves drooped forlornly in one corner. A square table strewn with tattered magazines sat in the middle. Though the hospital was nonsmoking, a faint hint of cigarette smoke still lingered, as though sealed into the walls along with the tears and grief of other inhabitants.

Surprisingly, only Brody, Dottie, and Dr. Krebs were in the room. Looking every day of her sixty-one years Dottie was resting her head against Dr. Krebs's shoulder. Brody sat apart on the other sofa, his elbows propped on his spread knees, his head in his hands. Dottie saw her first. Uttering a little cry, she leapt to her feet and rushed to the door. Grey stood as well and smiled a little. Summer smiled back before bending to kiss Dottie's cheek.

"How is she?" Summer asked as she and Dottie hugged, clinging a little in mutual fear before they drew apart.

"She's in surgery," Dottie said, her voice choking a little. Her tired blue eyes were damp, her lashes matted. "It's been almost an hour since they took her in."

Summer tightened her fingers around the strap of her shoulder bag. "What kind of surgery?" she demanded, whipping her gaze from one to the other.

Grey explained in a quiet voice, "The blow to the head caused a subdural hematoma. A clot."

Summer expelled air. The doctor sounded so matter-of-fact, but Summer saw the quick little flicker of worry in his brown eyes. Questions tumbled in her head, but one look at Brody's face dammed them in her throat. He needed gentleness now and support, not a rehash of the cold medical facts.

He had glanced up when she entered. Now he stood, his dark gaze fixed intently on her face as though searching for something. Taking a chance she walked directly toward him and didn't stop until his arms closed around her. She felt him sag against her for a moment before he steeled himself and let her go. "Thought you m-might n-not come."

Her heart broke. "Of course I came. I'm sorry I couldn't get here sooner. I had to call Joe's father and settle the troops." She manufactured a smile. "Sergeant Hingle said to tell you he'll be by to fill you in as soon as he's finished at the jail."

His jaw tightened. His eyes were sunken and dark, his face pale. His hair was disheveled, but his shoulders were so terribly stiff.

"Have you eaten?" she asked.

"Can't." The look in his eyes told her it would be a useless waste of time to push him.

"Then sit," she ordered, gently pressing on his shoulder. Surprisingly, he obeyed, tugging on her hand until she sat next to him. She saw Dottie and Grey exchange looks.

"All this talk about food has made me hungry," Dottie said softly, catching Summer's eye. "Can we bring you something?"

"Two black coffees, please."

"We'll be in the cafeteria if there's any word," the doctor said as he pressed his hand over Dottie's clinging fingers.

Brody watched them leave in brooding silence. Summer sat quietly, holding his big, rough hand in hers. His fingers were icy and stiff. He drew in a shaky breath. "I keep remembering how she used to come running across the yard when I'd come home. When . . . when she was l-little, she used to k-kinda w-wobble when she r-ran. And s-sometimes she'd f-fall." He ran his hand through his hair. "She'd look up at me with these big eyes and then hold up h-her arms."

"She'll do that again, darling. You'll see."

He closed his eyes. "I'm supposed to t-take care of people, damn it." He surged to his feet, his fists clenched. He walked to the door of the small waiting room and braced his hands against the frame, staring down the empty corridor. "It nearly killed me to let the system deal with Williams after Megan died. If Kelly dies, I don't think I can pull back—"

"She won't die," Summer cried, leaping up to go to him.

Brody saw the compassion in her eyes and knew what she wanted—his guts, spilled out on the floor. Fucking talk. Catharsis, the department shrink had called it. His mother had called it whining when he'd gone to her with a stinging backside and his father's curses still in his head.

"Brody, you're as white as chalk. You have to eat something." She lifted a hand to stroke his face. He felt his control start to go and grabbed her wrist. Tenderness would break him as nothing else could.

"I said I'm not hungry, damn it."

"All right, but come back and sit down."

It was flat out tearing him to bloody shreds, this need to pull her into his arms and bury his face in her hair. To let her hold him and soothe him and promise him the pain would go away.

"Go home, Summer," he said, turning his back. "Take care of your cat and your patients and let me take care of my little girl."

"Char and Manny will handle things. I'm not leaving you to wait this out alone."

He felt her gentleness. Her concern. All he had to do was turn toward her and she would be his rock. He nearly surrendered—until he felt the tears behind his eyes. He hadn't cried when Meggie died. He wouldn't cry now.

So he thought about the bruises on Kelly's face instead, feeding his rage, praying for it to kick in. Needing the edge that had kept his head high when his peers had jeered at him behind the teacher's back after he'd stammered out an answer. His protection when LAPD rookies he'd trained had been promoted over him because they could issue orders fast and clean in an emergency, and maybe, just maybe his stuttering might get someone killed. It was his salvation, that rage. Without it, he would start to shake and never stop.

He took a breath and made his voice hard, and the words slipped out easily. Like a blade slicing air. "I warned you this would happen, but you wouldn't listen. Just went ahead and brought that murdering asshole to my town. If Kelly dies, I'll never forgive you."

He heard the soft little cry in her throat as she drew in a shocked breath. He held himself still, his muscles rigid until he heard the muffled sound of her footsteps on the carpet. When he turned around again, he was alone.

* * *

Dottie was dozing on Grey's shoulder and Brody was drifting in a mindless state when the door leading to the OR swished open, jerking them to attention. Dottie's fingers dug into Grey's arm as Brody surged to his feet.

Dr. MacNeil was a bluff, whey-faced redhead with caterpillar eyebrows and freckles. He acknowledged Dr. Krebs with a nod before offering Brody a tired smile. "Your little girl is a fighter, Chief Hollister. She came through like a little champion. Baring complications, I expect her to make a full recovery."

"Thank God," Dottie whispered, her voice tremulous.

Brody gave thanks privately. "When . . . when c-can we s-see her?"

Dr. MacNeil smiled a little. "She'll be in recovery for a while. I'll have the nurse let you know when she's moved to ICU. You can peek in to reassure yourself, but she won't know you're there. Likely she'll sleep through the night. It's not unusual in cases of this kind for the patient to remain in a light coma for twenty-four hours, sometimes longer, but that's sometimes a good thing. Nature's way of letting the body heal."

"Paul's right," Grey hastened to assure them. "The important thing is that she *will* wake up."

Three hours later they moved Kelly upstairs to intensive care. She was still pale, still unconscious. Her head was swathed in a turban of white gauze and tape, making her look even more fragile. Brody had nearly lost it when they'd let him in to see her.

Slate Hingle had been waiting outside the door of the ICU when Brody walked out. He'd managed to stretch the five minutes they allowed into ten—until a nurse who could have whipped a platoon of delinquents and malcontents into shape ordered him out. It seemed his little girl didn't need him hanging around, getting in the way no matter how small he tried to make himself. But damn it, *he* needed to be near *her*.

"Before Doc took her on home Miss Dottie said I was to pour coffee into you and make sure you ate," Slate informed him with a wry grin. "Cost me more than I want to risk if she finds out I let you slide."

Brody managed a nod. "Coffee sounds good."

Though it wasn't quite ten, the hospital seemed bedded down for the night. Unlike the area outside the ER, which sometimes got so busy on the weekends the clerks stacked patients in the hall, this floor was almost too quiet. Only the sound of their boot heels on the linoleum broke the almost smothering silence.

The pale-green alcove that served as a waiting area was deserted, save for an elderly man with wispy white hair hunched over a Styrofoam cup cradled in big, work-rough hands. His name was Harold Pritchard, a fact that he had volunteered when he and Brody had exchanged a few words during the hours they'd spent sitting in silence. Mr. Pritchard's wife, Ethel Ann, had been driving back from visiting her sister in Wenatchee when her Civic had been sideswiped by a log truck.

"Any word?" Brody asked when the man jerked his head up at the sound of footsteps on the linoleum.

Mr. Pritchard shook his head, his red-rimmed eyes wearing the same blank look of disbelief Brody had seen far too many times over the years. Brody squeezed the old man's shoulder and offered a smile instead of the words he was too tired to manage. Mr. Pritchard's face crumpled before he pulled himself together. "I'm glad about your young 'un, Chief."

Brody nodded his thanks, and Mr. Pritchard went back to staring at his cup.

"That's got to be rough, sweating out your whole future," Hingle said as they turned the corner and headed past the nurse's station. "When I thought I'd lose Melinda after the babies were born I was so scared I couldn't even pray. Just kept begging God over and over for mercy." He gave Brody a look. "Guess you know some about that kind of praying, too."

"Some, yeah." Between prayers, he'd thrown in half-wild promises and more than a few threats. He doubted any of that mattered. He figured God tossed rocks at everyone, just to keep life interesting. Sometimes He picked up pebbles, sometimes boulders. Maybe it was luck of the draw. Ray Hollister had thought himself cursed with a sickly wife who might as well be barren, and a pathetic joke for a son. Brody figured God just naturally liked to mess with a man's mind now and then. The old bait and switch. Give him a few days of sunshine before tossing down the lightning.

When they reached the elevators, Hingle punched the button, then frowned and reached into his pocket to haul out Brody's key ring.

"Rich brought your Blazer over before the end of his shift. It's in the lot near the side entrance."

After pocketing the keys, Brody dug tired fingers into the knot at the back of his neck. Now that the worst was over he'd developed a real skull-buster of a headache. His belly wasn't all that solid either. He couldn't remember the last time he ate. There was a lot he couldn't remember, like whole hunks of time, he realized as he and Hingle rode down to the ground floor. What he did remember had him wanting to smash something.

He'd hurt the woman he loved with his heart and soul. To protect himself. To save his pride.

The cafeteria was all but empty, the line closed. In response to Hingle's query a balding, middle-aged man with a pallid moon face and a good-natured smile looked up from his spot behind the cash register and directed them to a bank of refrigerated cases containing sandwiches and salads wrapped in plastic.

Brody took a pass on the food, and after inspecting the selection, Hingle did the same. The coffee, however, was fresh and blessedly strong. Inhaling the aroma had Brody thinking of the week Summer had stayed in his house and the desperate look in her sleepy eyes in the morning as she went straight for the coffeepot. Lord, but she'd been cute, wrapped like a little mummy in that furry bathrobe, bare toes peeping out and her hair all soft and fluffy around her face.

He smiled a little, his face stiff from hours of clenching his jaw to keep from heading to the nearest pay phone to call her.

Only the nagging fear that he'd end up tongue-tied and mute kept him from dropping that quarter.

By tacit agreement they sat in the rear. Hingle waited until Brody had fortified himself with caffeine before filling him in. "First off, I talked to Assistant DA Labeck. He said to tell you it's a good bet Finley senior can make any bail the judge sets."

The white foam cup all but disappeared in Hingle's big hand as the sergeant lifted it to his mouth. Slate's eyes had the slightly glazed look of exhaustion Brody knew all too well.

Brody took a sip from his own cup and waited for the caffeine to hit. His mind wasn't even close to being sharp. His professional objectivity had been blasted to hell the instant he'd seen Kel lying white and still on the barn floor. The barbed tangle of emotions he'd been battling for hours twisted alive again in his belly. Tired as he was, he knew he had to concentrate on the job the town expected him to do

"Did you have Finley tested?" he said, wishing he'd thought to ask Kel's nurse for a couple of aspirins for the temple pounder that was getting worse by the minute.

"Urine only. By the time we could get someone to draw blood Melvin Bailey was throwing up more flack than Hitler's homeboys during WW Two."

Bailey again, Brody thought wearily. The hired gun in the thousand-dollar suits.

"McVey and Tong hauled in a biker who swore he'd been delivering dope to the r-r-ranch. Said he left it in a gunnysack under straw in one of the empty stalls. Didn't name the customer, but my m-m-money's on Finley."

Hingle sat bolt upright. "I'll get Fitzpatrick and his partner to toss every inch of that barn." He made a fist, lifted it a few inches over the table, then brought it down with a soft thump and drew a weary breath. "I should have thought of that first thing, damn it. I blew it."

"No, if there's any fault here, it's mine for not passing on the information. Guess I lost focus for a while."

"If you're right about Finley, the stuff should still be there. Or at least the sack."

"Be a hell of a motive if K-Kel walked in on him while he was snorting his daily fix," he said after taking another sip.

"Pretty much of a lock, I'm thinking." Hingle reached into his pocket and pulled out a cigar. He took a sniff, then reluctantly returned it to his shirt. One per day after his shift was his quota. "There's one more thing, Chief. About the Krebs boy. According to Dr. Laurence, the kid threatened to kill himself if Kelly broke up with him. Apparently showed your girl an antique dueling pistol and swore he'd use it."

Brody felt an icy jolt. It took a moment before he had breath to speak. "Jesus, he threatened to sh-shoot her?"

Hingle shook his head. "Himself. Suicide, like his old man. As soon as your daughter confided in Dr. Laurence, she went to Doc Krebs and the doc got his grandson into therapy. She said Kelly begged her not to tell you."

Brody was too tired to swear. But inside the words rocketed around his head. "If it's true, Mark could have some kind of sick obsession with Kel."

"It's been known to happen."

Brody thought about this for a moment. "Hell, Slate, I've talked to the kid. He didn't seem like a mental case. Anything but."

"That's pretty much my read. Still, Ted Bundy had a way with the ladies, too."

"Not funny, Sergeant."

"No sir." Hingle's mouth took on a grim look. "Dr. Laurence is a strong lady. Had me backed up against a wall in the jail while she banged away at me. Damn near had me convinced."

"You saying you think it was Krebs?"

Hingle shook his head. "My money's on Finley, Brody. He's a junkie. Probably whacked out or about to be. Either way he's dangerous."

Junkie. God, the word came so easily. Did it still hurt her when she heard it? Dumb question, Hollister. From a guy who'd sworn to kill the next man who called him a retard.

"I'm going to need you to handle things for a few days while I'm tied up here, so give McVey what you've got so far."

"Will do." Hingle rubbed his thumb over his cup, then frowned. "Did the surgeon say anything about amnesia from the blow on the head?"

"Just about guaranteed, he said. We won't know the extent till she wakes up. Even if she's forgotten what happened, there's a good chance her m-m-memory will gradually come b-b-back."

Brody stretched out his legs and tried to ignore the ache in his head. He was tempted to take some vacation time, give Hingle this horse to ride wherever it took him. Let the sergeant take the heat from Summer. No one would blame him. Not with his only child in ICU. Hell, a lot of people would blame him if he *didn't* step back from this one.

Brody drained his cup and glanced at his watch. In another ten minutes they'd let him see Kel again. After they threw him out, he figured to make a quick trip home to change his clothes and clean up before returning.

He got to his feet and picked up his cup. Hingle did the same. "Before you knock off for the night, call McVey and fill him in on the information on Krebs you got from Dr. Laurence. Tell him to check it out ASAP, then get back to me. In the meantime, I'll make sure Kelly isn't alone."

Slate looked surprised. "You think Finley—or Krebs—will try to get to her?"

"I'm too tired to think." Brody walked to the nearest trash barrel and tossed in his cup. Hingle followed suit. Then Brody headed upstairs.

From the moment he'd signed the papers in the recruiting office, he'd been struggling to be a man instead of a scared kid who never belonged. Problem was, he'd never been all that sure what that meant. His father sure as hell wasn't the ideal, rutting like a boar in heat to put another male Hollister in his wife's belly, then damn near ignoring her in between. Big Malcolm had been a good provider and a decent husband, but a lot of men had been maimed or killed on his logging crews because of the old man's refusal to provide decent equipment.

Brody figured a man stood by his friends, protected his family, and loved his woman with every ounce of strength God gave him. He didn't lie and he didn't use that strength to hurt someone weaker. It was damn humbling to discover that a guy could be six-five, two forty-five and still not measure up.

Tomorrow, he would go see her and start mending fences, he promised himself as he rang the bell outside the locked doors to the ICU. Tomorrow he would start over and he wouldn't give up until she was his again. As he heard the door click open, he made a mental note to tell Lucy to order a lot of roses.

CHAPTER 22

Summer sat rigid, her hand clamped around the phone receiver in a death grip. She'd phoned Judge Mandeville in order to let him know that Joe had been arrested again—and why.

"The police were here for four hours this morning, Your Honor," she said, after reciting the facts as she knew them. "As far as I could see, they searched every square inch of my barn. When I spoke with Detective McVey a few minutes before they finished, he admitted they'd found nothing to incriminate Joe— or any of the other residents."

"Well, that is a point in the young man's favor, certainly." She heard the judge clear his throat and pictured the man she'd met at the conference—thin as a greyhound and very tall, with a patrician face and a silver pompadour. But it was the shrewd blue eyes that she remembered most. She doubted Mandeville missed much that went on in his courtroom. "Where is Joseph now?"

So far so good. "He's still at the jail, sir. His attorney, Mr. Bailey, is arranging bail. I expect him back here sometime this afternoon."

"Do you think that's wise? Allowing him to mingle with the other residents while he's under suspicion? I'm thinking in terms of morale, you understand."

"So am I, sir. A patient who comes here is given a clean slate. A fresh start. That's what I believe, and that's what we try to make the patients believe. I'm not sure Joe truly accepted that at first, but after an admittedly rocky beginning, he's made excellent progress, especially these last two weeks. In fact, as our first patient, he's become a mentor of sorts for the newer residents. I think it would do irreparable harm for his therapists to play judge and jury at this point."

"I get your point, of course. Still, I'm mindful of my responsibility to the citizens of this state. What if Finley should decide to skip out on his bail? After all, it's not his money at risk."

"You have my word he won't run away," she said, trusting her instinct.

"Will you vouch for his innocence as well?"

Summer took a breath. "I can't do that, Your Honor. In my heart I believe that he is innocent, yes. The other boy had a far greater motive to hurt Kelly Hollister, though I don't believe it was premeditated or even intentional. More like a flash of anger, or another equally strong emotion. But nevertheless, there is always a chance that Joe was indeed responsible."

There was a pregnant pause during which Summer felt as though her rigid back muscles would snap. She'd been wired tight since the moment she'd heard shouts coming from the barn.

"I respect your willingness to stand behind one of your patients, Dr. Laurence," the judge resumed in a quiet, but firm voice. "But I have to warn you that if your judgment of this young man proves flawed, I would have to rethink my decision to refer offenders to your facility. In addition, I would be morally compelled to relate this experience to my colleagues."

Summer closed her eyes and wondered how much her reputation as a therapist really meant. In monetary terms, not nearly as much as a rock star's, certainly. Or even a tax accountant's. But to her it was priceless. Without it . . . An image rose in her mind of a grief-stricken girl huddling on the floor of her cell, clinging to a blanket still carrying the scent of the child she would never see again. She'd made a vow—then and there—to dedicate the rest of her life to trying to prevent other young women from experiencing that same hell.

"I understand, Your Honor," she said quietly but firmly. "I believe in my methods and I believe we've made progress with Joe."

"Very well." The judge cleared his throat again. "I'd appreciate it if you'd keep me posted."

"Yes sir."

Summer replaced the receiver with a shaky hand, then swiveled her chair to the side and looked out at the gnarled oak beyond the window. After a sunny morning, the clouds had moved in, bringing a dismal gloom to the summer landscape. The angry whine of a chain saw marked the morning's project—clearing away a sickly fir tree that had threatened to topple onto one corner of the barn. A lot easier than felling the dying giant slice by slice with the wickedly sharp axe Brody preferred.

Summer drew a long breath. She'd been so busy dividing her time and her concern between the ranch and the jail that she'd been fairly successful at keeping her worry for Kelly at bay. Calls to the hospital had been frustrating. *Out of surgery and resting comfortably. Satisfactory condition. No change.* Dottie's call first thing this morning to tell her that Kelly had briefly opened her eyes and recognized her father had been a godsend. Brody would have called her himself, Dottie had hastened to assure her, but he'd been home only long enough to clean up before heading back to the hospital a little after dawn. But he'd wanted her to know, Dottie had assured her.

It didn't matter, she told herself firmly. What was one more broken heart? Not even a blip on the cosmic scope of momentous events. Certainly she would survive. She would even heal. She was a respected professional with a Ph.D., for pete's sake. She had the skills, the coping mechanisms. The insights. Only a pathetically naive girl would cry herself to sleep because she'd fallen desperately in love with the wrong man. And Summer Laurence had stopped being a girl a long time ago.

"Summer?"

For an instant she thought she'd conjured up that voice. Just in case, she turned to see him standing like an awkward giant in the doorway, a bouquet of white roses clutched carefully in his big, rough hands. He was dressed the way she liked him best, in his old Wranglers and a navy polo shirt that showed off his magnificent chest. The dragon's tail curled from beneath the ribbed sleeve. Her heart stuttered, and for an instant she nearly ran into his arms.

"Hello, Brody," she said with the same cool smile she'd offered Anson Finley. "If you've come to help in the search, your men have just left."

One corner of his mouth lifted.

"McVey filled me in."

"Then you know they found nothing to even remotely implicate Joe—or anyone else at Phoenix House."

"It does seem that way." Brody took a tentative step into the small office, then halted when he realized he hadn't been issued an invitation to enter. Not that he intended to back down. Just tread carefully this time. "This used to be my r-room," he said, glancing around.

The walls he remembered as a dull gray were now a pale yellow and glowed softly, as though a little of the sun had been captured in the paint. Summer was like that, he realized. Bringing sunshine wherever she went. Along with compassion, he reminded himself. He was counting on that compassion. A thousand times he'd told himself a woman who could accept addicts and murderers could accept a fool. The fist that had twisted his gut into a knot on the drive from town relaxed a little when she didn't order him off her premises.

"First memory I have is of l-laying in this little iron b-bed and imagining that pine oak was a beanstalk." It was one of the good memories. He wasn't desperate enough to play on her pity.

"Dottie told me Kelly woke up." Pain shimmered in her eyes and he knew she was remembering Kel's still, white face. "I'm so glad."

"She . . . didn't do more than blink a couple of times, but Dr. MacNeil said it was a s-sign the swelling in her brain's gone d-down."

"She'll be fine," she said, picking up a stack of pink message sheets and sifting through them.

He'd never seen her so detached. Not even that first morning when she'd been dumping her distrust of cops all over him. Distrust she'd come by far too cruelly, he knew now. And he'd sure as shit done his share to deepen that distrust. But he intended to make it up to her. As soon as this mess had shaken down and the dust settled, he'd give her the ring and set about talking her into marrying him.

"S-Summer." Damn. He stopped and stepped forward to lay the roses in front of her. "I had to w-wait until Lucy opened," he said when she glanced up. Actually, he'd gotten Lucy out of bed—and paid double for the flowers.

She didn't smile. She didn't even look interested. "They're only a little wilted, so perhaps you can return them for a refund."

He took the hit. He deserved worse. "You're pissed and I don't b-blame you. I was an ass, but—"

"I'm not pissed, Brody. I wish I could be." The resignation in her voice tore at him.

"Honey—"

She put down the messages and looked up at him, her head tilted slightly, quizzically. She looked impossibly young and fragile in shorts and a cotton shirt. Tiny gold hoops glinted in her ears, and she'd been twisting the ends of her hair in that absent-minded way she had when she was deep in thought. God, he loved her. Flat out worshiped the woman.

"I won't be anyone's punching bag, Chief Hollister. I've come too far and worked too hard to build my self-respect."

"L-look, I know your feelings are hurt, and it's my fault. I'm s-sorry."

"Yes, you're sorry—now. I think you would always be sorry after you ripped off a piece of my heart." Her voice was too calm, too remote for his peace of mind. Anger he could handle. Even hurt. But not indifference.

"It was a b-bad time. I . . . didn't mean what I said."

"You'll never know how much I want to believe that, Brody. But I can't."

"Believe it, honey. I have enough t-trouble with words. I don't w-waste them on lying." He thought her face might have softened for a moment and took heart. But the coldness was back in her voice when she spoke again.

"You've gone through the kind of nightmare no one should have to endure, and I sympathize deeply. I even understand better than most the kind of scars it left on you." She eased her chin up and took a breath. He thought about the tremors that had taken her slender body when she'd been telling him about her baby. She'd lifted her chin then, too. Taking on the world with nothing but her grit holding her up.

"It's because I understand that I finally realized you'll never be able to truly accept me and my life's work," she said quietly. "Your rage against Williams and the prejudice it generated is too much a part of you. Maybe you even need it to survive, and God knows, I understand the price survival can exact."

He nearly told her of his fear of being weak. Nearly begged. Instead, he stood and took his punishment.

"I think on some level I always knew that you had the power to destroy me if I let you past my defenses, but you managed to throw me off guard. As I recall, I did mention once how formidable you can be."

He was almost desperate enough to take that as a compliment. "Shock does strange things . . ." he began, then stopped. How did a man explain a bone-deep terror of losing the respect of the woman he loved?

Needing to move, he walked to the window and looked out. The tree was still there, close enough for a small boy's arms to reach. His way out when he'd felt smothered by the hurt.

She loved him, damn it. She'd told him so, and she didn't lie.

"You want me to have Mark Krebs arrested?" he asked, feeling his way through the emotional minefield. "Is that what this is about?"

When she didn't answer, he turned to look at her. Her eyes

were shuttered tight against him. He'd done it again. Said exactly the wrong thing. "I didn't mean that the way it sounded."

"Of course you did." The bitterness in her smile tore at him. "Why not? In your mind all of us addicts are alike. Liars, cheats, master manipulators. And you're right. We are. Or were. It's part of the illness."

His throat closed, locked down tight on the words he needed. He took a step forward, only to have her stiffen and hold up her hand.

"Don't, Brody. We had our shot at something precious and special, and we blew it." She stood and carried a stack of folders to a red filing cabinet. After putting them on top, she opened a drawer, then stood silently staring at the files inside.

"I love Kelly, too," she said softly. "I wanted to be there in that room, adding my prayers to yours. I wanted to hold you and have you hold me." She laughed, a hollow, bitter sound. "I thought, really thought, I'd found someone who would accept me the way I am. Who would let me accept him. Equal partners. Lovers. Friends." She closed the drawer without bothering with the folders and turned to face him again. "I'm thirty-three years old, Brody. In my whole life no one has really wanted me just because. No one has ever looked past the bravado to the person inside and said, 'You know what, Summer Laurence, you're darned special.'"

When he couldn't stand it another minute, he walked forward, only to have her step back and fold her arms around herself. "Don't touch me. I won't let you touch me again."

He held up his hands, then let them fall to his sides. Please, he tried to say. One more chance. I'll show you every day how special you are to me, I swear. But even as he opened his mouth, his throat constricted and he felt the muscles lock up. He took a breath and tried. Nothing came out. Feeling as though he'd just been staked out to die a slow death, he nodded his acceptance of her terms, then turned to go. On his way past the desk he saw the roses—and a large German stein holding pencils and pens.

Before he even realized what he was doing, he picked up the mug. He'd already turned away when it hit the wall.

Summer had been in the RV changing Snowy's bandage when Char called to tell her Joe was back. After a few words with Melvin Bailey, who ordered her to refer all inquiries from the press to him at his bed-and-breakfast in Osuma, she hurried upstairs to Joe's room.

He was alone, sitting on his bed, his shoulders slumped. His sandy hair was disheveled, his face drawn and shadowed with a patchy growth of adolescent whiskers on his jaw and upper lip. Someone had applied a butterfly bandage to his split cheek. His right eye was black-and-blue and swollen nearly shut. The knuckles of both hands were puffed and raw.

"How are you doing?" she asked when he looked up.

"I'm kinda tired." He lifted a bandaged hand to rub his bruised jaw. "It's hard to sleep in . . . there."

Summer knew that all too well. "You can sleep now, for as long as you like," she said as she sat next to him.

"I wanted to kill that bastard when I saw what he'd done," he said, his voice harsh. His eyes were bloodshot from crying, and his face was gray.

"Tell me what happened. All I've gotten so far are bits and pieces."

"Like I kept telling that detective, McVey, the girl, Kelly . . . she was trying to talk to this guy and he was all wild, like on a bad trip, you know? All crazy and stuff. And, uh, she was crying and begging him to calm down." Anger darkened his face. He made a pass at his hair with stiff fingers. A mindless gesture meant to diffuse his frustration, she sensed. "I yelled at him to get away from her, you know?"

She nodded, sick inside.

"She saw me and tried to run. That miserable bastard grabbed her by her hair, and she . . . she slammed into one of those pillars." He closed his eyes and drew in a slow, harsh breath. "I thought she was dead."

"Don't!" she ordered. "You'll only make yourself sick thinking like that. The point is, you got there in time. And once Kelly can tell her father what actually happened, Mark will be punished."

Joe shook his head, his shoulders slumping again. Exhaustion came into his face. "Chief Hollister, he's . . ." He frowned, made a helpless gesture. "He wanted to take me apart. I saw it in his eyes."

"No matter what he wants or doesn't want, he's sworn to uphold the law," she said quietly. "Once you're proven innocent, he can't touch you."

He took a deep shaky breath, let it out. His fist clenched, then relaxed. "How . . . how is she? Is she awake yet?"

"Not fully yet. The doctor thinks it'll take a day or two. Maybe longer. But the important thing is, she *will* recover. You got there in time."

His gaze shifted toward the window. It was raining now, coming down in a dispirited drizzle. "What if she lies? What if she says it *was* me?"

Summer frowned. "Why would she do that, Joe? From what you've said, Mark nearly killed her. Lying would only protect him."

"Girls do dumb things sometimes," he muttered, looked down at the floor. "Like Cindy saying I . . . I raped her when she was the one who was always after me."

Summer felt a pang of unease. "Your girlfriend accused you of raping her?"

"After her old man caught us getting it on in the pool house." The defiant look had returned to his face. "My father paid him off. In stock options, I think. Cindy got a new TransAm."

"*Did* you rape her?"

"No. Maybe I was a little high, yeah, but I woulda stopped if she'd asked me, *only she didn't.*" The anger that flared hot one moment seemed to drain away the next. "You probably think I'm lying. Everyone always does. Maybe I am scum, like that detective said."

Later, when this was over, she would deal with the revelation he'd just made. It was possible he had raped his girlfriend when he was zoned out on crack. If so, he would have to take the consequences.

"You're not scum," she said, leaning forward a little so that he had to look at her. At this stage of his recovery, his emotions were still volatile, still subject to sudden flares of temper and bursts of resentment. Though she knew just how far he had yet to go, the fact that he had himself under control was vastly encouraging. "Joe, did you hear me? You're not scum. You're a young man who's made mistakes and is trying to rebuild his life."

"Tell that to Hollister," he muttered.

"It'll work out, Joe." She managed a smile as she got to her feet. "Hang in there. You're a great kid."

"Thanks . . . thanks for believing in me," he said gruffly.

"You're welcome. And remember what I said. Everything will work out."

He nodded, then drew in a long, shaky breath as she walked to the door.

Grey let himself into the house through the patio door and quietly latched it behind him. Mark's Miata was in its usual spot in the garage and the boy's room was dark. Grey wasn't surprised. It was nearly midnight, and the antidepressant Hank had given Mark made the boy sleepier than usual.

Grey was feeling sleepy himself. The stress and worry of the last thirty-six hours had taken a toll. He should have been home hours ago, but somehow, after he'd driven Dottie home from the hospital this evening, they'd ended up sitting at her kitchen table talking over tea and some strange sort of gritty bread she'd ordered from a commune in Sante Fe.

Though the stuff had all but stuck in his throat, he hadn't laughed so much in years—or felt so alive. It scared him a great deal to realize he still had strong feelings for a woman he should have forgotten long ago. He wasn't quite ready to label the light-hearted, almost giddy sensation inside him love, but he had a strong hunch he might be heading that way.

Chuckling a little at the randy thoughts that had been rocketing around in his head since he'd seen her again, he switched off the lights Mark had left burning, then headed up the stairs to his suite. Poor Mark. Life hadn't been kind to him this past year and a half. First Markham, and then his mother's affair with a fortune hunter, and now this terrible anxiety about Kelly. Thank God Brody had believed in the boy. Grey hated to imagine what might have happened if Mark had been arrested like a common criminal.

It was no wonder his grandson had been upset and edgy. Though only a patient's immediate family members were permitted into the ICU, Grey had arranged for Mark to see Kelly for a few minutes after Dottie had dragged Brody downstairs to the cafeteria for dinner.

The man was an emotional wreck, although Grey doubted anyone who didn't know him well would notice. It was the bleak look in his eyes, he thought. For the first time since Brody had been a child no higher than Grey's knee, he looked defeated. As though his will to fight had been trampled out of him.

Dottie swore he was in love with Summer Laurence and vice versa. Grey knew love did strange things to a man. Made him a little crazy sometimes. But the sadness Grey saw in Brody's face when he thought no one was looking didn't seem driven by love. More like . . . despair.

Mark's door was closed. Grey started to walk past, then paused. He smiled a little as he eased open the boy's door. It had been years since he'd tucked in one of his own, but he figured Mark would sense his love, even if he was asleep. His smile faded when the light from the hall fell onto the bed. The spread was still neatly in place, the pillow unused.

"Mark?" he said as he pushed the door wider. "Are you in here, son?"

Reaching out, he switched on the light, blinking a little against the glare. The shoe box he'd brought home to the boy was on the desk, open now and empty. A tightly rolled shirt sat next to the lid and several CDs were stacked nearby. A glint of

gold in a nest of crumpled tissue paper caught his eye and he
moved closer. It was a gold charm bracelet similar to one he'd
once given Sarah. He reached out a hand to touch the glitter, only
to freeze when his gaze fell on another spill of tissue. There, half
buried in the fold, was the missing cameo.

She was trapped, caught in that frightening, helpless state be-
tween full consciousness and deep sleep. The baby was crying,
her beautiful face obscured by the blanket, her tiny hands pum-
meling the air.

Summer struggled to leave the airless room holding her pris-
oner. Opening her mouth, she screamed, but no sound came out.
Curling her hands into fists, she pounded at the window. No one
came. The screams grew louder.

Why wouldn't the matron take pity on her? Couldn't she hear
that the child was in pain?

Summer twisted and turned, frantic to get to her child, but her
bounds held tight. The baby struggled, too, kicking at the
blanket. Summer called out, and the dream changed. Suddenly
she was at the hospital, looking at Kelly through the small
square window of intensive care. Kelly was on the bed, strug-
gling, crying. Screaming for help. Someone was with her, some-
one with large brutal hands and madness in his eyes. She
struggled to see the face, but the features were in shadow.

Summer opened her mouth to scream for help . . .

And jerked awake.

Gasping for breath, she fought to free herself from the sheet
twisted around her waist. Sweat beaded her forehead and pearled
between her breasts, and she felt light-headed. She tore a fingernail trying to get untangled, but finally she was free. After
lurching drunkenly to a sitting position, she reached for the
phone. Her hands shook as she punched out the number of
Brody's cell phone. It rang and rang, but there was no answer.
She swore as she broke the connection. Brody hated that phone
and left it in the Blazer more than he carried it. Thought it was
yuppie pretension and preferred the unobtrusive beeper. When

she got a dial tone again, she punched out the number of the hospital switchboard, memorized after countless calls. It seemed a lifetime before she was connected and transferred to ICU.

"This is Dr. Laurence." Mindful of the near-frantic emotion racing through her, she fought to keep her voice calm and rational. "I'd like to speak with Chief Hollister, please. You can find him in the waiting room outside the door." According to Dottie, he haunted the small space, staring at nothing while waiting to see Kelly again.

"Hold please, Dr. Laurence, while I check." The woman on the other end put down the phone . . . and never came back. After three full minutes of agony, Summer broke the connection. Seconds later she was throwing off the damp sheet and scrambling into her clothes. Since she couldn't sleep, she might as well drive to the hospital, and see for herself that Kelly was safe.

Brody was so tired, his vision was hazy. It was his second trip to the canteen outside the staff lounge on the second floor. The coffee was worse even than squad room sludge, but it was hot and had enough kick to keep him from nodding off in the chair while he waited for Kelly to open her eyes and look at him again.

It was an effort to put one foot in front of the other as he walked down the deserted corridor to the small alcove at the end. A little guy dressed in gray trousers and shirt looked up from the wide dust mop he was pushing as Brody stopped in front of the coffee machine. Habit had him registering the Fu Manchu beard and thinning hair, along with the sympathy on the man's weathered face.

"Long night, buddy?" the janitor asked quietly, leaning for a moment on his mop handle.

"Long enough," he managed, pulling out change from the pocket of his jeans. Sorting out the coins was an exercise in concentration that had him swearing under his breath by the time he figured out he didn't have enough. He was reaching into his pocket for a single when he noticed the light blinking on the change machine. It was empty. He uttered a rank obscenity. The janitor chuckled.

"Ain't that the way of it, though?"

Brody lifted a brow. "Don't s-suppose you have change?"

"Nope. I'm plumb tapped out. Good thing tomorrow's payday." With a shrug, the janitor went back to pushing the broom.

Exhaustion buzzed in Brody's head as he headed back toward the elevators. He was nearly to the lobby when he remembered the change he kept in the ashtray of the Blazer. It wasn't much. Only a couple of dollars in quarters, but it would be enough for coffee, and the fresh air would do him good.

The ICU nurse who responded to Summer's inquiry was brusque, and a little distracted as she told her that Kelly was no longer her patient. Because the teenager was stable and lucid, albeit terribly sleepy, they'd moved her to her own room after the dinner hour. While Summer cooled her heels in the hall, the young woman tracked down the room number. Two-seventeen. Two flights down.

Telling herself that Kelly was fine, she hurried back to the elevators, punched the button, then paced impatiently until the car arrived and doors whooshed open.

"Hurry up, hurry up," she muttered, pacing as the elevator moved downward at what seemed like a snail's pace. She nearly jammed her face against the doors before they opened. The nurses' station was empty. Light spilled from a room a few doors away and Summer heard the murmur of voices. No doubt the nurse was tending to a patient.

As she neared Kelly's room, she saw that the door was closed, unlike most of the others. Bracing herself to see Brody again, she put both hands on the door and pushed it open. The room was dark, but there was enough reflected light from the hallway to reveal a human shape standing by the bed.

"Brody?" She took a step forward, then realized her mistake.

* * *

One of the letters in the EMERGENCY ROOM sign had burned out, and another was winking as Brody walked past. The lot had been nearly full when he'd arrived. Now it stood virtually empty under the yellow lights. On the other hand the employees' lot across the access road was nearly full. He'd always hated working rotating shifts. Played hell with his metabolism and his marriage, especially when Kelly had been teething. He felt a jolt of sadness as he unlocked the Blazer and opened the door. Wearily, he climbed inside and collected the change. He was about to shove it in his pocket when a dark, late model Mercedes came rocketing toward him across the empty spaces, its lights blinding him for an instant. It was Grey Krebs, he realized, and something was definitely wrong.

"Brody, thank God," Grey said as he stepped out of the car. "Have you seen Mark?"

"No. Haven't seen him since yesterday. Why?"

In the garish light, Grey looked old and tired. His movements were jerky as he reached into his pocket. "I found this in his room tonight." He held out his hand and uncurled his fingers. Curious, and a little wary, Brody glanced down at the object on Doc's palm.

"Jesus, your wife's cameo."

Grey's sigh was eloquent as he returned the valuable keepsake to his pocket. "I don't want to believe Mark is responsible for the burglary, but I have to accept the possibility."

"Damn." Brody scooped his hand through his hair, then cast a professional look around. "No sign of the Miata."

"No, it was still in the garage when I left, but my pickup is missing. I park it on the street so I didn't realize it was gone until I started looking for Mark."

Brody noticed the cold then, seeping through the fog of self-pity he'd wrapped around his sorry self. Ice in July? The part of him that was still functioning beneath the weariness, the numb agony of loss, the self-hatred went on full alert. "Grey, S-Summer told my men about a pistol and some threats Mark made."

Brody saw the look of guilt on Grey's face and wondered what else was being kept from him. "He's been seeing Hank Gottlieb. The diagnosis was clinical depression exacerbated by fear of being abandoned. Hank mentioned something about control issues. Needing to be sure of his environment and the people in it."

The cold in Brody's bones exploded into a hot terror. "Christ, Grey, what if Summer's been right all along? What if it *was* Mark who slammed Kel's head against that post?"

"Oh God, no!" Doc exclaimed, but Brody was already running.

CHAPTER 23

A scream rose to Summer's throat. Somehow she fought it down. He had a pillow in his hands and was pressing it against Kelly's face. His hands were too close to Kelly's neck. One quick twist and she was dead.

As soon as the light hit him, he whirled around and Summer saw his face. "Shit!" he hissed when he recognized her. The pillow was still on Kelly's face. The girl wasn't moving. Summer felt her control start to go—and then she caught the slight rise and fall of Kelly's chest. Relief hit in a wave, nearly taking her to her knees.

"Don't move," he ordered, poised on the balls of his feet, ready to catch her if she ran. He was bigger, faster, stronger. She had nothing but her training to use as a weapon to protect Kelly—and herself.

"How is she?" Summer asked in a voice designed to soothe and calm.

"Asleep. She's asleep." He shot a fast glance past her shoulder to the empty corridor, and she could smell his fear. She told herself that Brody hadn't left the hospital. Perhaps he'd gone for a short walk to stretch his legs or downstairs for coffee and was even now on his way up. Somehow she had to keep talking until he returned.

"I don't want to hurt her." His voice was thin with panic as his gaze darted from her face to the bed and back again. He was a cornered rat in Levis and a Grateful Dead T-shirt, trying to figure out what to do now. Summer wanted his attention on her, not Kelly.

"Of course you don't want to hurt her. That would be a mistake, and you're too smart to make mistakes."

He sucked in air through his mouth, and the harsh sound rasped at her already taut nerves. Sweat beaded his brow and the bruises on his face stood out like black smudges against the pallor of his skin. Summer sensed that his control was balanced on a razor's edge. A mistake now would send him tumbling into a manic state.

"Close the door," he ordered, his voice quivering.

"Whatever you say," she soothed, careful to move slowly as she stepped forward and let the door swing closed behind her. The room was immediately plunged into semidarkness, illuminated only by the sliver of light coming through the slit in the partially closed bathroom door to her right.

"It's chilly in here, isn't it?" she said as she inched closer. "For such a warm night, I mean. Funny how that happens in the mountains. You're a city boy, aren't you? I grew up in San Diego where the mountains look more like Disneyland, you know? Like there should be someone taking tickets."

He blinked, then ran a nervous hand through his sun-streaked hair. "Shut up. I need to think."

Pressing her advantage, she took another cautious step forward. If she got near him she might be able to knee him in the groin. "Look, why don't we go down to the cafeteria and have a Coke, talk this out. Between the two of us I bet we can come up with a way to help you solve your problems."

He'd grown up with every advantage, the only son of rich parents. Spoiled and indulged, accustomed to charming his way out of punishment. She took another step, then stopped. His panic was nearly palpable, a dark and malevolent emotion pulsing between them. Somehow she kept her lips from trembling as she curved them into a nonthreatening smile. "So far, only you and I know you're here. I know what happened to Kelly was an accident. And I know you're scared."

His gaze darted to the door behind her, as though he expected Brody to come charging in. "The Chief will kill me if he finds out."

"How can he find out? You won't tell, and neither will I. If we can get out of here without being seen, of course." She frowned and pretended to think. "My car is parked in the rear. We could go down the stairs instead of taking the elevator."

He swallowed, his eyes glittering in the semidarkness. "It's a . . . you're trying to trick me." He glanced around, his eyes blinking too rapidly. Sweat ran down his face in rivulets now. "You hate me. You . . . don't care . . . no one cares. . . ."

"I care! And I want to help you."

"If you're lying, I'll kill you, I swear! I don't have anything to lose now. Not now. I'm—"

He broke off at the sound of a faint moan, and his gaze jerked back to Kelly. Summer felt a jolt of pure terror. She leaped forward, only to have him move faster. Even as her mind registered her mistake, his hands were on her throat.

Because the elevator was too slow, Brody took the stairs, racing up them two at a time. The nurse was just stepping into the corridor from a room near the door, and leaped back with a little cry as it banged back against the wall.

"Call security and nine-one-one!" he shouted as he ran past.

Earlier, he'd left the door to Kelly's room open. Now it was closed. His mind clicked into a cop's calm. Needing his hands free, he used his shoulder to push his way inside.

Crouched on the floor, his hands at Summer's throat, Joe Finley looked up, teeth bared, and his eyes glazed over with a killing rage. With terror sizzling in his head, Brody moved, smashing his forearm into the boy's throat. The teenager let out a shrill scream, letting Summer go as he clutched his own gullet and scrambled to his feet. Brody charged, spinning the bastard around, slamming him into the wall as the nurse came running in. He heard Grey shout something, saw Summer struggling to sit up. At the same time, he smashed a fist into Finley's chin. The bastard's head whipped back, hitting the wall with a resounding crack. Finley was unconscious before he fell to the floor.

Even though she'd drunk two large cups of steaming coffee in the doctor's lounge, Summer couldn't stop shivering. "Grey, are you sure Kelly's going to be all right?" she asked the doctor while Detective Tong scribbled something in her notebook.

Looking wan and tired Grey reached across the clutter of Styrofoam cups and dog-eared magazines on the low table to squeeze her arm. "She's fine. Slept through the whole thing."

Summer let her shoulders slump. Briefly, Grey had told her about finding the cameo and the terrible suspicion that had sent him racing to the hospital in search of Brody. Mark was still missing. Brody had his men looking for the boy. Grey had also put in a call to the boy's mother in Chicago, but so far there'd been no word.

Across the stuffy room Brody was standing by the window, looking out at the first whispers of dawn over the peaks. He'd split two knuckles when he'd hit Joe, and his left hand was grossly swollen, the skin already blotched with purple bruising. Grey had tried twice to convince him to go down to the ER for treatment, receiving only a cold stare in response. For the past thirty minutes, while Detective Tong and her partner spoke gently to Summer, he'd stood silently, saying nothing, his face closed and forbidding.

Glancing up, Detective Tong exchanged looks with her burly partner. "Did I miss any of the bases?" she asked, looking tired.

"Not that I caught." McVey shifted his gaze toward the window. "Chief? Anything we missed?"

Summer saw Brody's eyes turn her way and braced herself. "Nothing that can't wait." He sounded impatient and a little surly.

After she'd made sure Kelly was still alive, Summer had

fallen apart. Even her knees had crumpled. Brody had caught her before she hit the floor, then supported her while she'd sobbed, drenching his shirt with the tears she couldn't seem to control, all but choking him as she'd tried to climb inside his strong, sheltering body. His big hand had stroked her back while he waited patiently for her to stop shaking. And then, when she was steady on her feet again, he'd gently put her away from him. An instant later, he was all business, a quintessential professional, quietly and efficiently taking charge. Shutting her out as though she were little more than a bystander.

A stranger would have marveled at his detachment. She knew he'd just put a temporary barrier between himself and his emotions. A lone wolf wandering off when the battle was over to lick his wounds in some private place, growling ferociously at anyone who came close enough to sense his pain.

"That's it, then," McVey said, climbing stiffly to his feet. His grizzled hair stuck up in the back, and his blue dress shirt looked as though he'd grabbed it out of the laundry basket. His partner, on the other hand, was surprisingly put-together in tailored slacks and a tidy silk camp shirt. Both had been summoned, along with half the night shift, by Brody's call.

It had been almost an hour since Chuck Sawyer's dad and a skinny officer with a bobbing Adam's apple had taken a sobbing and broken Joe Finley to the jail. Another young officer named Fitz-something had remained behind, standing at attention near the door.

"I guess that's all, Dr. Laurence," Detective Tong said as she stowed her notebook in her shoulder bag. "Thank you very much for your cooperation." She rose, hesitated, then added in a sympathetic tone, "I know this must have been extremely difficult for you."

Touched by her solicitude, Summer managed a smile. "Thank you."

McVey nodded her way, the look he gave her far less

compassionate. Blaming her for bringing Joe here, she suspected. Holding her accountable because she'd defended him.

"Come on, Paulie, I'll race you to the parking lot," he said, holding the door open for his tiny partner.

"Five bucks says I'll make it to the street before you get that old junker of yours in gear," Tong countered as she sailed out in front of him.

Grey, too, got to his feet. Beyond the door, the hospital was waking up. "I'll take you home, Summer. You're in no fit condition to drive."

She nodded her thanks, aware, even as she fumbled for her purse and got to her feet, that Brody was watching her, a tight-lipped, dangerous stranger who could break her in two with one blow—or soothe her from a nightmare with amazing gentleness.

"I was wrong about Joe," she told him, because she owed him that. "You had him pegged all along."

One side of his mouth moved. "Is that supposed to make me feel better?"

She shook her head. Neither of them would forget this night— or, she suspected, the events that had brought them to this room. "No. I just wanted you to know that."

A muscle jerked in his jaw, and for an instant, she thought his eyes softened. Her heart leapt, only to falter when the hardness returned. "Go home, Summer," he ordered in exactly the same way he'd ordered Corporal Sawyer to haul Joe off to jail. "We're done here."

Brody flexed his injured hand, then scowled when a searing pain shot up his arm. Across the table in the musty interview room Pauline Tong gave him a wary look. It was the same look he'd been getting from damn near everyone in the last forty-eight hours. Like he was some kind of loose cannon, ready to explode.

He was entitled to be in a bad mood, damn it. The stitches

holding his shattered knuckles together had gotten infected and hurt like a son of a bitch, Phil Potter was pestering him for a comment on the series of articles he was running questioning the wisdom of locating a treatment center so close to a tourist Mecca, and he was getting sick and tired of people diving into the nearest doorway whenever he walked past. Even Max had threatened to give notice if he didn't stop stomping around like a bear with a sore paw.

What the hell did they expect him to do? He'd gone to Summer once and damn near groveled on his belly. How many ways could a man tell a woman he would wade into a gang fight unarmed before he would deliberately hurt her again? He'd been willing to stutter out an entire list if she'd given him the chance. Now it was too late. With just a few stupid words he'd ripped apart something rare and precious between them, and everyone was expecting him to fix it. But damn it, there was nothing he could do—and it was tearing him apart.

"Since Dr. Krebs refuses to press charges against his grandson, I figure the best thing to do is close out the case." Tong exchanged a long-suffering look with her partner before adding, "Unless you disagree, Chief?"

"Your case, your call," he said, shifting in the hard chair. He wanted to stop by the hospital to see Kelly before he headed home. Now that she was fully awake and improving by leaps and bounds, the fear that had kept him from sleeping had disappeared, and he was damn tired.

"Me, I think the kid deserves probation," McVey grumbled, tugging on the knot of his tie. "Four thousand dollars' damage in books alone, not to mention the hell he put his grandfather through, all because of a broken date."

"C'mon, Mac. You've been a cop long enough to know that people do irrational things when they're in love." Tong sighed. "I climbed a mountain once because I was trying to impress this gorgeous fireman I was dating in L.A. Darn near killed myself."

"Yeah, so how come you're still single?"

"He dumped me for some bimbo he met when he rescued her cat from an apartment-house roof. Told me she didn't intimidate him the way I did."

McVey laughed. Brody scowled. Mark Krebs hadn't killed himself as Grey had feared. He'd simply run away. Back to the mother who hadn't wanted him around. Brody knew what that was like. Hating yourself for still wanting to be held and comforted—and loved. Knowing it wasn't going to happen, and yet unable to stop hoping.

Grey had been a basket case until his daughter-in-law had called to say that Mark had shown up on her doorstep, upset and worn-out from his drive across the country. Grey had immediately flown to Chicago. Last Dottie had heard, he'd read Mark's mother the riot act about neglecting her son when he'd needed her the most and was bringing the boy home with him sometime tomorrow or the next day. He'd asked Brody's permission to let Mark visit Kelly, permission Brody had been more than pleased to give. No matter what problems Mark had or what grief he'd caused Kelly, the boy had saved her life in that barn. Brody was prepared to go a long way to repay him.

"If that's all—" He was already pushing back from the table when Max stuck her head in.

"Ted Labeck on line two for you, Chief. He says it's about Joe Finley. Apparently Mel Bailey wants to cut a deal."

Char's head snapped up, her brown eyes filled with outrage. "That's it? One count of attempted murder and one count of assault for trying to kill an innocent young girl simply because she was in the wrong place at the wrong time?"

Summer nodded. She'd just gotten off the phone with Joe's attorney. For once, the high-powered lawyer hadn't exuded arrogance. In fact, he'd been almost humble when he'd given her the details of the deal he'd hammered out with the district attorney's office.

"Joe serves a year on the assault, two to five on the attempted murder, and the county saves the cost of a trial and the appeals Bailey threatened to file." She struggled to contain her frustration. "It's not enough. Not nearly enough. Joe is a manipulator and a sociopath, and he deserves to do hard time."

"It's the system," Manny jeered as he pushed his chair back on two legs. "But he'll be in jail. And the original sentence will be changed, too. Too bad the bastard didn't break his frigging neck shimmying down that tree yonder."

Summer shifted her gaze to the oak that had been Joe's escape route, just as it had once been Brody's. Synchronicity of the most ironic kind, she thought. According to the disjointed story the detectives had gotten out of Joe, he'd bolstered his nerve with the crack he'd retrieved from the barn, then slipped away when everyone was asleep and caught a ride into town with a passing motorist. Pretending to be Kelly's older brother, home from college, he'd charmed a motherly nurse into finding out her room number, then waited in an empty room nearby until he'd seen Brody leave.

"Judge Mandeville also called this morning," she said, returning her attention to her two friends. "To say he's disappointed is putting it mildly."

Char frowned. "In other words, no more referrals."

Summer listened to the sound of laughter drifting up the stairs from the living room. It was Sunday, a light day for the residents. Because it was raining again, everyone was indoors.

"You might as well know now, he's talking about trying to shut us down."

Manny let the chair crash down on four legs. "Can he do that?" he asked, leaning forward.

Summer thought about the monthly operating budget and the amount remaining in the business account. "I don't know, guys. Four of our nine current residents came from his recommendation to the parents. If occupancy falls below five for three months in a row, we'll be broke."

* * *

Kelly was recovering beautifully. As Dr. MacNeil had predicted, she was a champion. After a week in the hospital, he'd pronounced her ready to go home. Her head was still wrapped in a bandage, and Brody had been given a list of instructions for her care.

"Dr. MacNeil made me swear not to go outside for a week," Kelly muttered to Summer as Brody settled his daughter gently into her own bed. Because Kelly had fretted about her shaved head, Summer had bought her a bright yellow cap decorated with a gay sunflower. Dottie had found a yellow top and matching plaid shorts, which Kelly had pronounced "totally gnarly" before adding that Tiff would be pea-green. Both Dottie and Summer thought she looked adorable, if a little pale.

"I assume Dr. MacNeil also mentioned that playing your CDs at full volume was definitely detrimental to your health," Summer said, satisfying her need to fuss over the girl she adored by adjusting covers.

A gleam appeared in bright blue eyes that were no longer shadowed by pain. In an ironic twist of fate Kelly remembered nothing of what had happened to her after she'd walked into the barn to discover Joe taking something out of a gunnysack in one of the stalls.

"Actually, I was kinda thinking that a mountain bike would be a really neat welcome home present," she said in a wheedling tone.

"D-dream on," Brody said gruffly, putting the bottle of pain pills he'd carried home onto the table by the bed.

A crafty look came into Kelly's eyes, and Summer smiled a little. "Ah, c'mon, Dad. You have to admit I was really good in the hospital. I did what the nurses told me and hardly ever complained, right?"

He lifted one raven eyebrow. "No mountain bike. At least until you're fully recovered."

Kelly pouted a little. "Then I have another idea."

"I'm not surprised," Brody said as he crossed his arms over his wide chest. Below the sleeve of his uniform shirt the dragon's tail twitched a little as he flexed his biceps. Summer thought about the first time she'd seen that dragon, and grieved.

"See, it's like this. Aunt Dottie and Dr. Krebs are already getting married next month, right? And I thought, well, that it would be really neat if you and Summer made it a double wedding."

Brody went pale, and for a split second his eyes took on the terrible look of a man stretched on the rack. Then he turned and walked from the room.

"I guess that was a dumb thing to say," Kelly muttered, her eyes wide with dismay as she stared at the empty doorway.

Summer tugged at the yellow sheet. "Nothing you say is dumb, sweetie."

"Yeah, but you love Dad and all, right?"

"Sometimes love isn't enough, Kelly."

"But—"

"Your aunt has made some brownies to celebrate your homecoming. Why don't I go down and get you a couple."

"Ralph Lentel is such a poop! I don't know why Mandy married him." Dottie rattled her teacup in the saucer and glared at her fiancé, who lifted one silvery eyebrow.

The Hollister household had been turned into a command post, with Dottie as a radiant but demanding sergeant-major ordering around her troops. Summer would have found it adorable if she hadn't been so miserable.

The big day was to be held on the last weekend before Labor Day, which was only three weeks away. Dottie was having four bridesmaids, the three other ladies of the Fearsome Foursome and Summer. Kelly was to be the maid of honor. Grey's medschool roomie, now a prominent cardiologist in the San Francisco Bay area, was to be the best man, and Brody was giving his aunt away. The wedding was to be in the same church where

Grey had once stood alone at the altar, brokenhearted. To replace bad memories with good, Dottie had told him.

"What's the reverend done to upset you, sugar?" Grey reached out to untangle the tiny silver stars dangling from Dottie's earlobe.

"He refuses to allow us to serve champagne in the church reception hall."

"Dot, the man is a Methodist minister. He could be defrocked."

"Oh, piffle." She sighed, then beamed as an idea struck. "No matter. We'll have punch."

Summer almost choked on her tea. "Dottie Hollister, don't you dare!"

Dottie's eyebrows lifted nearly to her hairline, and a look of innocence appeared on her face. "Do what, dear?"

"Spike the punch."

"But dear heart, think of the symmetry. Lucy will likely fuss a little at first, but she'll come around. Flossie will throw herself wholeheartedly into the spirit of it, and after a little persuasion, so will Mandy. After all, there's no law against sweetening a boring party drink with a few lively spirits."

"Works for me," Grey said, lifting the glass containing a double shot of Wild Turkey to his mouth. Surprisingly, Dottie herself had all but stopped drinking. It seemed that happiness had driven away her need to medicate herself with strong spirits.

"I think the lime silk is a wonderful choice for your dress, dear," Dottie said with a slightly vague smile. "You look so lovely in that color, although it's a little subdued for my taste. I myself am thinking of mauve with perhaps a touch of fuchsia."

"Princess, if you want to wear red, white, and blue spangles, it's all right with me. Just as long as you show up this time." Grey's indulgent grin told Dottie that he was teasing, and she let herself relax.

"Well, perhaps just a few bugle beads," she mused, winning her a groan from Summer and a throaty laugh from her fiancé.

"Lime, it is," Summer said, taking a sip of Dottie's favorite tea. It amazed her that she'd actually developed a fondness for the foul-tasting stuff. "I'll call Mrs. Stevens tomorrow and tell her to go ahead. What color did Kelly finally choose?"

"A lovely shade of lilac, and the cutest little cloche hat to cover her head."

Grey leaned back and crossed his legs. He looked very much at home in Dottie's living room. Content, Summer realized. After they returned from a honeymoon in Kauai, they planned to live in his house. "You once shaved your head as I recall," he said, caressing his soon-to-be wife with a fond gaze.

"Only because I was trying out this special red dye Lucy and I made up in chemistry class. Lucy forgot a step, and the stuff fried my hair."

Grey chuckled. "I thought you looked very fetching with peach fuzz."

Dottie blushed and bent forward to kiss him. Summer glanced into her cup, annoyed at herself for envying Dottie's happiness. She'd seen Brody twice since he'd saved her life. Once when she'd gone to visit Kelly in the hospital and then again on the day he'd brought Kelly home.

"How's Mark doing?" she asked when the couple drew apart.

"When I left this morning, he was painting the garage," Grey said with a note of paternal satisfaction in his voice. "Even considering the astronomical rates charged by painting contractors these days, he'll have earned enough by the time he finishes the house to pay off the insurance company."

"Oh dear, it's so beastly hot today," Dottie said with a worried look. "I hope the dear boy drinks plenty of water."

"He has water, princess. And a fridge full of snacks."

"I think you should be ashamed of yourself for suspecting that sweet boy of harming Kelly, when all the time he was pining with love." Dottie's cup rattled in her saucer as she took an agitated sip. "Of course, your finding the cameo did bring you to the hospital in time to warn Brody—even if you were warning him against the wrong young man." She gave a delicate little shudder. "It was such a close call. So many chances for tragedy."

"Dottie mentioned that a lot of the books Mark ruined were first editions," Summer said.

"At least a third of them, yes. I doubt I'll try to replace them. But I made Mark promise to read a book a week as punishment, and I get to pick the books." He grinned. "Dottie's making a list, starting with the classics."

"*Crime and Punishment* is first," Dottie said with a laugh. "Symmetry, you see."

Grey scowled. "Symmetry be damned. He made a mess of my house and darn near gave me a heart attack when I found the cameo." Grey glanced Summer's way. "As Hank keeps telling me, it was better that Mark took out his frustration against me by trashing my house than by hurting himself or someone else."

"As long as he's held accountable for what he did do."

"You haven't seen the size of my house," Grey said, chuckling.

Summer's own laugh was cut short when the back door slammed. Brody was home.

"We're in here, dear," Dottie called, turning expectantly. Summer felt nerves bunch in her stomach and took a quick sip of tea. It had been four days since he'd walked out of Kelly's room, and Summer hadn't seen him since.

"Thank God you're home," Grey said when Brody wandered into the living room. "These women have about worn me out with wedding preparations. Grab a chair and let's talk dirty."

Brody started to grin, and then he caught sight of Summer sitting on the sofa with fabric samples spread over the coffee table in front of her. His grin faded as he acknowledged her with a nod. It might as well have been a slap, for all the warmth he put into it.

"I'm about talked out today, but you go ahead," he told Grey quietly.

"You look tired, dear," Dottie said with a little frown. "Why don't you sit down and have some tea. I was about to make us some nibbles."

"Maybe later." He nodded, turned on his heel, and stalked up the stairs.

"I've never seen him like this," Dottie said, looking from Grey to Summer. "Not even when Megan was killed. It's like he's pulled into a tight knot inside. I thought that when Kelly came home he might relax, but . . ." She sighed. "Summer, you talk to him. He'll listen to you."

Summer put down her cup and picked up her purse. "It's time I got back," she said as she slung the strap over her shoulder. "Tell Kelly I'll stop by tomorrow around lunchtime."

The wedding went off without a hitch. Even Mother Nature smiled benignly on the reconciled lovers, producing a glorious sunny day and clear azure sky.

From the moment Dottie had asked her to participate Summer had primed herself for an avalanche of emotion. The church, the flowers, the organ music—she'd expected the sensory overload.

She hadn't thought to prepare herself for the sight of Brody Hollister's magnificent body attired in a black tuxedo, though. The man was flat-out devastating. A babe, she'd heard Tiffany whisper to Kelly during the reception. A babe who'd nodded curtly to her when they'd ended up in the foyer together before the ceremony started.

As soon as the newlyweds were on their way, covered with birdseed, Summer had gone back to the ranch, the wedding bouquet Dottie had pressed on her still in her hands. By the time she'd reached her RV, she'd been crying uncontrollably. Not even Snowy's attempts at comfort had soothed her. She suspected nothing ever would.

It was close to ten. Alone in the kitchen that seemed different somehow, now that Dottie had moved a few of her favorite things to Grey's house, Brody was washing his coffee cup in the sink when he heard a quiet footfall behind him. He spun around to find Kelly standing in the doorway, watching him with brooding eyes.

"I hope you're happy," she said as she pulled out a chair and flopped down.

"Happy about what? Your aunt's wedding?"

Kelly stuck out her lower lip. "No, about Summer leaving."

Brody upended the cup in the drain board and reached for a towel. He hated talking about Summer, especially now when the image of her in her wedding finery was still fresh and throbbing in his head. "Kel, cut to the chase, okay? I'm on duty at six-thirty tomorrow morning and I'd like to get some sleep."

"Just what I said, Dad. Summer's leaving. She told me this morning when we were getting dressed. She said she's only told Auntie and me, so far. And Char and Manny, of course."

Brody felt a pain in his belly. "Why?" he demanded, his tone harsher than he'd intended. Kelly didn't appear to notice.

"She said Phoenix House was a mistake and that she was going back to the place where she worked before."

"You must have m-m-misunderstood, baby. I thought she knew the town's going to give Phoenix House another chance."

"I know what I heard, Dad. She's leaving, and it's because of what happened with that jerk, Finley. On account of him trying to kill me and all. Summer feels like it's her fault, only she wouldn't feel that way if you hadn't yelled at her."

"I didn't yell, damn it! I . . ." He broke off when he realized he was shouting. "Hell," he muttered before flicking an embarrassed gaze toward his daughter.

"I hate that stupid Joe Finley," she exclaimed as she got to her feet. "You were going to ask Summer to marry you and then he had to go and ruin it all."

How the hell did she know? Brody hid his surprise behind a scowl. "Get some sleep, b-b-baby. You look tired."

"Oh Dad, I love Summer so much. And you two are perfect for each other. Even *I* can see that."

"Baby—"

"You laugh all the time when she's around, and you even look different. Like real handsome, you know?"

Brody felt heat climbing his neck. Handsome, hell. Maybe Kel needed glasses.

Kelly jerked open the refrigerator door and took out the milk carton. "It doesn't bother her at all when you stutter, like she doesn't even notice, and she's always finding excuses to touch you, like fixing your collar, and stuff like that." She found a glass before turning to look at him over her shoulder. "I saw her at the reception, watching you. She looked so sad." She scowled. "Aunt Dottie says it's all because of something called 'philosophical differences,' only I think you two are just scared of each other." She shot him a look that went to the bone. "I think it sucks."

Summer was brushing the hair spray out of her hair when she heard a vehicle pull in next to her van. As soon as she heard the impatient knock on the RV's door, she knew it was Brody, and her heart took off on a wild gallop.

"What's wrong?" she asked without preamble.

"You tell me," he said, jerking open the screen and vaulting inside. With a little cry, she stepped back before he bowled her over. He was wearing worn-out jeans and a torn shirt with grease smeared on the shoulder, and his hair was unruly and wild, as though raked through repeatedly by his blunt fingers. "Kel said you're leaving."

Her heart contracted. The decision that had taken her a lot of sleepless nights to make hadn't seemed totally real until this moment. "That's right."

"What about this place?" he demanded, standing very much the way she'd first seen him, with one hip cocked, a strong, powerful man who projected a vital, raw masculinity.

Too worn out to stand a second longer, she walked to the table and sat down. Because it was a warm night, she was wearing a skimpy shirt—and nothing else. She felt exposed and vulnerable.

"I'm sure Dottie can find another tenant. A children's camp, perhaps. She mentioned that once."

"You're giving up?" His tone was combative. Definitely surly.

"No, I'm correcting a mistake before someone else gets hurt." Brody heard the throb of emotion in her voice and felt it hit him below the belt. Damn, he hated it when she was hurting. He wanted to tuck that bright head under his chin and curl around her so that nothing could ever hurt her again, but he knew she'd only shake him off. She didn't want him to touch her. She didn't want *him*.

"I was so sure I had all the answers," she said, looking down at her small hands. Hands he longed to feel running over his body one last time. "*You* were unfeeling and prejudiced, while *I* was the compassionate one. God's gift to the poor, suffering victims. I was practically vibrating with self-righteous disdain. Told you off good and proper, didn't I?" She drew a shaky breath, and Brody clenched his fists to keep from reaching for her. "I'd apologize. I *do* apologize, but it's not enough. So I'm doing what you wanted all along. Leaving."

He took a minute to sort that through. "No way, Dr. Laurence. You're not laying this one on me." He leaned against the fridge and folded his arms. He could smell her, that light, swirling scent of flowers that made him feel as though he'd buried his face in a field of wildflowers. "Take my advice and do your running before Auntie gets back. It's going to flat-out kill her to realize she's backed a quitter."

She flinched, and he felt like a worm. "I'm not quitting. And she already knows." She looked at him and her eyes were as dull as her voice. "I told you, I'm correcting a mistake."

It was killing him to see her so lifeless. "Bullshit, honey. You're talking to a guy who knows all there is to know about giving up." He snorted. "Run away if you have to, but at least show enough guts to own up to the reason."

Instead of exploding at him with her claws extended and her eyes spitting anger she slumped lower in her chair. Damn, he was getting scared.

"I nearly got Kelly killed because of my blind stubbornness," she said, staring at the bouquet of marigolds in a blue vase on the small table.

"You were conned, Summer." He spoke carefully, watching her eyes, gauging her reaction. "Just like Calvin Williams conned me."

"I should have known better." The self-hatred in her voice seared him.

"Why? Because you're smarter than me?"

Her head shot up, and she jerked around to glare at him. "No, of course not! Because I'm a trained therapist. I should have seen the signs of antisocial behavior. They were all there. Char saw them. I thought she was overreacting." Her anger subsided. "No, that's not right. I *did* see the signs. I just ignored them."

"You wanted to believe in someone, Summer. A s-seventeen-year-old k-kid. You . . . hurt for him. That's not wrong. Because of you Finley got a second chance, and he blew it. But that's his shame, not yours."

She gave a bitter laugh that tore at him. "You're wrong, Brody. It wasn't compassion driving me. Anything but. No, it was plain old garden-variety ambition. Another sterling accomplishment to validate Summer Laurence, Ph.D. I wanted Phoenix House to work because it was *my* idea, *my* professional reputation at stake, not because I cared about Joe. Having him as a patient was a perfect opportunity, a kid in trouble, a rich father, a respected judge. Save the kid, instant prestige." She drew a shaky breath. "It was stupid and reckless and I . . . I'm afraid I'll do it again."

He sifted through her words, took in the bitter harshness around her soft mouth. He didn't want to see her go, and yet it was going to be hell on earth seeing her laughing over hairstyles with Kel and hanging out with his aunt. Sharing her sunshine with everyone he loved while he stood in the shadows, hurting.

"When Meggie died, I went a little crazy. Loaded my pistol with wad cutters, kissed my baby girl good-bye, hit the streets, looking for Williams. The bastard deserved to die. Nobody'd blame me. Hell, maybe I'd get a medal for blowing him away."

He winced at the memory he'd worked hard to shut down. "I had this plan. Find the son of a bitch, make him crawl before I gut-shot him, then watch him bleed out his life drop by drop, the way I was bleeding. Then, when he was d-dead, I was going to eat my g-gun."

He saw the horror drift over her face. She stopped twisting her fingers into knots. "You wouldn't leave Kelly. You're not that kind of man."

He snorted. Tomorrow, next week, the rest of his life, he'd probably wish he'd let her believe that. "Don't kid yourself. I wasn't thinking of her, only myself. I'd fucked up, thought I knew more than the streetwise cynics who warned me Williams was no good. Dumb-ass Brody Hollister knew more than the pros. And Meggie paid." He rubbed his hand across the sudden stab of pain in his gut. "Dying would have been easy. Living with my mistake, that was too hard."

He saw that hit, saw the sudden sheen in her eyes and the trembling of her mouth. "I know."

"I tried to run, Summer. Tried my damnedest."

"Why didn't you?"

He took a breath and felt his throat tightening. "I kept remembering the time Auntie broke my nose."

She tilted her head and blinked up at him. "Dottie broke your nose?"

He nodded. "With her fist. A short, neat jab. Damned efficient."

"But . . . why?"

"The speech therapist gave me an assignment to go into a crowded department store and walk up to a clerk, ask if she had a short-s-sleeved shirt, s-size extra large." He allowed himself a mocking grin. "In case you haven't noticed, esses are tough for me."

She smiled a little. It wasn't much, but it gave him heart. "It took me days to work up the guts, but finally I tried. Made myself pick a day when there was this big s-sale. Dottie drove me to the mall in Wenatchee and waited in the car." He felt the same oily sickness in his throat and swallowed. "I tried, but . . ." He shook his head. "Damn near had that poor lady in tears, trying to help me work through a few simple words. People were drifting away, hiding behind racks. I gave up and ran. Dottie could see right away I'd failed and refused to leave until I tried again. I threatened to run away, and she hit me. Then while I was mopping up the blood, she told me how much she l-loved me and . . . how proud she was of me for f-fighting back. Mushy stuff. Got my attention, though. By the time she was finished, I knew I'd rather face a bellyful of humiliation than another left jab."

Her mouth twitched. He wanted to kiss her so much he ached. "Dottie can be a little scary, I admit," she said with a laugh.

"She can be damned tough, too. Like you. Only in this case, you're being tough on the wrong person."

She shook her head, and he saw the sudden wash of tears come into her eyes. He'd blown it again. Damn. "S-Summer, Finley's not worth this. D-don't let him d-destroy what you've built."

"It wasn't him. It's me. I don't have what it takes."

He knew what would reach her, but it would also hurt her. Hurt her bad. He told himself it was the only way. Tough love, if he remembered right. Still he hesitated. When he realized he was damn near praying for his throat to close so the decision would be taken from him, he took a fast breath and leaped.

"Guess you were just blowing smoke when you laid there in that bed yonder and cried all over me about your baby, huh?" He forced a jeering smile to his face. "Damn, and I bought the whole con. That whole s-sad story about the . . . the p-promise you made to make your l-life count."

She shot to her feet, her cheeks draining of color. "I hate you for this," she shouted. "I . . ." Her face twisted, and she hugged herself, trying not to shatter. "I didn't want to love Kelly so much," she whispered, her voice thick. "I thought I could be her friend, give her my affection, but she's so special, so wonderful. I love her so much. It nearly killed me to lose my baby. If I'd lost Kelly, too . . ." Her voice splintered into a sob. Shaking, she turned away and took a step.

He couldn't stand it. He reached her in two strides, blocking her way. He wanted to hold her, but he kept his arms at his sides. "Don't go. S-stay and fight it through. Dottie will help. And Grey. A lot of folks, like Amos."

She lifted her gaze and looked up at him, her green eyes drenched and wide. "But not you?"

His throat closed up. The hurt that came into her eyes was a knife twisting in his belly. "That's what I thought," she said, brushing past him. Leaving him.

The hell with his pride, he decided, lunging for her. He caught her arm, spun her around, and crashed his mouth down on hers. He felt her stiffen, felt her hands stab at his shoulders, and then she was kissing him back, eagerly, hungrily. Making those wild little sounds in her throat. His body reacted, going hard so fast it darn near brought him to his knees. Before he lost all reason, he drew back and framed her face with his hands.

"M-marry me," he demanded, knowing it was too soon. Knowing she would say no. Knowing he would never be the same if he had to live the rest of his life without her.

"I hurt you," she whispered, her face wet with tears.

"Kelly needs a mom." Before she could refuse, he rushed to sweeten the pot. "I'll give you another baby. A dozen babies."

Summer heard the desperate note in his voice and didn't know whether to laugh or cry. "Brody—"

"God knows my aunt needs another niece to keep her busy. Now that she's quit drinking she has all this time on her hands."

"That is a frightening thought, I admit." Trembling, Summer

lifted her hand to his face and felt the strength of a man tempered to steel. He captured her wrist and kissed her palm.

"P-please," he said, his beautiful poet's eyes filled with so much naked longing it scared her a little.

"We'll fight," she whispered, her heart beginning to sing. "I'll make you furious sometimes."

"I'll handle it."

"I want at least three babies."

His mouth twitched. "I'll handle that, too."

"I love you. I love you so much."

His chest heaved, and for a moment his eyes wore the stark look of disbelief. The look of a lost boy who'd had to fight for every scrap of self-worth. "Don't even think of not believing me," she ordered, thumping him on his rock-hard shoulder. "Do you hear me, Brody Hollister? I said I love you, and I meant it. Now do me the courtesy of taking me at my word."

His mouth softened, then eased into a full-blown grin. "What the hell. A man'd be a fool to argue with a lady who's got herself plastered against him like wallpaper."

She felt it then, the erection that was a hard, promising bulge. Fire shot through her, driving out all the other things they needed to say. Promises, questions, a lifetime of negotiating. At the moment all she could think about was living with him, loving him. Giving him babies to spoil.

"Well?" he demanded, his grin fading.

"Well what?"

"Yes or no."

She smiled. "Yes, oh yes! Definitely yes, only—"

"No more talk," he ordered as he swept her into his arms and headed for the tiny bedroom. She snuggled closer, kissed his throat, his obstinate chin, his sensuous mouth. But when he tried to deepen the kiss, she drew back far enough so that he could see the love in her eyes.

"I thought I was healed. That I was whole. I know now there was still a piece missing." She lifted a hand and traced the line of his hard mouth. "You, Brody. The best part of my heart."

"You . . . are my heart," he said hoarsely before laying her gently on the bed.

And then neither of them said anything for a long time.

EPILOGUE

"Wake up, honey, we're here."

Summer smiled at the tender note in her husband's voice. "Mm," she murmured, burrowing against his shoulder.

"Honey, open your eyes for me."

She pouted and tried to snuggle closer, only to realize something was wrong. Frowning, she forced open her eyes, then uttered a little cry when she realized she'd only been dreaming they were home in bed. Instead, they were in the minivan, parked on a busy street.

Blinking her eyes wider, she sat up, then winced when the stressed muscles of her back gave her a little jab. Six months of carrying twins with her everywhere she went had taken their toll. But it was worth it. Two days ago, at her monthly checkup, Grey had pronounced her healthy and the babies thriving.

Brody had gone with her to Grey's office, then whisked her back into the minivan, kissed her in that no-nonsense way he had of staking his claim, and told her he was taking her away for the weekend. Kelly had already packed up everything Summer would need.

Now, two leisurely days of traveling later, they were in a picturesque town right out of the Old West, with ornate storefronts and wooden sidewalks. "Okay, big guy," she teased with a sleepy smile, "where are we?"

"Jacksonville, Oregon."

She nodded, then looked around, her curiosity simmering. In front of her was a two-story, redbrick structure with ornate windows and a look of nineteenth-century opulence. She loved it on sight. "Is that where we're staying, the Jacksonville Inn?"

He nodded, but the smile she'd expected to see, the smile that came easier to him now, was missing. "The bridal suite."

She felt a little thrill. If she knew her man, there would be roses waiting. White ones, with one red bud. "Your children and I love you very much, Chief Hollister."

"Hold that thought, honey," he said before leaning over to give her a hard kiss. "Now hang on, because there's something I have to tell you."

She felt a chill. Instinctively, she pressed her hands flat against her belly and one of the babies responded with a hard kick. "What?"

Instead of answering he sat back against the seat, his jaw tight. He tried to get out the words. "You were having nightmares. . . . I figured because you were worried about the b-babies." His face softened as he pressed a gentle hand against the swell of his children. "I couldn't stand it."

"I'll be fine," she hastened to assure him. "Once they're born, once I can hold them and know that no one will ever take them away."

He nodded. "I called in some markers in L.A. and . . ." He stopped to run his hand through his hair. He was wearing the blue oxford-cloth she'd bought him for his birthday and tailored slacks that did wonderful things for his handsome butt, a fact that she'd mentioned several times in the past with gratifying results.

"And what?" she asked, both curious and anxious. After nearly a year of marriage, she'd learned that Brody was even more complex than she'd thought. Brooding, generous, quixotic—a perfect partner who made her so happy she sometimes ached.

"Sweetheart, I . . . you know I'd n-never hurt you." Brody paused for breath. A man about to take a risk that might make his wife hate him had a right to stall, he told himself as he glanced toward the hotel.

"I l-love you more than my life, S-Summer. You know that, don't you?"

"Yes, and I love you." The trust in her river-green eyes scared him. In an hour he might see only fury. Or worse, unbearable pain.

"Your . . . your daughter is inside the hotel, working as a waitress in the restaurant."

Her face went white, and her hand groped for his. "You're sure." Her voice was a mere thread of sound, so faint he had to bend to hear her.

"Her name is Marina. Her folks moved here a year ago. Her dad is a doctor."

Summer felt a clammy wave of panic run through her. "Marina," she repeated softly. "It's a pretty name, isn't it?" Her mouth was dry, and she swallowed. "Have . . . have you seen her?"

He nodded. "A picture. She . . . looks like you, honey."

"Does she know . . . ?"

He shook his head. "I promised the guy who did the trace she'd never find out."

She couldn't seem to breathe. The babies were restless, twitching and turning. "I can't," she whispered. "I want to, but I'm afraid I'll say something. The wrong thing."

He grinned. "You won't. You can't." He leaned forward to press a warm kiss on her mouth. "I love you, Summer. You've given me more happiness than I deserve. Let me d-do this for you. Let me b-be there for you. L-let me help you take away that last shadow in your eyes. Please, sweetheart."

"It hurts, Brody. I don't know if I can see her and walk away."

He drew a long breath, then captured her hand and kissed it. "All right. We'll go someplace else for lunch."

She nodded, then bit her lip. "You'd go in, wouldn't you?"

She saw the flicker of his eyelashes. "Naw. What's the point?"

Of course, she already knew that this man was her rock. The man who should have been the father of the young girl inside the redbrick building. The man who would have died before tossing her to the wolves. "You'll be with me? And hold my hand?"

He took her small hand in his big one and entwined their fingers. And then he kissed her. "Remember what I told you? You're mine. No matter what, I'll never let you go."

"And you're mine," she whispered as she took a breath and felt the babies settle. *Your daddy is a wonderful man,* she whispered in her heart. *And he's all ours.*

Coming in March 1999!

HEARTTHROB
by Suzanne Brockmann

Once voted the "Sexiest Man Alive," Jericho Beaumont had dominated the box office before his fall from grace. Now poised for a comeback, he wants the role of Laramie bad enough to sign an outrageous contract with top producer Kate O'Laughlin—one that gives her the authority to supervise JB's every move, twenty-four hours a day, seven days a week.

The last thing Kate wants to do is baby-sit her leading man, and Jericho Beaumont may be more than she can handle. A player in every sense of the word, he is an actor of incredible talent—and a man with a darkly haunted past. Despite her better judgment, Kate's attraction flares into explosive passion, and she is falling fast.

Published by Fawcett Books.

Coming in April 1999!

DANCING AT THE HARVEST MOON

by K. C. McKinnon

At forty-five, Maggie McIntyre has been abandoned by her husband for a much younger woman. But some old letters in the attic from the first love in her life remind her of the precious summers she spent at the Harvest Moon dance hall so many years ago.

Now she is returning to Little Bear Lake, to the peace of the northern wilderness, hoping to recapture the woman she once was—and the woman she knows she could be again. But time has changed the place she knew. Until a second chance at love makes an unexpected appearance....

Published by Fawcett Books.